THE MAGIC RING

THE MAGIC RING

TOM MORRIS

A Journey of The Unseen

Book Six

Walid and the Mysteries of Phi

WISDOM/WORK
Published by Wisdom Work
TomVMorris.com

Published 2018

ISBN 978-0999352496

Printed in the United States of America

Set in Adobe Garamond Pro
Designed by Abigail Chiaramonte
Cover Concept by Sara Morris

To All Who Believe
And Any Who Even Suspect.

Contents

I

A Sunny Morning

Egypt: Many years ago.

To be exact, it was 1935. Strange things had been happening in Cairo, as well as in other parts of the kingdom and even across a broader section of North Africa. But more mysterious things were soon to come, and in ways that never could have been imagined.

A little café was itself strangely dark for such a sunny morning because it was, oddly, without any real windows, except for a couple of very high, small panes. It might have been chosen for precisely that reason. Large, round candles placed on the old tables inside provided almost all of its dim light. The small establishment sat in a part of Cairo where a great many Europeans of various backgrounds had settled. An old clock on the wall noticed by nobody was about to strike noon. Three men sat at a table near the back. One was a young city policeman in civilian clothes, on his day off. He had just arrived and taken a chair, minutes earlier. The other two were visiting from out of town and spoke with fairly heavy foreign accents.

"As our note explained," one of the older men said with a smile, setting his cup of tea back down on the table, "We're great lovers of animals, and are actually among the founders of a society for the protection of beloved household pets."

"Oh, that's good," the policeman replied. "I have a great dog."

"What kind?"

"He's a mutt, a little mixture of many kinds."

"That's the best of all."

"Yes. He needed a home. And we needed more family."

The man nodded and went on. "Good for you. I'm sure you enjoy his company."

"I do. We all do."

"We were so happy to hear recently that a big crime ring abducting animals here in Cairo and elsewhere was broken up, and apparently with all the creatures returned to their homes."

"Yes," the young officer said. "It was a great development. Everyone had been so concerned about the mysterious disappearances of so many animals. They were quite a source of speculation and worry and even grief throughout the city."

"I can understand that fully," the man said. Then he gave the policeman a look of great concern. "We were hoping to interview and perhaps provide a humanitarian award to someone who was involved centrally in the breakup of the crime ring. We'd love to meet anyone whose participation might make for a great story to be printed in the local newspaper with a human interest angle, something that could get more public attention for our benevolent cause."

"That sounds like a good thing to do," the junior officer replied.

The other man at this point commented, "We've heard that you were perhaps personally present at some of the interrogations of the suspected criminals."

"Well, I was just an observer mostly, but I took notes for the proceedings when several of the detainees were being questioned."

"Oh, I see. And did you hear anything about the involvement of anyone in the event of their arrest other than your fellow officers?"

"Sure, I heard the whole thing. Actually, there were no city police at the scene when the criminal activity was discovered in a big veterinary clinic at the edge of town and put to a stop. That was an activity involving mostly the king's men, guards from the palace."

"You say … mostly."

"Yes."

"So there were others—neither police nor palace guards?"

"There were a couple of young men there as well, boys, really, who were apparently instrumental in the take-down of the thieves, far beyond what could have been expected from anyone their age."

"Boys?"

"A couple of schoolboys in their early teens, I think. In fact, they were pretty much responsible for everything that happened that day. They were the real heroes."

"Oh? That's very interesting. Who were they? Did you get any names?"

"Actually, I didn't hear their names. We were just questioning the criminals—the alleged criminals—as to what had happened, and they didn't know the names of the boys, as you might imagine, but only that one of them had a dog named Giza that he had brought in for an examination at the clinic."

"Did the dog have an appointment for which there might be a record?"

"No, I don't think so. The man who talked about it seemed to indicate that it was an unexpected, walk-in visit, off the street."

"What was the dog's name again?"

"Giza, I believe—you know, as in the famous place not far away, the home of the Great Pyramid."

"Ok, good, very good. That helps. With that name alone, we might be able to identify and track down the boys."

"I could ask around at the station. They may have the names and contact information for the boys."

"Thank you so much for the offer, but that won't be necessary."

"You're sure?"

"Yes. There's no need. I think we have plenty to go on, thanks to what you've shared with us. It won't be a problem to locate them."

"I'm glad to be of any more service you might need. I do love dogs."

"Wonderful. But think no more of it! You've already been of so much help. We'll find the boys easily and interview them. I think the story of their involvement in saving so many animals would have a lot of human interest. It's just the sort of thing we were hoping to find. We could get the newspaper to do a big write-up and maybe raise the awareness of how our animal friends need us all to be on the lookout for them and protect them as fellow dwellers in the land."

"That's very nice," the policeman said. "I'm glad I could be of some help for such a good cause."

"Thank you. And, please, allow the tea and snacks to be on us—our treat and a small gesture of gratitude for your time and information."

"Oh, that's kind of you. I appreciate it," the policeman said.

"Say nothing of it," the older of the two men replied with a smile. And he knew that he meant more by the phrase than their young source of information could have guessed.

Four days later, the investigation launched by these men an hour after their brief meeting with the policeman had been concluded and had produced definitive results. They had a name and an address where a note could be delivered. Several of their associates had even come into town to help with the situation.

The sun was already making good progress along its charted course into the fresh new day. It was another sunny morning in eastern Egypt. The sky was a cloudless blue. The air was warm but not hot. There was no school on this day, and Walid had walked over to Kissa's house by himself to borrow a book from her dad. She wasn't home, but was out at the royal stables doing her regular training session on horseback with Hasina and their equestrian instructor, Hasina's mom, Layla.

Khalid had just shown the prince some books he was using for a new research project, and they sat a while and talked philosophy for about thirty minutes. The class recently had read Plato's Symposium, a famous cluster of conversations on the topic of love. After bouncing an idea off his teacher and getting an unexpected and interesting response, Walid sat in silence for a few seconds, building the courage to bring up something that had been on his mind. He finally said, "Khalid, may I ask you a very personal question?"

"Surely. I will, of course, choose whether and how to answer."

"That's fair. Ok. I was just wondering, if you don't mind. How did you first know you wanted to marry Hoda?"

"Oh, my goodness. That's indeed a personal question."

"I'm sorry. I shouldn't have asked."

"No, no. It's Ok." He paused for a second and then said, "For you, I think I'll answer. And the response is easy. I quickly knew I wanted to marry Hoda. The first time I looked into her eyes, I saw God."

"Wow."

"Yes. That was my response as well." Khalid was sitting across from Walid at a small table, his elbows on the top and his hands together, with fingers interlaced. At this point, he separated his hands in a slight gesture, while tilting his head a bit to the right. He added: "But equally important with what I saw was what I felt. I sensed in that instant the loving embrace of the source for all things."

He smiled at the memory and again paused for a moment. Then he continued. "Anyone can see Hoda's great physical beauty. It glows for everyone to enjoy. It's a beacon and shines its light on both the best in this world, and even things beyond our world. But there was, in addition, something special between us early on. Hoda feeds me the divine energy that it takes to live this life fully. She's my constant encouragement, a best possible companion, and my most wonderful connection to the source and reason for all."

"That's amazing. She said pretty much the same thing about you."

Khalid laughed. "Oh, you've already spoken to her about these things? I see. And now you come to me for a second opinion."

"I hope you don't mind."

"No. It's fine. You're a bold man."

"It's just that this is a part of life I'm trying to understand better."

"That's good. It's a bit hard to put such things into words. But I'll continue to try, because there's more to say."

"Really?"

"Yes." He paused for a few seconds, and then continued. "Hoda and I connect on a deep level. And there's something that passes between us. We bring each other the glory. I hope you can understand what I mean. That's the gift graciously given to us. She conveys to me the fire and radiance of the sun. She says I reflect it back. I bring her cool water from deep wells. And she always gives it back to me, whenever I need it. We also offer each other solid ground on which to stand. She provides for me—and I know this sounds strange, but please bear with me—she gives me the freedom and lightness of the air in my spirit. And I offer to her, in turn, a wind at her back to help her walk with confidence the path that's hers on this earth."

"That's just so great," Walid said quietly.

Khalid paused and then went on. "I shouldn't say any more, but I will mention one other thing, again, because it's you who's asking. I don't think I would tell anyone else this, and I would ask that you keep it confidential, but there is something additional and important."

"Ok."

"There was a kiss we had after we had known each other for a while, and it was truly a sacred thing. The world around us melted for a moment. Time slowed and stopped for the most wondrously full and extended instant, if that makes any sense. I was convinced, in the richness of that experience, that there has never been a kiss precisely like it in all of human history. It was as if cosmic forces touched then and sealed our destiny to be together. There have been many, many more such moments, just as powerful, over the years."

Walid let out a huge breath. "Man," he whispered.

Khalid laughed again and said, "Why the sudden rush of air from your lungs, and perhaps also from your soul, my young friend?"

"Because I think I understand what you're talking about and

I do know, as sure as knowledge can be had, that such a moment in its own special uniqueness is awaiting me—some day, when the time is right."

"Yes. When the time is right."

"I just want to be good enough for it, noble enough, worthy of it, and capable of making the most of the treasure it will bring."

"Good. Very good! That's the right perspective to have. I would expect no less of you. This is why I chose to tell you such things."

"Are you up for one more personal question that's about something completely different?"

Khalid smiled skeptically and said, "This may be risky, as I now know, but I think the answer is still yes, and yet with the same condition, of course."

"Ok. So, why … aren't you … Phi?"

"What?"

"Why aren't you a member of Phi?"

"What do you mean?"

"You sure have so many of the sensibilities of Phi. And everything you just said about you and Hoda sounds like a very special and distinctive case of Phi meeting Phi."

Khalid looked both blank and puzzled. "Wait. I'm sorry. It sounded like you used a Greek letter just now to name something, but what did you mean by it? What is this Phi you're mentioning?"

"Oh! I'm sorry! It's, it's …" Walid sputtered, as his mind reeled and his assumptions were all completely confounded in an instant.

Khalid looked even more perplexed, and then he laughed loudly and said, "I'm kidding! I'm kidding! It's my bit of Mafoolery for the day!"

"You almost gave me a heart attack!" Walid said, now laughing also.

"I know all about the most special club of all clubs, of course! But I just had to put you on the spot in response to your questions which have put me on the spot, and see your reaction." He laughed some more and said, "It was well worth seeing!"

"That's the best anyone's gotten me in a long time!"

"I'd like to thank Oxford and Yale," Khalid replied. "I'm fast on my feet, as they say—as long as we take feet to be thoughts, as a classic idealist might."

Walid laughed now, as well. "Yeah, I'd say so." He shook his head in mild astonishment. "And you know about Mafoolery."

"I listen well."

"You got me even better than Mafulla does."

"Excellent. That makes my day, in fact. But now, I should answer your question. It's worthy of a reply."

"Ok, good."

"Not everyone who is firmly immersed in the fellowship of the mind is Phi."

"You know about that, too."

"Yes. My life is all about the fellowship of the mind. But I'm not Phi. It's unusual, or extremely rare, even among those who are quite advanced in matters of mind and the spirit. I want you to understand this. Not all of us have the same gifts and responsibilities. Always remember that. Some people—like Hoda and Kissa and you and Mafulla—are specially blessed, or perhaps also burdened, by the abilities that qualify you as Phi. Of course, even the burden is a blessing for those who receive it well."

"And it's often true in life that whether something is a burden or blessing is up to us," Walid responded.

"Exactly," Khalid said. "The fact that you're surrounded by so many Phi can give you a false impression that it's much more common than it really is. And, trust me, it's not common at all."

"I had a conversation with the king back in the desert, before he was recognized as king, that almost made me later think that everyone is born with at least some Phi qualities—although I didn't know about Phi at the time."

"We're all born with great and important qualities that few ever develop, and some of these are attributes that Phi have in unusual abundance. But we're all different."

"Yes, but what do you mean by that in this particular context?"

"Everyone who comes into this world capable of thought and love is qualified for the fellowship of the mind. And that's a very big thing. It's a potential that most people sadly never develop and realize. And then, as I understand it from what Hoda tells me, Phi is a level of traits beyond this that can be even more developed. Being Phi, she says, doesn't make a person better or more valuable, in herself or himself. It just makes that rare individual differently abled, or capable, in this life. And connected with that is an opportunity and obligation for service to others in quite distinctive ways."

Walid frowned and almost insisted, "Are you sure that you don't have these particular abilities—the Phi attributes?"

"Yes, I'm sure, at least up to this point in my life. And that's absolutely fine. I have no regrets about it, whatsoever. I've been entrusted with many other wonderful abilities and I enjoy developing them and using them for the benefit of other people as well as myself."

"You're a really good philosopher and a totally amazing teacher."

"Thank you. I try to use my mind well. I do think I have a disposition for teaching. And I strive to keep sharp—physically, and mentally fit. I feel that my work is blessed by creativity, accuracy, bits of depth, and some measure of excellence. But I'm not one of those who can tell at a distance or in a dream when something dangerous is happening, while also dodging a bullet that's coming my way." Khalid smiled. Then, he added, "I can certainly give Hoda a headache, and I'm sure I have many times, but not the way she could give me one, if she chose!" And at that, they both laughed again.

"I guess we do all have different talents, or at least different clusters of talent," Walid commented.

"Yes, our profiles of talent may be as distinctive as our fingerprints. Some of our abilities come from our bodies, and some from our souls. The key to a happy and fruitful life, in my opinion, is to make the most of the talents you have and not to go around moping about one or two or more that you haven't been given. We can truly enjoy the differing gifts of others. We can celebrate their personal abilities and skills."

"Yeah, I'm sure you're right."

"Look at it this way: Life isn't a crass competition of capacities, with the winner being the one who has the most, and most fully develops them, seeking superiority to all others. That would be a grim way to live. And it's not our purpose. Life should be more like a celebration of the wonders of existence, with each of us taking joy in our own form of being, and in each other, perhaps even more."

"I like that way of looking at things," Walid said, truly impressed.

"I do, too," Khalid replied. "And, with that as our foundational perspective, then a healthy sense of competition can fit into the picture in appropriate ways. We can spur each other on to develop ourselves, viewing each other as positive standards and goads and inspirations. But we should never feel jealous and envy another person's basic talents, or even his accomplishments. In order for competition to enter our lives in the healthiest possible way, it should be a motivational mindset that's absolutely devoid of any negativity."

"That makes sense," Walid said. "I think Mafulla and I are often competitive in the way you describe, in a form that's completely positive. And because of it, we encourage each other to grow."

"I'm sure," Khalid said. "True friends help each other along the path and make each other better."

Suddenly, there was a loud knocking at the door. And then a very familiar voice called out, "Khalid! Walid! Is anyone here?"

Khalid got up with a puzzled expression on his face. "That's Mafulla," Walid said, as he rose, too. They both walked toward the door, where the young man stood, looking very concerned and even agitated.

"Hi Khalid. Good morning. Can I talk to Walid for a minute?"

"Sure, Mafulla. Walid, you boys can talk outside, if you'd like."

"Thanks," Mafulla said, as Walid walked the rest of the way up to the door and opened it, stepping out.

"What's wrong?" he asked, as their teacher disappeared back into the house to give them more privacy.

"It's Malik and Haji," Mafulla replied. "I think they might be in serious trouble, and bad danger."

"Why? What's happened?"

"A sealed note was left on my bed by Kular a short time ago. It was in Malik's handwriting. It says that he and Haji were sent a message by someone who claims he can provide definitive information about who was behind the animal abductions they helped to stop, and what this individual is planning now, and where he can be found."

"No way."

"Yeah, and here's the bad part. They were given a remote location to go to in the industrial district and were told to come alone, and if they did, they would get all the information they could want."

"Uh, oh. They're not going, are they?"

"Unfortunately, they are. In the note, Malik said they're going this morning, and he gave me the address in case anything might happen."

"Oh, man. What is it?"

"Here it is." Mafulla showed Walid the note.

"I can't believe it. That's near one of the warehouses that was used by Ari Falma and some other local criminals in the past."

"Yeah, I made the connection, too."

"Does the king or anyone else know about this?"

"I don't think so. I went to tell the king but he wasn't anywhere in the palace. He was off somewhere at a meeting."

"I wish we had time to go back there to get one of the Phi guards to come along."

"They're apparently all with the king and Masoon and Hamid at some meeting away from the palace, across town, and in the opposite direction from where Malik and Haji are."

"Are you sure? I mean, it would really help to take one of them with us, if we could."

"Yeah. I'm sure. I asked."

"We could even use some regular palace guards for backup at this point. Any help would be great."

"I don't think there's time for even that."

"Oh, man. Ok. I guess we do need to get there fast. They could be in bad trouble really soon." Walid turned back to the house, walked up to the door and opened it, and said in a loud voice, "Khalid? I have to go now for a bit. Can I come back and get the book later?"

A voice came from inside. "Sure. I'll see you later. Just try to be careful, whatever emergency now calls you into action!"

Walid thought to himself, "How did he know it's an emergency?" But then, as he walked down toward the street with his friend, he said to Mafulla, "That address is a good half hour to forty-five minute walk, at a fast pace, and maybe more. I think we need to jog."

Mafulla agreed right away and both boys began to run at a measured pace down the street in the direction that would take them ultimately to where their friends were having a mysterious meet-up with whatever individual or group had contacted them.

"Good thing we're both in shape," Mafulla said.

"Yeah. I just hope we get there soon enough."

"Hey, remember, those guys are The Wild Camel and The Silver Sabre," Mafulla reminded Walid.

"Yeah, but a legendary monster is on the loose, and a trap is a trap."

"You think it's him?"

"I hope not. I sort of doubt it. But still, I kind of feel like he's behind whatever this is, and whoever is involved."

Just then, they turned a corner onto a main street and, as they looked both ways before crossing the broad avenue, they saw a car coming toward them, headed in the direction they were going. Mafulla moved closer toward the pavement and stuck his thumb up in the air.

"What are you doing?" Walid asked.

"I saw this in a movie," Mafulla said. "I'm hitching a ride for us."

"You're what?"

"Hitch-hiking, using a hand signal and asking the driver of the car to stop and take us at least part of our way. If he's seen the right movie, he'll know what I'm doing."

The car actually slowed down, and then so did the boys. The driver rolled down his window. "Hitch-hikers Paradise!" he called out to Mafulla.

"You've seen it!" Mafulla exclaimed.

"Yes! Good movie! Hollywood! Do you need a ride?"

"We do. We're going to the industrial area," Mafulla said.

Walid added, "And we need to get there faster than we can jog."

"Ok, no problem. Hop in! That's what they say in the movie!"

"Unbelievable," Mafulla said. The boys ran around to the other side of the car and Walid opened the passenger door.

"Thanks a lot," Mafulla said as they got in, with him in the back, and Walid in the front, beside the driver.

The man looked at Walid and said, "Do I know you from somewhere?"

"I don't know," Walid said. "Where would you have seen me?"

"I deliver food supplies to the Grand Hotel. I work for the company called Kingdom Food."

"I've been there to eat a few times," Walid said, "at dinner."

"No, that's not it. I also deliver to the palace weekly."

"Maybe that's where you've seen us," Mafulla replied. "We go to school there." Something told him to be careful in what he said. Or rather, something just told him generally to be careful right now, and he interpreted that inner caution to mean that he should give only this sort of partial answer to the man's question.

"Oh, Ok. The palace," the man said and pulled back onto the street. "That could be it. Now, what address are we going to?"

Walid showed him the paper, and he began to pull forward and shift gears as he looked at it. And then, within maybe three seconds, he drove into the next intersection without looking first for cross traffic. He had distractedly glanced down again at the address, and a large truck coming from their left with its horn blaring slammed into them, broadside, with the sound of a thunderous explosion, crushing the left front side and the driver's door inward.

2

SUDDEN DISASTER

EVEN WITH THEIR NOW WELL-DEVELOPED PHI ABILITIES, neither Walid nor Mafulla had even remotely seen this coming. Just like the driver, they were distracted. They had been paying insufficient attention to their surroundings for a span of seconds. And a disproportionate consequence of this completely normal lapse of awareness then seemed to leap out of nowhere and pull them instantly into an unexpected vortex of crushingly loud and damaging violence.

The truck that collided with them had been going at a high rate of speed. As a result, the forceful shock of concussion was terrible, as metal smashed into metal and two windows blew out of the car where the impact was greatest. Walid and Mafulla both had that instant experience of time quickly slowed and suspended as the car they were in spun around and wobbled as if to flip over in the next second that would tick them into their oncoming fate.

Disasters have a way of orchestrating their own self-contained world. It's as if the event creates a new gravitational field of space, time, and awareness around itself. No one watching from outside the experience will notice it. But anyone on the inside of the catastrophe will find that the normal flow of the immediately surrounding environment has altered dramatically. It's like a crack opens up in the cosmological constants of the mundane. The dice of destiny are tossed in slow motion, and no one who is living in the middle of that extended moment can know what the result of the roll might be.

Outside of town, Kissa and Hasina were on their horses, riding fast around a stationary target, a large thick post set deep into the ground in the middle of a huge open area near the royal stables. And they were shooting at it, at this point, with military revolvers, taking turns roughly two to three seconds apart, and trying to keep their bullet holes in a level line around it. Layla was watching them closely, but from a distance, when she had the first hint of something wrong that was happening, or perhaps about to occur, not too far away. She waved an arm up and down and blew a loud whistle, and the girls in response slowed and stopped their horses and turned them toward her. She motioned them to come to her.

"I'm stronger since our ride across the desert," Hasina said to her best friend, as she turned her horse toward where her mother was, and began to walk him in that direction. Kissa followed along. "In fact, I think I'm much stronger."

"I am, too," Kissa replied. "Legs, arms, and all over my body, through the whole core," she added.

"Yeah, and it's not like we hadn't already been working out all the time and really hard," Hasina said.

"It's just different," Kissa mused. "We suddenly started using our muscles in new ways and they grew."

By then, they were within loud speaking distance of their teacher. "What's up, Mom?" Hasina called out.

"Come closer," Layla said, and she gestured again. The girls did as they were asked, without thinking that anything might be wrong. They rode right up to their teacher, who was sitting on her own mount.

"How were we doing?" Kissa asked.

"Very well," Layla replied. "You're starting to get the feel of the horse's movement, up and down, and how to compensate for that with your aim and body movements, and your timing."

"I felt like it was flowing more today," Hasina said.

"Good, I'm glad," Layla responded, and added, "but that's not why I called you over."

"Oh, my," Hasina said, and in just that moment, she looked shocked. Then, she twisted her body left and right, peering into the distance as well as she could, looking for what might be the source of the sudden awful sensation she had just felt.

"Oh, no. What is it, Hassi?" Kissa asked, as she suddenly felt cold, with a shiver all over and inside her body. "I feel something awful."

"Stay calm," Layla said. "I had a strong premonition just now that Walid and Mafulla are in some sort of immediate danger, and if you just felt something this moment, either of you, I want you to know that I did, too. And I sense that the danger is rapidly growing."

"But, how could that be? Walid's with dad at home," Kissa said.

"And I think Mafulla's supposed to be spending the morning in his room, reading," Hasina added, her face showing both perplexity and great concern at the same time. "How could they both suddenly be in danger?"

"Something changed their plans," Layla said, simply. "I have no idea what it is, but they're together now and something traumatic or endangering just happened. Our job this second is to send them love and power and healing and protection. They need our help."

Across town, the high level meeting in a private room at the Grand Hotel had been going well. The king looked up from an official document he was reading and preparing to sign. He looked up and then sat very still, staring straight ahead with absolutely no expression on his face for five or six seconds.

"What is it, Your Majesty?" Hamid asked, with a look and tone of concern. He gripped the arm of his chair.

But before he could answer, Masoon said, "Oh. There's trouble."

"Yes, as soon as you spoke, I sensed it," Hamid said. "I mean I felt something."

"You're both right," the king replied in a calm voice. "There's serious trouble."

"What is it?" Paki asked, as he and Omari immediately rose from their chairs, ready for any action. Amon, who had been next to the window, instinctively looked out, quickly searching the broad view below him for anything that might serve as evidence of what was going on. Across from them, Hoda remained seated and looked straight at the king but, like him, with no expression.

Amon turned and said, "What's happened? Where is it?"

The king then held up his hand as if to stop or pause everyone, and to calm them for what he was about to tell them. But first, he said only the word: "Wait."

Three other people in Cairo had exactly the same thought as the king, and Masoon, and then Hamid, and at almost exactly the same moment, with roughly the same feelings attached. And none of them took action. No one prepared to take action. They seemed to be held back, as by an invisible hand. Only the king and Hoda didn't feel any measure of concern about this strange, shared sense of alarm and restraint. They had advanced to the point where they had a way of accepting anything, it seemed. And in this, they were far beyond most of their associates who could in any way be thought of as close peers. Both of them knew deep in their hearts something that most people are unable ever to believe. However incredible it might seem to us, and especially at difficult and even traumatic times, things most often tend to happen just as they need to take place. The power that works behind all else can alone help us accept that and be at peace.

Only the king fully knew, at that moment, that there were four young people very close to their hearts who were all in imminent danger. And he consulted that knowledge for what might be done.

The crashing, almost deafening cacophony of the accident that had instantly filled the boys' ears and bodies and souls now gave way to a thick, nearly opaque silence, if only for a long, broad moment. The driver of the car they were in had lost consciousness and was slumped over in the seat, bleeding badly. The prince felt the light of his mind dim and fade and flicker away, and then reawaken. But everything was still, for the moment, a confused blur. He couldn't remember now how he got outside the car, to be standing on the edge of the street beside the crumpled vehicle, gripping the shoulders of Mafulla, who was bent over in front of him and almost doubled up.

"Are you Ok?" Walid asked his friend and coughed loudly. There was no answer and he yelled, "Mafulla!"

"Yeah, Yes. I'm Ok, I think," Mafulla said.

"How … did we get out here?" Walid exclaimed, in a stunned voice.

"Defenestration," Mafulla answered. "You pulled me out some window, from the back seat. Or somebody did, and you're the only one here, so it must have been you. That's all I know."

"You're bleeding."

"Defenestration isn't often easy or pretty."

"I'm sorry."

"No, you got me out. I'm glad." Mafulla straightened up and glanced at the car he had just escaped, thanks to his friend. He said, "Look at the front end of the car. It's smoking badly. I've read about this. The whole thing might burst into flames any second. We need to get away from it."

"What about the driver?" As Walid said this, he suddenly became aware of the shouts of men's voices in what at first sounded like the distance, but coming closer. Then he rose out of his mental fog a bit more and noticed someone dressed in what looked like military clothes, pulling the driver out from the other side of the car.

He then heard a loud voice with an urgent tone yell, "Boys! Get away! Away from the car!" Two men instantly appeared, practically flying around the back of the sedan. They grabbed both Walid and Mafulla, who were still too stunned to move much on their own, and pulled them away from the side of the badly damaged car and then pushed them back behind it and down the sidewalk as quickly as they could.

The next instant, there was an explosion and flames leaped from the engine compartment under the hood of the car, as well as the entire underside of the vehicle. The two men helping Walid and

Mafulla shoved them downward to protect them, as they also ducked low to avoid any flying debris. One of them said, "Oh, man!"

The other commented, "That was too close!"

"Is everybody all right?" Another individual then came toward them.

"Yes, yes, I think so," Walid said. Mafulla nodded his head.

"Get them farther away! There could be another explosion," the man shouted to the two who had first moved the boys from the side of the now dangerous car. He was pointing, it seemed, a good distance from where they were now located, still in a protective squatting position. They quickly moved several more feet farther from the car and right away there was a smaller, secondary explosion, with the sound of glass shattering and being propelled through the air.

"Whoa! That was scary!" Mafulla said, as he looked up from his now once more hunched over position.

"You're bleeding!" The man who gave the orders spoke to Mafulla, as he got closer to them.

"Yeah, but I don't think it's bad. My friend here pulled me through a window, and some of my skin was unsure about leaving. I think it wanted to hang onto the broken glass as I slid out."

"Yes, yes, I see," the man said, as he looked more closely. "And I think you're right. Nothing seems deep."

"Thank you, so much," Walid said. "Thanks for getting us away from the car. I wasn't thinking clearly."

"You're welcome. And of course I'm very sorry about the crash. The driver of your car just pulled right in front of us unexpectedly, and we were going quite fast, since we had the right of way and were trying to stay on a tight schedule. We didn't notice in time that he wasn't going to slow or stop."

"I understand," Walid said.

"You're sure you're both Ok?" the man asked.

"Yeah, I'm pretty sure," Walid answered. And then he said, "Are you guys Egyptian military?" He was just starting to get his complete vision and mental clarity back and was, in a sense, asking the obvious.

"Yes. I'm Rashid al-Suki, captain in the army, third division."

"Thank you, Captain. I need your help."

"You do?"

"Yes."

Captain al-Suki looked back around to the scene of the accident for a moment and then returned his attention to Walid and said, "The men have just signaled to me that our truck can be driven. Most of the damage happened to your vehicle. And we need to leave as soon as we can. We're under serious time constraints. But I'm happy to be of help—quickly, in any way possible. What is it that you need, my boy?"

"First, is the driver of the car Ok?"

"He seems to be unconscious still, but alive, and there are no visible traumatic wounds. He's bleeding a lot, but it looks superficial. He may have a concussion. His cuts are being tended to by one of our men. And I think he'll be fine. Is he a friend or relative of yours?"

Walid said, "No, but I'm glad to hear he's alive. We actually don't even know the name of the man, but we would want the best help and medical treatment for him. We had just hitched a ride with him not a minute before the accident."

"Hitched a ride?"

"Yes, we're also in a big hurry. We have to go and maybe save the lives of two endangered friends, and we were running to get to them when we saw this car and got the driver to stop for us to give us a ride to the industrial district where a dangerous situation is right now likely taking place. The driver was just being helpful. There may be an attempted murder underway soon, with two very good friends of ours being the intended victims, unless we get to an address out on Commerce Avenue quickly."

"That's quite a dramatic story you're telling."

"All true, I'm afraid. And, I feel terribly bad about interrupting your schedule, especially if you were in a hurry, but our situation is urgent and we really need you to take us to Commerce Avenue, right away."

"I'm so sorry, but I'm afraid we can't do that. We're on strict orders."

"I can issue new orders. I'm Prince Walid Shabeezar, nephew and heir of His Majesty, King Ali Shabeezar."

"What?"

"I'm Prince Walid, and I can issue new orders for you."

"I'm … I'm … sorry, my friend, but it isn't within the scope of my power to accept your impressive identification claims here on the street with no appropriate context or evidence, or form of confirmation. You realize, I'm sure, that this is a fairly extreme assertion you're making, and one that, if false, could get you boys into a lot of trouble."

"Yes, thank you, Captain, for your kindly worded expression of caution. I know the consequences of such claims made falsely. But I can assure you that I am the prince, and know quite well your general, Masoon Afah, and Dr. Hamid, his second in command. It's their sons, Haji and Malik, our good friends, who are in danger."

At this point, two other soldiers had walked up behind the captain, joining the boys and their other two colleagues who were already there and now standing slightly behind the boys. "Ok, I have to admit I'm impressed that you know the names of the two top officers in the kingdom's military. Most people of your age, or any age, would not. But still, even if you are who you say—and I know you must realize the objective unlikelihood of such a thing, from my point of view: The prince of our kingdom and another boy asking for a ride on the side of the road and getting into a car with a man they don't know. Then you tell me a story about two murders being imminent and the two endangered individuals happen to be the sons of our top two officers. It's all just so far-fetched. You must realize that I'm under official orders and would get into a pack of trouble if I were to just take your word as to your identity and your need. I'm sure you can understand."

Walid nodded and said, "I totally get it. But this is truly an emergency, Captain."

"Still."

"Ok, I have to show you something privately. May I?"

The officer hesitated for a moment and then said, "I suppose so." He looked at his nearby men and said, "Please, give us a minute." They nodded and turned and walked away, toward their truck.

Walid turned to Mafulla and said, "Reversos."

Mafulla was at first confused. Did Walid mean they were going to go all Viper and Storm on the captain? That couldn't be. It wouldn't make any sense. But without understanding any other reason why, he instantly complied with his friend's request and the two boys simultaneously clicked over their watchcases, revealing the backs of the watches. But Walid immediately put one finger over the lower part of the back where the Phi symbol was engraved, as if to cover it, and then extended his arm out toward the captain and, following him, Mafulla did all of this, too.

The officer looked down at the reverse side of their watchcases and saw the crown engraving on each of them, the official crest of the monarchy. He was aware that they were both also covering something, but the crown got his immediate, full attention and he quickly said, "Oh, my goodness! I'm … I'm … so sorry! Please forgive my wariness, Prince. We … we're fully at your service. What can we do for you and your friends?"

"Thanks. I need you to take us quickly to an address."

Walid clicked his watchcase back into its normal position, as then did Mafulla. The prince pulled the notepaper from his pocket and handed it to the captain. "We need to get there as fast as we can."

"Yes, Your Highness," The captain replied and, turning to his men, said, "Everyone, in the truck! We're on a new, urgent mission. This young man is Prince Walid Shabeezar, and he needs our help."

The men standing nearby looked completely surprised. But one soldier who was still in the truck stuck his head out the door and shaded his eyes to see better, and within two seconds shouted, "Prince! I was with you in the desert, on the trip to your home! I didn't even see you just now!"

"Hey! Sure! I recognize you!" Walid shouted back. "You're Amin, right?"

"Yes! Yes, I am, Your Highness! You remember me!"

"I do! Good to see you, Amin! We're now on a rescue mission. Please, get everyone to load any weapons you have with you!" Then he turned to the officer and said, "Captain, I'm sorry, I should have let you issue that order."

"No, it's quite all right, Prince. Time is of the essence, it seems. Let's get into the truck and you can explain the situation to me as we go."

"What about our poor driver, the man who was giving us a ride?" Walid asked.

"Oh, the driver. I almost forgot him in all this excitement." The captain looked over at one of his men who was still tending to the fellow, now lying in the sand well away from his car, but showing some hopeful signs of movement, and called out, "Omar! Stay here with the man until someone comes along, and get him to the hospital as soon as you can!" The soldier nodded his understanding.

They walked quickly up to the truck, climbed into the back, and after the captain had given his driver the address, along with instructions to park a block short of the destination, he joined the boys and five other men in the back. Including the two soldiers up front in the cab of the truck, there were now eight military men supporting Walid and Mafulla in their effort to go save their friends from what might be a very dangerous situation. Their presence as backup would turn out to be needed even more than Walid realized.

The truck pulled off and began to rumble down the street on its new mission. All the soldiers in the back with the prince and Mafulla listened intently as the boys related their story about the good friends who were now in grave and mortal danger. They told the men all that they safely could, without revealing too much about the power that ultimately might lie behind the challenges they were going to have to confront. But the boys warned them well about the threats they might all face in a very short time.

The captain listened carefully and then instructed his men to carry extra ammunition with them when they left the truck.

The situation they were about to enter would measure up to all the warnings that were being given, and would involve for the two young men speaking these cautionary words more than they could currently imagine. The prince and his best friend really had no idea of exactly what they were about to witness. And it would be, in many ways, at least for Walid, a much bigger shock than what they had just experienced.

3

A Big Revelation

Mafulla's father, Shapur Adi, was outside his shop arranging some pots with flowering plants to decorate the front entrance. He had just exchanged greetings with the Sakat brothers, Mumar and Badar, a few minutes earlier and was back to work on this sunny morning, whistling a little tune as he moved the various pots around to achieve his desired effect. He thought he was now alone.

A man quietly walked up behind him and said, "Excuse me, sir."

"Oh! Yes, hello!" Shapur turned and said, "I didn't see you there! Good morning to you."

"Good morning," the man replied. "I don't want to disturb you or keep you from your work, but I'm trying to find a Mr. Sayid Kaza."

Shapur looked at the man with surprise and then kindness, and he said, "I'm so sorry to bear this news, but Mr. Kaza has passed away, not very long ago."

"Oh," the man replied. "I regret to hear that."

"Did you know Kaza?" Shapur asked the stranger and then added, "He was a wonderful man and was like family to us."

"Yes, I did know him, many years ago, but only briefly. He and my father once studied under the same teacher, when Mr. Kaza was young and my father was a bit older. I'm here in the capital for some business and I thought that perhaps I'd look him up."

"Well, I'm sorry that you won't be able to see him and visit," Shapur said. "Even at his advanced age, he was in very good health, and his mind was extremely sharp. But most of all, as you may know, he had a kind and wonderful personality. He was like a member of our family for all these years."

"I see. What took him from us, if I might ask?" the man said. "Was it just one of the many blights of advanced age, those maladies to which we all eventually become vulnerable?"

"No, not at all. He was hale and hardy to the end. I'm afraid his life was taken quite suddenly by violent criminals."

"Oh, my," the man responded with a look of surprise.

"Yes. It was a shock for all of us and we still haven't gotten over it."

"How sad."

"Indeed."

"Such, on occasion, is life."

"Oh, please forgive my manners. I'm Shapur Adi, proprietor of this humble shop."

"It's nice to meet you. My name is Osvaldo."

"A pleasure, Mr. Osvaldo."

"I appreciate your gentle way of passing on to me the unfortunate news."

"I hope it hasn't spoiled your day," Shapur said, with great sympathy.

"Thank you, Mr. Adi. I thank you. I never knew him well, but I'm still deeply sorry to hear of his passing. I should be off, now, and let you get back about your business. Again, I didn't mean to disturb your work."

"No, not at all."

"A good day to you."

"And to you, Mr. Osvaldo."

As the man walked away, Shapur had a strange feeling, but could not have said exactly what it was. The man was very polite, but there was something different about him, and unsettling, that his surface manners couldn't completely hide. Shapur suddenly felt like he needed to sit down. He was even a bit light-headed and felt oddly tired, despite what had seemed like a good night's sleep. And he had been fine just minutes earlier.

A short distance away, Reela Adi also felt something unusual, a particular twinge of attention that shifted his consciousness in a sudden and disturbing way. He looked up from his desk where he was reading, and he had the thought impress itself on him that he should visit his brother as soon as he could. He got up from his chair and looked at his watch, then glanced out the window before turning abruptly and walking briskly out of the room, through the front door of his home, and down the street in the direction of the marketplace, and the Adi shop.

A minute earlier, Mafulla had just turned to Walid inside the back of the noisy military truck and said, "We need to check in with my dad."

"Ok," Walid said. "Any particular reason?"

"Yeah. Something's up—nothing urgent, I think—but I have a feeling that something's going on we need to know about."

"All right then, as soon as we take care of this, whatever this is."

The brakes squeaked and the truck slowed and pulled over to the side of the road, parking one long block from the address on the note from Malik. Walid looked over to the officer in charge and said, "Captain, if you would, please take half the men around to the back of the building, and let us have the other half for the front and the near side."

"Are you sure, Prince? Have you done anything like this before?"

"Yes, unfortunately, too many times, and all successfully, I'm happy to say. We have much more experience in such matters than our age would suggest."

"Good. I'm sorry to question you in that way, but I want you to be safe. I feel responsible. I'm sure you understand."

"Yes, certainly."

"When should we enter the building?"

"I'll post a sentry at the corner close to us. As soon as we give him a hand signal and it's conveyed to you, breach the back loudly enough to get all the attention of anyone inside. Then, we'll go in the front and make the rescue. Don't shoot near the two boys our age in there. Anyone else, if they come at you with hostile intent, feel free to take them down, or out, whatever you think is required. We'd like to be able to question someone about who's behind this, but your safety and that of our friends is our first concern. This is primarily, and most importantly, a rescue mission with what could be strong resistance."

The captain said, "Agreed," and then jumped out of the truck, quickly assigning his men to the two groups. He led his own few up the road and off to the right, down a narrow lane alongside the address of their destination. Walid and Mafulla took the other men straight up the broad avenue, walking at a brisk pace, but not running, so as not to attract any more unwanted attention than might be inevitable.

The whole area seemed quiet, even deserted. It was the day of the week when commerce mostly gave way to religious observances and family time. That's why the boys were off from school. There was no traffic of any kind at the moment, and the buildings they were passing on both sides of the street appeared to be either abandoned, or else shut up for the day. They didn't see anyone on their walk to the door whose address they carried.

The meeting place, 1218 Commerce, was a medium-size warehouse building whose front door had not been closed fully by the last person who passed through it. When Walid arrived there and saw the door cracked open, he wanted to do some quick surveillance before giving the sign for all to enter. He signaled to Mafulla and two of the other men to go to three of the closest windows and try to get a look through them while he carefully checked inside the front door. He then gave a third soldier whispered instructions to stand at the corner of the building, watchful and prepared to relay a signal for the other group to enter the structure from the back.

The prince then silently pushed the door open a little more, and from where he stood, he could hardly believe what he saw. Through a shallow front room, a short, broad hallway, and a wide-open inner door beyond it, he could now see into a large open space with pallets of boxes stacked up high, far in the back. And there, well in front of the storage, were Malik and Haji hanging by their feet, upside down, tied with ropes and with their heads about waist high above the floor, just visible from where Walid now stood. He could see the barrel of a rifle on the left pointed at them, but not the man holding it. And on the right, he glimpsed the shoulder and left arm of another man from behind, and then heard him yell at the boys, "Tell me now!" His voice boomed out with aggravation. But they were silent in response.

"This is your last chance!" The man shouted again. Malik and Haji showed no expression, as far as the prince could see at this distance. Then the man doing the shouting walked more into Walid's view, and he was clearly holding in his right hand a metal pipe, maybe three feet long and three inches around—some sort of plumbing pipe or other conduit, hollow on the inside, but clearly made of thick metal. The man suddenly swung the pipe at Haji's ribs, and what happened next was something that had Walid doubting his own eyes.

Haji, hanging upside down, grabbed the pipe before it could hit him, and he held on to it for a second or two as the shocked man tried to process what had just happened. But then, things got really strange. If he could believe his eyes at all, Walid would have sworn that he saw the pipe light up and glow reddish orange, and the guy whose swing of it had been interrupted yelled out in pain and fell away from it, letting go and waving his hand fast in the air, up and down, as if to cool it off or shake off the pain. He was also doing a sort of crazed pain dance where he stood. He shouted, "Ow! Ow! What was that?" Haji, at the moment still suspended by his ankles, somehow instantly twisted his body and slung the pipe that then flew like a spear straight at the guy to his right, or Walid's left, who was holding the gun he had seen, and the prince could hear a shout of pain as he now saw the gun clatter to the floor.

There were other bellowing voices and three more men with guns immediately appeared, crossing Walid's line of sight. Before anything else could happen, the prince dashed back to just outside the front door and gave a hand signal frantically, three times. The soldier at the corner mimicked what he saw and within about four seconds, Walid could hear crashing noises, as of windows breaking in the distance toward the back, and lots of gunfire coming from the rear of the building, likely at this point just intended to draw attention and clear a path.

Walid motioned for Mafulla and the group of soldiers with them to follow him through the door, holding up five fingers for the number of adversaries he had seen. Despite a dull throbbing in his head from being upside-down so long now, Haji had a sudden feeling and looked up in Walid's direction, and seeing them come through the door, he alerted Malik, saying, simply, "Viper. Storm."

Without hesitation, before Walid was even through the front room and into the intervening short hallway, the prince made a violent up and down hand gesture toward Haji and then aimed his borrowed rifle fast and shot twice with unbelievable accuracy, cutting both ropes in two and dropping his friends to the floor, where they were able to catch themselves, thanks to the anticipation that his gesture had produced.

Malik came down hard not far from a man who was in a low crouch, already shooting toward the back of the building. He tackled the guy so quickly that a normal observer would not have been able to see how he could have landed on the floor, popped up, leaped over, and taken the man down so fast. The adversary's gun fell to the cement floor and Malik scooped it up, using the butt of the rifle in one smooth motion to slam him in the head so hard that he was instantly left without further awareness.

As Walid ran through the short hall and entered the big open area, he caught sight of another man, unseen by Malik, who was about to grab him from behind and shove him, face down, toward the floor. But Malik rolled to his left as he lurched forward under the man's weight, even before he hit the floor, so that he was already recovering from the tackle before he was completely down. And as he turned over, one leg shot up and out toward his opponent, and the heel of his foot got the guy as he was coming down, right on the side of his head, exactly at the temple. And that was it, for now, for one more of the enemy. But Walid then saw a man nearby raise a gun, and he quickly shot first to hit the weapon, which fell to the floor. The man yelled out and dove down behind some boxes for cover.

Haji meanwhile, in the few seconds during which all this had been happening, had grabbed a loose gun off the floor and, doing his own dive and roll, shot another man twice who was just about to pull a trigger, point blank, on him. Bullets were flying all around. But the rescuers were all there, of course, for an extraction and not mainly a battle. So Walid at that moment yelled, "Guys! Come with me!" as Mafulla stepped past him, aiming an army rifle over to the side of the room where a man had just turned toward Haji with a revolver raised up and pointed at him. Mafulla, like Walid, quickly shot the gun that the man was holding out of his hand before he could pull his trigger.

The soldiers with them rushed through the door and split two to the left and two to the right, at this point shooting at any visible target over the age of the two young men to be rescued. Amin, the military man who had been in the security detail on the trip to Dromeda, then saw the guy that Mafulla had just disarmed bend over and reach for his gun with his other hand, and as he came up with it, the soldier took him down with two quick shots.

Captain al-Suki and his group in the back had eliminated three shooters as they first entered the building. One of his men was slightly wounded in the shoulder and one had been shot in the leg, but, although he was in a lot of pain, he was in no real danger and could still get to cover, where he continued to fire on the enemy.

Malik and Haji were now moving toward Walid when, suddenly, the man Haji had taken down with the pipe thrown as a spear slowly rose up on their left and reached for his weapon. But, on the other side of the boys, far away off toward just beyond the edge of the open space and behind a tall stack of pallets, another hostile gunman at that same moment fired a shot straight at Haji's lower back. Walid happened to be looking at his friends and waving them toward him when this happened. With his peripheral vision, he saw the shooter and the muzzle flash right before he heard the shot and knew that if the guy missed Haji, he would likely hit Malik, who was right beside him, maybe lagging behind only by half a step at the most. The shooter could even possibly get them both. And, at that instant, Haji fell forward and to the side, while Malik fell backward and Walid had a surge of alarm jolt through his body and thought to himself, "Oh, no."

Life was about to teach Walid once again one of the main lessons he still had to learn so thoroughly that it would become a part of the way he experienced everything that happened around him. The lesson was that things are not always, and even not often, what they seem. His two friends and crime fighting colleagues had fallen as they had not because they were both hit by the shot that had been fired, but rather, on purpose and with precise timing, intentionally protecting themselves. Even though Walid had seen Kissa do this, and had done it himself, he didn't at all expect to witness any such thing here. And so the real truth didn't occur to him. The bullet had split the difference between the boys as a result of their moves, barely missing them both. And to the prince's astonishment in the next moment, the same slug took out the adversary who had just picked up his rifle, ripping into his lower gut and collapsing him to the floor where he had stood, to fight no more. Three kingdom soldiers simultaneously from two sides then stopped the other shooter behind the boxes with their own violent fusillade of fire.

Walid and Mafulla had run forward and now stood next to their friends, rotating their bodies and weapons, scanning the open area for dangers, as Malik and Haji both jumped up, each gripping a rifle of his own. And now, they began doing the very same thing, as they also began to move slowly toward the front hall, crouched down and alertly watching for any danger. The building was almost quiet at this point, aside from the sounds of boots on the floor, converging on the wounded and the dead. Then a voice called out.

"Back, clear!" Captain al-Suki shouted.

"Front, clear!" one of the other soldiers with Walid answered.

"This side, clear!" Walid heard from his right.

"Over here, clear!" he now heard from the left. And at that sound, he could feel his tense body begin to relax.

Two soldiers immediately ran over to one man who was on the floor but stirring, their guns on him. His hand slowly moved toward his face, as if in a pain response, setting off no warnings in the minds of the soldiers, but then his fingers went into his mouth, and someone yelled "Cyanide! Stop him!"

He was poisoning himself with a capsule he had carried, so that he couldn't be questioned and possibly reveal anything under interrogation. Within seconds, he was having seizures, convulsing, and then, in a very short time, due to the amount of poison he had ingested, he collapsed and died right there, in front of them all.

Amin saw one other man making the same movement toward his face. He ran and dived down toward him, but was a split second too late. The same sort of capsule was chewed and swallowed. And that act ended the possibility of answers on this day.

At that same moment, in two different places across town and beyond the town limits, the king, Masoon, Hamid, Hoda, Layla, Kissa, and Hasina all knew to varying degrees that the danger for their friends had now passed. Layla brought the girls out of their meditative state of prayer and assistance as they sat beside their horses, and began to speak softly with them about what had transpired. They still didn't know the details, but realized with full assurance that something very bad, and even a few tragic possibilities, had been avoided. Their close friends were safe.

Walid and Mafulla were now standing with Malik and Haji outside the big open space, in the front entry room to the building. "Are you guys Ok?" The prince asked this with great concern.

"Yeah, but no thanks to my friend Malik!" Haji replied, a bit out of breath, and with a mock look of alarm and irritation.

"What?" Malik said, surprised.

"You always insist that we should wait 'until the right time' before we make a move!"

"So?"

"So, whenever I'm hanging upside down by my ankles with guns in my face, I'm naturally thinking, 'Couldn't the right time have come a little bit before this?' I mean, really."

"We had to catch those guys by surprise," Malik explained. He added, "Surprise worked better than anything else."

"Yeah, as the last bit of blood was draining out of my brain," Haji replied.

"But, admit it: All's well that ends well!" Malik responded.

"Yeah, thanks to our friends here and the Egyptian army!" Haji replied.

"Hey, one way or another!" Malik said, still getting his breath. And then he commented to his complaining friend, "But when the time did come, you surprised that guy pretty well, you know?"

"Yeah, I did."

"Ok, look," Walid said, in a lower voice. "There's some stuff I have to ask you about later."

"Sure, boss," Haji replied, sort of knowing that it might be one of his own actions that had piqued Walid's curiosity. But, was this going to be like the masked crime fighter confrontation that had happened not so long ago, and yet, now flipped around? That had been quite a dance of apprehension and uncertainty, squeezing out bits of tightly held information in a context of surprise and confusion. In this moment, though, Haji wondered if he should just come clean about whatever Walid might ask.

Right then, before anything else could be said between them, the captain came up and announced, "Prince, I'm sorry to report that every one of the enemy is dead."

"Oh, that's really too bad," Walid said. "I'm sorry also. What a waste of life. And now, in addition, we can have no answers to our questions. But we did what we had to do."

The captain then said, "The last two took their own lives with poison. I've heard of it, but had never seen it before. It's such an extreme act. There's always a reason to live."

"That's a terrible shame," Walid said.

"If I may ask, Your Highness, who exactly were these men and what were they doing?"

"They're enemies of the state, trying to force information out of my friends, here, who as sons of important individuals, and fellow students in the palace school, might be assumed to have knowledge of things that these men must have wanted to learn."

The captain looked over at Malik and Haji and said, "I'm so sorry, I should have introduced myself and expressed my great relief that you're safe. I'm Rashid al-Suki, captain in the army, third division."

"Thank you, Captain," Malik said. "It's nice to meet you. We sure do appreciate the rescue."

"Yeah, thanks Captain. Things were getting a little dicey before you got here." Haji did a small salute to the officer, who nodded back at him and then turned toward Walid again.

"Your Highness, you say those men were trying to get information. If I may ask: What sort of information would they seek from your friends and fellow students? What were such men wanting to learn?"

Walid thought for a second and said, "Some things concerning the king and your general, Masoon, I would imagine. This is Haji Afah," Walid said, pointing to one of his friends. "He's the son of Masoon. Our other friend here is Malik al-Nasir, son of Dr. Hamid. We're old friends."

"A great honor to meet you both."

"The honor is ours," Malik said, as Haji nodded.

Then Walid continued, "These violent men were trying to get information concerning the details of a recent operation, I strongly suspect. Masoon can provide more background later. If you could right now task some men to clean up the scene, I'll need for you to take us back to the palace as soon as possible. And the bodies of the fallen will need to go to the army coroner's office here in town for any possibility of identification. But we all have to get back to the palace quickly."

"Yes, Your Highness, immediately."

Far across town in the marketplace, Reela Adi walked up to the Sakat brothers' sandal shop and saw Mumar in the door. "Mumar, my friend, have you seen anything unusual across the street today?"

"Hi Reela. No, I can't say that I have. Should I have?"

"I'm not sure."

"Is everything all right?"

"I'm going over to check on that now. If I need you for anything, I'll come out front and wave. But I'm guessing that I won't."

"Oh, Ok. We're here if you do need us, and we'll be watching closely," Mumar said. Reela nodded and did a little gesture with a salute-like motion of his hand. He then crossed the street and walked down it just a bit and, turning into the area in front of the shop where he saw his sister-in-law, Shamilar, right inside the door, arranging some small decorative vases on a table. Some were a deep red, with intricate patterns. One was a beautiful bright green.

"Hello there, my dear Shamilar!"

"Reela! This is a nice surprise!"

"Thank you. It's always good to see you."

"What brings you to the shop?"

"I have a quick question to ask you."

"Certainly. Ask me anything."

"Have you noticed any activity different from the usual today, or anything strange around the shop?"

"No, not at all," Shamilar replied. "It's been a very normal morning so far. Why? Is something wrong?"

"No, there's nothing to worry about. I was just wondering if anything odd or unusual has happened around here today—anything at all that was somehow out of the ordinary."

"Well, I've been in the back most of the morning and just came out front. Shapur was out here since we arrived, and just now went into the back room. Maybe you should ask him."

"Good idea," Reela said, and turned to go into the back of the store.

"You're sure nothing's wrong?"

"Not a thing to be concerned about," he said and smiled, as he walked quickly toward the back.

Shapur was sitting in a chair, bent over a large box, as if he was going to open it. But he was at the moment simply propping himself up on it. Reela came in and said, to the top of his brother's head, "How's my favorite business man?"

Shapur looked up. "Oh! My goodness! Reela! My best brother! To what do we owe this honor of a visit?" He had a good smile for the unexpected guest.

"I … just thought I'd stop in," Reela answered. "But now that you ask, I do have a question for you."

"Sure, shoot!" Shapur replied.

"Have you seen anything unusual today? Has anything odd or out of the ordinary happened, up until now? Anything at all, however small."

"Why do you ask?"

"To tell you the absolute truth, I'm not sure. But I just had a very strange feeling."

"What do you mean?"

"I had a sense that something may have happened around here and that I should check on you."

"Well," Shapur said, and paused a moment. "There was a man who came by and surprised me while I was working outside the front entrance, arranging some pots and plants."

"What did he want?"

"He was looking for Kaza, not knowing he'd passed."

"Why was he looking for Kaza?"

"He didn't fully explain, but did say that his father and Kaza once had the same teacher, many years ago. That's how he put it."

"So, he actually gave no specific explanation for the purpose of seeking out Kaza?"

"Not really."

"Did he give his name?"

"Yes. I introduced myself and then he reciprocated and said his name is Osvaldo, a Mr. Osvaldo."

"Interesting. That's not a common name around here."

"No, it's not."

"Is that all he said?"

"Yes, it is."

"Did he speak with any discernible accent?"

"There were hints of something."

"Could you make it out?"

"No, I'm afraid not. It was almost redolent of too much, as if many accents had become blended in a strange and distinctive way, and then the blending had been masked. But that sounds strange to say."

"Interesting. What did you think of him?" Reela asked.

"Well, now, that's indeed a bit curious. I had some sort of an odd feeling immediately. I can't really put it into words. But there was something unsettling about him, I think, something … and I hate to say it, but it was almost sinister. Maybe it was just his face, or his eyes, or something else about him."

"Osvaldo."

"Yes. And when he left—and I know this is going to sound very peculiar—but I realized I was suddenly quite exhausted and even a bit dizzy, though earlier, ever since I got up this morning, I had been perfectly fine."

"That is indeed odd."

"It is. I had to rest for five or ten minutes and then I was a little better, more like my normal self."

"Good, I'm glad."

"I'm still a bit off. And it happened when the man left. But that was likely nothing but a coincidence."

"It certainly could have been. You look fine now."

"For an old man," Shapur joked.

"For any man," Reela responded and smiled. And then he said, "Ok, thanks for this information. I'll make some inquiries as to who this Osvaldo might be."

"Is there something wrong? Is there anything I should know about?"

"No, no, not at the moment."

"You're sure?"

"Well, I just had a strange feeling that I should come in today and check on you. It may be nothing. But I'll look into this name and get back to you if I learn anything."

Reela and Shapur had no idea who this man was that had darkened the doorstep of the Adi shop. And if they did find out both his identity and his purpose in Cairo, one of them would be shocked and the other, simply terrified.

4

SOME EXPLANATIONS

CAPTAIN AL-SUKI DROPPED THE BOYS OFF AT THE MAIN GATE of the palace. Walid assured him that his important help would be acknowledged with gratitude and rewarded by the monarchy, as would that of his men. The prince then said his goodbyes to all the soldiers and reminded them that the deceased should be taken to the military coroner's office for finger printing and any identification that might be possible. The captain promised that he would see to it right away and left with a small bow and quick salute to the young man.

Walid then led Mafulla, Malik, and Haji through the front gate and toward the main entrance of the palace itself, shouting out greetings to various guards as they passed near them. But about halfway to the front doors, he pulled his friends aside to a small fountain flanked by two benches close together. "We need to stop here and sit for just a minute before we go in," he said, and Malik and Haji looked at each other. Mafulla just seemed surprised. "Have a seat, everyone."

"Ok. What's up, boss?" Haji asked, as he slowly sat down on the nearest bench.

After all three of his companions were seated, Walid, still standing, looked at Malik, and then at Haji, and explained, "I ... saw what happened at the warehouse before I got you guys down from the ropes, and also once you were free, and at the end."

"You ... did?" Haji said, with a cautious tone. Mafulla appeared to be completely puzzled. But he didn't say anything.

Malik responded, "Well, we didn't see you at first, I guess. We were sort of upside down for a while and it was a little hard to see everything going on. But we had those guys just where we wanted them."

"It looked like they had you just where they wanted you," Walid replied.

Malik laughed and explained, "Well, you know, there's an up-side to upside-down, or downside-up," nervously making a little joke. Then he added, "It was a great setup for what Haji's dad likes to call a turnaround."

Walid smiled and was not at all surprised to hear this. "I know exactly what you're talking about."

Haji then jumped in and explained again, as he had earlier, "Malik always wants us to wait for the right second before we go all Wild Camel and Silver Saber on anybody, and with so many guns aimed at us today at first, I guess you could say that I was a little more favorably inclined than usual to go along with his wishes."

"Yeah, for once he didn't want ... to jump the gun," Malik said, and looked over at Haji with a grin.

"Oh, bad pun for a good plan," Haji said and added, "I just wish that waiting until the right time didn't always involve letting things seem to get so completely out of control."

"Yeah, but remember: It's the perfect preparation for a turnaround. When things look unbelievably bad, that's often when the best new opportunities open up. And we're then able to flip the situation."

Walid listened to all this and thought that both these guys must have learned a lot over the years from Masoon and Hamid. But he needed to take the conversation back to where he wanted it to go. He looked at Malik and then over at Haji and said, in particular to him, "I saw the pipe the guy swung at you when you were waiting for the right time."

"That would have hurt," Haji replied. "I took it as a clear sign that the right time suddenly had come, at that very moment."

"Yeah, and I saw it all as you caught the pipe mid-air—even though the guy had swung it suddenly and fast—and then, when you were holding on, it looked like it was glowing or something, almost like it was instantly as hot as fire. And that was quite a big surprise to me."

"Well."

"The guy who had swung it just couldn't hold on to it for a second more, like it was every bit as hot as it looked."

"Oh, yeah."

"He dropped it like it had badly burned his hand. And yet, you were holding it as well and you seemed fine."

"Yeah. I had no problem, and it felt fine to me. Maybe what you saw was just the light reflected in a strange way and, you know, the guy could have had a bad cramp or a seizure or something. Stuff like that happens when things get crazy." Haji said all this with hesitation, and he seemed a little uncomfortable, and even a bit nervous.

The Golden Viper took a deep breath and said, "Look, this is me, Walid. I have to ask you something and you have to tell me the truth. We're all for one and one for all. Remember?"

"Yeah, sure."

"I'm your friend. I'm the Viper. And I'm your personal, one and only prince."

The Wild Camel and The Silver Saber looked at each other and Mafulla studied their faces, still completely clueless about what was going on but remaining silent until he found out. Walid didn't pull the princely status thing very often, except maybe in fun. And he looked completely serious at the moment.

The first in line to the throne of the realm suddenly reached down to his left wrist and flipped his Reverso watchcase over, clicking it into its face down position. And then he stepped closer toward his two school friends, lifting the back of the steel case up near to their faces, as he had earlier with Captain al-Suki, but this time without covering any of it. He first showed it to Malik for a couple of seconds, and then to Haji and, looking at The Silver Saber, he asked: "What do you see here? Tell me."

Haji seemed completely stunned. He took a breath and said, in a strained voice, "Wow, that's … really nice. I've never noticed the back of your watchcase before. How did you …" And then, he became totally silent as his now rapid pulse pounded hard in his neck and ears, and deep in his chest.

Walid asked again: "Please, tell me, Haji: What do you see?"

"Um, Ok, well, a really cool royal crown engraving that looks pretty amazing and must have cost a lot, and …" Haji looked up at Walid and over at Mafulla and back at Walid. "There's also, a nice … letter from the … um, Greek alphabet." His mouth got really dry and his stomach did a big flutter and he stared at Walid for maybe three seconds without speaking, and then looked really serious and in a low voice asked, "Are you … Phi?" He had something like utter and complete uncertainty and a real hesitation in his tone.

Mafulla was nearly as surprised as Haji at what Walid had just done, and still didn't know what was going on. And he was strangely unable to hear Haji's question, which he didn't process or grasp immediately. But he trusted Walid for whatever was going on and wanted to back him up. So, just like earlier in the day, he also flipped his case over with an audible 'click,' and Malik instinctively looked down toward his wrist. He stared at the back of Mafulla's Reverso and said, in a near whisper, simply, "No way."

"What do you mean, 'No way'?" Mafulla responded.

"Are you?" Malik looked at Mafulla, and at his watch, then at Walid, and at Walid's watch and said, "Oh, jeez. It's just that … wow. I didn't ever think."

"Do you guys know what this means?" Mafulla asked.

Haji took a deep breath and let it out. "Yeah. Yeah."

Malik said, "We do."

"Because of your dads?"

"Well," Malik started to reply.

But then Haji said, in a lower voice, "I guess … this explains a lot, a whole lot. You two … both … are … Phi? I had no idea. I guess it never even crossed my mind. Well, once or twice, maybe, about you, Walid, because of your uncle, the king, and because of a couple of things I've seen you do. But now that I know, I guess I'm really not all that totally surprised. Well, still a little bit, or maybe more than a little, about … you know, you, Mafulla." He glanced at the youngest of the palace Phi and said, "Sorry, man. I mean, don't get me wrong, I've seen you do some great things, too, but I just thought you were sort of unusually strong for your age and wiry, and agile, but I had no idea. And it's sort of a shock. Sorry."

"What are you talking about?" Mafulla said. "I could fry your brain right now like a scrambled egg."

"But you won't," Haji said.

"No, you're right. I like you and admire your brain and will leave it just as it is—no more scrambled than it might already be at the moment."

"And I could maybe make the bench crack up under you," Haji said in a soft and kind voice. "Or burst into flames, despite being stone. But that would be pretty unpleasant, as well."

"Wait. What?" Mafulla said and looked at Walid, now speaking to him. "You saw something back there at the warehouse, and you didn't tell me about it?"

"Yeah, I saw a few things too strange to mean anything else."

"But. Why didn't you say something?"

"We were a little busy with dodging bullets at the time. I had to file it away until now. I didn't want any of us getting shot as we pondered the enigmas of the moment."

"Oh, enigmas. Nice," Mafulla said. He then looked over at Haji again and he said the only thing he could think of that would make sense of what Walid had just done and how Haji had just responded. "So. Ok. Let me get this straight. You're both Phi, too?" Then he looked at Malik. "Both of you guys?"

They were completely silent for a few seconds and then Haji spoke up and let out a deep breath and said, "Yeah, both of us."

Mafulla and Walid looked carefully at these two good friends. "Why didn't we know this?" Walid sort of asked both of them at the same time.

"Yeah," Mafulla said. "Why the big secret?"

"We didn't know it ourselves … I mean, about ourselves, until a little while back, not that long ago, and we sure didn't know about you, either," Malik said. "And … we had been sworn to secrecy."

"Who swore you to secrecy?"

"Amon," Malik said.

"Why Amon?" Mafulla asked. "Why would he do that?"

"He's our … main Phi trainer," Haji said. "We work out with him on a regular basis."

"But, I don't get it. Why would anyone, especially somebody like Amon, keep a secret from us? He's our friend. Why couldn't we know?" Walid asked. "Why wouldn't anybody tell us?"

"I have no idea," Haji said, "We didn't know about you, either. But we've violated our promise just now to keep this information to ourselves only because it's you guys. I figure that the prince maybe outranks everybody else in this sort of thing—except the king, of course, since Phi serve the people by serving the senior Phi, who is, nicely enough in this case, our king, and serving his enlightened monarchy. But that also means you, the prince, the number two in the whole royal deal. And I guess, Mafulla, you're sort of almost number three or something—maybe three and a half, or something at least semi-official, and I know that you guys know Amon really well, so … I'm sort of sure it'll be Ok, probably."

"You're sort of sure?" Walid said.

"Well, almost sure—or, at least, pretty confident, nearly."

"Why do you think they kept you guys from knowing about us, and us from knowing about you?" Walid was still trying to understand all this.

Malik replied, "Maybe, I don't know, for security and our general safety? It could be that they try to keep Phi of roughly the same age, especially us young guys, in something like separate networks, sort of, so that if somebody dangerous finds out one identity, or pair of identities, that won't necessarily compromise a whole generation of Phi, or a big part of it. That's my best guess."

Walid thought for a second and said, "That actually makes a lot of sense."

"Can you dodge a bullet?" Haji asked Walid.

"Yeah, if I have to," Walid answered.

Haji then looked at Mafulla, and Mafulla said, "Not me, of course. Wiry and agile alone wouldn't get the job done. So I just look straight at the bullet and identify myself by name and it realizes I'm not really worth shooting and it sort of misses, on its own."

At that, Haji laughed and then suddenly punched straight at Mafulla's face as fast and as hard as he could, and Mafulla caught his fist mid-air and deflected it away, but without causing any pain.

"Wow!" Haji said and grinned. "Great move. And I didn't just decide you weren't worth hitting. You stopped me fast. Super quick and awesome."

"You're pretty fast, too," Mafulla said, clearly impressed.

"Thanks. But you guys are probably way ahead of us, I think, I mean, in the training."

"Maybe a little," Walid said. "But I saw you both dodge that bullet toward the end, back there in the warehouse."

"Yeah," Haji said. "Extended proprioception. That was the first time with anything going that fast. But we've dodged so much other stuff in practice sessions, and even as the Camel and Saber, that it was sort of instinct, I think. Still, I wouldn't go around at this point assuming I can do it. That's pretty advanced. Total avoidance is always better, whenever possible." Mafulla nodded in agreement.

Then the prince asked, "Did you guys help us out in any way when we were away, on the trip to Dromeda?"

"I think so," Malik answered. "Hoda at one point got us into a meditation session in the university library, right at a table there. We were showing her some research we were doing about the animal stealing criminals, and she suddenly said that she felt there was a need and that we should help, and she led us through what she wanted us to think and picture in our minds. I guess she's a big meditator, and sort of mystical."

"Yeah, that's the truth," Walid replied. "I want you guys to know how much we appreciate you and Hoda sending us that help. It made a big difference. We needed it. And Hoda always knows when we need something like special help."

"Wait a second," Malik said. "Is Hoda more than just a really mystical meditator? Is she maybe also possibly … Phi?"

"You don't know about Hoda and Layla?" Walid replied, with his face showing that he was even more surprised.

"Hoda and Layla?" Now, Haji was sounding confused.

"Yeah, they're both very senior Phi."

"Really?" Malik said.

Then Haji added, "Ok, so, we were both maybe a little suspicious about Hoda, but Layla had not come to mind at all in that way."

"What do you mean that you were a little suspicious about Hoda?" Walid asked.

"Well, she sort of seems to have an aura or something around her all the time and, you know, we had noticed all the meditation stuff she's always doing. And, maybe you haven't heard about this yet, but Hoda sort of healed Jabari's monkey Manni from some sort of strange, intense sudden ailment or attack while you guys were away. And she did it by leading us through another really odd meditation where we had to do a visualization thing."

"I've seen Jabari since the trip," Walid replied, "and he did say that something weird had happened to Manni after the big veterinary clinic battle—I mean, after you guys shut the whole operation down, and that Hoda had somehow helped the little guy through it. He also mentioned that you two were there, too, and that you meditated along with Hoda, and him and his mom. But he didn't go into many details."

"Yeah, Hoda happened to come over to visit Jabari and his mom while we were at their house checking on Manni and retelling our story about the big action in the clinic. And this strange thing happened, first to our favorite monkey and then it started in on us—I mean, a really bad head pain," Haji explained. "It freaked Manni out, and us too. When Hoda did what she did and it worked—a bunch of stuff about imagining a pyramid and its power—we were pretty sure she must be something at least almost like Phi. But no one had told us, and the world is pretty strange, so we thought maybe she was just really super mystical or something like, I don't know, an alternative shaman sort of healer, but we sure wondered."

"What's a shaman?" Walid asked.

"It's a spiritual healer, like lots of tribal groups have in different parts of the world," Haji explained. "I've read all about those guys."

"And, yet, we didn't know what to think," Malik jumped in and said. "Plus, we were afraid to ask anybody. I mean, we assumed that if they ... wanted us to know, they'd tell us. And now, I'm glad you've finally done it, I mean, spilled the beans about Hoda. But, Hasina's mom, Layla—I had no idea. She's obviously a beautiful lady, like Hoda. And she seems really smart and kind and special, completely full of positive energy, but I never even thought of her being Phi."

Walid paused a moment and said, "Who else in Phi do you know about?"

"Well, we know about our dads, of course, and the king. We found out when Amon told us that we were being invited in."

"But not before?"

"No, not at all," Malik said. "They had kept it really quiet, our whole lives. We had no idea. We had never even heard about Phi. We just knew that Masoon and dad were super strong, committed to total fitness, and really smart, mega military types, but kind people at the same time. And we had both always wanted to be that way, too. But we had no clue about Phi."

"Did you know about Paki and Omari?"

"Yeah," Haji said. "Amon first told us about them, too. They've also helped out in our training."

"But you didn't know about the ladies?"

"No, not at all—not until you gave away the big secret just now."

"Oh, man," Walid said and looked very worried.

"What?" Mafulla asked.

"Maybe I just really sort of compromised an important separation between Phi networks by talking about Hoda and Layla."

"No," Mafulla interjected, "I'm sorry, but I'd say you just pretty much single-handedly destroyed any separation of networks, smashing it to total smithereens, like a rampaging ox in a delicate pottery shop—an image, of course, that makes any Adi shudder. And we also now know that the separation wasn't just about same age networks."

"Oh, man."

"But, what does the king always say?" Mafulla asked.

Walid looked stumped, but said, "You can't blame a mule for breaking a rule?"

Mafulla replied, "No, I've never heard him say that. But it seems true enough, anyway, and oddly appropriate in the present instance, of course." He then explained. "The king always says that things happen when the time is right. Remember the famous phrase, 'When the time had fully come.' That applies here, I think."

"Oh, yeah. Maybe so."

"No 'maybe' is allowed here. Look. We often get information just when we need it, or right before we need it. I'm guessing the fact that this has happened now is a sign that the time for any separation of our Phi networks, at least, to the extent that it existed, is over."

"You think?" Walid responded.

Mafulla continued, "Yeah, I do."

Malik said, "That makes sense to me."

Haji said, "It does."

Mafulla continued. "The separation must have served its purpose, you know, during our period of greatest weakness, through our early training. But, now, this is a sign that we're developed enough and we're all strong enough to know."

"Ok. Ok, I get that," Walid said. "That makes a lot of sense."

Malik spoke up and said, "Do your parents know about you guys?" He was clearly still getting his head around all this.

"My parents do," Walid answered, "but not Maffie's."

"How about the girls? How about Kissa and Hasina?" Haji added. "Do they even suspect anything about you guys or their moms? Or do you think they've ever even heard about Phi?"

Walid looked at Mafulla. Mafulla looked back. And then Walid took a deep breath and said, "They both know."

"Really?"

"Yeah. Totally."

"Are you sure that's safe?" Haji asked.

"Yeah," Walid answered. "They're both totally trustworthy, really strong, and they both have Phi skills I don't think we could even touch."

"Wait! Whoa! Slow down! They're Phi, too?" Malik said and looked even more surprised than ever. "I had no idea there were girl Phi!"

Walid now looked puzzled, as he replied, "Well, sure. Their moms are Phi, like we just said. And they were once girls."

"Yeah, Ok, that's true. But I didn't know that until just now, either, and my brain's still not working well enough for me to get a grip on all this. And, plus, I do know that Phi isn't always passed down in families from fathers to sons, or I guess mothers to daughters, or maybe even through aunts or uncles—sometimes, but not always. I just never imagined there would be girl Phi our age."

Walid said, "Well, Kissa and Hasina come from many generations of Phi. It's actually pretty amazing how far back it goes in their families. It could be that this is why they have such deep skills. And from what I've heard, they all started young in their earliest manifestations of those abilities."

Haji now asked, "Are there other girl Phi, or other grown women Phi, in addition to Layla and Hoda?"

Mafulla said, "We don't know for sure. But we think so. Remember all the people in the lobby of the big hotel in Alexandria the first night we were there on our school trip?"

"Yeah?"

"Well, a lot of them were Phi, we were told, and there were several ladies in the area."

"I remember one girl about our age," Mafulla said. "She was standing with an older woman."

"Interesting," Haji said. "Very interesting. And one night, while you guys were gone on the recent trip, we saw Hoda and Khalid walking to dinner at the Grand Hotel, and they said they were going to meet with an old friend of Hoda's, a lady she mentioned was her teacher or mentor or something. Maybe that's another, older, senior lady Phi."

"Man, we haven't heard about her," Mafulla said. "I wonder how many of us there are in the kingdom?"

"It can't be too many, but it's got to be more than we know," Walid speculated. Then he asked Haji, "Did anyone tell you yet what happened in Dromeda?"

"Only that the bad guys took off when they knew you were coming, and you found a lot of stolen animals and returned them to their owners. And, you know, Hoda said you needed help of some sort at that one point where we joined in."

"Hmm. Maybe you should know more, and then everything might make a little more sense."

"There's more?"

"Yeah, a lot more."

"We'd love to know," Haji said and looked over at Malik, who nodded.

"It's pretty amazing," Mafulla said.

"Yeah?"

"Totally. But I'll let my friend here tell you all about it."

"Good. So, tell."

"Ok, then, here's the story," Walid said as he now sat down on one of the two benches and began to relate the entire tale. He told them as quickly as he could the highlights of everything that had taken place, all the strange and dangerous stuff, both on the trip generally, and at the ambush where he thought Kissa had been shot. And he recounted the strangeness of mysterious village and how their time there ended with the huge, bizarre experience they all had at the end, before the trip back to Cairo. He also told them at least the basics about The Book of Phi, The Ring of Phi, and The Stone of Giza, as he related the tale—things they had not yet been brought in on.

The Camel and the Saber both sat mostly silent until the very end of the story, looking stunned for pretty much the entire duration of it. Then they spoke. "Oh, man," Haji first said.

"That's totally freakish and unbelievably crazy," Malik added.

"The whole thing really gave me the shivers, the total heebie-jeebies, just hearing about it all—especially the fire stuff, and the monster legend, and then what happened at the end," Haji added. "I mean—you guys went through all that?"

"Yeah," Walid said.

"How powerful, really, is the king? I mean, really." Malik said, in amazement.

"Well, he used The Ring of Phi," Walid said.

Haji scratched his head and said, "Yeah, but still. And I thought the normal Viper and Storm stuff was awesome. This is way, way beyond anything like that."

"It was pretty wild and totally weird," Mafulla said. "On a cosmic scale of one to ten, it was about a two-thousand."

"I bet," Malik replied.

Haji said, "I'm also amazed at hearing about the ring, the book, and the stone, along with the crazy stuff that happened on the trip."

"Yeah, it's all pretty wild," Walid agreed.

Mafulla quickly added, in a spirit of grace and friendship, "We wished out loud a couple of times on the trip that you guys had been able to come along with us. But then we remembered to be glad that you were here in town taking care of business while we were away. We just didn't know that we had left a couple of fellow Phi in charge of the crime fighting enterprise in our absence. And we had no idea at all that you guys would end up playing such a crucial role in breaking up the whole animal theft ring. But now that makes total sense. That was true tip-top Phi stuff and legendary League of Crime Fighters."

"International," Malik said, with a smile.

"Yeah, international," Mafulla, laughed, echoing his own original addition to the name they had taken on for their new joint venture to stop crime in the capital.

The Golden Viper, The Windstorm, The Wild Camel, and The Silver Saber were, of course, the founders and, at present, the total membership of The League of Crime Fighters, International. As a fun, made-up club or group, it was really just a commitment of mutual support and encouragement that sprang from the crazy unexpected event where they had discovered each others' secret identities, as well as their parallel history of similar activities in helping to rid the city of crime, or at least, any instances of it that they happened to come across during their normal activities. It was now, to their mutual complete surprise again, a sort of junior Phi club, so far involving only, but not of course all, the younger Phi in Cairo.

"One for all and all for one," Walid repeated with a smile.

And then the other three echoed the phrase in near whispers, and so did Walid, as they all reached out their right hands into a classic, four-way hand stack. Two palace guards passing by at a distance looked over at them, but they continued walking toward the front entrance of the palace, as one of them spoke to the other. The boys didn't notice them at all. "Let's go see the king," Walid then said to his friends.

"Oh, man. I'm a little concerned," Malik said.

"Yeah," Haji added.

"Don't worry," Walid reassured them. "Here's the plan. I'll go in first and talk to him, with Mafulla. You guys can wait outside with Kular for a few minutes and have a snack or something, and maybe then come in to see him, too." They all agreed on this way of proceeding, and got up and walked into the palace together.

Across town, Reela Adi stood at the reference desk in the University of Cairo library and said in a voice barely above a whisper, "Excuse me." The librarian on duty looked up at him with a pleasant expression, and Reela asked in a bit louder tone, "Are you able to discover from any sources in the library if there is anyone in the city or the kingdom with the last name of 'Osvaldo'?"

The man answered, "Well, we have various birth and tax records on file here, and I could look those over for you, or give you access for your own search."

"I might like to do my own search," Reela said, "If it's not too overwhelming."

"What was the name again that you're looking for?"

"Osvaldo."

A young man just then bringing the reference librarian a stack of books looked over and said, "Did I hear the name 'Osvaldo'?"

"Yes," Reela answered. "Do you know anyone by that name?"

"I do," the young man said. "He's Osvaldo Pugliese, the great tango pianist and composer from Buenos Aires, Argentina."

"Oh, I'm looking for someone with that as their surname, their family name—and perhaps someone Spanish."

"There are a lot of Spaniards in Argentina."

"Yes, I know. But I need one who's here in town." Reela smiled.

"Osvaldo Pugliese is here in town! He's playing this week at the Foxtrot Club, all the way from Argentina. And this is his last night to be with us."

Reela smiled. "Well, that's very nice, but I'm not searching for a musician by the name."

"You should be! He's really great. I heard him two nights ago. You should go tonight. Do yourself a big favor. The tango is pretty incredible. And he's the best, really the best."

Reela now grinned at the young man's enthusiasm and said, "Thanks for the tip. I just might go." And then he thought, "Why not?" He hadn't had a night out in a long time. And he loved good music. The Foxtrot was a very elegant supper club and venue for both music and dance, frequented by the more fashionable side of Cairo society and a certain wealthy international clientele. It had been at least a couple of years since Reela had gone there. He suddenly felt a growing desire to visit, perhaps after he did his research. He had no way of knowing that the real discovery of value on the topic of his concern would take place not here in the library, but among some of the most elegantly dressed ladies and gentlemen of the kingdom, in one of the most unlikely of places for the detective work he was undertaking. But the biggest clues to hidden truths are often found in surprising places.

5

Tango and the Truth

The El-Bay house was filled with wonderful aromas. Hoda walked into the kitchen with a big smile and said, "Shumar, you're so good to us!"

He smiled back. "It's my pleasure, mom." He was busily chopping vegetables to be cooked later on. And already, the stock for a soup was simmering on the small stove. The aroma filled the room, and was beginning to make its way through the entire house.

"Well, I'm glad you're here. Thank you so much for all the help this afternoon."

"You're quite welcome. It's good to get away from work and hang out with you guys and lend a hand now and then."

"But then you come here and also work." Hoda laughed.

"It's not work here. It's different," Shumar replied. "It's pure fun."

"I'm glad to hear that. And we all benefit! Now let me ask: Will you and Baqid be around this evening? Can you join us for dinner?"

"Oh, I wish we could," Shumar replied. "But we had to change the night we go out with friends this week. Tonight we're planning to go to a couple of the clubs for dinner and then music."

"And yet, you still come and do dinner preparation for us."

"It's one of my gifts. Plus, I'm such a good son, you must admit."

Hoda laughed and said, "Yes, you are. So, where are you and your brother going with your friends this evening?"

"First, we'll go to The Nile Club for dinner and then, later on, we'll stop in at the Foxtrot for the music."

"Oh?"

"There's a famous tango musician playing there, and I think this is his last performance before he goes back to his native South America."

"Good. I'm glad you'll get to hear him." She smiled and raised her eyebrows. "Are you going to tango?"

"Well, that depends. It's a tremendously tangled tale—about the talented teacher I'm taking to tonight's tango." He grinned at this display of his own alliterative ability and then said, "But you know me: I am a dancing fool. With the right partner, there'll be gossip all the way back to Buenos Aires."

Hoda laughed and said, "Whatever you do, I hope you have a great time."

"What's my brother going to do to have a great time?" Kissa asked this as she walked into the room. "I didn't hear."

"He's going out to some clubs tonight with friends and he'll hear a famous tango musician play at the Foxtrot. And—who knows—he may even have a chance to dance!"

"What's tango?"

Shumar answered as he scooped the vegetables from the cutting board into a bowl, "It is a fiery, provocative music, with great rhythm, and it accompanies a dance that's quite dramatic." He did a funny spin with a bend move and ended in a momentarily frozen pose with the knife above his head, and that made Kissa laugh. Then he said, "It all started during the last century in Argentina and Uruguay, but it has European and African influences. From what I've heard, the guy playing tonight is one of the very greatest tango musicians alive."

Kissa then sighed and said, "If I could just age faster! I can't wait to be able to go to the supper clubs with my own friends and hear music like that!"

Hoda laughed. "You'll one day wish you could age slower, much slower, so be content. You're at a great age."

Khalid just then walked in and heard Hoda's words and said, "Yes, you're at a great age … for taking the puppies outside. They need a little time … in nature."

Kissa laughed and said, "Ok, Dad. I'll take them out right away."

"Take Shibby, too, of course. She'll help you watch them."

Kissa sighed and said, "Shumar gets to go dancing, and I'm on doggie duty."

"It's not all glamour and music and elegance in the world," Khalid replied with a smile. "But, then again, Shibby does have a pretty glamorous brood now. And the little whimpers of the pups can be quite musical if you listen properly."

"You're right," Kissa agreed. "I can hear the concert starting up now. I'd better get moving."

"Yes, please, before they're moved first!"

"Khalid!" Hoda playfully scolded with a smile.

Upstairs at the palace, Walid and Mafulla had been with the king in his sitting room for more than thirty minutes, reporting everything that had happened since the prince was with Khalid at the El-Bay house, mid morning—from Mafulla's urgent visit with the note, to their first hitch-hiking experience, with its surprising accident, to their rescue assault on the warehouse with army back-up. Walid told the king about the metal pipe, the glow from it, and then what he had seen Haji do with it. He spoke also about how the two boys handled themselves in the gunfight and then, finally, with a touch of trepidation, he reported the conversation that they had just gone through on some palace benches outside. The king listened quietly and with complete attention, asking only an occasional question along the way. His head had nodded slowly at some of the points in the story. And now, Walid was about to wrap it up.

"So, I wanted to apologize to you, Uncle, Your Majesty, if I've done something wrong in revealing our Phi status to Haji and Malik, and asking them about theirs. I was just so surprised at what I'd seen, and maybe I wasn't thinking as clearly as I should have been. I guess I ought to have asked you, first."

"No, no, it's quite normal and perfectly all right," the king replied. "You're correct in the belief that we had established separated networks, as you well put it, of the younger Phi, for the sake of security and safety. But all four of you have proved that you're now beyond the need for that extra measure of caution. I'll make sure to let your older Phi friends know, in each of those networks, right away. The cat is officially out of the bag."

"I love that expression," Mafulla said. "But I've always wondered how the cat got into the bag in the first place."

"Not now," Walid said.

"I was thinking curiosity, but there's another saying about that."

"And it's an unfortunate one," the king replied, amused at Mafulla's stream of consciousness here, as always.

"Yes. Curiosity killed the cat. But I'm thinking rather that it bagged the cat. And although there is a colloquial usage wherein what is bagged is indeed eliminated, I suspect we can eschew that tangled tie at the present time and just answer our question in the simplest way."

"Simple is often good," the king said with a smile, playing along. "And the one thing curiosity tends to eliminate most reliably, whether simply or not, is perplexity. And the simple truth of my reaction to all that you've told me is that I'm proud of what you did today, both in saving your friends and in following your own curiosity to learn the deeper truth about them."

"Thanks, Your Majesty," Walid said.

"Yeah, thanks," Mafulla added.

"You're quite welcome," the king responded.

Mafulla then added his own additional expression of relief by saying, "You know, Your Majesty, you're always … just … so incredibly understanding about everything."

"I thank you for those kind words, Mafulla. It's easy to act in an understanding way if you do understand. When our eyes have been opened and we see even a glimpse of the true big picture for things, that vision of our overall context, along with the confidence and compassion it breeds, allows us to be, in most matters toward those around us, as you put it, incredibly understanding. We're then comfortable enough to have a certain trust in the way things play out and develop. Too many people run around shocked and panicked or angry and worried because they're untethered to the deepest truths. So, they don't see others truly. And this is often also because they don't see themselves truly, either. And, as it's well been said, the truth can set you free. It liberates us in a variety of ways."

"I'm still learning that," Mafulla said.

"Yes, you are, and that's good," the king replied. "One of the most wonderful things about a life well lived is that we're always learning." He took a sip of his tea and sat in silence for a moment, and then continued. "I do want to congratulate both of you on the brave and well-executed rescue assault. I still have to remind myself now and then that your skills are at a level not normally to be expected from even the best young Phi until five or six years beyond your current age, at the very earliest. You're both extreme prodigies. And I'm glad. I certainly wish, however, that, despite your extraordinary level of development, you had been able to take a Phi contingent with you as backup. But, in this most unusual case, and unknown to you at the time, you had Phi waiting for you onsite. And of course, it was very prudent to bring along the soldiers you met, by accident, as most people would say. But we know that coincidence is quite often the disguise of something much more interesting and important."

"We do," Walid said. "And it was vital to have those men with us, given the number of adversaries we faced."

"Yes. I'm glad you teamed up with them."

"They all performed bravely and well. I'm not sure we could have done the job as safely without them."

The king replied, "I'll make certain that they're recognized for their valor in service to you and the kingdom."

"I guess we have one huge question to deal with," Walid said. "Who exactly are these guys that attacked Malik and Haji, how did they find our friends, and what are they up to?"

"Three huge questions," Mafulla said. "But, who's counting?"

"What? Oh, yeah, you're right," Walid turned and replied with a smile. "I should pay more attention in our math lessons."

The king asked, "Were the boys themselves, Malik and Haji, able to shed any light on those questions?"

"In the truck on the way back, Malik mentioned that the man who spoke the most to him had a thick accent and it sounded Spanish, which almost certainly connects them to our mystery villain, that Santiago character. And then, right after that, what Malik told us was said first thing to them sort of seals the deal that it's our monster."

"What was that?"

"He reported that, when the guys all initially jumped them and had about eight guns on them at the same time, one of them said, "We want to know who helped you break up the veterinary clinic operation, who tipped you off about the place, and also who went on the trip to Dromeda. We want names!'"

"Yeah," Mafulla added, "and then Haji said they told the guys that nobody helped them at the clinic. They did it alone, except for a small monkey, until some palace guards showed up at the end, and they didn't need anybody's tips. Plus, they had never received an official list of travellers on the trip to Dromeda, since they didn't go, and so they couldn't answer that one at all helpfully, either."

The king said, "Well, we can then be certain that Santiago is behind this. And knowing what we do about him at this point, his aim is likely nothing any more complicated right now than mere revenge."

"Really?" Walid asked.

"Sadly, yes. He wants to punish anyone who's interfered with him. But then, he'll surely also proceed with his larger plans, whatever they might be, in some new way. The boys did well to deny his men any useful answers, especially since they couldn't have known at the time that none of the interrogators would make it out of the building alive. They did very well."

"Yes, sir, so well that it got them hung up by their ankles, Your Majesty." Mafulla replied.

"And then your Phi sensitivity and guidance got you there at the perfect time to see what you saw and do what you did."

"It's sometimes a little spooky how that works, and how the accident got all woven into everything and gave us the help we'd need."

"It also slowed you down so that you'd not get to the meeting place too soon," the king pointed out.

"But if we had gotten there sooner, the guys wouldn't have been strung up by their feet," Mafulla said.

"Yes," the king said, "and then Walid would not have seen the first and most obvious sign of Phi ability which, it now seems, he was supposed to witness and recognize. The time had fully come, and it was right. So your arrival, for an important reason, had to happen exactly when it did. You made it there for the precise moment that awaited you."

"That's just too much, I mean, when you think about all the timing involved and how we got to where we needed to be just when we needed to be there," Mafulla replied.

"Some people call it synchronicity, and some speak of serendipity," the king said. "Many invoke the notion of luck."

"Yes, sir. In the old days, I would have said we had amazing good luck."

"I'm sure. But is luck a rich enough concept? I think not. I believe true synchronicity, or in another sense serendipity, involves something much deeper and more interesting, as you know—that could even be characterized as a wellspring of purposive intention bubbling beneath the façade of apparently unrelated events." He paused for a moment and said, "We're blessed when we live in tune with the deeper forces, energies, and signs around us. And then we can bless others. It's a bit like a dance to unheard rhythms produced, possibly, by something that's mystically akin to what Pythagorus called 'the music of the spheres.' And that means, in this case, the spiritual symphony that's always playing for those who have ears to hear it, based on a score composed by the greatest genius, and then performed under the most meticulous direction, but yet, with plenty of freedom for creative interpretation and nuance along the way."

"I like that image," Walid said. "It's pretty wild and insightful."

"Yeah, it makes me think," Mafulla agreed. "If we'll just listen, there is a symphony."

The king said, "We should seek to develop the capacity deep within us to listen and hear, or feel and live the music. We don't know precisely what piece will be played next," he said and paused with a smile. "But, as things are going, I would tend to expect something dramatic—and quite dramatic, indeed."

The boys nodded in agreement, and the king then said, "I think we should bring in your friends now and put them at ease. Otherwise, they might eat too many of Kular's rich cookies and as a result, grow sluggish—which would not be good for ... international crime fighters."

Mafulla's mouth fell open and he said, "How did?" before realizing that he needn't ask. He just added, "Never mind," as the king smiled. Mafulla had realized, long before now, that the king often had odd, uncanny knowledge. He didn't know everything. In fact, no one in this world could literally know everything. But Mafulla now understood that Ali could know many things without the normal expected channels of perception, evidence, or testimony serving as intermediaries between his mind and whatever facts drew his attention.

Across town at his home, Reela Adi pulled a box down from a shelf in the closet, placed it on a table, lifted off the lid, and looked down at the most elegant pair of sleek black shoes, gleaming from the perfect polishing they had been given before they were last stored. He smiled and picked up one of them as he remembered the last event where he had worn them—the welcome reception for the man who, at the time, had just come to the capital as the new ambassador from Tunisia. It's too bad that he was not at all what he was supposed to be, and that he had been involved with such corrupt people. Reela thought on it all for a moment. The man's associations and activities had led to his brutal death and the tragic, untimely demise of his son, a boy just a little older than Mafulla and Walid. But that reception itself had been quite a night. In the old days, such shoes as these would have been worn at least two or three nights a week, if not more. Now, they often sat patiently for months in their box within a dark closet, waiting for some excuse to come out and glow. Tonight was as good an opportunity as any these days for a man whose work no longer involved lavish evenings of entertainment and, sometimes, intrigue.

Reela dressed fully, except for his bare feet, then pulled on some new thin dark socks he had just purchased, and finally eased his toes into the soft black calfskin, custom handcrafted British Balmorals that would carry him to his destination and, perhaps, even across the dance floor. He whistled a tune as he splashed a small amount of cologne on his face and then considered himself in the mirror. "Older, indeed, but not too old," he said to himself. "Aged to perfection?" He laughed aloud and thought, "Perhaps. But likely, even a bit more."

Within a couple of minutes, he walked out his front door and down the street, looking forward to what the evening ahead might hold. Tango. It was a recent innovation. He had read about it and heard some talk of it and was eager to experience one of the most highly acclaimed top practitioners performing it, from all the way across the world. Osvaldo. Reela was still haunted by the name that Shapur's brief visitor had given him when he came to the shop looking for old Kaza. What an interesting thing that it was also the name of this famous musician. Life seems to play its tricks, now and then, and provide us with little winks along the way, as we seek our aims and goals.

The night air was a touch cool. Reela's stroll through the early evening didn't take long. He lived close to some of the nicest entertainment locations in town. The Foxtrot Club could now just be seen a block or two up the street. People were already arriving for dinner. The show would follow. Reela approached the front door, smiled, nodded at the doorman, and walked in. High ceilings and light wood trims that were almost the color of desert sand welcomed him. A large Persian carpet of dark green, festooned with intricate patterns of red and gold, padded his steps as he made his way toward the spot where an elegantly attired older man granted admittance to those whose names he had in a book, as well as to a few others whose presence he thought might brighten the evening. Lots of happy conversations and occasional laughter spilled out from the large room up ahead. Waiters waltzed around through the spaces between tables, smoothly putting down plates, picking up gleaming cutlery, and filling glasses and cups. The tinkling of silver, crystal, and fine china already provided its own music to the night.

The gentleman with the reservations book gave a quick expression of recognition and, moving out from behind his post, approached Reela that moment with a smile, a small bow, and a word of greeting. He then led him quickly though the inner doorway, by several groups of seated guests, and over to a table for two with an excellent view of the stage. Reela thanked him and reached out his hand with a generous show of appreciation in the form of a substantial Egyptian banknote, and an even broader smile appeared on the man's face as he bowed again, backed away, and turned, snapping his fingers twice. Two young waiters came spinning around nearby tables with trays held high and, dipping down, placed small plates of breads and olives and cheeses on the crisp white linen, with cool water and strong tea poured into a glass and a beautifully decorated cup that were already at the table. One of the men handed their guest an elongated rectangular menu with ecru pages set into rich burgundy leather and inscribed in a broad calligraphic script, and then he whirled away again and dis-appeared, along with his associate.

Reela was accustomed to sitting and enjoying a meal alone, at least, since his official retirement from a long career in the Foreign Service. And tonight he expected to be no exception. He looked around the room, took a sip of tea, and glanced down at the menu. But before he could begin to survey the selections available for dinner, the owner of the establishment came over to his table and greeted him warmly.

"Mr. Adi! Very nice! Reela! It's so good to see you!"

Reela pushed back his chair and stood and, with a big smile said, "Hector! How are you? It's good to see you again, too."

"What a great treat to find you here this evening! It's been far too long! What brings you back to our humble establishment, which of course, as you know, is also the best of its kind in the world?"

"Ah! Yes!" Reela laughed. "It's been too long since I've been able to visit. This is certainly one of my favorite spots on earth."

"You're most kind."

"I've heard that you're having some fine music tonight, and I was curious to come and enjoy it, along with your always excellent culinary delights."

"I thank you for your gracious words. We have wonderful music almost every night. But you're right. Tonight's performance is indeed special. Where have you been? I haven't seen you in ages."

Reela sighed and said, "Business takes me many places and, at my age, it's become a little tiring."

"Listen to you! You're still at the peak of your powers. I can tell by just looking at you. Where have your travels taken you recently?"

"Tripoli, Tunis, Algiers—mainly to some neighboring capitals."

"Did you happen to visit The Sands Club while you were in Tunis?"

"No, I'm afraid that, during the recent trip, I had no night life whatsoever."

"That's too bad."

"Yes, it is. The work I was doing was a bit too demanding. I haven't had an evening out, in forever."

"Well, please, relax and sit back down. May I join you for a moment?"

"Certainly, it would be a pleasure."

Hector Gravas pulled out a chair and sat down opposite Reela, and then motioned a nearby waiter to the table. "Chill us some bubbly from Bin 31 and bring it right away, would you?"

"Yes, sir! Immediately!"

Reela laughed and said, "You're extravagantly generous, my friend."

"Wait till you see what it is!" Hector laughed as well. "I want you to taste the magnificent Salon '28."

"Oh! I haven't had it. But I've heard great things. Champagne at its finest, they say."

"It's very nice. I keep it for special occasions and very special guests. We have to celebrate your newfound freedom to join us again now, presumably out from under the more taxing burdens of international mystery and your long-term job of keeping the world safe from danger and disorder." Reela chuckled some more and his host continued, "We must make this visit well worth your time and perhaps you'll come back soon and bring some of your many fascinating friends."

"Hector, you're too generous. I didn't even expect to see you tonight. I thought you and Lisandra were in Capri for the season."

"Ah, you know, things change. That had been the plan, as it is this time every year. But the opportunity presented itself to spend a few weeks in Paris with friends and family in the coming days, and you know how Lisandra loves Paris. We just couldn't be away for both. So we'll head off to the city of lights soon and then do Capri, perhaps, in a few more months."

"Both are good places to be," Reela said.

"Yes. It will be nice to visit them both this year."

Reela nodded and thought for a moment and said, "My old friend, you most likely have a wider set of acquaintances than anyone else I know, throughout the city."

"My network is nearly as wide as my waistline these days."

Reela laughed again and said, "Perhaps it's you whose business involves danger."

Hector chuckled as well. "Yes, and at my age, I should be more careful. So, tonight, perhaps only one glass of the champagne!"

"It sounds like it will be a memorable one."

"Yes."

"I may have two glasses."

Hector laughed loudly and said, "Good! I insist!"

"Now, I need to ask you a somewhat serious question."

"Anything for my old friend."

"I'm looking for a man in the area who introduces himself with the name of Osvaldo, not a common name around here. Do you know such a man?"

"Like our star performer tonight?"

"Yes, but as a family name. He may be a recent arrival or just a visitor to town."

"What's his nationality?"

"I don't know."

"Nothing comes to mind. But I'll ask around." Gravas then learned in across the table and said in a conspiratorial voice, "First, tell me: Will it be extremely unhealthy for this man if you locate him? Could I lose a potential customer?"

Reela laughed and said, "You confuse me with my younger self."

"You can't fool an old fool like me," Hector replied. "I know who you are. The tiger doesn't change its stripes."

The champagne came at that point, and after a moment to view the label, followed by a gentle pop and pour, both men drank a toast to good health, good friends, and a great evening. Reela was very impressed with the vintage, and both men waxed poetical in seeking to name the aromas of the nose, along with the subtle flavors lying in wait beneath the bubbles. Each laughed jovially at the other's efforts.

"We're no poets, my friend," Hector said, chuckling.

"No, but we appreciate a good wine," Reela responded.

"That we do. I'm glad you like it."

"Spectacular!"

Hector spoke a few more words to his guest and finally excused himself for a bit to go check on things, promising that he'd be back later. Reela thanked him again for his generous hospitality and thought to himself what a good idea it had been to come out tonight. He ordered his dinner shortly after that and, when it came more quickly than he would have expected, he enjoyed every bite of it tremendously. The champagne was perfect with it. The waiters were also especially attentive, and during the course of the meal, four other old friends or current acquaintances stopped by the table for varying lengths of time to say hello.

Then, just as dessert was put down with coffee, a small orchestra took the stage, and a couple of minutes later, an announcer said, "Ladies and Gentlemen, the Foxtrot Club is proud to present, on his world tour all the way from Argentina, the leading composer and pianist of tango in our time, Mr. Osvaldo Pugliese!" There was loud applause all throughout the club, along with some shouts and whistles. And a young man of about thirty walked across the stage, nodded his head in recognition, gave a small wave to the room, and took his seat on the bench of the gleaming black grand piano that was awaiting him in a prominent position, next to the other musicians who were already in place. At his direction and count, the first song started, and Reela knew right away why he had such a reputation.

In no time at all, several couples were up on the dance floor, and all of them seemed to know exactly what they were doing. It was an amazing sight. The drama of the dance was quite a thing to see, and it suited the music perfectly. The end of the first number brought an enthusiastic ovation and even more dancers to the floor in front of the stage. Now, the evening was in full swing.

Reela had noticed several younger people come into the room during the first tune, and he instantly spotted Shumar El-Bay, and then his brother Baqid, among them. Shumar stood out in any crowd. He was clearly his mother's son, with a striking face and ample dark hair combed back in the European style. "This is a man for the movies," Reela thought to himself, even though he had seen him before many times. But tonight, Shumar looked even more dashing than usual.

Baqid, almost as handsome as his brother, reflected more his father's features and had, as a consequence, a serious look of high and almost scholarly intelligence. Their entrance attracted quite a wave of fleeting attention throughout the room, even though the music was playing and so many couples were moving in thrall to its beat. Three very attractive and elegantly dressed young ladies about the age of Shumar and Baqid, along with a male friend, had arrived with them. And they all now made their way across the room to a table on the far side of the large dining area.

Hector suddenly slid into the chair again opposite Reela. "How do you like the music?"

"He's very good," Reela answered. "And this tango style is certainly captivating. There's a great drama to it."

"Yes. I thought you'd enjoy it."

"I just had an idea—a feeling, really."

"Ah. Many people do when listening to tango. And there's a lovely lady here tonight to whom I could introduce you, a good friend of mine."

"No, no, that's not the idea or the feeling," Reela laughed. "Or, at least, not the one on my mind."

"I see." Hector smiled with an expression of amused disbelief.

"I'd like to have a moment to talk with our featured musician, Osvaldo, privately, just the two of us, but only briefly, during whatever break he might take. Is that possible?"

"You know the owner of the establishment. Anything's possible."

"Well then, how about it?"

"I'll get the two of you together during the first break. And then, if you're interested, there's still the lovely Yvette. And I believe she can tango."

Reela laughed again and said, "It takes two to tango."

Hector chuckled and nodded and then got up with a smile and said, "You're a quick learner. And she's an excellent teacher of many things, or at least so I've been told." Reela shook his head at his old friend in mock amazement, and Hector turned and made his way back across the room, between the tables.

A little more than thirty minutes later, the proud owner of the Foxtrot Club appeared again, smiling and laughing and escorting Osvaldo Pugliese over to the empty chair at Reela's table, weaving their way around a great many well-wishers and diners exclaiming praise for the young man and his music. With a firm grip on

Osvaldo's arm, Gravas made quick introductions as Reela stood, and then with a word to excuse himself from their company, he had a waiter bring some new cold and refreshing drinks for the enjoyment of the two.

"Thank you so much for stopping over," Reela said to the man. "I'm immensely enjoying your music this evening."

"Good! That's nice to hear! The music is from my heart," Osvaldo replied.

"Yes, and also the heart of the world," Reela said. He then added, "Because of both those truths, it touches all our hearts as well."

"That's beautifully said. You're most kind," Osvaldo replied, and at Reela's prompting gesture, they both sat down.

"Look," Reela said, "I don't want to detain you when you most likely would prefer to be resting."

"It's quite all right. I'll rest when I'm dead."

Reela laughed and said, "One never knows." He then cautioned with a smile, "We may be called upon to be even more active in the next adventure."

Osvaldo also laughed. "I suppose that might be true. But then, I'll insist on higher pay and longer breaks!"

"Good, good," Reela replied with a chuckle. "Perhaps we'll unionize the afterlife and negotiate for a few other extras, as well."

Osvaldo laughed again and raised his glass, and Reela continued by saying, "Cheers." After a sip of his drink, he said, "Now, if you don't mind, let me ask you something that's totally out of the blue."

"Ok, shoot."

"Have you ever met anyone who has 'Osvaldo' as a family name?"

"That is out of the blue! Let me think. No, I can't say that I have."

"Do you know any other Osvaldos at all?"

"Yes, a few back home."

"All first names?"

"I believe so. But … wait. Now that I think about it, there was one fellow I met a few years ago who had Osvaldo as his middle name. He was from Spain, if I recall, but was in Argentina for a while."

"Who was he?"

"A very strange man. He made quite an impression. He came to the home of a great musician I knew. They had met at some sort of spiritual lodge, some kind of retreat for creative artists and mystical types. We were sitting around having drinks at my friend's apartment in the city, and this extremely odd and almost scary fellow dropped by for a visit."

"You say he was almost scary?"

"Yes. He was extraordinarily intense, clearly a man on a quest. Not really a pleasant type at all. He was all wrapped up in seeking energies, as he put it. It was almost as if, in his presence, you felt your own life energy being sapped, or actually taken away by the man. I'd even go so far as to call him a spiritual vampire, as odd as that might sound. He was a strange one, indeed."

"Oh, my. He must have been dreadful," Reela replied. "Do you happen to recall his full name?"

"Yes, yes, I do, now that you ask. It was Juan Osvaldo Santiago."

Reela was greatly surprised at hearing this name, Santiago. It was one that had been shared with the prince and Mafulla during their trip to Dromeda, not long ago, in connection with a mysterious individual who had lived for a time not far from Walid's home village and had been abducting animals on a large scale throughout northern Africa, and perhaps in Spain. He was thought to be on a relentless quest of spiritual access and power, to be used for his own nefarious purposes. And he did seem to have extraordinary abilities. Some even suspected this Santiago to be the living incarnation of an ancient legend, traditionally referred to simply as, "The Legend of the Monster." It was a tale about a deeply damaged and perverse individual who lived his life in pursuit of superhuman energy and strength in order to wield ultimate control over others.

"Do you happen to know whatever became of this man, this Santiago, after you met him?"

"No, not really. It was rumored he travelled the world. But just two days ago, I overheard one of the musicians here use that name. As I walked by the stage after a practice, I distinctly heard one of the men say to another, "I spoke to Santiago yesterday," but at the time, I thought nothing more of it. Perhaps it's a complete coincidence and he referred to some other individual."

"Who were these men? Are they on the stage with you tonight?"

"Actually, no. They were both Spaniards, as I now come to think of it—Moors. They suddenly left us that afternoon without advance notice, and we had to hustle to find replacements for them."

"Do you know their names?"

"No, I'm afraid I don't. But someone in the band most likely might, if you'd care to ask around."

Reela said, "Something tells me that this Juan Osvaldo Santiago of whom you speak could be the individual I'm seeking. And if he is, then I have some independent reason to believe, from another source, that he's indeed currently here in Cairo—but for what purpose, I have no confident answer. My only confidence is that it's not good—not good at all."

6

THE MUSIC TEACHER

IT WAS A BREEZY MONDAY AFTERNOON. THE MARKETPLACE was thinning out from the usual morning rush, and things were temporarily quiet in the Adi shop. Shamilar had been in the back for a few minutes to help with the unpacking of some recent stock, and she suddenly thought she heard voices out front. Walking quickly back into the main part of the store to give assistance to any shopper who might have entered, she was delighted by the sight of two faces just inside the door.

"Kit! Khata! It's so good to see you! What a nice surprise! What are you lovely young ladies doing out and about today?"

"Oh! Hi, Madame Adi," Kit said with a big smile. "We're both out shopping with Khata's mom."

"Please, Kit, call me Shamilar. And you say Rama is here?" Shamilar exclaimed, looking quickly around the store.

"Yes, but she's still next door, negotiating over something," Khata said with a laugh. "It may take a while."

"She's like me, very prudent with the family resources," Mafulla's mother said. "It's one of the many reasons we've been such good friends for years. We always share tips on where to get a bargain. Now, are you two simply spending some time browsing around while you wait for the great negotiator, or is there something I could help you with?"

"Mom just got us a piano, and we need a beautiful vase to go on top of it," Khata said.

"She got the piano?"

"She did! And I'm so hoping to take lessons soon," Khata gushed.

"Rama told me she was seriously considering a purchase," Shamilar replied, nodding her head. "I'm glad she made it." She then smiled conspiratorially and said, "I bet she got a good deal."

Khata laughed and replied, "Yes, she did. The whole family's excited about it. And mom thought it might be nice to have a pretty vase to put on the new piano, something nice that we could fill with beautiful flowers—nothing too big, but not too small, either."

"Oh, I have some lovely ones over across the shop, and a few that might be just the right size. Let me show you." Shamilar motioned over to one side of the store, and began to walk the girls over there.

"You always have such incredible pottery and glassware here," Kit said, adding, "and so many other nice things."

"Thank, you, Kit. We try to carry the best."

Khata said, "Mom's turning my older brother's bedroom into a study and music room, now that he's moved out."

"We're all so proud of him," Shamilar said. "And that's a good use of his room. I'm sure his time in the army will send him on many adventures and give him good training in the new radio and electronics field where he seems so talented."

"That's what he's hoping, and mom and dad, too."

"Let me ask you something. Do you have a music teacher yet?"

"No, I'm afraid not. We're hoping to find a good one soon."

"Well, I have some news." Shamilar again broke into a big smile. She then added, "And, I'm so excited."

"What is it?"

"I wrote my sister Muriel two weeks ago, and since she's a great music teacher, I happened to mention that your mom, my good friend, was talking about getting a piano for your family. I also told her about you and how I thought you might need a good teacher soon. I asked if she knew anyone in our city who would be appropriate. She knows all the best people in music. And then, I got the most surprising and wonderful reply from her just yesterday."

"What did she say?" Khata asked.

"Well, it was better than I ever could have expected! After years of living in Alexandria and traveling so much that I hardly ever get to see her, she's moving here to Cairo in just a few days!"

"Oh, that's really nice," Khata said.

"Yes," Shamilar replied. "It's great news. I haven't been able to see her in ages—far too long—and in addition to being a renowned performer in her own right, for which she travels extensively and often, she's widely recognized as an absolutely first rate private music teacher, and she specializes … in the piano!"

"No way!" Khata said. "Do you think she would give me some lessons herself? I'm sure mom will pay whatever she charges!"

"Subject to serious negotiation?" Shamilar said with a smile.

"Without negotiation! I'll see to it," Khata replied. "I would absolutely love to learn from someone like her."

"She indicated in her letter that she would be delighted to be asked."

Kit said to her classmate, "That would be a great idea, Khata, and since you know her sister here, the most kind Shamilar, she might go a little easier on you than some teachers and really give you great personal attention."

"Yeah, I bet," Khata replied to Kit and then turned back toward her favorite shopkeeper to say, "This is a really great development. I know we'll definitely ask her as soon as she arrives. What's bringing your sister to town?"

"I'm not exactly sure. It's all so sudden. But she did say something about her husband's business causing him to relocate to our fair city and, despite her regular work with the symphony in Alexandria, she's gladly embracing the move and seems excited about reconnecting with the family here and expanding her circle of musical associates."

At that point, Rama El-Noor walked into the shop with a big smile on her face. "Success!" she said, and put a large bag down on the floor.

Shamilar laughed and asked, "Did the poor merchant next door have to pay you to take whatever item in his shop you were acquiring?"

"Almost! But close enough," Rama said with a laugh. "I think his last and final discount was just to get me out the door."

"Ha! Well that would never work with me. I always like you to stay as long as you can."

"I would not in a million years use my top secret shopper tricks on you, dear friend," Rama said. "Your prices are already reasonable, and I know that all the profits go to a good cause—the wonderful Adi family, with its immensely deserving members."

"Good! That's very good. I'm sure I could never withstand your superior negotiating powers," Shamilar said. "I would fold, instantly. In fact, I'm already thinking about just giving you some-thing now. See how effective you are?"

"You're funny!" Rama replied, as she walked over to hug her friend. "How are the children?"

"Great! A mother could not be more blessed. Sasha is a delight, as always, and Sammi's doing very well in school like his older brother, Mafulla."

"And how is our favorite best friend of the prince?"

"As rambunctious as ever, I think—and always clever, like his father. But since they've been back from the trip across the desert, I haven't seen him as much as I'd like. The boys seem to be busy with a number of important projects in the palace."

Rama reflected: "I suppose Prince Walid's role in helping the king is increasing as time goes on, and with Mafulla always at his right hand, I'm guessing that his role in kingdom affairs will also expand."

"Yes, it's just so unexpected for all of this to be going on, as I've often told you. We're so proud of him."

"You should be. It couldn't happen to a nicer boy."

"We all like Mafulla a lot," Kit said, adding, "and, of course, the prince. They're both really nice. I think Mafulla is just so funny."

"True. Too bad he's totally taken," Khata added, looking over at Kit and making a universal gesture with her hands that clearly said, "Oh, well. What can you do?"

"Hasina is a wonderful young lady," Shamilar said. "I'm so glad the two of them are such good friends."

"And, anyway," Kit said to Khata, "I think at least one young man in the palace already reliably has his eye on you."

"Well, we don't talk about such things around M-O-M-S," Khata said, making a face.

"Oh? Who might this be?" Shamilar asked, playfully.

"It's all rumors," Khata replied, embarrassed.

"No, it's all Haji," Kit said.

"Masoon's son?" Shamilar responded, clearly impressed.

"Yes," Rama said. "Can you believe it?"

"Mom!" Khata exclaimed.

"I hear things," Rama explained. "But I'll honor your reticence, young lady, and let the matter drop, for now."

"Jeepers, Mom," Khata said.

"Very impressive," Shamilar replied. "The son of the top general in all the kingdom. Quite a catch, to be sure, but then again, so are you! Of course, for now and henceforth, my lips are sealed."

"Just so hers are, too, but of course not with a kiss," Kit said, pointing at Khata, and she made them all laugh.

"Stop it!" Khata whispered loudly to her friend and laughed again despite herself, while dropping her face toward the floor and shaking her head.

Rama quickly said, "So, on to other things!" She looked around and commented, "By now, Shapur would normally be out here carrying on with us. Where is he today?"

"Oh, the poor man is home with tummy trouble. And it has nothing to do with my cooking, I can assure you."

"Never!" Rama said with a smile.

"I don't think I've ever seen him looking quite so bad."

"You think he caught it from someone? I've heard an intestinal problem is going around."

"That could be. So many people come and go from the shop."

"Yes, they do."

"He woke up this morning and didn't feel well. It took all my powers of persuasion to convince him to stay put and let me run the show today. You know what a dedicated hard worker he is."

"Indeed. I don't think I can recall ever seeing him in repose. He's always on the move, talking with customers or spiffing up the place."

"You're right. But today, he looked like he could use a good rest. If he doesn't feel better tomorrow, I'll convince him to go see a doctor."

Across town at the palace, Walid and Mafulla had spent the first two hours after class with Kissa and Hasina in the library, where all four of them had to read some assigned essays for the following day. The boys were now walking back to their private quarters in the palace.

Mafulla said, "I really like what Khalid explained today in class about the quality or personal characteristic of consistency, at its best, being a sort of flexible harmony."

"Yeah, a flexible, adaptive form of harmony," Walid added.

"And I loved that three-fold diagnosis of what he called persistent inconsistency, people acting over a period of time in a way that's contrary to their own goals and values."

"I agree," Walid said. "I think that really nailed it. Let's see if we can get it right."

"Ok."

"So. When anybody continues to act in a way that's inconsistent with what's in their own best interest, it's either out of ignorance—a failure to think through the consequences of their actions, so that they don't realize they're being inconsistent."

"Or indifference," Mafulla said, "in which case they know, but for some reason don't really care that they're self-sabotaging."

"Or inertia," Walid concluded, "where they may understand

the nature of the inconsistency, and they care about it—sometimes really worrying about what they know is going on in their lives. But they still keep doing the wrong things from the incredible power of what we most often call habit."

"Yeah. You got it." Mafulla then paused for a second and remarked, "I thought it was really insightful when Khalid said that to avoid any ignorance, or unawareness of inconsistency, it takes a clear conception of what we're supposed to be doing and an alert mindset constantly paying attention and acquiring new knowledge."

"Yeah. And I also loved his point that to keep indifference at bay, you need to truly care about your goals and values," Walid added. Then he paused for a second and said, "I guess, when you have a real passion for what you're seeking, you won't ever tend to be your own worst enemy and self-destruct through totally passive apathy."

"It amazes me that two words can be very similar and yet totally opposite in what they mean," Mafulla said.

"What two words?"

"Passive and passion, which apathy is a lack of."

"Oh."

"A person with passion is active and engaged and has an enthusiastic commitment. A person who's passive is the opposite. He's inert, unmoved, unmotivated, inactive."

"That is strange," Walid agreed.

"Yeah, but back to our solutions."

"Ok."

"To really avoid destructive forms of inertia, the sort of passivity that lies unmoved in the ruts of habit, Khalid said you have to keep agile, active, flexible, and adaptive," Mafulla recalled.

"I guess that about sums it up," Walid concluded. Then he thought for a second and made the observation, "This all fits in really well with what the king taught me long ago about the universal keys to success in anything we do—especially in difficult pursuits."

"Those seven things that you then taught me, professor," Mafulla recalled. And he added, "Ok, so let me do it," and he immediately adopted what he imagined was a more intellectual voice. "To position ourselves as well as possible for success in any challenging endeavor: we need a clear conception of what we want, a strong confidence we can attain the goal, a focused concentration on what it will take, a stubborn consistency in our actions, an emotional commitment to the importance of what we're doing, a good character to guide us, and a capacity to enjoy the process along the way." Mafulla looked at his friend and did his now famous and completely expected double eyebrow jump.

"Good. Perfect, in fact," Walid said. "The king would be proud."

"And I actually remember that stuff, not just to recite it for the edification of my friends or the amazement of my peers, but whenever I'm working really hard at something. It's like a great checklist. Those ideas have often helped me zero in on what it takes to make the most of my time and energy in a tough challenge."

"Yeah, I agree. These few concepts, or conditions for success, have helped me a lot, as well," Walid said. Then he concluded, "I really like the useful, practical side of philosophy."

"I do, too," Mafulla replied. "I mean, the theoretical stuff can be crazy interesting at times, no doubt about it, but I always eventually have to tie it back to real life concerns, or at some point it starts feeling like I'm just playing some sort of elaborate mind game."

Anyone who saw these two walking down the hall and carrying on this conversation would have thought they were talking about a new car, or an exciting football match, or their girlfriends, and not about some philosophical ideas they had discussed in class. But that was just further testimony as to how lively the minds of these two students were. They could get excited about anything they recognized as important. And they were very fortunate at their ages to have a keen sense already of what really matters in life.

Right then, a palace guard spotted Walid from an adjoining hallway, and called out, "Prince! What a relief! We've been looking for you! There's an important meeting in the king's sitting room in about five minutes and he wants you and Mafulla there!"

"Oh, Ok! Thanks!" Walid answered and, turning, said to Mafulla, "I wonder what's going on?"

"No idea, let's pick up the pace. We always seem to slow down without realizing it when we're talking philosophy."

"True. Deep thought can call for a slow walk."

"Or even standing completely still for the entire length of the idea to be articulated."

"Also true," Walid replied. "I think Socrates was known for that. He could stand in one spot all night long, just pondering."

"My hero," Mafulla said.

"Really. But for now, we should pause the pondering and move more quickly."

They began jogging down the hall, then took the stairs two at a time, and ran almost all-out for the last stretch to Kular's office. Coming through the door first, Mafulla said, "Hey, Kular!"

"Mafulla, I heard what sounded like a stampede or possibly a footrace going on outside my door just now."

Walid at that point also appeared and said, "I always let Mafulla win!"

"Ha!" Mafulla laughed.

"We've been told there's a meeting."

"Yes, let me announce your arrival," the head butler said, as he walked to the inner doorway and disappeared for a moment. Popping back into where the boys were now standing, he reported, "His Majesty awaits you," and held the door open for the two of them.

Walid was first through the door and was surprised to see the king sitting with Masoon, Hamid, Bancom, Reela, Hoda, and Leem Hadad. Everyone except the king stood up as Walid walked in, followed by Mafulla. "Your Highness." Masoon spoke the words in a low voice and did a quick nod of his head. That always made Walid smile.

"Boys," King Ali said with a quick smile, "please have a seat."

Walid grabbed the closest chair and Mafulla sat in one next to it, as the others then returned to their seats. The prince nodded to them all and gave a little, almost embarrassed, wave of his hand and then turned to the king and said, "What's going on, Your Majesty?"

"It seems we face a very serious development. Reela here has just reported to me that, prompted by a strange feeling, he went by to see his brother Shapur and asked him if anything unusual had happened around the shop. Shapur reported that a very unusual man had visited him briefly outside the store not an hour earlier, looking for Mr. Kaza. The man said that his father and Kaza had studied with the same teacher for a time, long ago. Shapur told him of Kaza's passing, and the fellow expressed condolences and then left. But Shapur was troubled by him in a way he couldn't understand, saying that the short conversation they had seemed to have drained him of all his energy. He reported that he actually felt a bit sick and had to take a nap afterwards. Before the man had left, Shapur fortunately introduced himself by name, and the man responded by calling himself Osvaldo."

"Is dad Ok?" Mafulla asked.

Reela spoke up and said, "Apparently, he's fine now, but he did feel exceptionally odd in the man's presence and totally exhausted, and even a little nauseous, afterwards. He said it was very strange. He took a bit of a rest later and said that it fully revived his spirits."

"That's weird," Mafulla commented. "I'm glad he's all right."

"Yes. We all are. And now it gets more interesting," the king said. "Reela began a search for any local man with the family name of Osvaldo and, while at the library, he was told about an Osvaldo Pugliese, a famous musician who was visiting to play at a local club. He then went to the club and met the man and in conversation about other people named Osvaldo, Mr. Pugliese told him about a very intense and unpleasant individual who once visited Argentina, and the house of a musician friend of his—a man he actually met, named Juan Osvaldo Santiago."

"Santiago?" Walid said with great surprise.

"Yes. Pugliese remembered him as a most intense, unpleasant, and difficult character who was completely fixated on questions of spiritual energy and power."

"Wow. That sure sounds like our recent bad guy," Mafulla said.

"You're right," the king replied, and then he continued. "Osvaldo the musician had heard, earlier in the day—now, this was Saturday, just this past Saturday—he overheard a man who played in the band speaking to another musician about recently having talked to someone he called Santiago."

Walid looked over at Reela and back at the king. The king said, "Those two musicians mysteriously disappeared shortly after their conversation was overheard. We've now learned their names, but we can't find them anywhere in town. It's as if they just vanished. And so, we have strong circumstantial reasons to think then that this man, this Osvaldo that Shapur met and spoke with, may be our adversary, the mysterious Santiago. It seems that 'Osvaldo' is his middle name, and he's actually now here in Cairo."

"Oh, no," Mafulla said, adding, "And dad met him, in person and alone? That gives me the creeps. What's he doing here?"

"I suspect that he's here, at one level, for simple revenge, to get even with anyone who participated in the breakup of his criminal activities and his larger plan that depended on them, starting with your friends Malik and Haji, who, of course, escaped his most recent effort at retaliation, thanks to your valiant rescue mission."

"And we all do thank you two for that," Masoon said.

"Yes, we do, indeed," Hamid added, and said, "We're very grateful for the courageous and effective assistance you gave our sons. We're also quite proud of you both, as well. From everything we've heard, you showed both great courage and considerable prudence in rescuing the boys."

"Thanks," Walid said, "but I'm not absolutely positive they needed our help. They fought like a small army themselves. But our arrival with a supporting cast of well armed kingdom soldiers probably speeded up their safe escape, at least a little bit, and made it less problematic than it otherwise might have been without the help."

Both men smiled at Walid's words and nodded their appreciation for his humility, as well as for speaking so confidently in praise of their sons. The king then said, "Santiago is apparently aware that the palace was well represented on the trip to Dromeda. But he doesn't yet know the identities of everyone who was involved in thwarting his elaborate scheme. He is likely aware that Walid and I once lived in the village, and may infer or otherwise realize that we were both at the compound there to rescue the animals. But we have to assume that everyone who went on the trip, and anyone that he even suspects might have gone, is now officially under threat by him."

Walid looked over at Hoda. "Are Kissa and Hasina safe?"

"Yes. They've been in the library studying. I'll go get them in just a bit and escort them home, now that I know all this. I'll make sure they're always accompanied outside the palace while this guy is in town."

"Oh, man," Walid said, as he felt a jolt of adrenalin shoot through his insides with a shock and icy tremble. His mouth grew dry with apprehension, and a look of great concern appeared on his face.

Mafulla quickly said, "We left them in the library more than twenty minutes ago. They said they were going to take off in five minutes and walk down to the Kingdom Luxury Goods Shop just to look around for an hour or so before they went home. And that's a pretty good distance, maybe fifteen or twenty minutes away at a normal walking pace."

Halfway through his sentence, Hoda stood up and began to move quickly toward the door, and said, "I'm sorry. I have to go."

Hamid, sitting closest to her, jumped up to follow her, saying to the others in the room, "Please excuse us both."

"Take palace guards," the king said, and as he stood up, everyone else rose, and Hoda and Hamid disappeared through the door, as the doctor called back, "Thank you, Majesty."

Omari was ambling down the hall toward Kular's office when Hoda and Hamid emerged into the large passageway. Hamid said to him, "We need an emergency escort of Phi and palace guards, fully armed, and immediately."

"Yes, sir," the man answered, as he stopped to turn around and accompany them. "Count me in, and Paki's downstairs now."

As they walked at a brisk pace down the hall, Mafulla and Walid came running out of Kular's door with permission from the king to join the escort or rescue or whatever it might be that they were now launching. Walid started counting to himself, having seen Omari and heard his mention of Paki and now said to himself, in the recesses of his mind: "Ok, Hoda, Hamid, Omari, Paki, me, Mafulla—six Phi, plus guards. That should do it." He then spoke up loudly, "The king says to go out the side door and palace cars will be waiting for us, to get us there fast."

"I hope we're fast enough," Mafulla whispered to him.

"Yeah, listen, remember, they're both Phi," Walid whispered back, as they were now walking a few feet behind Hamid and Omari, adding, "So, actually I guess we'll have eight Phi to face whatever we might encounter at the shop, if anything."

"Yeah," Mafulla said. "That should be more than enough for pretty much any possibility. But I'm starting to get a bad feeling."

"Guys," Walid said loudly. "Do you mind if we actually jog or run? We need to get there quickly."

Hamid looked back at Walid and motioned toward Hoda, who was walking at a rapid stride in the front. "She's already there," he said. "Follow her pace. She knows what she's doing."

7

A Shopping Trip to Remember

"It's so great that our moms are giving us a little more basic freedom these days to go and do," Hasina said to Kissa as they walked briskly down beautiful Nile Avenue toward one of their favorite shops.

"It really is," Kissa replied. "But, of course, Hoda still says that a lady should be careful, and that advice is meant to include even us. I mean, we can clearly handle two or three bad guys at a time, maybe four, but more than that might be difficult."

"You're funny," Hasina said, with a laugh. "But I guess you're right. We should clearly avoid areas in town where small armies of accosters, molesters, or muggers might congregate."

Kissa laughed and said, "You're pretty funny, too, Hassi, especially since you've known Mafulla."

"He's sort of contagious,' Hasina replied.

"Yeah, but in a completely good way that doesn't involve any rashes, fevers, or sneezing fits," Kissa joked.

"Ha! At least, most of the time!"

Kissa laughed again. Then she said, "So, did you say Ara told you there's a new shipment of scarves and shoes at the shop?"

"Yes. And Mr. Arumbar said that any of us from the palace school can have a twenty percent discount on anything that just came in."

"That's very nice of him."

"Yeah, I think he really appreciates the extra patrols the king has been sending around since that attempted robbery the Viper and the Storm broke up a while back."

"During our joy ride in the new Rolls Royce," Kissa said, as she mentally saw herself in the car. "Imagine, back then, that we didn't know what the boys were continuing to do … in their spare time."

"A lot's changed," Hasina mused.

"Yes, it has."

They walked up to the shop and Kissa held open the door for her friend, as they entered one of the finest stores for ladies in all of Egypt. "Welcome! Welcome to the shop!" Ali Arumbar called out from the counter in the back.

"Thanks, Mr. Arumbar!" Kissa replied and waved.

"Is that Miss Kissa El-Bay?" Arumbar shaded his eyes and squinted toward the front of the store.

"Yes, and my best friend Hasina is also with me!"

"Oh, two of my favorite young ladies in all of Cairo—no, all of North Africa—no, all of the known world!"

"Ha! You're funny and kind, sir! We're here today because we've heard that you have some new scarves and shoes just in."

"From Paris and Milan!" Arumbar said. Please, come and I'll show you. I have the scarves displayed already in the glass case here in the back. And the shoes are right now over to the side. I'm making room up front for them later today so that, tomorrow, they'll be my most prominent display."

"Good! Then we get to see them before they attract too much attention," Hasina said.

"Yes, you came at just the right time. And it's a quiet hour of the day for the shop. Most ladies who are, in age, a bit farther down life's road are getting dinner ready for their families, or are finishing up their workdays outside the home. And most young women are … well, doing whatever young women do in the late afternoons!"

"That would be … homework," Kissa said.

"Yes, I forgot—homework!"

"I wish we could forget it," Hasina commented.

"Oh, I'm sure you do an excellent job on it."

"Thanks. We try."

The girls didn't notice yet, but four men had just walked up to the front door of the shop. Two others were a few feet down an alley behind the store, standing beside a dark green truck. Three of the men out front quietly entered the door. One stayed outside on the walk to make sure that no one else would go in. A small bell jingled and one of the three closed the door behind them.

"Oh, gentlemen shoppers, surely here to find something for a lady," Mr. Arumbar said to the girls as they gazed down into the glass case, admiring the beautiful, multi-colored scarves neatly arrayed on two shelves. He waved toward the new arrivals.

"Welcome! Welcome to my humble shop!" he called out to the men. "I'll be right with you. We have some of the best selections in town." He walked around the counter while the girls continued to browse. Turning back to them, he said, in a low voice, "Excuse me for just a moment. And by the way, feel free to pull out anything you'd like to look at more closely. The light's better over at the side window there." He pointed and smiled as he left.

The men who now stood at the front of the store, looking around, could not from their vantage point see the girls, who were all the way in the back and blocked from view by several large displays of fashionable clothing and accessories.

"How may I be of assistance to you gentlemen today?" Mr. Arumbar had a big smile on his face as he rounded a large clothing display nearest to the men.

One of the men said, "Greetings to you. First: The two young ladies who just entered the store, moments ago—one of them dropped something on the sidewalk that appears to be of value, and I wanted to return it to her. Is she here?"

"Yes, yes, right in the back. I'm sure she'll appreciate your kindness. Please, follow me," Arumbar said and, as he turned, one of the men hit him in the back of the head with something, crumpling him to the floor and rendering him unconscious.

At that very moment, far away from Cairo, five burly men were rapidly packing up the entire contents of a large, beautiful home in the nicest neighborhood of Alexandria, Egypt. Its residents were about to make a sudden move south to the capital city. Muriel al-Baki walked into the room where her husband sat at a desk, apparently deep in thought. "My dear husband, you must gather the rest of your things. We need to be going soon."

"I'm not sure this is a good idea," he said.

"It's too late for that. And I have my orders," she replied.

"But the business is flourishing here."

"Yes, thanks to all your hard work and our important connections. But the one who is responsible for most of those connections needs us now, and we have to rise to the occasion. You have experienced men to run the business here while we're away."

"But we don't know how long this will take."

"No, we don't. It's not our need to know."

"You can be so focused on what you consider to be your duty."

"You can, too. You know what ultimately gives us a hope for the future we've always wanted. The reality is what it is."

"Yes. Yes. I suppose you're right." He sighed.

"So it's best to keep your eyes on that and accept whatever's asked of us in the meantime."

"What have you told your sister?"

"That your business is requiring us to move."

"I see. And what of the girl?"

"That's developed most remarkably, since the Cairo Phi lady named Layla first mentioned her to me in a note and asked if I might visit, teach her a few things about the piano, and in the process subtly evaluate her for membership status in the group."

"I remember how it started. But how does it all stand now? I've been so distracted that my recall of more recent things is unreliable at best."

"Well, at first, I wasn't allowed to say much about it, as you may remember, just that we had orders to move, and it was an important assignment, and it involved a girl named Khata."

"Yes, yes, that I know."

"After the note from Layla about the girl, my sister then also mentioned her in a letter and said, like Layla had, that she would be in need of a piano teacher, and that she's a student in the palace school. That was something Layla had not revealed in her note, if she knew it. But how could she not? I realized right away that I should pass on that crucial information, and I knew from the start what my assignment would be."

"You do tend to get the big jobs."

"Yes. And in this one, everything has worked out much easier than I ever could have dreamed."

"How so?"

"The girl's mother and Shamilar are such good friends."

"I see."

"Because of that, I'm completely trusted and have been given an open-ended invitation to teach the girl in her home. And then, as you know, the house nearby was found for us, and a renter for this one, and all so quickly."

"Yes."

"The one who gives us assignments gives us, also, the means we need."

"So it seems."

"We'll start the music lessons, the girl and I, shortly after we arrive, and under the cover of those, I'll do what I've been asked, and what I've been told." Muriel smiled.

"Do all of the relevant Phi know what you've been asked by this lady, Layla?"

"Yes, apparently, and they seem to think the lessons will be a perfect cover—or, in their minds, a nice opportunity—for what they've asked me to do."

"And the leader?"

"You know I don't call him that. He deserves more."

"Well, I refuse to call him what you call him. I'll refer to him as 'The Grand Poobah' if I like."

"Please don't joke in a derogatory way. It's quite inappropriate.

And remember, your attitude may not be as private a matter as you might like to think. It could get you into serious trouble."

"Regardless, I'll take my chances. What about him? Does he know all these details?"

"Yes. Of course he does. He also thinks that serving as the music teacher is a perfect guise for what he wants me to do and for the information he needs me to get."

"It is quite amazing—the fact that both sides think your teaching the girl is a good idea and that it will further their individually specific and mutually contradictory interests." The elegantly attired man shook his head in near disbelief.

"Indeed. Powerful forces are clearly in play. Things like this don't just happen by accident. So, you see? We're obviously being moved in the direction we should go."

"Maybe."

"Stop being so recalcitrant and grumpy. Put away the procrastination. You know what's best for us at this point just as well as I do."

"I certainly don't know it in quite the ways you apparently do."

"But you do, nonetheless, know."

"I suppose so."

"You certainly understand how eager I've been to serve in some exceptional way and stand out, and perhaps position myself for bigger things. The sooner this begins, the better."

The man just let out a long sigh and said, simply, "Ok. All right. I'll be ready in half an hour, or possibly less."

In Cairo at that very moment, in his private sitting room on the second floor of the palace, the king was still speaking with Masoon, Bancom, Reela, and Leem.

"Leem," he said, "we need you to help us locate Santiago, and as quickly as possible. He's likely to be a major threat."

"Yes, Your Majesty. I'm honored to be of assistance."

"He's staying somewhere. He's getting food and eating somewhere. He's directing the movements of other men, either in person or by some form of communication. These are all vulnerabilities and access points for us."

"I can get on that right away, Your Majesty."

"And perhaps you could task Ibrahim, first thing, to work on finding those two musicians. They may be a key to Santiago's whereabouts."

"That's good. It will be less dangerous for him than a direct search for Santiago, and I'm confident he can handle it."

"The two of you will have any support you might need from me. Just ask."

"Yes, Your Majesty. Thank you. I'll not hesitate."

Reela then said both to Leem and the king, "I have some old friends here in town who are also good at this sort of thing. If I could introduce you to them, Leem, I think they might be of help."

"Excellent," Leem responded. "I'm always open to good partnerships."

After a moment, Masoon spoke. "Majesty, I think I should mobilize some of our elite forces to be on alert, and to be present on and around the palace grounds, in perhaps a few carefully inconspicuous ways."

"That's a good idea, and one that has helped greatly in the past."

"I can also provide escorts for the students in the palace school, and even post guards near their homes—but unobtrusively, of course."

"Good. We shouldn't alarm the parents, but such a measure of caution would indeed be prudent, and I think it should be put into effect right away." The king stood, and so did the others.

"I can initiate that immediately, Majesty."

"Please do, Masoon. I thank you."

The king gestured that Masoon could leave, and then he turned to Reela. "I also thank you, good friend, for all the information you've supplied to us."

"It's my pleasure and honor, Your Majesty."

"I would ask you and Leem to keep in touch with me through Bancom, as the situation develops."

Reela responded, "Yes, Your Majesty," as did Leem.

Bancom said to both of them, "We'll keep the communication

lines open at all times and be here to coordinate all activities, as needed."

The king then concluded, "Thank you all for coming today. Let's resolve this situation as soon as we can."

"Certainly," Reela said, and the others then echoed his response. The king walked them to the door and they made their way together down the hallway, continuing to talk of their most imminent plans.

Ali then turned to his head butler and chief assistant and said, "Kular, I need a few minutes alone, unless there's anything of the utmost urgency."

"Certainly, Your Majesty," Kular said, and the king disappeared back into his room.

Some distance away, the palace cars were closing in on their destination. Walid was nervous. He turned to Hamid and said in a low voice, "Do you really think Kissa and Hasina are still Ok?"

"Yes, so far, up to now," Hamid replied, right away.

"They are," Hoda said from the front seat. "But we have only a short time to intervene. There are several men, and one has power."

Hearing these words frightened Walid for a moment, as he realized what the girls might face. Mafulla felt the same twinge and a rush of cold deep inside him. A man with power—they both wondered exactly what the word meant in this context, coming from Hoda. But each of them guessed that she had sensed something like Phi power. And that was a cause for great concern.

Walid then said to Hamid and Hoda both, "Mafulla and I have been inside the shop, as I know you have, Hoda. There are no clear lines of sight—too many large displays of clothing and accessories. I think there's a back entrance, and there's a window to the right side, as you come in, most of the way back."

"Three men just entered the shop, seconds ago," Hoda said, softly. She otherwise seemed to be in something like a trance. "One more is out front, and two are in the back. So we have six awaiting us."

Walid quickly said, "They may have poison capsules, to prevent their capture and interrogation—cyanide, like what we saw when we helped Malik and Haji. I think we need to question them at this point, at least a couple of them. So, we should be watchful."

"I agree," Hamid said.

The cars now pulled over to the side of the road and parked nearly a block away from the Kingdom Luxury Goods Shop, just out of sight around a corner from the main street. Walid, Mafulla, Hamid, Hoda, Omari, Paki, and four palace guards with the most senior rank all got out of the cars, initially. The guards at this point were to stay with the cars and position them, once anything began to happen—one near the front, and one at the rear.

"Hassi, something's wrong," Kissa whispered. Then she said, "Triple Double." Instantly, the words, 'Prepare, perceive; anticipate, avoid; concentrate, and control' ran through Hasina's consciousness like a mantra of readiness. Kissa was standing near the window at the moment, holding two brightly colored scarves in her hands, and had just been comparing their patterns in the extra light that was available there. Hasina was beside her. Two tall and wide displays of clothing blocked them from the view of anyone near the front of the shop.

Hasina saw a four-foot-long stick leaning against a table, about three inches around, with a small metal hook on the end, probably used by Mr. Arumbar to reach the hangers for clothes that were displayed high up on nearby racks. She bent down and grabbed it and walked back a few steps to lift a large heavy tapestry away from the wall and stand behind it. It had a dark, subdued geometrical pattern and it reached from near the ceiling to within a couple of inches of the floor. The bottom of the tapestry was in deep shadows, so she reasoned that her feet in dark sandals under it wouldn't be too obvious. Some dust behind it almost made her sneeze, but she caught the reflex in time and made herself stay quiet.

Kissa, meanwhile, pretended to continue on in her shopping. She picked up and looked at various items as she scanned the area for anything else that might serve as a weapon. Mr. Arumbar's voice had obviously gone silent up in the front, and she knew that was not a good sign. She heard other mumbled voices and some shuffling of feet. Suddenly, she had a tactical idea and walked briskly and even a bit noisily over to the proprietor's desk in the back, behind the large glass display case, with the demeanor of an employee busily taking care of things.

When the first man appeared around a tall clothing display, she greeted him in a cheerful voice that completely concealed her true feelings, "Oh, hello. I'll be happy to help you with anything you need." But, having smiled and said this, she held up an index finger, and continued to walk back toward the desk, adding, "I just have to find something and I'll be right with you."

What then caught her eye behind the owner's desk made her think the words, "I can't believe it! Good old Mr. Arumbar!" She had been hoping to find a letter opener or a paperweight or anything she could use as a projectile or weapon of any sort. But after the attempted robbery of his store some time back, from which he was saved by the heroic intervention of the Viper and the Storm, those two famous crime fighters who had mysteriously appeared at just the right time, he had kept a loaded revolver in the desk on an easily accessible shelf, and Kissa could now clearly see it. Her relief matched her nerves.

In an effort to approach and come closer to the young lady, but without in any way alarming her, the man said, "I have an item that might be of value to the store and wanted to get your appraisal of it. I'd like to show it to you, if I could."

"Good. That would be nice. And I have something I'd like to show to you as well," Kissa said, as she pulled the gun from the shelf and raised it toward him, holding it steadily aimed at his chest.

The man began to lift his hands up in what he meant to seem like a gesture of surrender, but at that moment, another voice said, "I don't think you want to do that." Kissa looked slightly toward her right and saw a second man. And this one also had a gun in his hands, pointed directly at her.

"I agree," a third man said, from far to her left, near where she had been standing earlier in front of the window. She quickly glanced in that direction. He had a gun raised as well, and was walking very slowly toward her.

At that precise tick of the clock, Hasina silently came out from behind the tapestry, and flung the stick in her hand hard like a spear at this third man's back. He suddenly stepped to the side, almost before it was out of her hand, slightly turned, and actually caught it with his left hand, without even completely seeing it before the catch. Extended proprioception and lightning reflexes, Hasina thought, as her mouth went totally dry and her brain nearly froze from the sheer unexpected shock of what she had just witnessed. That was not supposed to happen. Criminals and street thugs just can't do such things. It was pretty advanced stuff. She didn't know what they were up against.

Kissa had turned and also seen this, and had a similar inner reaction of confusion and shock. But she kept her gun aimed at the man right in front of her, and in the tradition of Walid, she said with a tone of no emotion whatsoever the words, "Lucky grab." The man to her left, now holding both his gun and the intended spear, was at this point facing Hasina. And he laughed out loud, in a brief moment of what sounded like true mirth and an almost grudging respect for the voice and attitude of the girl who had spoken. The gun in Kissa's hand was now starting to grow strangely warm. That drew her attention and divided her focus, but her gaze remained on her adversaries.

Outside, Hoda walked briskly down the sidewalk, now arm-in-arm with Hamid. He spoke to her and she laughed, as if they were on a normal stroll down the street. As they approached the front of the store, the man standing beside the door held up a hand and said, "Sorry, the shop's closed today for inventory." Without a word, Hoda walked up closer to him and stared into his eyes for maybe three seconds. His initial reaction was awe at her beauty, like it typically was for any man who caught a first sight of her. And her eyes were mesmerizing—deep sparkling pools that drew him in and put him into something like an instant hypnotic trance. He was floating on air, then on water, and then he crumpled to the sidewalk, sliding down the outer wall of the store and into a seated position, as his neck went limp and he lost all consciousness, without a struggle.

Hoda silently opened the door, crossed the threshold, and stopped a few feet inside. The small bell did not jingle, as it otherwise almost always did. Hamid had stayed back for a moment to search the unconscious man's clothing. But as he did, an impulse suddenly prompted him to look up, and he saw Hoda from behind as something like a glow seemed to surround her body, an aura of faint light that appeared to extend out from her in all directions. He had not seen anything quite like it ever before. It evoked in him, right away, something like a sense of wonder and a surge of intense curiosity.

An ancient Greek catching full sight of her at that moment would have thought that Pallas Athena, the goddess of just war, had just stepped onto a field of battle. Anyone from India would have been sure that this was Kali, dark mother divinity of power, annihilator of evil, and foremost among the ten fierce tantric wisdom goddesses. A Viking or Norseman would think of Freya, the goddess of beauty and war. And any native Egyptian from centuries ago would recognize instantly the strange forces embodied here that went far beyond anything we could even begin to imagine as possible in our modern world of surface appearances and superficial strength.

The power now coming through Hoda was almost tangible and projected itself throughout the large store, far beyond her immediate aura. It made all three men at the back of the room instantly turn toward the front to see what was happening, as if being pulled around by a force they couldn't resist. Two of them could see only what looked like an eerie light on the walls and ceiling. But they also felt a cold shiver run through them like a warning. Only the man holding Hasina's stick and his own gun could see the source of the light between two tall displays of merchandise. And he knew in that moment what had just appeared. Or to put it more accurately, he alone had a clue. But even then, he had no idea about the full range of force now confronting him. It took him only a split second to decide to empty all six bullets into her on the spot. He would aim so that no small movements could evade the spray of deadly metal.

His first great surprise was that the trigger was stuck, almost as if it had been welded in place. It wouldn't move. The gun couldn't fire. He dropped it onto the floor with disgust and a loud clunk. Kissa suddenly realized that her revolver, Mr. Arumbar's gun, which had been getting hotter by the second, had now cooled down in her hand. She was glad for whatever was happening at the front of the shop that had drawn attention away from her, but also focused her mind on what she might have to do in the next few seconds, and made a quick assessment of the immediate situation around her. The man still directly in front of her had no visible weapon. The one to her right had a six-shooter that was now pointed toward the front of the store. Kissa without hesitation moved her gun to the right and fired a single bullet to shoot the weapon out of the man's hand, whirling around then to disarm in the same way the man now holding the long stick.

But as she was pulling the trigger, he was already swinging the stick. The second thunderous bang of her gun almost kept her from seeing something in the next split second that she found hard to believe. The man had begun his swing of the long stick before her finger had even squeezed the trigger. And now that the bullet was making its way invisibly fast toward him, she heard a sound of metal on metal and a spark flew from the end of the stick.

This strange man had actually hit the bullet with the metal hook on the end of the pole and changed its trajectory just enough that it missed him and did no damage at all. It merely embedded itself harmlessly into the wall beyond him, not far from where Hasina had just bent over to pick up a metal rod that was holding up a clothing display, in hopes of using it for self defense or some form of attack. The man paid her no attention but now swung the wooden stick around a bit more until it was pointed at Hoda, and then something happened that went far beyond anyone's wildest expectation, or what could even be imagined. What looked like a stream of fire, or a wide streak of electricity, even a form of lightning, seemed to shoot from the end of the stick, off its metal hook, and right at Kissa's mother.

The man whose gun had been shot from his hand had already begun to move toward Kissa, seeing that she was now distracted, as he pulled a long and menacing knife from his belt. But at that same moment, Omari and Paki, followed closely by Walid and Mafulla, came through the back door just in time to see the streak of flame shooting across the room toward Hoda. Mafulla fired his gun twice at the man with the fire stick and missed, due to a quick and elusive movement on the part of this startling and formidable adversary.

Instantly, the thoughts exploded into Mafulla's consciousness: "Streaming fire. Extended proprioception. Who is this?" But then, for a third shot, he aimed into the air four inches away to the left of the man and fired, as Paki shot at him dead center, and Omari instantly fired three inches to his right, as if by agreed coordination. The target now stepped directly into the path of the fifth bullet and took it in his shoulder with a loud grunt, completely distracted and stunned by what Hoda had just done, at the previous instant.

Not even Hamid, still staying back, had ever seen or even heard of what they all witnessed in that striking moment. Hoda's arms were raised to the sides, and instantly there was something like a torrential downpour of rain inside the store, but so strong that it was more like an aerial flood coming from or through the ceiling. But that doesn't even come close to describing what was more like a massive, thunderous waterfall, instantly appearing in front of them all and drowning, dousing, and neutralizing the fire, or thunderbolt, or whatever it was that had been hurled at her from the metal end of that otherwise ordinary stick. And a sound came up from deep within her lungs at that instant, something whose pitch and power seemed to rise up and shake the building and bring a wave of fear even to the hearts of each of her extraordinarily powerful friends.

There was a sudden earsplitting, overwhelming noise of booming outside in echo to her shout, a sound that could be felt as well as heard, as if the strongest windstorm ever to hit a desert was raging around them all with a power that could destroy the entire building they were in, despite its heavy stone walls. The large window in the wall near Hasina instantly and loudly exploded inward, as glass shards and hot blinding sand, along with large rock fragments shot straight at the man who had sought to eliminate the protective mother who stood before him.

The searing, compressed wind that was rushing through the shattered window frame must have been howling and blasting forth at two hundred miles an hour or more, but with a bizarre precision that was as weird as its sudden existence, spanning little more area in width or circumference than the measurement of the window frame it had burst through. It was a powerful column of air exploding furiously through a now gaping whole in the wall and focused directly on the torso and head of the man at whom it seemed to be aimed. It ripped the wooden stick from his grip, and sent it slamming into the far wall of the shop, imbedding it into the stone like a large nail hammered hard through soft and pliable wood.

Hasina jumped backwards, away from the heavy focused wind and flying glass. And Mafulla grabbed her and pulled her back toward the rear door. At that moment, the stone of the wall near the window, and the wood and tile of the ceiling overhead, and even the outer roof materials above it blasted inward and downward at the same time with implacable, catastrophic force and collapsed precisely on the man who had held the stick. No proprioception could help. All of these hard, unforgiving objects tore like weapons through his skin and muscles, and instantly broke most of his bones, including his back and even his skull. They ripped into his internal organs, and buried him deep in a massive pile of rubble. This was a form of assault that he clearly could not have anticipated or escaped. The altogether indescribable, overwhelming roar of it all then suddenly ended, leaving everyone's hearing strangely muffled as they reeled inwardly to try to regain their senses, focus their minds, and understand some bit of what had just happened around them. For a moment, it even seemed hard to breathe, as if the oxygen level in the room had been depleted.

The other two intruders were at this point bent over gasping, and in a complete panic at the fury that had taken out their superior and hit them both hard with flying debris. No more than three seconds had passed since the additional group of Phi had entered through the back door. But those large, ample seconds full of force and wonder contained sights they had never seen and a form of power they had never even imagined.

Walid regained his breath and moved quickly to help Kissa take down the knife wielding man, who at that juncture seemed almost too paralyzed with shock and pain to put up much resistance. But the prince could have just stood by and watched, because Kissa got to their adversary before he did, and with two vicious kicks and a precision punch to his throat took him down and extinguished the light of his awareness. Omari instantly doubled over the other man, knocking him out, face down on the floor, and he and Paki quickly searched the clothing of these two for poison, due to Walid's earlier warning. They found one capsule on each of them, in a pocket, which they immediately took away from the now inert bodies.

Hamid had done the same thing with the man outside, who was currently tied up tight and gagged. So, fortunately, three cyanide capsules had been kept from doing their intended jobs. These three men would, as a consequence, have to endure an interrogation, and perhaps answer some questions and provide insights into what was going on, who was behind it, and why it was happening.

No one in the room saw the two gun barrels that suddenly appeared in the choking swirl of dust near the back door, and that were pointed straight at Hasina and Mafulla. But then, everyone heard the four loud percussive bangs that were clearly the sound of gunfire.

8

DEATH AND DESTRUCTION

REELA STARTED JOGGING SLOWLY DOWN THE STREET, FOLLOWING his instincts. He didn't know where he was going, but felt he had to get there faster than a normal walk would achieve. And, despite his age, he was still in very good physical shape. A mental vision, quite vivid, had just gripped his attention. He saw Mafulla's face, then a gun, and then a bullet—not in one picture, or a complete scene, but in three separate flashes, one after the other. That's when he turned around, looked up and down the street, and started a jog in the direction opposite to the one in which he had been walking to the home of a man he had known and worked with in his days of intelligence activity years ago, both in Egypt and abroad. Now, his mind was a temporary blur. He knew he had to follow the strong pull he felt in connection with what he had seen in his mind's eye and not let questions distract him from whatever he needed to do. Years of training had taught him to honor his intuitions and eliminate that mental chatter that could dilute or cover over the deepest promptings he had learned to heed.

The king had just experienced the exact same flashes in the inner theater of his mind, but more vividly. He stopped, mid-sentence, in what he had been saying to Layla, who was sitting in a chair across the desk from him. He slowly rose from his own chair, planting his hands firmly on the dark wood desk in front of him, and in that moment made his mind completely blank. Layla stood hesitantly as well. She wanted to speak, but somehow knew that it was best to remain silent. He listened. He waited. A long five seconds passed.

"Kular!" He called loudly toward the outer room.

"Yes, Your Majesty." The butler opened the door, with a very serious look on his face. He had not heard this tone in the king's voice before.

"Get Bancom. Tell him to radio Masoon to rush to the Kingdom Luxury Goods Shop on Nile Avenue where the prince is, and as soon as possible. He's needed, and should go in person, with men."

"Right away!" Kular disappeared and walked down the hallway at a fast stride.

"Did you see it?" Layla then asked the king.

"Yes, I did. Mafulla."

"I saw it, too. What does it mean?"

"I can't tell yet. But moments before, I felt something different."

"What?"

"A major use of power beyond anything I have ever felt outside my own actions, and then, an … extinction of some sort, as of power, and … as if something had just left our world."

"You don't think it's Mafulla, do you?"

"It's … so extraordinary, what I felt, that I'm not sure what to think."

"Do you need to go?"

"No."

"Are you sure?"

"Yes. But Masoon should be there. There's a reason. There's some reason."

"Is Hasina all right?"

"What do you feel? What do you sense?"

Miles away, the first thing Hoda and Hamid saw from where they were at this moment, both rushing toward the back of the store, was a rifle falling to the floor, and then another one, and two bodies collapsing forward into the room. The Phi holding weapons now had all of them pointed at the back door. Hoda's gaze in that direction was intense and ready. And at that instant, through the doorframe, two palace guards in uniform appeared, guns raised and held forward, as one yelled, "Is everyone Ok?"

Mafulla had twisted and fallen backwards with Hasina in his arms. They had hit some large broken stones on the floor where they fell, but could feel nothing. Hamid pulled a small pouch from his pocket as he moved quickly across the piles of rubble in the shop, leaping and scrambling over the stones and wood that had just killed and buried their powerful adversary.

He pulled The Stone of Giza from the inconspicuous pouch as he now dove down toward the two young bodies in front of him. Neither of them was moving. The moment was suspended in its fullness. "What happened?" It was a low voice, nearly a whisper, tinged with pain, as soon as Hasina saw Hamid.

"Are you Ok?" Hamid quickly asked.

"I think so," Hasina said. "There were gunshots and Mafulla pulled me down, and my shoulder hit a piece of stone. But I think I was so battle juiced I couldn't feel anything for a few seconds. And I had the wind knocked out of me. But now, I'm starting to hurt. And my hearing is a little muffled."

"That's normal." Hamid responded and then he saw blood on the side of Mafulla's chin and cheek, as he lay motionless, face down in the debris littering the floor. "Hold this," he said to Hasina, placing the stone into her hand as he turned to look more carefully at Mafulla. He gently put a hand on the boy's shoulder and pulled him upward, from the floor.

"Mafulla! Mafulla!"

"Oh, no, no."

"Mafulla!"

The boy groaned. "What happened? Where's?"

Hamid looked up and yelled to the room, "Both are Ok!" And he reached down and turned Mafulla over so he could see him better. And then he replied to the question. "We thought you might have been shot. But it looks like you just split your lip badly when you dove down and hit the floor. Are you all right everywhere else?"

"I'm in pain almost everywhere else," he said. Then he asked, "Did Hasina get hit? Where is she?"

"No. I don't think so," Hamid replied. "She's here. She's fine. I see no other blood on either of you. I think all the shots were palace guards taking out some new adversaries before they could pull their own triggers on you two. They apparently had snuck in the back door and were aiming for the two of you specifically, or so it seemed to me, in the split second I caught sight of the guns the men were holding. Then I heard the shots and saw them go down. I think they may both be dead. It's likely. Just a second." Hamid looked back at Hasina.

She turned her head a bit and said, "Is he Ok?" Hamid knew she was concerned about Mafulla.

He replied, "Yes, it's just some superficial stuff. And I think our medicinal gem has had time to work on your bruise. Let me take it and give it for a minute to our smashed up friend here."

Hasina opened her hand for Hamid to retrieve the stone, and he turned to Mafulla and said, "Here, take this." He put the bright green stone into the boy's hand.

"Am I that bad?" Mafulla asked and groaned, as he took the stone.

"No, but it's more blood than would be expected from just a split lip. It's a bit profuse."

"My body can be overly dramatic," Mafulla said. "It likes the attention."

Then, gripping the stone tightly, he now turned slowly over to face Hasina and said, "Ow. Are you sure you're Ok?"

"Yeah, I just got hurt from falling onto a broken rock. But a few seconds with the stone seems to have taken most of that away."

"I'm really sorry. It's my fault. I didn't want you to get shot."

"I'm glad. I appreciate your quick action," Hasina said. "I'd rather be sore than dead, or severely injured. The floor's basically a good place to be when bullets are flying through the air." She rolled over and leaned up a bit to see him better and said, "Oh! You've got blood all over you. And your lip looks terrible!"

"Yeah, thanks. And you have lots of dust and splinters in your hair … and … I don't mean that in a critical way, because … it all sort of looks cute."

Hasina laughed and moved over more to grab Mafulla and partially hug him, and they both said, "Ow!"

"Oh, man!" Walid exclaimed, as he walked up with Kissa. He grimaced at Mafulla and said, "You look … bad."

"Yeah, after about ten minutes in a lady's shop, the blood sort of starts draining from my face. But, normally, not quite like this."

"Ha! Mafoolery. That means you're fine—or, at least, no worse than usual."

Mafulla picked up a piece of relatively clean looking cloth from the floor and wiped it over his mouth and chin and was shocked at how much blood there actually was. "Man, remind me to eat some protein when we get back. I think this calls for goat cheese on crackers."

Kissa was standing behind Walid and, all of a sudden, she looked up from Mafulla toward a figure standing a few feet away from them and said, "Mom!" She squeezed Walid's arm and ran over to where Hoda was waiting and watching, to hug her and be hugged. The two of them embraced each other and then Kissa started crying. "I don't know what you did or how … but you saved us! Thank you! Thank you so much! You saved us all!"

Hoda was back to normal in her appearance at this point, looking almost like she just stepped off the cover of a fashion magazine, or finished up an ordinary shopping trip with friends at the Luxury Goods store, apart from a light covering of demolition dust that was all over her and, of course, aside from her feet that were soaked from maybe half an inch or more of water on the floor throughout the shop. But she did also look a little subdued, or even tired, which was not something that anyone was accustomed to seeing with her.

"I'm so glad you're Ok," Hoda said. "I was concerned."

Kissa hugged her again and kissed her on the cheek and said, "I can't believe what happened!"

Hoda took a deep breath and let it out. "I'm sorry for all the drama and destruction," she responded, quietly. "There was no other way to stop that man quickly enough."

"He had power," Kissa said.

"Yes. A lot," Hoda replied.

"You had more."

"Yes."

"A totally scary, unbelievable, whole lot more."

"Thankfully."

"I want to be like you."

"You are."

"No, I mean, like that."

"You will be."

Kissa tried to take that in for a moment, and said, "Really?"

"Yes. I think so."

Kissa then asked: "Who was that man?"

"I've never seen him. We'll have to find out."

Just then, Mr. Arumbar began to wake up, groaning and rubbing the back of his head. "Oh! Ouch! What happened to me?" He then looked all around as he sat up on the floor, his clothing all soggy, and said, "Oh, No! What's this? No, no, no. It's a nightmare, a total nightmare! What's happened to my shop?"

Hamid had just helped Mafulla and Hasina get up off the floor, and now immediately turned his attention to the older gentleman, as he briskly walked toward the front of the store. He said, "I'm so sorry, Mr. Arumbar, but a small army of men chose your shop for the scene of a battle today. They were soundly defeated, but it left a real mess."

"Oh, no! All my merchandise! What will I do? What will I do?" the poor man said, as he rubbed the large lump on the back of his head. "Ouch. Ow! The whole building! It's torn apart! I can't afford this! I can't fix such a disaster! I'm ruined!"

Walid walked up at that point and said, "Don't worry, Mr. Arumbar."

"Why? Who are you?"

"Prince Walid Shabeezar."

"You're the prince?"

"Yes. And I'll take care of your place here."

"What do you mean?"

"We'll rebuild it all for you very quickly. We'll have everything cleaned up and as good as new, or better, within days and at no cost to you. I promise."

"Oh! Your Highness! That's so wonderful! I had no idea you were here. Thank you so much for your words of assurance! I would not know what to do without your most gracious and kind offer."

Mafulla had also walked up, and at that point said to his friend in a low voice, "Should you ask the king about this first?"

Walid said, "No. It's Ok. He's letting me have a lot more authority these days, as you know. We can take care of it."

Walid helped the old proprietor up off the floor and spoke with him for a couple of minutes more as Omari, Paki, and Hamid went over to Hoda and Kissa with Mafulla and Hasina. One of the palace guards came up to Walid and said that he was trained in emergency medicine and would like to look quickly at Mr. Arumbar's injuries. The prince thanked him and, reassuring Arumbar once more, walked over to join the group of Phi who were now gathered around Hoda, hugging her and patting her on the back and thanking her. They talked for three or four minutes, and then heard a noise outside the front door and, of course, this got all of them to turn instantly and prepare themselves for anything that might happen next.

At that moment, three armed men, guns at the ready, came through the door. The third was Masoon. Hamid looked over at him with relief and smiled, and said, "Ah! Welcome, friends! You missed some real excitement here earlier."

"Is everyone Ok?"

"Yes, thanks to Hoda and some of our best sharp-shooting palace guards."

"Good! I'm glad." He looked around and said, "What happened?"

In response, Hamid took him by the arm and steered him away from the soldiers, whom he asked to watch the front of the shop, and away from Mr. Arumbar and the palace guard attending to him. He then told Masoon in a hushed voice about everything that had taken place, and recounted what he had seen of Hoda's actions and their wild results. He also explained that there had just been an attempt to shoot Mafulla and Hasina after everyone thought it was all over, and that their vigilant palace guards had prevented what could have been a terrible tragedy.

Masoon said, "Well, the king sent me, so even though everything seems to be over, I'm sure there's a reason I'm here. We need to figure out what it is."

Just then, Walid walked up to them and, overhearing his friend's words, said, "There is indeed a reason. I'd like our military to rebuild this shop as quickly as it's humanly possible to do so, within a matter of days. And I'd like for that to start before the sun goes down. Everything has to be as good as new, or even better."

Masoon smiled and nodded and said, "Yes, Your Highness. As you wish. One of the men I've brought can actually oversee it personally. He has extensive training in construction and finishing work. I'll walk through the shop with the owner and him before we leave, and we'll see what needs to be done. I'll personally provide all the resources necessary. We'll even put up a sign later today for customers that says, 'Remodeling Underway. Opening Soon Better than Ever, for Your Greater Convenience.' How's that?"

"Very good," Walid said and laughed. "Only you would think of that."

Masoon looked around and said, "There appears to be some serious damage, but oddly limited in scope, as I look more closely. Most of the building seems to be intact."

"Yeah, Hoda was pretty precise in the wild demolition she created in response to the enemy," Walid explained in a low voice. "She did what it took to take down the main bad guy, but nothing more. And he was a man with serious power, so if she hadn't acted in such an extreme but focused way, I can't imagine what might have happened. I just didn't know anyone could do what Hoda did. I didn't realize such stuff was even possible."

"It's not the result of even the most advanced normal training," Masoon nearly whispered. "From what Hamid just told me, it was far beyond any of that. It was … distinctive."

"Can others do that?" Walid asked in a near whisper, as well.

"A few, perhaps," Masoon said and Hamid nodded his head. "But from what I know, just a few, ever. It's extremely rare. It takes an unusual, very special, and rare individual, like Hoda, or the king."

Walid looked interested. Masoon added, "You may be able to do such things, if necessary, some day."

"What?"

"You're a Shabeezar."

"But."

"There are no further explanations."

Walid thought for a few seconds to try to take this in. Then a sudden realization came into his mind and he said, "The four elements were in play. I just realized that."

"What do you mean?" Masoon asked.

"The man attacked Hoda with fire, she defended herself with water, and then took down her adversary with wind from the air and stone from the earth."

Masoon looked impressed. "Three in response to one. That's Hoda."

Reela Adi walked in through the front door at that moment, just as Omari and Paki were leading a prisoner over to the main debris pile that two palace guards had already been digging through. The man in their grip was the one who had been stationed at the front door to guard the shop while his associates were inside. He was now once more conscious and was tied up, hands and feet, but the ropes on his legs were loose enough so that he could walk, and yet not run. Paki had pulled a large cloth out of his mouth, and stood holding him tightly, as Omari bent down to remove some final pieces of wooden beams and broken stones from the head of the deceased individual who had used such power before Hoda stopped him.

"Is this man Juan Santiago?" Omari asked, as he pointed at the body.

At first, their prisoner remained silent. "Is this Santiago?" Omari repeated. Still, he was mute. "You must tell me now. Is this man Santiago?"

"Yes," the man replied.

"This is Juan Osvaldo Santiago, and he's dead?" Omari said.

"Yes," the man responded. "I don't know how, but yes."

"Well, that would explain what happened," Omari said to Paki.

"I guess the worst of all this is over, then," Paki surmised.

As soon as he had walked into the ruins of the shop, Reela made his way around some of the piles of merchandise on the floor and the few wet clothing displays that still remained upright. Looking over at Mafulla who was now standing and talking with the others, he saw that his beloved nephew was apparently fine. With a bit of perplexity in his mind, he then felt drawn to go over to where Omari stood.

Mafulla saw him and said, "Uncle! Uncle Reela!"

Reela smiled and held his hand up in greeting, and yet then lifted his index finger into the air, as if to communicate, "Just a moment," and he walked up to Omari.

"Juan Santiago," Omari said to Reela, as he pointed to the dead man under the debris.

Reela looked down at his face for a moment, and then slowly began to remove more wood and stone and some varied items of clothing that had been blown off their display from a nearby rack and onto this man's body, and that were still lying there, piled on top of the corpse. He stood back up and looked him over carefully, and said, "No. No, this is not Juan Santiago."

"It is Santiago! You fool! He's Santiago!" The bound man hissed in a voice of outraged disdain.

"Quiet!" Paki said and jerked him hard.

Reela explained, "I recently received from my brother a full description of a stranger here in town calling himself Osvaldo, and then an identical account of his appearance from someone who once, in Argentina, met the Juan Santiago we seek, and this is not the man who was described to me, identically, by those two highly credible sources." He said, calmly, "This is someone else."

"It's Juan Santiago!" The man now nearly shouted. "It's Santiago!"

"Stuff his mouth! Gag him again!" Omari said, and Paki began to do exactly that.

Masoon noticed something from a distance, and walked up to the man who was now being held by both Paki and Omari. He looked at the individual closely and said, "I have a question. Were you ever in the Egyptian military? Nod if the answer is yes."

The man just stared at Masoon with great anger in an effort to be defiant, but after their eyes had met for less than two seconds, he averted his gaze downward and meekly nodded once.

"Do you recognize this man?" Omari asked Masoon.

"I thought he looked familiar. But it's so unlikely that I would ever have seen him, apart from the fact that when the revolution happened and the king retook the throne, we had to purge some officers, junior and senior, whose allegiance was only to their own greed, as it was fed by the former monarch. A few enlisted men had to go, too, because of their connection with those officers, and I think this man was one of them. So our Santiago character, if he's behind this, has at least one former military man of ours in his command, and that's a fact that could be important to know." He thought for a moment and added, "There was more than one reason I was supposed to be here today at this stage in the course of events."

Hamid had come up now and was hearing all this. "I wouldn't have recognized the man at all," he said.

"Yes. There's a reason for many things, despite any appearance to the contrary," Masoon said. "This is knowledge we were supposed to have today." Turning back to Omari, he gave the order, "Take this man away, to the palace jail for more questioning. And explain to him, along the way, how it's strongly in his interest to cooperate with us and give us the information we seek."

On the second floor of the palace, the king and Layla had been sitting quietly in his office, in a deep meditative state. "Mafulla and Hasina are safe. They're fine," the king said.

"Yes, thankfully, all of ours are well," she replied. "Hoda prevented something terrible. And then your guards saved Hasina. She and Mafulla have had some pain, but nothing bad."

The king took a deep breath and let it out. "There were deaths."

"Yes."

"And there was a departure of someone with power."

"I felt it, too," Layla responded. "But I didn't know at first what I was feeling. I wonder if it was Santiago."

"I sense that there's still a threat," the king answered. "It's a bit diminished for the moment, at least, but it continues. Extreme resources are being expended. I believe our ultimate adversary most likely may still be with us."

"What of our friends, and Hasina? Will they come back here now?"

"Yes. Can you stay?"

"Absolutely."

"May I have Kular bring you something to eat or drink?"

"No, thank you, not until Hasina's back here and I can see her and we can decompress. I started to say 'decompose' and that's almost what it seems like." Layla laughed. "Sometimes you feel like you're going to come apart when someone you love is in danger, or has just been in jeopardy, and you couldn't physically be present to help."

"I understand," the king said with a smile. "But you do very well in such circumstances, or actually, in all circumstances."

"Thanks. I suppose so. And yet, you know, being a mother comes before everything else."

"Yes. But you're both a Phi mother, and the mother of a Phi."

"It helps a lot," she said. "And still, while I may not actual-ly worry with frantic anxiety, as most other mothers without my knowledge and resources would, the amount of existential concern can still be great, and even a bit draining at times like this when we're separated."

"Yes. The knowledge and resources do help, though, and quite a bit, I'm sure," the king replied.

"More than I could ever say," Layla responded and took a deep breath. "If everyone would just open themselves to the deeper truths about life and the positive powers available to them through their hearts and minds, the world would be a vastly different place."

"Yes, it would. And we may hope for that, one day. I'm an optimist over the long run," the king said.

"And, in the short run, we spread whatever positive perspectives and good energy we can," Layla replied.

"Enlightenment takes place one mind at a time, one soul at a time, one heart at a time," the king added. "And that one change alters everything."

Kular came into the room and waited until the king looked over at him, and then he said, "I'm so sorry, Your Majesty, but I just had to ask: Is everything all right?"

"Yes, yes it is, Kular. Why do you ask?"

"It was your tone of voice earlier, Your Majesty, when you had me send for Masoon. And then, an envelope just arrived at the main gate and was conveyed up to me a couple of minutes ago."

"What was in the envelope?" The king asked, with a look of curiosity.

"Well, there was an outer envelope and an inner envelope. The outer one was addressed to 'The King's Assistant.' So of course I opened it. And inside it, there was another envelope." Kular held it in front of him and looked down at it. He explained, "It says on the front—and I'm so very sorry that I have to read this aloud: 'To the Soon-to-be-Deceased King Ali Shabeezar.' What a terrible thing for anyone to write! I feel awful about it. Should I open it for you?"

"No, thank you, Kular. Please just bring it over to me and I'll open it myself," the king said.

Kular walked across to the king's desk with an expression of great concern and handed him the envelope. He then turned quickly and nodded to Layla, who almost imperceptibly nodded back.

The king took the item and held it in both his hands for a moment, considering it, pondering its odd form of address, and sensing anything about it that he could. Then he tore open one end. There was a single sheet of paper in it, which he carefully slipped out. And on the paper, there was one simple, hand-written sentence. The king read it aloud.

"I'm waiting for you right now at the main gate. Sincerely, Juan Osvaldo Santiago."

9

THOUGHTS AT BREAKFAST

MAFULLA OPENED THE DOOR AND SAW THAT WALID WAS already sitting at the breakfast table, eating a bun and sipping strong tea. "Well, this is new," he said as he walked by his friend and grabbed a plate for himself.

"What's new?" Walid replied.

"You up first—you, in here already, eating. How many times have I had to beg and bother you to get out of bed in the morning? You're the late sleeper. You're never here first."

"I've been up first a few times."

"Well, I can't remember any. Nevertheless: What's up?"

"Me."

"Ok, and also joking already. So, the brain cells are at work, although still, given the quality of the humor, not that many."

"I couldn't sleep. I was lying in bed a long time this morning thinking about everything that happened yesterday."

"Yeah, it was a lot."

"First, I was so worried about Kissa and Hasina before we got to the shop. Then, there was all that over-the-top Hoda stuff that I still haven't really processed, mentally or emotionally."

"Me, too. Both things."

"And then, there was the whole envelope-for-the-king business. I was not prepared for that at all."

"Yeah, I know. It was probably one of the strangest, out there, freakiest days of all time. And that's really saying a lot for us." Mafulla moved over to the sideboard and began putting fruit, cheese, and bread onto his plate. "It's sometimes like we live in an alternate universe, and even in that world of weird, yesterday was just wild."

"True," Walid commented. "And yet, I guess it's the genuine real world that we live in, and most other people seem to be living in a shiny, superficial shadow-land, where you can't even begin to see most of what's going on in the true cosmic drama."

"Good point. Well said. And I think we should talk about all of it. But let's save the stuff about Hoda for when I've had a little tea," Mafulla suggested. "Let's start with the envelope."

"Ok. I mean, it's just too bizarre that, as it turned out, a guy not much older than us wrote that note in front of the main entrance guard, put it in the envelope, then in another larger one, and gave it to the guard to take to Kular. And then, after a couple of minutes, he just walked away, and so far as anyone can tell, simply vanished."

"And he presented the letter that he wrote like he's Santiago," Mafulla said. "I mean—that's how he signed it."

"Yeah. And you don't even know yet what Kular told me this morning, a little while ago when he brought in the food."

"What?"

"So, mid-day yesterday, two city policemen picked up an old guy who was passed out drunk on a bench in that park where we first saw The Wild Camel and The Silver Sabre in action, you know, when they rescued that lady's dog from the animal thieves."

"Yeah?"

"And they took him into the police station—the drunk guy— and when he regained consciousness and sobered up, they talk- ed to him about why he was there, and then released him with a warning about public intoxication."

"So, this story is going somewhere interesting?" Mafulla said with a skeptical look.

"Yes, be patient. So when the paper came out this morning,

there was a small write-up and it's over there," Walid gestured to a side table. "In the normal 'Crime Report' section, it says that an old man was picked up in the park inebriated. I like that word. And it reports that the identification he had in his pocket listed his name as … hold on to your fig … Juan Osvaldo Santiago."

"No way."

"Yep."

"So, the lookout guy yesterday that Paki and Omari dragged into the shop … he identified the dead man who had all that strange power as Juan Santiago. And he kept insisting on it. And the guy at the gate, a little older than us, signed that strange note as Juan Osvaldo Santiago. And now a drunk old man had ID on him that says he's Juan Osvaldo Santiago."

"Super, super strange."

"So maybe the lookout wasn't lying to us in the shop after all, despite what Reela told us."

"What do you mean?"

"Maybe the dead guy was named Juan Santiago. Maybe there's a small army of guys suddenly in town named Juan Osvaldo Santiago."

"But … why?"

"I guess, to make it harder for us to find the real one, to give us lots of false trails to follow, maybe."

"Oh. Ok. Wow. That's pretty smart."

"Yeah. It is. Somebody's being really smart."

"No, I meant you, for your reasoning."

"Oh, Ok. Thanks."

"I'm really rubbing off on you."

"Ha. Yeah. So, if I'm right, then when Reela or Leem or anyone looks for somebody in Cairo by that name, one that's otherwise been really uncommon around here, they'll now find it all over the place."

"But why the note to the king?"

"Bad guys with attitude like to taunt their intended victims."

"Yeah?"

"Sure. Remember the bomb in the basement?"

"I'll never forget that."

"And then remember the fake wires in the tunnel later on, taunting us. It was to undermine our confidence, and make us feel like enemies were everywhere and had access to the palace and us at any time."

"Ok, yeah, I remember all that like it was yesterday, and I do remember how it made me feel."

"Maybe the real, original Santiago is doing the same thing, trying to undermine us, get into our heads, sort of taunt us, and evade us as long as he can, all at the same time. And this is going on while he plans whatever he really has in mind for all of us."

"But these aren't just a bunch of guys he found on the street and gave fake IDs to. That guy in the shop had scary power."

"Yeah, I hope there aren't a lot more like him. Maybe he was the real Santiago's main student, or associate, or something."

"If the real Santiago has more power than that, I'm concerned."

"Yeah, but remember what the king did outside Dromeda."

"True."

Walid thought for a moment and said, "There will probably never be anything stranger than that."

"I hope not," Mafulla said, "but yesterday was pretty impressive, too, and also a big win for the home team and, I'm sure it's got to rank pretty high in the all-time chronicles of locally caused cosmic fireworks."

"Yeah. It was. If I didn't know Hoda so well, if she wasn't almost like family, I would have been scared half to death just by the way she looked. And there was this sense of power way beyond everything in this world that seemed to shoot out her eyes and, you know, emanate from her whole body."

"Emanate is a nice word," Mafulla said, between bites. "Good job with that one. Score another one for the home team."

"Thanks. I'm obviously trying to catch up with you, but that's likely hopeless, or as you would say: inevitably futile." Mafulla smiled at that, and gave a thumbs-up, as Walid continued. "Still,

I've come to realize that a rich, wide vocabulary is a great resource, and doesn't have to be as good as, or better than, somebody else's in order to be valuable. It's not a competition."

"Another astute observation. Superlatively sagacious," Mafulla said in reply.

"Ah. I appreciate your positive words, which clearly constitute a case of … supererogatory kindness." Walid pronounced the word carefully and smiled, admitting, "I've been waiting for a chance to use that one for a month."

"Ha! It was well used, and worth the wait," Mafulla said.

"You know what it means?"

"Sure. Beyond the call of duty, more than would be expected, or exceeding what's necessary," Mafulla answered.

"Boy, your knowledge of words is really …"

"Supererogatory," Mafulla said.

Walid sighed big-time and said, "Well, there you go. I waited weeks to find an appropriate way to use that word, and you got the job done again within about ten seconds."

"What can I say? It's one of my talents, and I daresay, a considerable part of my distinctive charm. You have your own virtues. It's not a competition."

Walid laughed again and said, "That's a good thing. But I'm guessing that, with your formidable linguistic firepower, you have to be careful not to use too elevated a form of speech with those who might not grasp the particulars and subtleties of your meaning."

"Yeah. It's a concern. In a book I was reading not long ago, the author cautioned against the use of overly advanced language with, as he sort of disdainfully put it, *hoi polloi.*"

"That must be a synonym for 'Walid Shabeezar,' because you got me with that one. I mean: I know hoi, like when you've got an unexpected pain in your back, but *hoi polloi?*"

"Greek, of course, for 'the people,' meaning the common run of humanity, the crowd, normal folks, individuals who aren't among the elite cognoscenti, the few educated to an advanced level."

"Oh."

"It's kind of an aristocratic phrase with a touch of arrogance to it, and people nowadays who use it a lot tend to be all hoity-toity and high-falutin' and pedantic. But there are also people who just use it to sound smart and don't really know what they're doing."

"What do you mean?"

"Well, you can tell because they'll often say 'the *hoi polloi*,' not realizing that '*hoi*' already means 'the,' and so they're being clumsily redundant in their phrasing, and saying, of course unknown to them, 'the-the people.' Does that make sense?" Mafulla then got up to get more tea from a nearby table.

"Yes, professor. Thank you. But I never thought I'd hear ancient Greek words and the expression 'hoity-toity' in the same short discourse."

"You just never know what you might experience next, in my linguistic presence, within my unique conversational orb," Mafulla said.

"I truly never know," Walid agreed.

Across town, Khata's mother Rama El-Noor was having breakfast. And she began reading a note that had just arrived. Suddenly, she called out to Khata, who was still back in her room, doing some homework. "Sweetie! Good News! There's very good news!"

"What is it?" Khata responded, as she rolled off her bed and began to walk out of the room and in the direction of her mother's voice.

"Your new music teacher will be in town tomorrow, and the day after that, before she even gets completely unpacked and settled in to her new house, she'll begin your piano lessons!"

"No way!"

"Yes! She says so in this note that just came in the mail. And the best thing of all is that the house they're moving into is only a block away from here! Can you believe it?"

"What a coincidence! That's amazing! It's going to be so convenient," Khata said. "I can't wait to start!"

"It is pretty incredible how all this is working out," Rama said. "Ever since I got the idea to buy the piano, everything's just fallen into place in the most wonderful ways."

"How did it even enter your mind to get us the piano in the first place?" Khata said, "I mean, other than the fact that I've always talked about music and pianos since I was little. What set you off suddenly to find one and buy it now? I never thought to ask before."

"I guess it was seeing the one at Layla's house not long ago. That was the first time I had paid attention to how well made a piano can be, and how elegant it can look, with the beauty of the finely finished wood and the dramatic contrast of the keys. When I said something in admiration of its visual beauty there in her home, she sat down and played for a minute or two, and I was just overcome with the music. She's really good. That's when I got a sudden urge to have one in our home as well. So, that's what set me off, as you say."

"I didn't realize it was Layla's piano and her playing that did it. I'll have to thank her."

"Yes. I even mentioned your interest to Layla at the time, and she told me how good she thinks you'll be at the piano, and what a difference she believes it can make in your life."

"She said that?"

"She did. Her encouragement meant a lot. The playing and her words both had an impact. And then, when she said she'd even help me find a great piano at a good price, how could I resist?"

Khata laughed and said, "Well, I'm glad you didn't resist."

"And now, what impresses me to no end," Rama said, "is how much you've taught yourself in the few days since the piano's been here. Layla was right! You're a prodigy."

"I don't know about that, but it is fun, and it feels natural to me. It's all about the patterns of sound and patterns on the keyboard, and it does seem to come easily. I can't wait to really learn about it all and get lots better."

"Well, that will start very soon," Rama said.

"Yeah. I'm so glad!" And with those words, Khata walked over to the piano, sat on the bench, and began to play a sequence of notes and chords that she had been working on. Each note seemed to touch something in her soul. It was almost as if the piano was a doorway into a place of the spirit where Khata could feel deeply at home, and at peace, and yet exhilarated, all at the same time. The polished wood, the cool touch of the keys, and the magical sounds vibrating through the instrument all conspired to take her somewhere she had longed to go. And Layla somehow had sensed all this.

What Rama and Khata didn't know was that, while Layla was genuinely and sincerely trying to be helpful, and really believed every word she had said about the piano in this young girl's life, she'd also had something else on her mind. She saw Khata's interest in music as an ideal way to get a member of Phi, one that the Khata didn't know, into her life now for a time, in order to evaluate her for a possible invitation into the secret order. Invitations were, of course, rare, and easier to decide on when a candidate had clearly shown Phi abilities repeatedly over time and was also from a Phi family lineage, as Walid, Kissa, and Layla's daughter Hasina all were. Even though Phi abilities didn't always run in families, that still seemed to be more common than not. So, both these facts were judged to be relevant when assessing how deep any apparent Phi traits might go in a possible candidate's mind and heart. Senior Phi members were looking for a kind of potential that could be grounded only in some fairly impressive realities.

The problem was that Khata had experienced most of her uncanny insights, warnings, and knowledge-beyond-the-norm while alone, and typically had not spoken of these things to anyone, except on one or two occasions. But in one particular instance, witnessed by Hoda, the power seemed especially strong in Khata, and deep. There were no known members of Phi in her family's background. But the king had also experienced some distinct intuitions about her, and so had Hoda, on more than one occasion. So, an impartial evaluation was very important at this point. That, at least, was the recommended process, as outlined in The Book of Phi. Ideally, at least one member of the society that Khata didn't previously know should quietly evaluate her over a period of time.

When the king had mentioned this need to Layla, Mafulla's aunt, Muriel al-Baki, had immediately come to mind.

Muriel, despite her age, had never advanced much beyond level-one Phi training and, in fact, it was fairly early during her level-two work, many years ago, that she had to suspend her lessons due to her suddenly busy concert schedule. Her Phi sponsors in Alexandria understood this and had allowed her to initiate a pause in her general physical and spiritual development for the sake of her overwhelming musical gifts and their use for the greater good of her family, community, and nation. After all, it was one of the core purposes of Phi to encourage all members to make their distinctive contributions to the world. It was clear when the time had come for her to devote herself to performance and travel. And then, her life in the intervening years had never seemed to let up in its extraordinary schedule, so she had not ever had the chance to resume her formal training in the order. But she was still officially a member of Phi, and she was trusted by the Phi who knew her, although not many had recently enjoyed any contact with her, again, due to her demanding schedule and extensive travels.

Layla had met Muriel a few years earlier and had greatly admired her musical skill. As a senior Phi, she also knew of Muriel's status. So, when the question of evaluating Khata had come up, she instantly thought of the girl's interest in music and Muriel's expertise. Little things that Layla had said recently, both to Rama and to their mutual friend, Shamilar Adi, had planted all the right seeds, and Layla's plan to bring Muriel and Khata together seemed to be coming to fruition, though in a much more extensive way than she had even hoped.

The king had put Layla on the task, initially, because of her close friendship with Khata's mother. Ali trusted that Layla could find someone who would be able to do the evaluations that were called for as a preliminary to any decisions that would have to be made about Khata's gifts and potential relationship to the Phi of Cairo. She was a sensitive and thoughtful girl, and keenly intelligent. And even though the king had some solid indications to go on, he would never move rashly in such a matter. Various forms of testing would have to be done, unobtrusively and ideally without any prior or concurrent revelation of what was happening. Questions would need to be asked in such a way as not to be thought of as too strange, or as in any way out of place. With a few potential members, the king had experienced an immediate intuition of total recognition. With others, he had started with a small suspicion, as he had with Khata, and had then taken action either to confirm that feeling or to see beyond it.

In order for a Phi evaluation to be administered properly, it had to be done almost like an ideal psychological test over an extended period of time. Any awareness on the part of the person being examined, or any alertness, to there being something strange underway could skew the results and give inaccurate findings. If anyone known to Khata had tried to do the testing, there would not be the necessary distance, or objectivity. Because the young lady's social circles involved in some way almost all the local Phi of Cairo, Layla had hoped to recruit someone from outside town. And the person had to be able to meet Khata in a way that seemed natural and for a good reason. Then, the Phi member would have to interact with her for an extended amount of time, with ample opportunities to ask pertinent questions. This was, of course, a combination of conditions normally hard to satisfy. But the idea of a music teacher for her ticked all the right boxes and would work quite well, in addition to providing Khata with something she would love, in itself, and that would forever enhance her life, regardless of how the evaluation went.

Layla had been around Muriel al-Baki several times, and had recently suggested to her in a letter only that she come to Cairo on an extended visit where she could meet Khata and spark the girl's already deep interest in music, perhaps give her some piano lessons, and make certain determinations along the way about her overall personal abilities relevant to Phi. She had no idea that the famous musician would actually move to town shortly after their brief correspondence. And, of course, she had no absolutely no clue that Muriel would also be working for another source, for his own ends, and would be manipulating her new relationship with Khata to gather extensive information about the palace and all the Cairo Phi.

No one outside Muriel's immediate household could possibly guess that her travels as a performer had exposed her to people and forces that had slowly undermined her character and, by now, undercut almost everything that was supposed to be involved with being Phi. She was the only member of Shamilar's family in their entire history ever to be enticed and drawn in by what we can call the dark side of life, due to an overwhelming personal ambition and unquenchable desire for greatness and adulation. But she never thought of what she had experienced and become involved with as representing spiritual darkness, or as being in any way wrong, which is a common tragedy.

When she met a strikingly intense man who loved music so much, she had no idea what he would bring to her life. He began to introduce her to the deeper levels of what she cherished and to which she was devoting her life. He helped her see beyond the sounds and the tonal and rhythmic beauties of music, as well as far beyond the mathematics and aesthetics of it all. He took her deep into the soul of music. And as a result, she was entranced and completely hooked. He taught her that spiritual energies could be accessed through music and then used for personal transformation and great power. What she had learned from him was exciting to the point of near inebriation. A forceful enthusiasm and even giddiness was blocking any form of self-examination or questioning that alone would have had a chance to turn her away from what the real Juan Osvaldo Santiago wanted for her and, most importantly, from her.

It was Muriel who first told Santiago about the palace school student Khata El-Noor and the opportunity that she had been given to evaluate the girl for Phi abilities. He had heard many reports of this secret society over the years and had some knowledge about the king and prince and their powers. He had worried about how they and the gifted and unnamed others in their sphere might hinder his plans. Desperate for quick connections to the palace and hungry for any knowledge about the Phi of Egypt, he jumped at the chance to use Khata, and thus Muriel at the same time, for his own purposes.

Of course, he had many other creative and independent plans to gather the knowledge he was seeking. But this was an unusual and important avenue for him, so he had instructed Muriel to move to Cairo and probe the young girl for any information that might be useful to him. He told his musical acolyte that she was uniquely positioned, in her depth of soul and in her rare personal talents, and now with this new opportunity, to do for him, for the cause of spirituality on earth, and even for her beloved domain of music, more than any other individual alive could do. He insinuated in every way that success in this endeavor would bring her status, power, and wealth beyond imagining. He even conjured a promise of eternal significance for her life, if she performed this one task well. And she was enthralled.

Muriel had to keep secret from her family and friends what had by now become a total loyalty to Santiago. But he had woven a web of lies both around her and within her so that, as a result, she felt certain that, in serving his needs, she would ultimately be serving her family, friends, kingdom, and even the society of Phi in ways that they would not yet be able to recognize as being greatly in their own interests, throughout the long term. In addition, she was thrilled at the thought that, alongside her spiritual master, she would have special access to knowledge that she had been told was not shared by even the most advanced Phi. She would be special. Osvaldo, as she liked to call him whenever she didn't just use the word 'Master,' had made her believe that she could become something like a new spiritual queen of the realm, once his plans had all come to their proper completion. And, as he knew, the secret thrill evoked in her by this prospect would move her to do anything he asked.

Santiago had always been a master manipulator, knowing that

the royal route to moving people was to discover what they already loved and show an equal or greater excitement for whatever that was, while intimating a special status in that regard and making promises to them that would set their hearts afire with an overwhelming sense of new and magnificent possibilities. Everyone wants to feel important. We all want to be appreciated for who we are. And we naturally aspire to make a difference in the world, far beyond what normally seems to be available to us. It's our true nature that prompts these desires, which are really spiritual needs. A shrewd manipulator like the real Juan Osvaldo Santiago understood those needs deeply enough to be able to use them for his focused purposes.

Because of this, Muriel's move to Cairo was creating a cluster of dangers that no one yet anticipated. And the treachery would play out faster than anyone could ever imagine. People who thought they had seen it all would be shocked at what they would very soon see, and also at the consequences they would face without being able to see.

Back in the palace, at the breakfast table, Mafulla had a concerned look on his face and had grown silent for a few seconds. The prince noticed. "What?" Walid said. "What's going on? Is something bothering you?"

"It's nothing," Mafulla said.

"No, it's something. What is it?"

Mafulla just looked away from Walid and stared down at the table and took a deep breath and let it out. "I don't know."

"I think you do. So. Tell me."

10

Beyond the Box

"It's Hoda," Mafulla said, looking back up.

"Ok. Ok. What about her?"

The younger boy let out a big breath and said, "Well, It's just that I think I haven't fully come to terms with what happened yesterday. We may need to talk for a minute about all that I-can't-believe-what-I'm-seeing stuff that went down in the shop." Mafulla clearly had the extraordinary events of the previous day weighing on his mind.

"Hey, it's hopefully my future mother-in-law. I'm the one who should be worried," Walid said.

"Very funny," Mafulla replied. "I'm serious. It sort of threw me."

"And you're not as easy to throw as you once were," Walid said.

"Goat cheese and heavy lifting," Mafulla replied. "But listen, I need to be honest about this. The stuff that happened in the shop went way, way beyond anything I ever would have expected. I mean, I was ready for Hoda to give the guy a paralyzing migraine or something, but not for what happened. It was a huge shock, and I have to admit, sort of scary to the max. What did you think of it all?"

Walid took a bite of cheese and said, "Remember what the king told us after the Dromeda trip?"

"About what?"

"The story of the box."

"Oh, yeah, of course I remember. I like that story a lot."

"Me too, so if you don't mind, let me review it quickly in basic outline."

"Ok. But why?"

"It's relevant. And I want to see if I can get it right," Walid said. "I think we need to have the details fresh on our minds for me to be able to say what I want to say about Hoda."

"All right. Go to it." Mafulla crossed his arms and put his elbows both up on the table, as he prepared to listen.

"So. Imagine that there's this race of tiny beings, extremely small intelligent creatures who for generations have been born and have lived their lives and then died in a very, very large box."

"Miniscule beings," Mafulla offered, while biting into a fig that he had just plucked from his plate.

"Yeah, miniscule. And it's a huge box. But let me go on."

"Absolutely. Good start. Proceed."

"The box has everything in it that the beings need. Or so it seems."

"Yeah. It's well stocked with good stuff."

"Exactly. But, at some point, one of the tiny people starts wondering aloud whether there's anything outside the box. And lots of the other box people say things like, 'How can you even ask that? We get our whole concept of "in" and "out" as we live our box-enabled lives and experience stuff here, throughout our Box World. Maybe the concept of "outside" can't even apply to the box itself. It probably just makes no real sense to ask about whether there's anything outside the box, or Beyond the Box.' The other little people are puzzled, and some are even irritated by this guy's curiosity and his questions."

"Yeah, I like that part," Mafulla said, now munching on a cracker. "He's so much like the guy Khalid told us about, the first philosopher, according to Socrates in the myth of Plato's Cave."

"He is. He's not satisfied with living in the cave, or the box."

"Yeah. He's asking if there's something more. But go on."

"Ok. So, this one guy is wondering whether there's anything outside the box. And many of the little creatures think the question makes no sense. But others are intrigued by it. And, maybe, shortly after the issue arises, there come to be both Beyond-the-Box Believers and Beyond-the-Box Skeptics. And there are maybe those who think the whole issue is dangerous and should be avoided. But then a few brave souls actually try to get out of the box, but nobody ever makes it until, one day, there's a character who has, strangely, disappeared for a while, and he suddenly shows up again and says, 'Guys! You won't believe it! I've been outside the box! There's a whole giant world out there! An entire, mind-boggling universe! This box is so small by comparison to the greater reality that there are no adequate words for it! It's tiny! It's a speck!'"

Mafulla spoke up. "He's got to be excited by a discovery like that."

"Really, for sure. But some of the box people are outraged and offended by this announcement, and yet still he continues on. He says: 'Look, this is really good news! We don't just live in this speck of a box! We actually live in a vast, unimaginably big and diverse overarching reality in which the box is only a teeny, relatively microscopic part. There's so much stuff out there, and beauty, and possibility!' And when he says all this, most of the box dwellers don't believe him for a second. They claim he's gone out of his mind, not out of the box, and that as a result he's just talking crazy."

"But then, a few are different," Mafulla jumped in again and added. "See? I remember the story pretty well."

"Yeah, you do. A few of the others are willing to listen, and at first take it sort of on faith that there's a bigger outside world, and they follow this guy around and listen to what he says, and eventually a few of them somehow manage to get out, too. And they see it all for themselves, everything he's told them. And stuff happens to them outside the box that can change them … forever. And then, when they go back inside the box to tell their own tales of discovery, they find that they have knowledge and insights and maybe even abilities and stuff that no one with limited box experience and thought can possibly understand. And so they aren't believed, either. But they know by their own experience that it's all real."

Mafulla, looking impressed, lightly clapped his hands three times and said, "Good job."

"Thank you."

"As a metaphor, it's amazingly apt."

"Apt?"

"Good. Appropriate. Accurate. Telling." Mafulla was nodding slowly as he said this. He then continued on, and reflected: "I guess your point, and it's a good one, is that Hoda's been way far out of the box, in and out now for a very long time. So, whenever she's back inside, here in Cairo or anywhere in this box of a world that we love and know so well, and she faces a big enough need, there are likely going to be some outside-the-box things happening that are pretty stunning and wild to normal box dwellers like most of the rest of us."

"Yeah," Walid said. "But, then why was it so unsettling to you, and even more than a little bit to me? I mean, we're not just box-bound people. We go out of the box, too."

"Sure, a little bit, and pretty far compared to most people, and maybe even compared to most of those who get out at all, I'm thinking, but, I guess, not like Hoda or the king, and a few others," Mafulla said.

"That's true," Walid acknowledged. "And that's my point. We shouldn't be scared about what we saw, or troubled by it, or thrown, but just awed and maybe even encouraged by how much there must be out there, beyond the box and how it can be a source of great power."

Mafulla then took a long sip of tea and commented, "I'm glad you reminded me. The story does speak to what I was feeling."

"Good. I thought it would."

"I also like what the king told us later that same day about the various dimensions of reality, as he explained the box metaphor—that there are these three dimensions of space we know so well ... length, width, and depth, or height, whichever up or down word you prefer ... and then there's the dimension of time, with its before and after; past, present, and future; then and now, and yet to be. And these four dimensions together of space and time, along with the physical world they measure, are like a big box for most people. We live and move and think inside them. But what if there are more dimensions than just these? What if the life of the soul, or the ultimate self, as our deepest personal foothold in existence, is really and properly on another dimensional plane, with its actual roots outside the earthly box? That's what the king seemed to be saying."

"Yeah, I know," Walid replied very quietly, almost whispering.

Mafulla at this point stood up and started pacing, and said, "Ok. So. Here's the idea. The soul, or the ultimate self, the inner core of the person is not literally to be found in our bodies or in our brains, and it's not located any physical distance from our bodies or anything in our bodies. Its home is in a dimension or metaphysical space, so to speak, outside the box. But it has a mind that's grown up in connection with the brain I have in this physical box and so it can easily see things through this mind as if everything was in the box."

"Yeah. The earthly body is a part of this box world, and the mind that's formed by the operation of the brain is a part of this box world, but the soul or core self that has the body and mind, the soul that experiences through them and is expressed through them is outside this box and in another dimensional reality." He paused and added, "It's an idea that really stretches me." Walid then scratched his head as if the thought actually made him itch.

Mafulla continued. "And of course the same is true of heaven, the soul's natural home, properly understood. It's no physical distance away, or up, or down. It's not in this cosmic, physical box at all. And when the western religions say that the soul exists now and that it will exist tomorrow and into an everlasting future, they really mean that, within its embodiment in a human form, within the four dimensional reality that structures this world, as it experiences life through this sort of body, along this worldly time-line, there will be no point in this world's story or time-line when it—the soul itself—will cease to exist, regardless of what happens to the body. The soul, though, will at some point in box time leave the embodiment it has had in this box, its temporary home-away-from-home, but it won't stop existing and experiencing in it's most fundamental form and dimensions of being, in its eternal mode and its ultimate home. And it's really, in itself, not confined to this four dimensional box at all, even while it's having and experiencing life on earth, but is instead most fundamentally real in its own proper plane or sphere of dimensional existence."

"Wow, that was a mouth full, professor," Walid said, and then he added, "I can't believe you can remember all that so exactly. But then, again, it's you."

"Yeah, well."

"No, really. Excellent performance, as usual, in recalling precisely what the king said, and in saying it all the way he did. I don't think you missed a single twist of it, and I know I couldn't have recited it all nearly as well. Your memory is pretty impressive."

"You're just being nice," Mafulla said. "But feel free to keep it up. I wrote all this stuff down when I got back to my room that night, right after the king told us, and I've reread it a few times since then. But, oddly, I didn't think of it at all when the Hoda thing happened, or even right afterward. The experience was just sort of overwhelming. And you've brought it all back with your retelling of the story."

Walid said, "Hey, we all have habits of thought. Just because we have a new idea, even a big one, and even if we've reflected on it a bunch, we still can forget it temporarily when we're confronted with a situation where it applies, especially if the situation is totally crazy and confusing. We naturally fall back to old habits of thought and feeling, almost like we hadn't ever come across the new insight at all."

"Yeah, it's strange, but true," Mafulla agreed. "Habit is really strong here in Box World. We're all too often just creatures of habit. We expect things to happen the way they've happened before, with nothing really or radically new. We're boxed in by habit."

"Absolutely," Walid agreed. "And we need to do something about that. We need to get used to thinking outside the box. And so ... when we get involved in some of our stranger Phi stuff, and when Hoda goes all Greek goddess on some guy, we need to remember that we're operating—but mostly, that she's operating— from the deepest resources not only of normal worldly dimensions, but also out of other dimensions that are far, far Beyond the Box. The power she used comes from way outside the box and can blow away stuff that's in it."

"Yeah, for sure."

"And it can be super scary to see this happen, because stuff like that just doesn't go on here in the box very often at all. And this is due to the fact that most people live their normal box lives inside ordinary Box World most of the time and never get out of it, or even really believe that anything like the bigger, broader reality exists."

"Well said." Mafulla encouraged his friend. He had gotten out of his chair and had been pacing around as they spoke, but he now stood still, leaning on the back of the chair, taking it all in.

"Thanks," Walid replied. "And what's neat, or maybe weird, about the box story, is that it's sort of the opposite of the ancient Greek myth of Pandora's Box, the tale of the woman who opened a box that was never supposed to be opened, and out came all this scary stuff, but then at the bottom of it, after all that, was hope. In the king's story about a box, we live in the box, and it's what's outside the box that can be so scary and yet, that's also where our greatest hope is."

"Very nice," Mafulla said. "Except that ... it was really Pandora's Jar."

"What do you mean?"

"The Greek word meant large jar, but when this Dutch guy

named Erasmus first translated it into Latin, a much more widely understood language for Europeans than Greek was a few centuries ago, he made a mistake and thought it meant box."

"So Pandora's Box is really Pandora's Big Jar?"

"Yep."

"I didn't know that. And how do you?"

"I read a lot," Mafulla said. "And I get around, at least here, inside the box."

"Apparently a lot more than I do," Walid said. "Pandora's Big Jar. Who knew? But everybody since then has called it 'Pandora's Box,' so I guess my comparison is still a good one."

"Yeah, quite appropriate," Mafulla said. And then he added, "Almost … jarringly so." And that got the double eyebrow jump.

"Ha!"

The boys then sat in silence for maybe thirty seconds, which was unusual for them in the middle of a conversation. And finally, Mafulla spoke again.

"I wonder how big, how enormous, how vast it all really is," he said.

"What all?"

"All the stuff outside the box."

"Oh." Walid said, "I don't even know how to start getting my mind around it. I mean, in reality, the actual box of our physical universe itself, of course, is huge beyond imagining, from what the astronomers and other scientists are now saying. So I'm sure we can't even begin to fathom how much is beyond the box."

And that's when the biggest of all ideas hit Mafulla, and then seconds later Walid, in a flash of revelation and with a sequence of thoughts that left them both completely stunned and full of astonished awe. At first, Mafulla was so overwhelmed by it that he couldn't speak. Then he just said, "Oh. Oh wow."

A second before his own understanding, Walid just said, "What?"

In a nearby part of town, Reela Adi climbed a few steps and looked up at the address on the door and a nearby sign to make sure he was at the right building. Opening the outer front door and stepping into an inner hallway, he saw an interior door on the left, and stenciled on it in black was the name, "The Cairo Detective Agency." He knocked twice and waited.

"Come in!" A loud voice boomed out and came through the door in only a slightly muffled form.

Turning the doorknob and entering slowly, Reela saw Leem Hadad leaning back in his chair with his feet up on the desk in front of him. "Reela! Come in!" he said, adding, "It's good to see you!" He quickly swung his feet down from the desktop and stood up to greet his visitor.

"I'm sorry to interrupt what must have been a major bout of detective work going on just now, pondering the mysteries," Reela said.

"It's no interruption whatsoever." Leem said with a smile. "I was just winding down with the pondering and getting ready for some action. Please, have a seat." Leem gestured to the chair immediately in front of his dark wooden desk, and Reela, also smiling, sat comfortably.

"I thought I should check in and see if you'd made any progress."

"Oh, good! I wanted to thank you anyway for the connections. The two old friends of yours were quite helpful to me."

"So, you're hot on the trail now?"

"I've been hot on far too many trails," Leem said. "Your former colleagues had some good suggestions, and they're even asking around for me, likely, as we now speak. But in the meantime, I've been working every angle I can think of, and I've turned up both too much and not enough at the same time."

"Oh?"

"Yes. Ever since we learned of the young man using the name Juan Osvaldo Santiago—the one who wrote the king that very strange note—and found out about the man in the park with the same name on his personal identification, and then concluded that the man killed in the fight with Hoda may actually have also had the same name as well, we've discovered much more."

"Good. What have you uncovered?"

"There's apparently a small army of Juan Osvaldo Santiagos in

Cairo at present, and most of them don't directly work for the original, and have never even seen the man himself."

"How can this be?"

"There are apparently at least three men bearing the name who do indeed work directly for the monster, if I can call him that."

"I sometimes don't know what to make of ancient legends, but his actions are certainly monstrous," Reela said, "so it's fine with me."

"I feel the same. So, I've learned that these three men were apparently told to recruit some other individuals to bear the name for six months or more, and for a fee. They were given identification cards and moved into various new apartments, for which they would sign the lease with their new name, and they were instructed to go introduce themselves to the local grocers, shopkeepers, and others, also using the name, with a cover story of some sort that they moved here recently from Spain, or Argentina, or, in one case, Sweden."

"Sweden? With that name?"

"Yes, if you can believe it."

"What do you think our foe is up to with all this?" Reela asked.

"On one level, he seems to be just seeking to hide himself in a crowd so as not to be found. He's created what communication experts call noise. He's given us too many trails of apparent evidence to chase and track, too many Juan Santiagos leaving their mark around town so that we'll waste time on them that could better be spent finding the real thing, the man himself."

"I suspected at least some form of that was happening," Reela replied.

"But I think there's more," Leem confided.

"What else?"

The former policeman gazed at his desk for a moment and said, "I've come to believe, but, now, I have to admit that I don't yet have any direct evidence for this yet—although there is some historical precedent for it—I suspect, I should say, that the original Juan Osvaldo Santiago has some scheme going on where he rewards his top followers with his name, once they attain a certain level in their discipleship, or advanced training with him."

"Really?"

"Yes. It's still just an old detective's guess, or better, a hunch, but it would explain the adamant insistence of the lookout man at the luxury shop, when he was so outraged at any assertion on your part that the dead man was not named Santiago. Now, this agitated individual, by the fervor of his response, I infer, is in some way a proper part of their organization and not just a goon hired for the particular job. His voice, as you described it to me, betrayed that something was at stake for him. He could have been playacting, deceptively, but in his tone and actions, again, as you conveyed them, there seemed to be more going on, much more. I thought carefully about everything you told me. He was very worked up about the matter, as you explained."

"Yes, he was. He seemed deeply offended that I was denying it."

"Then there are reportedly three men—with three different physical descriptions—who've been out recruiting others to take on the name temporarily. Those recruiters, each of them, introduced themselves to their potential recruits as Juan Osvaldo Santiago and produced official looking identification to back it up. That's what the ordinary and random recruits whom we've found and questioned have told us."

"I see."

"They've also told us that each of the men said the name with an almost haughty tone of pride, as if it meant something of great value. But of course, to the ordinary Cairo recruits, it meant absolutely nothing."

Reela nodded in understanding, and Leem continued. "I have a feeling that these few Santiagos who are apparently working directly for the master, as they think of him, or the monster, in our estimation, were given new names at a certain point as a sign of newly acquired status within their ranks. And that took place before this whole mess started happening in town. They acquired the master's name as if it was being acknowledged that, in some sense, they're now somehow equals to him, or on the same basic level."

"That's very surprising," Reela said.

"Yes. But there's an angle here. Given the psychological profile that we've put together, based on our adversary's recent actions and on the old legend of the monster, it would seem that the original Santiago could never truly recognize anyone as even roughly an equal, not even close."

"That's what I was thinking," Reela replied.

"And yet, here's the twist. He puts on this little charade, or big one, as the case may be, to motivate his top followers to stay loyal and do whatever he requires. They know how highly he thinks of himself, and so for him to confer on a very select few of them his own name, well, you can imagine the impact and the motivation that this must have on them all."

"Ok, I get it," Reela said.

"It's very shrewd," Leem said and then he continued. "We heard the full report about the strange power that the man in the luxury shop, apparently one of these top disciples, seemed to display in his confrontation with Hoda. So, a guy like him could easily be led to think he was actually being recognized as in some broad sense an equal. And now, the assigned task of at least three of these top disciples has been to hire some normal men to take on the name, temporarily, the same name that they are so immensely proud of, while the original Santiago hatches a plan here and carries it out."

"I think I can see where this is going."

"I knew you would."

"There's got to be a sense in which it's psychologically hard for these true disciples to pay ordinary people to adopt the name that they're so proud of having been given as the result of their extremely hard work," Reela suggested.

"You're totally right," Leem answered. "It's a name they worked so long and hard to receive as a great reward. And finally, they've achieved it, and they've been basking in the honor."

Reela interjected, "But they're now out on the street paying absolutely unworthy types to take on this very same name, their new exalted name, for six months or more, and for money."

Leem concluded, "It must really bother them, deep down, even though they're surely working on orders that have been explained to them masterfully by the real Santiago."

"So, his top guys are out there at his command, doing something that at a deep level diminishes their own status."

"Yes, and I'm guessing they're really bothered, maybe even offended, and this could create a weakness or vulnerability that we can use."

Reela contemplated the idea for a few seconds and then said, "How many Santiagos of true status do you suppose there are? Do you think that now maybe it's just the three you've inferred from the descriptions of recruiters you've heard?"

"Actually, I would guess that there are more—not a lot, but a few more of them."

"What makes you think this?"

"Well, so far we have physically come across, all told, six men in town identifying themselves as being named Juan Santiago, other than the adversary who died at Hoda's hand. Under our questioning, as I've indicated, the six gave three different descriptions of the man who they say recruited them into this ruse, in each case introducing himself as Juan Osvaldo Santiago. And none of the descriptions matches the dead man in the luxury goods shop."

"So that would give us at least four, until his demise," Reela said.

"Yes. But if my hunch is right about the use of the name in this cult—and that's what it is, I should emphasize, just an intuition, but a strong one—then there could be a few more of what we can call status Santiagos running around. Or, I might be way off, and there were just the four. And now only three remain. We simply don't know."

"How do you think we can find the real, original Santiago?"

"I have an idea," Leem said.

In the breakfast room, upstairs in the palace, Mafulla's hands still gripped the back of his chair at the table. He seemed more than a bit thunderstruck, as anyone might appear who had just experienced a possible cosmic revelation of unparalleled proportions. He said, in a very low voice, "I wonder if there could be ... beyond our closest box, our immediate normal world of experience within this physical universe, something almost like another box out there, a totally different and even richer reality surrounding us, and then … one beyond it, and maybe even another beyond it, and on and on."

Walid looked impressed and said, "Oh! This could be what the king was talking about, or at least beginning to touch on, when he told us a while ago that a secretly coded passage in The Book of Phi had revealed there's a nearby spiritual realm or dimension of existence whose overall magnitude stands to ours in the famous golden ratio, or Phi, of 1.618 to one—more than half again bigger than our seemingly endless physical universe. Maybe it's like a box, too."

"Yeah, and … then maybe there's another realm standing in the same relation to that one, another box, and then another, and another, and another."

"Well, that's pretty mind boggling," Walid said. "And, maybe even a little scary."

"Unless it's all like an ascent to greater forms of goodness."

"What do you mean?"

"Do you remember when Khalid had us read some stuff about each of the seminal religious figures of history, and we read the four Gospels about Jesus?"

"Yeah, sure."

"There was this one statement he was recorded as making that really hit me at the time, and it's haunted me ever since."

"What's that?"

"The translation was, 'In my Father's house, there are many mansions.' Remember that?"

"Sort of. Yeah."

"Well, I did some research on it."

"You and Set amaze me, how you do that so often."

"Hey, breadcrumbs marking the path to truth, my friend—you have to follow them to see where they lead."

"I'm glad you do."

"Thanks. And I always tell you. So you can relax and just be princely."

"I appreciate it."

"Anyway, when I read about the passage, I found out that the original Greek is pretty interesting. It really means something like, 'In the overall structure for living that my Father—meaning God—has created, there are many dwelling places,' and the Greek here can actually mean 'temporary stop-over lodgings' like places you would stay for a night or two, or a week, or a month, on a very long trip or journey."

"Like hotels, or campsites in the desert?" Walid said.

"Yeah, sort of like that, but on a much bigger scale. So the idea is that, maybe, the spiritual realm outside our box has layers and layers, or boxes and boxes, or universes within universes within realms for us to visit, and dwell in for a while, and then move on to experience even more."

"Oh, man. I get it. I totally get what you're saying. That is an amazing thought," Walid said, feeling almost dizzy with the concept. "It means that there could be so much more out there to discover and explore, more than we can ever imagine."

"More than enough to keep us busy doing and being and learning and growing, and maybe, forever," Mafulla said.

"For sure," Walid agreed. "And people who are totally curious about stuff, those of us who are energized by the quality of curiosity, are the ones who're eager to explore the box we're in and learn about it, and maybe look into whether we can catch a glimpse somehow of other boxes out there that can teach us new stuff, as well."

"Yeah. Curiosity and openness would be like the fuel of exploration for all the boxes."

"And you know, when you really think about it, it could be that the first box, the closest one that we live in, isn't even the physical universe."

"What do you mean?"

"Maybe the closest box that we get all trapped in is the psychological world we've inherited and constructed, the one made up out of our social beliefs and our daily perceptions and interpretations and assumptions. That's the one I think Socrates and

Plato were so worked up about—you know, with the image of the cave that we're all metaphorically living in, mistaking shadows for realities."

Mafulla said, "Yes! Yes! I think you're right. Both those guys, Socrates and Plato, wanted to get us beyond that subjective box of shadows—you know, peel back the illusions and get a grip on the true realities outside the cave, or the box, that await us and our recognition. That's how Khalid put it that day in class."

Walid said, "Yeah, it is. So maybe the first box around us is a subjective, psychological thing, a social and perceptual world of insights mixed with images and illusions and shadows. Then, beyond that, we get the objective boxes, so to speak, the reality boxes. And among them, the first real measurable box is the actual physical universe in all its unimaginable intricacy and strangeness and enormity. And then, there's whatever the closest spiritual reality beyond all that might be. That's where the golden ratio kicks in metaphysically. And then, beyond that, who knows how far it might go, on and on?"

"Yeah. And on and on and on, maybe," Mafulla said.

"So," Walid concluded, "when we're all caught up in our perceptions and assumptions and habitual illusions, in the tight little subjective box around us, we can just begin to guess and discover what lies beyond, in the true reality of the world, and then in the spiritual dimension that alone ultimately allows us as souls, as centers of consciousness, action, and love, to exist and really flourish, as Aristotle would say."

"Ha! Now you sound like me, quoting The Philosopher," Mafulla replied. "And, of course, also in using words like 'metaphysically' without any prompting, which by the way, was very nice."

"Yeah, for once! And, thank you."

Mafulla then thought for maybe five seconds in silence. Finally, he said, "And that guy in the shop—the guy Hoda had to take out—the power he used showed that he had been way out of this first box, and out of the second, and maybe more," Mafulla said.

"Apparently, and to a truly unsettling degree," Walid replied.

"Which just makes you wonder. What's the real Juan Osvaldo Santiago like?"

"Yeah."

"How far outside the big objective normal worldly box has he been, and what's he brought back from the other side?"

"That's worth wondering about," Walid said.

"But not worth worrying about, right?" Mafulla said.

"No. Worrying would get us in trouble with the king," Walid said, adding, "and only that would really be worth worrying about."

"Ha! Maybe the truth is that worrying is always a subjective thing, and maybe at most a box one activity, or at worst, a thing of the first two boxes. The people who go beyond these two boxes, the farther away they get, the deeper, or higher, or whatever metaphorically, then the less room there is in their lives for anything like worry at all."

"And that explains the king."

"Yeah, really, and Masoon for sure, and maybe Hoda in all her total calm," Mafulla said. And then he added, "You know, I just had another thought."

"What is it?"

"I wonder if some of the gods and goddesses of myth and lore around the world were once real people, long ago, like Hoda and the king, really senior Phi types, and some of the other people around them were so stunned at what they saw them do that they thought of them as nearly divine, and then other stories and legends grew up around them, and within a generation or two, you get a complete divinization of them."

"Divinization?"

"Yeah, a sort of enhanced memory of them as even more than they were, and then they eventually become the pantheon of all those gods and goddesses that are like real human beings, but enhanced."

"That's an interesting thought. So, there was a reality behind the myths, and it was Phi."

"Yeah. And what about the bad gods? I mean, there is some

pretty bad behavior attributed to some of them in more than one tradition, and there's stuff about demons in some."

"True. Maybe some of those stories come from real life power from far beyond the box, used in evil ways."

And that brought Mafulla back to his original big concern. He said, "So, I'm still wondering what the answer is to the big bad guy question in our own place and time. How far has our ultimate adversary, the monster, gone? What powers does he have?"

"Unfortunately," Walid said, "I guess we're going to find out at some point."

"Yeah, I suppose you're right," Mafulla agreed.

But neither of them had any idea how soon they would learn the answer to this question, or the way it would present itself.

II

PARTY PLANNERS

THE NEXT DAY AFTER SCHOOL, THE BOYS WERE SITTING around the table in the room where they always had breakfast. But this time, they were enjoying an afternoon snack and conversation about an upcoming date on the calendar.

Walid shook his head skeptically. "I don't know. The whole idea of a surprise birthday party for the king seems to be a very doubtful proposition. He always knows when something's afoot."

"Or a cake," Mafulla added, flashing a silly grin.

"Funny," Walid said, but with a face that said, maybe not.

"He's not omniscient," Mafulla commented.

"True, and he keeps insisting on that, but he reads people really well, and I think if all of us who are closest to him were holding back the same secret, he'd know what it was ... and who first thought of it."

"You're probably right," Mafulla said. "So, why don't we plan instead a no-surprise birthday party?"

"We could do that," Walid replied. "But of course, that might actually surprise him—you and me, real party planners."

"Not bad. You're almost catching on to the cleverness thing."

"I try."

"But I guess we need to be sure the king will even want a party, with all this scary Santiago stuff going on."

"Hey, threat management is just a normal part of the job around here."

"I guess."

"I don't think the king ever obsesses over stuff like that. You know, he spends most of his day doing normal, routine royal work, like there's no monster threat out there at all."

"True," Mafulla conceded. "Nothing worries him. Nothing scares him. He's Mr. Cool, or King Cool, I should say."

"Wisdom has its benefits." Walid added, "I think he'd enjoy a party, and maybe it would be the most fun to try something really different."

"Like what?"

"Like ... I don't know, why not ... lunch outside on the palace grounds and with games?"

"What games does the king like?"

"Well, for sure he likes bocce ball."

"Ok. And you know how Malik and Haji are with bocce ball. Plus, I think their dads play. So, we could get a good game going with that."

"And I've heard the king talk about badminton. I think he really wants to learn how to play that."

"I've read about badminton," Mafulla said. "It sounds like a great little game, with a high net and lightweight racquets, and that little feathered birdie thing you hit."

"The shuttlecock, I think it's called," Walid said.

"Yeah, that's it, but I like to call it a birdie. You know, I can see myself yelling out 'Bye, Bye Birdie!' and smashing it high. Then, 'Be Good, Birdie!' and plinking it barely over the net. And then, hitting it hard, 'Birdie Bang!' 'Birdie Boom!' and stuff like that, while I play. And if it ever hits me in the head, 'Ouch! Birdie Beaned!' The official name doesn't lend itself to all the clever chatter that I already have planned. And that's pretty important."

"I see. Then, birdie it is."

"You can beg a birdie. And berate a birdie. 'Bad Birdie!' It's endless."

"I get it."

"Ok. Good. So. Does the king have any badminton equipment around here anywhere?"

"I don't know. I've never seen any."

"Well then, there's the gift for the man, or in our case, the monarch who has almost everything."

"Huh. Actually, that's a really great idea. And at the party, he gets a chance to learn how to play, along with us, and we'll read up on it in advance, all the rules and everything."

"Sometimes I'm amazed at how brilliant we are," Mafulla said.

"Yeah, when we aren't being total idiots," Walid replied.

"Also true," Mafulla admitted. "But maybe idiocy is the great swamp from which the blossom of brilliance can best bloom."

"Ha! Well said. I may need to quote you on that. It's Masoon's turnaround, and in an almost poetic form."

"Yeah. Masoon's turnaround."

"Idiocy—at least, our kind—can lead to brilliance; confusion can lead to clarity; chaos to new forms of order; failure to success; despair to hope; fear to courage; humility to the heights; nobility to simple service—and, maybe the other way around—service to significance. And it likely goes on."

"All very nice turnarounds," Mafulla said, suitably impressed.

"I don't know why, but something just jumped into my head."

"What?"

"Maybe it was the mention of idiocy and brilliance, or because of the idea of a turnaround, but did you know that Hamid has a cousin at the university?"

"No. Is he a professor?"

"Yeah, and get this: He's got this big research project going on to find uses for ... wait for it ... you'd never guess it ... sand."

"For sand?"

"Yeah."

"Uses for sand?"

"That's right."

"You're not joking."

"Nope."

"Ok. I thought sand was already pretty useful. I mean, it holds the desert together, right? It gives camels something to walk on. It measures time through every hourglass in the world, and even here in Cairo, it normally provides us a place to stand, whenever we're outside and not on pavement, which probably includes sand, and the city pavement around here itself sits on sand. Plus, in a big storm, the wonderfully useful stuff exfoliates us pretty effectively."

"It what?"

"Exfoliates. It removes dead skin, unneeded epidermis, superfluous surfacing from the outside of our bodies."

"Ok. True, all true, but I think Hamid's cousin is looking for hidden uses of sand, esoteric transformation repurposing, or else something similar."

"Oh, that's impressive: esoteric transformation repurposing."

"Something like that—I read about it recently somewhere, in one of the king's papers I think. There's a grant proposal."

"I like it. But can you imagine when this guy was a kid? His mother's asking him what he wants to be when he grows up, and she's thinking maybe a doctor, or a lawyer, or a teacher, or a shopkeeper, and he says 'I want to study sand.' That just might have given her pause. 'Yeah, Ok, take this broom and go study it all you want. First research project: How it can be esoterically transformed in location from inside to outside the house.' At least, he'd have a purpose in life, maybe even a repurpose. Poor kid."

Walid laughed. "He could have had different dreams as a kid. Sand may have come later. I suspect it's more of an acquired taste."

"Yeah," Mafulla conceded, "You're probably right. And still, for most of us, it's both unpleasant to the palate and yet also tasteless. I mean, I got a mouthful in the desert on a windy day, a couple of times, and that pretty much guaranteed I'd never have too high a view of the stuff. I'll leave it alone if it leaves me alone. It's hard to think of it as being interesting enough to study."

"True. But curiosity has no bounds. And, you know, there may be more to it than we think. I was just reading about an American scientist with an African heritage, George Washington Carver, who recently got famous for finding over a hundred ways to use ordinary peanuts."

"Really?"

"Yeah. It actually may have been over two hundred ways. And, I mean, think about it. Philosophers have always studied the obvious and commonplace. There's nothing more obvious and commonplace around here than sand. Maybe something like extended research can end up producing some remarkable insights and even revolutionary uses for it."

"That would be a massive turnaround."

"So true."

"There's sure plenty of it."

"We won't run out anytime soon."

"Aha!" Mafulla said, suddenly, and lifted his right index finger high into the air.

"What?"

"We ourselves may have discovered a new use for it, just now!"

"Wait. What do you mean?"

"It will be the setting for the king's birthday celebration! No party in the palace this time around, but rather an outdoor Soiree on the Sand!"

"Nice! There's our catchy title: 'Soiree on the Sand.' That'll work."

A short distance across town and in the apparent safety of her very own home, Khata El-Noor was in some ways as nervous as if she were sitting next to a poisonous snake. And, in a sense, she was. But she didn't know it, at least, not consciously.

On one level, she was really excited and happy to be ready to start her first formal piano lesson. But at a deeper level, she was agitated and almost frightened. She thought it was just performance anxiety and the commonly unsettling nature of the new when it first crosses our paths. But, on the contrary, she was experiencing an operation of the very abilities that Muriel al-Baki had, on one level, come to test.

After some preliminary pleasantries, her new teacher said, "We're going to start in a few minutes with the names of the notes sounded by the various keys, and introduce you to what are called octaves. But first, let me ask you how much you've played before now."

"Not much," Khata said. "I mean, since mom bought the piano, I've sat here a lot and just messed around with it, finding patterns and making up little tunes."

"How do you feel when you do that?"

"I was a little hesitant at first, not wanting to play something that would sound stupid, but then that worry went away fairly soon and I really started enjoying it."

"Does your state of consciousness shift in any way when you play?"

"What do you mean?"

"The way your mind feels—is there any difference when you play?"

"Well, yes, I guess it does feel different."

"How would you describe it?"

"Sometimes, it's almost like I go into a little bit of a trance and time seems to slow down or even stop, and the music sort of touches my soul. I feel lighter inside. It's almost like I'm floating. And I'm not even really playing, yet."

"That's good. Does anything like this ever happen when you're just listening to music and not playing?"

"Yeah, all the time. But playing puts me in to it deeper, I think."

"This is very good," Muriel said. "It shows me that you'll be a natural with performance."

"Really?"

The famous teacher turned a bit on the bench and said, "Yes. There's no doubt about it. And, if we can wait a few moments more before we begin to touch the keys together, let me ask you something else."

"Sure."

"This will help me to understand more fully the role that music plays in your life and how it might fit in with other things."

"Ok."

"Here's the question. Are there any other times that don't involve music at all, when your consciousness seems to shift, and becomes something different from what it is during a normal, routine day? Do you experience any such times at all?"

Khata felt a rush of something almost like panic, as the moments flashed before her mind when she had known about something going on at a distance, or about something that was yet to happen, but she pushed the panic down and took a sharp breath to maintain her composure. "Sure, now and then." That's all she said.

"At special times, or just without any apparent reason?"

"At special times," Khata said and looked down.

"It's Ok. You don't have to talk about those times. But they don't involve music?"

"No."

"Do they ever involve thoughts of events or people?"

"Yes. They do."

"Good. I myself often have thoughts about something that might be going on at a distance from me, or that might happen the next day, or the next week. And it's an amazing thing that these thoughts often turn out to be true," Muriel said. And then she added, "Some of the greatest musicians have reported such thoughts."

"Really?" Khata was intrigued. Muriel's bait had worked.

"Yes, very great musicians often report such thoughts and commonly say that these special states of consciousness had a role in their lives years before they began to play an instrument like the piano, or violin, or flute, or even the guitar. It was like their minds have an openness to realities beyond the mind that include music, but go beyond it."

"I didn't know about that," Khata said, in awe of what might be a sign that she could indeed have an exceptional talent for music.

"Very few speak about it freely. They seem almost embarrassed to possess a gift that not everyone appears to have. But it's indeed a real gift and when I manage to get them to talk about it, they look relieved to share their story with someone who understands."

Khata then said in a very low voice, "One time, I knew what some friends were going through, many miles away from me, friends who had been kidnapped. It was almost like I was seeing a movie of what they were experiencing, and not just on the outside but on the inside, too. And I could even feel the feelings they were having and it was hard because it was a bad situation, and I cried a lot during it."

"Wow. That's amazing and very good. It's just what I'm talking about," Muriel said. She smiled sympathetically and thought to herself that this was going to be much easier than she had even hoped. Khata was almost too susceptible to simple manipulation, and this was a strong sign of her inner nature—that she's an honest, innocent girl who could be moved and molded by a subtle enough approach. Interestingly, that was just how Muriel herself was, at the same age.

"There have been other times, too, but not normally so dramatic, and yet whenever one of my friends is in trouble, I somehow seem to know," Khata intimated hesitantly.

Muriel nodded and said, "That's good. It helps you to be a much better friend. Now, if it's still all right, I'll ask one more thing."

"Ok."

"When we create music, we make things happen both with our minds and with our bodies. But it all starts in the mind. And, sometimes, what happens in and through the mind seems to go far beyond what our bodies appear to be capable of doing. At least, that's experienced by most of the truly great musicians I know. Have you ever had the sense of making something happen beyond what you think your body was capable of doing?"

"Hmm. I've never really thought about it, but maybe."

"Good! These are all strong indicators that you should indeed be my student and that we'll be able to do great things together."

"I'm so glad!" Khata said, momentarily forgetting her anxiety.

"I am, too," Muriel echoed. "When I learned that I was moving to Cairo, I was hoping to meet some excellent musicians here and teach a few very promising students, and it seems like we're off to a great start already, just you and I."

"It's really exciting for me. And I'm sure eager to learn."

"Ok, then, let's end our philosophical discussion for the moment and turn to the keyboard."

Khata had managed by now to block out most of the unease she had been feeling. She was instead allowing her hopes and dreams, fueled so expertly by this new teacher, to fill her heart and mind. And her emotions were now, as a result, inhibiting an important exercise of the very powers that the teacher was probing to discover. Because of that, she had never been in a more vulnerable and dangerous position than she was in right at this moment. And she wasn't able to sense her vulnerability at all. Muriel had learned from a master how to weave a spell of fantasy and illusion, although she had no idea that exactly this had so profoundly been done to her. Prisoners of fantasy can't often recognize their incarceration from within the dream.

"I'm so sorry to interrupt," Khata's mother said as she stuck her head around the doorframe and looked into the music room. The sound of her voice shattered the thick cocoon of special feeling and hope and focus that Muriel had woven around her new student.

"No, no! It's no problem at all. We had just finished some necessary preliminaries and were about to turn to the practical, hands-on side of the lesson," Muriel said, completely hiding the flash of shock and irritation, even bordering on anger, that she felt about what she considered to be this abrupt intrusion.

"I'm just going out for half an hour or so to the store," Rama said, pleasantly. "Khata's father and I have been planning a little party to celebrate this first piano lesson, and I forgot something I wanted to have for it. It's just going to be the family and a few neighbors I thought you'd like to meet briefly, since you just arrived in town, if you have a little time after the lesson. We'll serve drinks and treats for everyone, and it won't go on long. It will be very informal, quite casual."

"Mom! That's so nice! Can you stay, Muriel?"

"Oh, certainly! I'd love to. I'll have roughly an hour, or a little more, after our lesson before I have to run on to my next appointment, which won't be nearly so much fun. I have to meet with a carpenter first, a man who'll be doing a few things for the house, some small changes. And then I'm on to see a rug merchant after that. The new place is larger than I realized, and we need two more floor coverings. But, yes, I'd be delighted to stay here a bit longer for the party."

"Good! Excellent! I'll let you two continue. I'll be back shortly," Rama said, completely unaware of the danger Khata now faced.

A few miles away, Reela Adi leaned back in the main visitor's chair at the Cairo Detective Agency and spoke to Leem Hadad, the proprietor and head detective. "However smart this Santiago fellow may be, I can tell you one thing."

"What's that?" Leem asked.

"He's not as smart as he thinks he is."

"How so?"

"Well, with all these honorary Santiagos and fake Santiagos that he's spreading around town to make himself harder to find, he's not giving us the mere dead ends he apparently had in mind, but rather a wealth of new leads and trails and hints to follow."

"You're right," Leem said, immediately.

"And I'm sure he hasn't thought it through," Reela added.

"Yes," Leem agreed again. Then he added, "Each of these men we find has some sort of tie back to him, however direct or indirect, and they're all going to help us track him down."

"That's correct."

"We'll learn a lot about the original from the fakes. And it usually takes only one small bit of information, sometimes trivial in itself, to turn the tide of an investigation like this."

"Absolutely," Reela said. "The rightly famous Law of Unintended Consequences is already transforming our adversary's efforts at elusiveness into a wealth of evidence for us."

"I've seen such a thing many times in my life," Leem commented.

Just then, there was a soft knock on the door. "Come in!"

A lady appeared and said, "Mr. Hadad, there's a call for you."

"Oh, really? Ok, thank you! I'll be right down." Leem got up from his chair, motioning for Reela to stay seated. And as the lady closed the door to disappear down the hall, he said to his guest, "A nice fellow with an office on this floor lets me use his telephone. Give me just a minute. I'll be right back."

"Certainly," Reela said, and as Leem left the office, he reached over to a table and picked up the latest edition of *The Kingdom Daily News* and began to look over the headlines. Within no more than about a minute and a half or two, the proprietor was opening the door again and coming back into the office.

"Bancom was calling from the palace," he said to Reela. "The king would like to see us a bit later today, you and me."

"Did he say what it's about?"

"No, only that he wants us to meet him at the Grand Hotel."

"I see."

"Here's the information. I wrote it all down."

"Interesting. I wonder why the hotel and not the palace."

"Bancom seemed to be in a hurry, so I didn't ask any questions."

"That's all right."

"I did mention that you were here, since he said he was about to call you, too, and I told him I'd simply give you the message."

"Good."

Leem glanced at his watch and said, "I was hoping my nephew Ibrahim would come by while you're here, so that we could both get his report on what he's discovered today in his pursuit of the two mystery musicians."

"He's due in here soon?"

"He usually comes by this time of day. I actually expected him a little before now. Would you like another cup of tea and maybe some biscuits? We could give him a few more minutes before you have to run—of course, only if you have the time."

"Yes, no hurry. There's something I have to do before joining you and the king at the hotel later, but it won't take long and can wait."

Leem got out a biscuit tin and a small plate, and popped the top of the tin, offering Reela his choice from a number of very appealing cookies. He looked them all over and then took two and put them on the plate. But before he could take a first bite, the door opened suddenly and loudly. It was Ibrahim rushing into the room.

"Uncle Leem, it's awful!" He looked over at Reela and said, "Hi, Reela," and then turned back to his uncle with an expression of great intensity, and almost one of panic.

"What is it? What's wrong?"

"It's Ben! I can't find him anywhere. He's just disappeared!"

Leem got up from his chair with a look of serious concern. "Where was he supposed to be?"

Ibrahim looked over at Reela and explained so both of them would understand. "One of my friends was to bring him home after school today—you know, Ahira—as he often does on days I have work, but when I got to the apartment shortly after they should have arrived, there was no one there, and no sign of anyone. I've checked all around and even asked neighbors, and no one has seen him."

Leem looked over at Reela and said, "Ben's a young boy we adopted back in Alexandria when he was out on the streets, living on his own, and he's become a wonderful member of our little family. He's in school now, here in Cairo, and he's living with us."

"Yes. I've heard of Ben. The prince speaks highly of him. Is there anything I can do to help?" Reela asked.

"No, I don't think so—at least, not at this point. But we should leave immediately and continue to look for him. It may be nothing. The two of them could simply have gone out for a treat or to shop. Ahira can be a bit spontaneous at times. But it's unusual for him to take Ben out without leaving a note on their whereabouts and expected return. The boy has homework, and Ahira knows that Ibrahim always stops by the apartment a bit before now to check on him."

Ibrahim said, "Ordinarily, I wouldn't be so concerned about such a thing, but in light of the kind of people we're investigating now, I like to be doubly or triply cautious. I think we should go straight to the apartment and make a beeline from there to the school and stop by any place they might have visited along the way." Then he added, "I don't want to be a worrier, but I feel really nervous about this."

"Yes, I feel a bit odd about it, too," Leem said, and then turned to Reela. "We should go. But, please, take your cookies."

"Thanks, I will. Look, I have to walk right by the main police station on my quick errand," Reela told them, as they were all now walking out. "I'll stop in and ask them for some extra patrols in your neighborhood right away—I have friends there—and I'll tell the men to be on the lookout for Ben. What was he wearing today?"

"The same as usual," Leem said, and looked over at his nephew for confirmation or correction.

Ibrahim said, "He has on the same white outfit as always, and that all the children of his school wear. I'm afraid there's nothing that stands out about it. But my friend Ahira wears a bright red scarf around his neck or shoulders. That makes him easy to spot."

"Ok, that should help."

"And here's our home address. I've scribbled it on this scrap of paper," Leem said as he handed the note to Reela.

"Got it. And good luck on your search," Reela responded. "I hope he turns up quickly. But just in case, I'll get my police buddies on it right away. And after that, I'll see if I can find you and help look for them."

"Thanks, Reela," Leem said. "It would be helpful. We'll start near the apartment and then take the main street toward the school."

"Yeah, thanks, Mr. Adi," Ibrahim also said as they turned down the street in the direction of their apartment, and Reela went off toward the main city police station several blocks away.

Reela wasn't even a minute from the office when a thought came vividly to mind. "I do hope this has nothing to do with Santiago." But as soon as this sentiment was entertained, he had an eerie feeling that he had just identified the source of the problem that was intended to create for them all a great difficulty.

12

THE LOST BOY

"KISSA!" HODA CALLED OUT AND THEN WAITED A MOMENT. "KISSA?"

"Yes, Mom?" Her voice came from a distance.

"You just got something in the mailbox. It looks like it's been hand delivered."

"What is it?" she called out from back in her room.

"I don't know, but your father and I also received an envelope that's just like it. Come and see."

Kissa popped out of her door, followed by Hasina, and she nearly ran up to her mother to learn what the mystery in the mail might be. She said, "Have you opened yours, yet?"

"No, I was going to let you go first."

"Oh, good," Kissa replied as Hoda handed her the large envelope with her name on it and she whirled over to the nearby desk where she picked up an opener to slit the thick paper down the side. She spread apart the edges of the envelope just enough to be able to pull out a piece of heavy card stock ivory colored stationary from within it.

Hasina was at this point looking over her shoulder. "What is it? What did you get?"

"It says, 'Soiree on the Sand: A Birthday Party Fit For A King' and it has a cute drawing of people having a picnic outside, and ... what's this net thing?"

"Ooh, that's a drawing of a badminton net!" Hasina explained. Then she read and summarized more of the invitation aloud. "It says, 'Come for Food and Fun and Games' and gives the day, date, and time for the party. Wow, it looks like this will be really different from the sort of birthday party you might expect for the king."

"Yeah, not all formal and fancy and inside the palace," Kissa agreed.

"I wonder if I got an invitation, too," Hasina said.

"You silly! Of course you got an invitation!"

"You think so?"

"I know so! I bet yours has already been delivered to your house."

During this little exchange, Hoda had been opening her own invitation and, pondering it, she said, "It does look like a lot of fun. And, did you happen to notice the bottom of the card?"

Kissa looked down and read the very small print: "Prince Walid Shabeezar and Mr. Mafulla Adi—Party Planners, Extraordinaire."

"Ha!" Hasina said. "I should have known this was their doing."

"Truly," Kissa said. "It has The Dynamic Duo written all over it."

Hoda put her invitation down on the table and said, "Well, the most important aspect of all this for the moment is that it gives us an excellent reason to go shop for some new and appropriate clothes."

"Really?" Kissa exclaimed in voice of genuine surprise.

"Of course! How many 'Soiree in the Sand' birthday parties for a king have we been to in the past? I'm sure we'll need new outfits for this special event, something dressy but sporty at the same time."

"Well, you sort of temporarily put the Kingdom Luxury Goods Shop out of business," Kissa said, and that made Hasina laugh out loud.

Hoda smiled and replied, "I'm sure they'll be better than ever with all the construction and remodeling the prince is having done. I've gone by there recently just to check up on things. And they'll reopen soon enough with lots of new and exciting merchandise. But I was thinking more along the lines of a possible trip down to Madame Alexander's."

"Madame Alexander's?" Both girls exclaimed now at the same time. "Really?"

"Yes. Felice always has in the latest fashions. I think the occasion calls for something casual but continental, and from Paris, don't you?"

"Oh, wow!" Kissa said. "That's the most exclusive ladies' shop in town, and in the whole country!"

Hasina made a face and said, "I don't know if mom …"

"Hasina," Hoda interrupted her, "This is my treat, Ok?"

"Do you mean it?"

"Yes. I want to take you girls shopping and it will be my treat, in more ways than one. Plus, I promise, no massive destruction this time." At that, both girls laughed.

Upstairs at the palace, Walid was in his room writing an essay for class on the ancient epic of Gilgamesh, a poem that many say conveys the oldest story that has been passed down to us, from about 2,700 BCE. When the tale begins, we're introduced to Gilgamesh, a king who is part human and part divine. He's also handsome, smart, charismatic, and powerful. But he's completely self absorbed and totally selfish in his actions. He meddles in the lives of his subjects and exploits them in completely improper ways. His people, as a result, feel terribly oppressed by him and pray to the gods for a solution to their problem. The answer the gods come up with seems at first to work, and then it just creates new problems. And yet, ultimately, it does work. They send Gilgamesh a rival, a man who is in many ways his opposite, but also has great power.

The king is a man of the city. He's cultured and sophisticated. His new rival, Enkidu, is a man of the country who dwells in the forest, is a bit innocent, uncultivated, and raw, and has been living among the animals as his only society. The wilderness man eventually hears of the king and his more nefarious activities and comes to town to see it all. Enkidu is incensed at what he witnesses. The two of them meet and fight furiously. It's an epic battle beyond anything the people have ever seen, with their king in the end barely prevailing and subduing his new adversary. Then, as a surprising turnaround, the two combatants, in stunned admiration of each other's physical prowess, quickly become the best of friends.

In lots of ways, the story then becomes the first buddy caper. The new friends get so involved in going out and doing things with each other that, basically, Gilgamesh has no extra time for causing trouble in the kingdom, and so at this point leaves his people alone. His oppressive activities stop. So, initially, what the gods did seems to have worked. But then, the king and his friend go on a quest together to violate the natural order of things that has been established by the gods. They cut down the trees in a sacred cedar forest and kill the forest's divinely appointed guardian. And they get into layers of trouble because of it. As a final punishment, the gods take the life of Enkidu.

As the result of losing his one friend, Gilgamesh has to confront for the first time in his life the tremendous challenge of our common human mortality. He comes to a new and deeper understanding of the often-difficult departure that ultimately awaits us all. The death of his friend causes him to develop a vision for his own future that sends him on a frantic search for answers, and perhaps to find a secret to eternal life. His quest fails in providing what he wants, but it ironically gives him what he most needs. By the end of the story, this formerly abusive monarch has become a different person, a surprisingly good king whose public works, as predicted in the epic itself, will be remembered forever. And because of the story and its preservation down through the ages, they are.

Khalid had asked his students to write a short essay on what turns Gilgamesh around. Walid read the story twice and began to formulate an answer. He was just doing his introductory paragraph, succinctly summarizing the ancient tale, when there was a knock at his door.

"Come in," the prince said.

Bancom stuck his head around the door and said, "I'm sorry to interrupt you, Prince Walid, but Reela Adi just called in from the main police station with a message for you."

"What's Reela doing at the police station?" Walid asked, puzzled.

"He stopped by a few minutes ago to file a missing person report and to get some of his old friends there to help look for the individual he's seeking."

"Who's missing?"

"The young boy who's a friend of yours, Ben Hadad."

"Ben? Oh, no. What's happened?"

"It seems that one of Ibrahim's friends was to pick him up from school today and take him home while Ibrahim was finishing some current investigative work. But when Ibrahim arrived at the apartment, there was no sign of Ben or of the friend."

"Why does Reela think they're missing in a way that requires a police report and police involvement?" Walid asked this while standing up from his desk chair.

"The circumstances make it suspicious, from what Reela told me. Ibrahim is convinced that his friend, Ahira Setti, the one entrusted with Ben's safety, would never just take the boy somewhere without leaving a note or word with a neighbor. And when Ibrahim went home to see Ben, enough time had passed since the end of the school day that there was no way they could have been just slightly delayed on the way home, stopping to get a treat for the young man or anything like that. And, of course, Ibrahim and Leem both have been working hard quite recently, trying to track down that man Santiago, following suspicious people and asking questions."

"Does Reela think that someone connected to Santiago has followed them, discovered where their apartment is, and has maybe now kidnapped Ben to have leverage to get them to stop their work?"

"Yes, that's exactly what Reela suspects," Bancom said. "He wanted you to know that this is going on, in case you might have any insights, and because he knows how fond you are of both Ben and Ibrahim."

"Thanks, Bancom. I'll go tell Mafulla right away." With those words, Walid walked quickly up to the doorway and added, "Maybe there's something we can do to help."

"Great," Bancom replied and turned to go, with a short bow. Walid patted him on the shoulder as he passed by, and while the older man went back down the hall toward the main staircase, the prince headed straight for Mafulla's room in the opposite direction. The door was already open.

"Gear up, Stormie," Walid said.

"What?" Mafulla had been on his bed, reading the Gilgamesh story for the third time.

"Ben Hadad has gone missing, and your uncle suspects that Santiago's behind it, or at least, his men."

"No!" Mafulla practically leaped off the bed and said, "This is getting to be more than a little aggravating. Let's go help find him."

"My thoughts exactly. And I'm thinking … fully armed. We'll leave a message with Kular for the king. He's in meetings with many of the government ministers today, offsite at the Grand Hotel. We shouldn't disturb the session, which is pretty important, and we can't take the time to go there first and wait until they have a break."

"Yeah, you're right, good thinking." Mafulla walked over to his dresser and opened the top drawer. "I'll be down in a minute." Walid walked out of the room and back down to his.

Across town, the music lesson had just ended. When Muriel and Khata came out of the room, they could already hear voices in the front area of the house. "There you are!" Rama said, as they appeared down the hallway. "Muriel, come and meet some of my closest neighbors."

There were platters of goodies set on tables all over the room— great cheeses and biscuits, figs, and hummus, and nuts and olives of various kinds. There were teas and coffees and juices, and bright, beautiful arrays of flowers had been put here and there throughout the light filled room. "Mom! This is great!" Khata said.

"It is quite nice, indeed," Muriel remarked, in admiration of her host's skills for so quickly putting together such a wonderful little afternoon party. "I love all the flowers."

"Thank you," Rama said. "They're from the neighborhood florist. I was hoping you'd like them."

"They're simply spectacular," Muriel said in response. "You have all my favorite colors."

Rama's smile was beaming at this nice compliment, and she began right away introducing Muriel to the other guests. Everyone was glad to meet her. Many of the ladies greeted her with a hug and a kiss on the cheek. A couple of the men who had gotten off work early for the occasion spoke of their love for her musical talent, having heard her in concert on trips to Alexandria or elsewhere.

An older man began to tell her stories of his own days as a musician, playing the arghul, a traditional woodwind instrument that was a bit like a clarinet in sound. Many decades earlier, he had performed with it at a club, to accompany its well-known bevvy of belly dancers. "I was a young man then," he said. "And I did love the music, and the dance! Of course, at that age, I loved the dancers even more!" He laughed as he said this, and Muriel smiled and commented on the ancient heritage of the arghul and it's place in Egyptian culture.

Ara's mother was also there, and at this point she was introduced to Muriel who, learning that she had a daughter in Khata's class, began asking about the class, the school, and the other girls. She wanted to know all their names and whether any of them showed an interest in music. Rama joined in and Muriel gained a lot of information in a short time about the palace school, the class of girls, and about Hoda and Kissa, and how the two of them can trace their ancestry back to Cleopatra. Muriel was fascinated and asked lots of questions.

After all the guests had been greeted, and now that many of them were talking with each other, Muriel managed to get Rama to herself off at a punch bowl in the corner of the room. "This palace school I'm hearing about sounds interesting," she said.

"It is," Rama agreed. "It's full of children from very accomplished families who are in one way or another serving the monarchy and, of course, the kingdom."

"I would imagine that many of the king's top people are represented there," Muriel said.

"Yes, and their children are such an intelligent and talented group," Rama replied. "We're very blessed to have Khata in such a place."

"Your husband serves the king, then?" Muriel asked.

"He does. He's the Minister of Commerce for the kingdom now, and he loves his job."

"It must be fascinating, with people from so many nations doing business in the kingdom these days."

"Oh, yes, it really is," Rama agreed with a quick smile. "Zaman has to work long hours. It's ironic. His name, of course, means 'time,' and yet now he has so little time of his own since taking over the position."

"I can imagine," Muriel responded.

"But he finds the job to be intellectually challenging and personally rewarding. He's of course deeply honored to be of such service to the king. And because of his work in the palace, Khata's getting a remarkable education."

"I'd love to meet all the girls in the class," Muriel said. "Perhaps I could come in one day and talk with them about music and its role in a full and balanced life."

"That's a marvelous idea," Rama said. "The girls would love it. I bet that their teacher, Hoda, would jump at the chance to have you visit and give a presentation. I'll mention it to her very soon, the next time I see her."

"Wonderful," Muriel replied. "I want to be of real service to people here, now that I'm in Cairo. And I've seen the difference that a love for music can make in a young person's life. It would be a true joy to share some of my perspectives with the girls. And, of course, as you might imagine, I've never been in the palace before. That alone would be fascinating for me."

"Well, we'll make sure it happens soon," Rama assured her. And Muriel smiled with a sense of great triumph. Khata, by contrast, standing not five feet away felt a twinge of something she couldn't identify, but then it passed as Ara's mom walked up to her and asked her about her first official piano lesson.

Elsewhere in town, a couple of the boys from the palace school were about to get involved in something big. Malik and Haji had taken time off recently from their occasional crime fighting patrols, or rather, their long walks around town where they tried to pay close attention to everything they saw and intervene whenever it could be useful. Since the huge and unexpected battle at the veterinary clinic, they had broken up one mugging and rescued a boy's cat from a tree. But recently there had been nothing more eventful than this that required the attentions of The Wild Camel and The Silver Sabre.

Today, though, would be different. Malik had asked Haji to go with him for a walk and to take their sand masks, just in case. They were three blocks from Haji's house and turning onto a major avenue when Malik said, "I don't know what it is, but today I really feel like we're supposed to be out and about."

"As soon as you asked me to take a walk, I sort of felt the same thing," Haji said.

"Then keep your eyes peeled for anything that we might be out here to stop or to help with," Malik reminded his friend.

"I will," Haji responded. They walked on for about five minutes just talking about school and Gilgamesh and a recent project, before anything interesting came their way. And what caught their attention was a car.

"Hey, look! One of those new convertibles I was just reading about," Malik said and pointed at a gleaming automobile that was coming down the avenue.

"Wow, nice," Haji commented, as they both stopped walking just to look at it. "How cool would it be to have a car like that?"

"Super cool," Malik answered. "It would be like being a character in a movie."

"That's for sure," Haji said.

"And I think it would be a major lady magnet," Malik added. The car passed and the boys began to walk again.

"A lady magnet—you know, I bet you're right," Haji replied. "Ladies like good style."

"To the max: they seem to like stylish clothes, beautiful jewelry, flowers, art, great cars, elegant homes."

"Yeah, it sounds pretty expensive. How do you pay for all that stuff?"

"Well, some of them make their own money, of course, but I guess you have to get a really good job yourself."

"Doing what?"

"I don't know. But our dads have pretty good jobs."

"Yeah, we should ask them about it."

"Well, I'm not sure I would want to be a doctor like my dad, although in a big city you could do a lot of good and probably get paid well."

"Why wouldn't you want to be a doctor?"

"For one thing, pretty much everybody you're going to help doesn't really want to see you, at least at first. People really try to avoid doctors."

"I guess."

"Who would ever be excited to go and see a doctor?"

"You have a point. But if somebody is in bad enough pain or sufficiently sick, they're going to be desperate for your help."

"Yeah, but then you're dealing with people who are already in lots of misery, which is not the best, most positive and calming influence for doing your work well. It's just not pleasant."

"But then, when you help them, you'll have accomplished something important and they'll be really grateful."

"That's what my dad says. And then people give you all sorts of things."

"Like convertibles?"

"Well, not that big. More like goats and food and books and stuff."

"Look, it's a great thing, being a doctor. I'm just saying don't rule it out."

"I won't. It's not like I have some great alternative that I've already identified as the job I want."

"It'll come. You'll figure out what you really want to do."

"You think?"

"Yeah, you know, that's what Amon often says. We're each here for a reason, and you just have to be patient to find out what that is, and sometimes you never fully know, at least in your conscious mind. But if you're open and eager to make your proper difference in the world, you'll get on the path you're supposed to be on. You're probably even on it already, although you don't necessarily recognize it. You're being prepared for what you're here to do."

"Yeah. That makes sense."

"It does. And remember, we're still young. Our job now is to be students and learn. And maybe we'll soon discover what we want to do when we're the age of our dads. I think we're already learning some pretty great things with Khalid, and with our Phi training, and just in day-to-day life, generally."

"Very true," Malik said. As the boys reached a corner, he looked both ways for traffic. And to the right, three buildings down, he noticed a car parked on the side of the street with its motor running. He could see the exhaust coming from its tailpipe. Something made his gaze linger for a moment more, and in that instant two men came out of the building, practically dragging two boys with them who were struggling to get out of their grip. One of the boys was a little older than Malik and Haji, and the other was quite young. Malik reached over to touch Haji on the shoulder. "Sand mask," he said and pulled on his own that instant, as he began to jog down the street toward the car.

The two large men were now trying to get the boys into the back seat of the vehicle. The older boy was shoved in violently, but the much younger one was holding on to the doorframe with his hands and even his feet. He was fighting and obviously yelling, but Malik saw that he had something stuffed in his mouth, and a cloth tied around his head, holding the gag in place. So his attempts at shouting were greatly muffled, and yet still audible.

The Camel and the Sabre were halfway there when the smaller boy was finally pushed into the car and the two men jumped in as well. Then they took off—practically the moment the crime fighters reached the back bumper. Malik actually had his hand on the metal of the tail end of the car when it accelerated and sped away. Haji stared at the license plate and memorized the number. Malik stopped, with his heart pounding. He felt a jolt of disbelief and disappointment that they were just barely too late to intervene and help. He then struggled with the thought that he should give chase on foot, as the car disappeared around a corner two blocks down from where they now stood.

"Which door did they come out?" Haji asked.

"What?

"Which doorway here did they use?"

"That one, I think," Malik said, pointing. Haji went straight over and, opening it, saw a dim hallway whose only light seemed to come from a transom in the door itself. There were three interior doors along the hall, one on the right close by, and two on the left side, farther down. The first door, nearest to them, the one on the right, was slightly ajar. Haji pushed it farther open and it made a loud creaking sound. He then pushed on it a little more and stepped into the doorway just enough that he could peek in.

He looked to the right and saw nothing of note, just the front of what appeared to be a mostly bare room with a wooden desk and chair, up against a really dirty window. And then he turned his head to look left and what he saw, to his great surprise, was the open barrel of a gun pointed right between his eyes, five inches from his face.

13

Two Shots

THERE'S AN INTERESTING THING THAT OCCASIONALLY HAPPENS. Someone's name comes to you out of the blue, and as a result you get in touch. You find out that he has some sort of a problem and that you, of all people, might be in a position to help. Or maybe an old friend is going through a difficult challenge and you don't know about it at all, but her name suddenly pops into your head. You reach out and it's just the encouragement she needs. How does this work? Have you ever wondered? Could there be something like a spiritual beacon that broadcasts a friend's need, or perhaps better, narrowcasts it to the right person, or special few, who best can help?

Is this phenomenon confined to problems? Or does it also work with opportunities? There could be vastly more signals or promptings of need and new direction available to us in this world than we might imagine. Perhaps we can develop a capacity to be more sensitive to them and not shrug them off or dismiss even quite subtle hints when they sneak up on us, but rather learn to pay attention to such inklings and respond at the right time, as well as in the right way.

The members of Phi in Egypt have long seemed to be notably gifted in this skill. Some appear to be born especially sensitive to these signals. All develop the art or skill as a part of their training. It involves taming the chatter of the conscious mind, getting beyond the noise of everyday life, and deeply paying attention—truly noticing the little nudges that come into the soul as room is allowed for their arrival. When we properly access the thought beyond ordinary thought, interesting and important things happen.

Walid and Mafulla were walking fast toward the school where young Ben Hadad was a student. They had been talking about him as they left the palace, went through the front gate, and turned onto the street. But now, a few minutes later, their conversation had drifted to other things. Mafulla looked over at his friend and asked, "Is the new Gilgamesh essay meant to be one of our competitive assignments?"

"Yeah," Walid answered. "Khalid's going to pick a 'Best in Class,' like he's been doing recently, and then read it out loud to all of us."

"Well, we have two shots for the home team to win," Mafulla said.

"That's true, but, you know, Set's been writing some pretty awesome papers recently," Walid replied.

"I agree," Mafulla said. "Still, I think I'll be able to do a nice one this time, and I could always tutor you on yours and, you know, edit whatever you come up with and shape it into a respectable result."

"Hey, I think mine will have a decent chance, too, and without any outside editorial input."

"If you say so. I guess a prince writing about a king has an edge."

"Yeah. But we still shouldn't underestimate the competition. Like I said, there's always the hyper-philosophical Set to contend with."

"Yeah. There's always Set. And I'm glad. He's got a lot of great insights. Some days, I learn as much from him as from Khalid."

"I know what you mean. He's a natural with close analysis, and those amazing little nuggets of wisdom that can help you see a situation in a totally new way."

"Yeah, he's almost like a new superhero of the mind. I think of him as Perspective Man."

"Ha! I like that! Perspective Man strikes again, illuminating the path for mere mortals."

"So, speaking of illuminating the path, what exactly should we do to help find Ben, once we get to the school?"

"I don't really know yet. Maybe we should start at the building and do some concentric circles covering the neighborhood around it."

"Ok, that's a possible plan."

"Yeah, though actually, I'm not sure. As soon as I said it, I had this strange sense that we'll be led where to go, but let's start that way."

On the second floor of the palace, Walid's parents were in their comfortable sitting room. Rumi was at the desk, looking over some work, and Bhati was standing behind him, with her eyes on the same papers. She lightly squeezed her husband's shoulder and said, "I'm glad the boys asked us to help plan the king's birthday party."

"I am, too." He looked up and smiled. "Their basic idea was truly excellent, a real stroke of genius."

"Yes. Walid and Mafulla are impressively creative."

"They are. And I think Ali will have a lot of fun at an outdoor party like this. But there is, indeed, a little too much preparation work for the boys to have done it alone. It shows me how they're maturing, to realize that and ask us to help."

"This has been a time for lots of maturing, with all that the king is asking Walid to do. And I think Ali's idea to involve him more in governance at this stage has shown him so much about the life of the kingdom and, actually, life itself. Responsibility provides for growth."

"I agree completely."

"Do all the figures look right on the catering sheets?"

"Yes, I think we'll have plenty for everyone. The kitchen always does a great job with these events."

"They do. And I think you said that you have someone already lined up to bring in the sporting equipment and set it in place, ready to go?"

"Yes, I did. Kular's taking care of it all, with some of the men from the motor pool and the stables who've volunteered their time."

"Good."

"We'll have bocce ball, badminton, archery, and even horseshoes available, plus some music. Oh, and there's going to be an area for a simple ring toss geared to the small ones, and also a space for football displays of skill. Mafulla asked for that to be added."

"Nice."

There was a light knock on the door, and Bhati walked over to answer it. "Hamid! My second favorite doctor! Please come in!"

"Hi, Bhati. Thanks." Hamid smiled and stepped into the entry.

"You have your doctor's bag with you, I see."

"Yes, we're going to be doing some vaccinations throughout the palace today."

"Oh, is there a problem?"

"No, not at all, just routine care for the kingdom's leadership. Rumi's going to make the rounds with me for the next hour or so, if you can spare him."

"He did mention some palace work coming up."

"Everyone gets two shots today."

"Ouch. Ouch."

Hamid laughed and said, "I don't think they'll hurt. You'll feel a tiny little sting in the upper arm, barely perceptible, then another one, just as minimal. That's all."

"So, are you here simply to get my husband, or are you planning to ask to see my upper arm?"

"No, no, no. I'll leave that to the man of the house. But I'll give him his shots first, so you can witness his brave reactions."

"Good! In that case, let me bring you in to see him. He loves to show off his great courage."

Across town, the search for Ben was fully underway. Reela had just greeted a shopkeeper at a grocery store a few blocks from the boy's school. He'd found the man sweeping the walk outside his store. Leem and Ibrahim were directly across the street, speaking to the owner of a small rug shop who was standing outside his front entrance. Reela said to the grocer, "Excuse me. I hate to bother you during your work, sir, but may I ask you a rather urgent question?"

"Certainly. It's no bother."

"I'm out looking for a missing boy, the wonderful, adopted son of my friends over there, across the street." He gestured toward Leem and Ibrahim and then said, "The boy is about this tall," holding his hand to his lower chest level. "And he dressed in white and was with a young man who's older and who was wearing a red scarf, the last that we know. Have you by any chance seen them today?"

"Oh, yes! I did see them both!"

"You did?"

"Yes! They were right over there." The man pointed across the street and down a bit. "I'd come out to arrange some fruit in this display, and happened to notice them. I think it was the bright scarf. That's not seen very often on a young man, so it caught my eye. And there was a boy with him, about the size you indicate. And also there were two older men."

"Two men?"

"Yes. There were two men with them. One was walking beside them and was holding the arm of the younger boy, and one was walking behind, with his head down a bit."

"Did you see a weapon of any kind?"

"A weapon? Oh! No, my goodness, no, or I would have called for help."

"Which way were they going?"

"West, that way," the proprietor said, while pointing to their left.

"How long ago was this?"

"I'd say maybe an hour ago or perhaps a little less."

"Did you notice anything else about them?"

"Not really. As I said, it was just the bright red scarf against white that drew my attention. I looked over for no more than a quick couple of seconds and then got back to work. Nothing else stood out, or in any way made me suspect that anything of importance was going on with them. A flash of red and a group walking—that's all it was."

"Thank you so much for your time and the information. You've been very helpful," Reela said.

"Happy to be of assistance. I hope you find the boy soon."

This was the first sighting they had learned about, and Reela had to tell Leem and Ibrahim right away. He crossed the street immediately and, as Leem glanced up toward him, motioned for him to come over. The older detective stepped toward Reela, and then his nephew, seeing them, thanked the man he was speaking with and walked quickly to join them as well. Leem looked at Reela expectantly and said, "You've learned something?"

"Yes, let's walk and I'll tell you," Reela answered, as they all began to move again down the street in the right direction. "I talked to the grocer and he said the boys were here an hour ago or less, on this side of the street, in the company of two older men. One of them had Ben by the arm. They went this way."

"You're sure it was Ben?" Ibrahim asked.

"The shopkeeper recognized the red scarf Ahira was wearing. That's what drew his attention initially when he'd come out to sweep."

"Good. That's Ahira, all right."

Leem said, "What should we do?"

"Well, we need to keep walking in this direction, but we can likely hurry by this next block or two. There's no reason to think they stopped here. As I said, they passed this way almost an hour ago, so they could have gotten a long way from here, or they could have entered a building somewhere closer. Unfortunately, we have no idea where."

"That's true."

"But it's a big city, so we've at least narrowed our search with this crucial piece of information. If we can find a policeman or a place with a telephone, I can get the officers who are helping us to concentrate their efforts around here and search just in this sector of town. Maybe one of us will see something."

Leem said, "You know, there was one of the men we traced several days ago, one of the fake Santiagos, who worked at an office maybe half a mile from here in this direction, over on a side street about four or five blocks down. And they have a telephone."

"We should go there," Reela replied. "Right away. That may be the place."

"Yes," Leem said, "I agree. "When we get close, I'll recognize which street it is and then we'll turn right. The place of business is the Land of Wonder Travel Agency. That's what the sign outside says. Even if it isn't in any way connected to the disappearance, we can call in to the police from there."

"That's good," Reela said. "But with a fake Santiago recently there, I think we should be prepared for more than a simple phone call. I have a strange feeling about it."

Only a few feet away, and just outside the doorway Malik had walked through, Haji must have seen the gun that was now pointing in his friend's face. From where he was, he loudly yelled, "Ow!" as if he had suddenly been hurt, and then he repeated "Ow, Ow, Ow" and lurched into the office, stumbling on purpose across the floor, right by Malik, and then collapsing dramatically onto the floor. This was all a ruse, of course, meant to attract the attention of the gunman, if only for a second, away from Malik's head. And it worked perfectly. The astonished gunman couldn't help but look down at the writhing and groaning boy for the fraction of a second it took Malik to hit his hand, pushing it upward toward the ceiling.

BAM! A thunderously loud shot was fired inadvertently into the plaster of the ceiling as The Wild Camel then punched hard into the man's midsection, now that the gun was tilted up and away from his face. "Oof!" The gunman was caught totally by surprise and staggered backwards, but still held on to the revolver. The Silver Sabre jumped up, grabbed a heavy paperweight from the desk near him, and threw it right into the man's jaw, causing him to drop the gun that now clattered to the floor. Malik and the man then both dove for it at the same time. Their assailant was a little closer to it, so he got there a split second sooner and grabbed the weapon off the floor. But at the same time, Malik took hold of his forearm and jerked it upward. There was a loud second shot that now blew out the window, shattering glass into the street. The gun went flying again, and the two of them dove once more for it.

At that moment, Walid and Mafulla came rushing in through the door, but only Haji saw them. Malik had just tripped on a chair and hit the floor hard as he scrambled again for the deadly pistol and grabbed the man's arm. For a split second after he clamped onto the guy's elbow, the breath was knocked out of him and he released the man's arm as he fought to suck in air. That was all it took for the man to snatch up the gun again and turn it once more toward Malik's face.

No one even saw Mafulla pull out the military knife and throw it hard, somehow, handle-first, into the side of the man's head, hitting his left temple at precisely the right spot before he could squeeze the trigger of the gun a third time. That dropped him like a sack, turning out his lights as instantly as the projectile found its mark. He went from leaning up to cracking his head on the wooden floor as he fell over. With a single violent twitch of his entire body, he was now both immobile and unconscious.

Haji had also scrambled toward the guy's loose gun after flinging the paperweight and seeing it hit its mark and then fall to the floor, but the desk in the way had slowed him down. Now the three upright boys, were all over the gunman, taking the revolver out of his limp hand, as Malik coughed twice and then began to breathe normally.

Before they realized that anyone else had entered the office, Reela Adi was standing over them, saying, "What in the world just happened here?"

"Reela!" Walid exclaimed, at about the same time that Mafulla also did. "This guy was going to shoot Malik! Mafulla stopped him!"

"I tried," Haji said. "And I slowed him down and he dropped his gun. And Malik went for it, but the gun went off and shot into the ceiling. And then Malik knocked it loose again and dove for it and tripped and fell hard and somehow had the breath knocked out of him. And the guy was about a half second from shooting him in the face when Mafulla saved the day, for sure."

"I had to be careful, since I didn't know who the guy is, or why he was shooting at our friends," Mafulla said. "So I tried to eliminate the threat without fully eliminating the man."

"That was wise," Reela commented.

Haji quickly added, "We saw Ben and Ahira! They were taken out of this building, just minutes ago, gagged, and they were pushed into a car. We gave chase as soon as we saw, but they got away, and then we came to check out this building where they had come from, to see what could be here, and the guy with the gun surprised us."

"Well then, you certainly did the right thing," Reela said to Mafulla. "This man is our only lead, our only source of information as to how we can find Ben. We should tie his hands. Who has something?"

"Here, take my belt." Leem had just walked in and had been looking around the room for any clues about what was going on, and, hearing Reela's question, he'd quickly loosened his belt and handed it to him.

Reela took it and began to tightly tie the man's wrists, saying to the detective, "Is this the guy you told me about?"

"Yes, yes, it is—another of those men named Juan Santiago, and clearly now not just some ordinary guy hired off the street merely to take the name, which is what he told me when I found him. His actions are certainly those of a hardened criminal."

"Well, you're right. He's no innocent, paid name-bearer, for sure. As long as we have him, we have a path to finding Ben." Reela then looked at Walid, who was closest to the unconscious man's face and said, "Shake him. Rouse him if you can."

Mafulla said, "Leem? You somehow know this guy?"

"We came across him a few days ago when we were in the process of first discovering that there seem to be many men in town now going under the name of Juan Santiago."

"Oh?"

"Yes. I believe that some are so named as a symbol of status by their leader, the real Santiago. Others have been hired by those status Santiagos to bear the name for a time, six months some have said, for a large payment."

"Why? What's going on?"

"Well, We think the original Santiago's trying to give us lots of false trails. I met this guy in pursuit of anyone named Santiago and he claimed to have been paid to take on the name, for reasons he said he didn't know, and merely on his end, for the money. But now, his violence and his presence here where Ben and Ahira were being held tell a different story. There's much more to his involvement than he wanted me to think."

"He's obviously not the original Santiago," Mafulla said.

"He can't be the real thing," Walid agreed.

"No, not by a long shot," Reela said. He doesn't fit the physical description we have, and he's clearly not imbued with tremendous powers of any kind. So, he could be a paid thug, also given the name of Santiago, just to muddy the water, or he could be a 'status Santiago.' But if so, he's apparently very low down the chain of those so honored, since you've not mentioned any exercise of unusual power on his part in the struggle you experienced."

"What? What's this?" The man spoke for the first time with his eyes barely open. "Who are you?"

Reela said, "No, the question is: Who are you, really, and what were you doing with the two boys here?"

"I answer no questions."

"You'll answer mine."

"You ... dream well in the daytime." He said with a slow, groggy voice, but still tinged with menace.

"Where have the two boys been taken, the ones who were here?"

The man just looked at Reela and didn't answer. "Tell me now and save yourself a lot of trouble. Where have the boys been taken?"

The guy actually made a feeble attempt to spit at Reela. No one could believe it. Here he was just regaining consciousness, tied up, and in a room facing several adversaries, one of whom he had just repeatedly and unsuccessfully tried to shoot. He's being asked some simple questions. And, in response, he seeks to insult and show his utter disdain for his questioner.

Leem had already picked up the phone that sat on the desk in the front of the office, dialed the operator, and asked to be put through to police headquarters for a matter of the highest urgency. "Hello? Yes, this is Leem Hadad, former Chief of Police in Alexandria, now working as a private investigator here in Cairo. My friend Reela Adi came by your office earlier today to ask for help in finding a young boy and his friend, who have apparently been kidnapped. Yes. Yes, I know. And we deeply appreciate it. But now, we've found a place where the boys had been held until just a few minutes ago, when they were seen being forced into a car and taken away. It's the Land of Wonder Travel Agency, just off Memphis Avenue on Sixteenth. We've captured a man involved in the kidnapping and are starting to question him. We need someone to come arrest the man, and we need all your officers to be on the lookout for the car. Just a second."

Reela looked over at everyone and said, "Boys, what did the kidnappers' car look like?"

Malik replied, "It was a dark blue sedan, two door, newer model, license EK245."

"Did you hear that? Dark blue, two door, newer car, license EK245."

"Headed which way?" Leem said to Malik.

"North."

"North. Yes, about ten minutes ago. Yes. Thank you."

Walid and Ibrahim meanwhile had lifted the man to his feet.

Reela stood looking at him. "You'll tell us first your birth name."

"Wrong again." And at that, the man started to laugh and then to cough loudly, and on about the fourth cough, he groaned, and tensed up, and bent over and his knees buckled and he collapsed to the floor, slipping mostly from the grip of both Walid and Ibrahim, although the prince continued to maintain a bit of a light hold.

"What's wrong with you?" Reela said. "Get back up." The man was unresponsive.

"Get up!"

Ibrahim grabbed him better under his arm and said to Reela, "He's completely limp."

Walid added, "I don't think he's breathing."

"What?"

"He's not breathing! Something's happened!"

Walid and Ibrahim laid the man on the floor and Reela checked for a pulse in his wrist, and then his neck.

"I can't believe it."

"What?" Walid asked.

"He's … dead. He just died."

"No! No! That can't be!" Mafulla said, "He told us nothing about where Ben's being taken. We're back … where we started."

14

THE GRAND HOTEL

THE LARGE SUITE IN THE GRAND HOTEL WAS FULL OF LIGHT from the big windows and the tall French doors that opened out to a wide balcony. Four men sat in the spacious living room. The newly arrived guest spoke. "First of all, thank you so much for meeting me here, Your Majesty. It was just too dangerous for me to go to the palace."

"You're quite welcome. Our relations with your country have been good and strong for a very long time," the king said. "It was my pleasure to arrange this little offsite session. But may I ask why you have such a concern about visiting the palace?"

"Certainly, Your Majesty," the man replied. "We have reason to believe that one of our citizens—a very strange and violent man, I'm afraid, and with a following or cohort of associates—may have harmful intentions toward your monarchy and various individuals within your realm. We suspect that he has people watching the area around the palace, and anyone widely known from his home country seen there ... well, there would likely be some unfortunate consequences."

"Would this be a man who, we've come to believe, goes by the name of Juan Osvaldo Santiago?"

"Yes. That's the man. For a time, we know that he was going back and forth between a compound we think he built in the western part of your kingdom, and a place of retreat that he has in the south of Spain, also remotely located. He's been in our country recently, but we think he's here now."

"We've come to the same conclusion," the king replied. "But why do you think he's now in Cairo? What would be his purpose, or reason for coming here?"

"I've heard he's very angry about something that happened recently in your kingdom."

"Oh?"

"Yes, and he's seeking revenge on anyone who thwarted some plans that he had well underway. There's much about this that we don't know. But I've also heard that he's in search of something, some item that he believes to be held in safekeeping here in Cairo, and perhaps even in the palace."

"What would he be seeking?"

"That, I'm afraid I can't answer. I've heard only that it involves an artifact of legend that's rumored to convey some power or else some knowledge beyond what's normal. But you know how rumors are, and how unreliable they can be."

"Do you have any idea how we might locate this man, this Santiago?"

"I have some relevant thoughts, but what I have to say may strike you as foolishness."

"I can assure you, I'm very open minded."

Just then, there was a knock at the door and a guard opened it, stepping for a moment into the hallway. "Your Majesty, Reela Adi and Leem Hadad are here," the guard announced into the room, bowing.

"Yes, please, invite them in," the king said.

"Your Majesty, we're so sorry to be late getting here," Reela said as they walked in. "We've been dealing with an urgent and unexpected situation."

Leem at that point explained, "Our boy Ben disappeared, and we've learned that he's been kidnapped by people affiliated with that man, Santiago."

The king said, "Walid left me a quick note that Ben had gone missing and that he and Mafulla were going to join the effort to find him. Have you made any headway in discovering where he is?"

"Malik and Haji saw him being forced into a car a couple of miles from here with another young man, a friend of Ibrahim who had picked Ben up at school today. The car sped off before our friends could intervene. The boys went into the building from which Ben had emerged and were confronted by a gunman who fired two shots but then was subdued by Mafulla, when he and Walid arrived on the scene, hearing the gunfire."

"The boys are all right?"

"Completely."

"So, you have the man in custody, being questioned?"

"No, Your Majesty, I'm afraid not," Leem answered.

"What happened?"

Reela said, "I began questioning him, and while he was attempting to show great disrespect to us all, he apparently suffered a massive heart attack or a stroke, or some other sudden physical calamity that removed him from our world. And this happened before we could get any answers."

"Oh, my," the king said.

"But the police are looking for the car that took Ben and Ibrahim away. We have a detailed description and license number."

"That's good."

Leem said, "We made sure the police got all the information they need and we quickly stopped by my office on our way here. There was a note that had been left for us about Ben."

"Do you have it?"

"Yes, here it is." Leem took a paper from his pocket and handed it to the king.

"This is all so odd."

"It is, Your Majesty. And as you'll see, the note simply says that if I ever want to see Ben again, I must cease to pursue the investigation I'm now engaged in, and I must make sure that no one else continues it in my place."

"I see," the king said.

"Of course, I'll do no such thing," Leem assured the king. "Santiago's sure to be found. And I'm going to do everything I can to make certain that it happens as soon as possible."

Masoon spoke from his chair, where he had been sitting quietly until then, just listening. "Leem, I'll be happy to provide you with all the resources you might need."

"Thank you, Masoon. Your offer is appreciated."

The king said, "We were just about to hear from our visitor who's with us today. This is Señor Carlos Sanchez, Director of Intelligence for Spain, who apparently has a view on how we might find Santiago."

Reela walked over to shake the man's hand and Sanchez stood. "I'm Reela Adi. It's a pleasure to meet you," Reela said, as they shook. "I served long ago in a position similar to yours in our own kingdom."

"Oh, Mr. Adi, I'm well aware of your storied service to Egypt. It's my distinctive honor to meet you. I've heard many things about you over the years."

"Half may be true," Reela said with a smile.

"No, no—I also believe the good things," Sanchez said, and that gave Reela a small chuckle. But then, their visitor added, "I'm sorry to joke at a time like this. I know that the situation you face is serious."

"It's quite all right," the king said, adding, "I believe in the worth of mirth," as Reela nodded his agreement.

"Indeed," Reela added.

And the king explained, "We're serious in such situations, but rarely somber. We have faith that we'll prevail, and our spirits are typically kept up by that conviction."

"Oh," Reela said to Sanchez, "May I introduce my friend and colleague, the former Chief of Police in Alexandria, Leem Hadad?"

Sanchez shook his hand as well, and greetings were exchanged briefly. The king then looked at Leem and Reela, and said, "Both of you, please take a seat. And, Señor Sanchez, if you would, make yourself comfortable once more."

And as they all sat, their visitor said, "Thank you, Your Majesty." He then turned to the newcomers and explained, "The king had just asked for any ideas I might have about how Santiago could be located here, despite being a master of deception and keeping his whereabouts generally unknown when he perceives it to be in his interest to do so."

"Yes, anything could help at this point," Reela replied.

"I had just warned His Majesty that the one hint I can provide might sound terribly foolish, but I assure all of you that I'll convey it with complete sincerity and a serious intent."

"And we'll take it as such," Leem assured him.

"It may even sound a bit crazy."

"Not to us, I can assure you. Please, speak freely," the king said.

A short distance away, Walid, Mafulla, Malik, and Haji were at that moment walking down a street that intersected with Sixteenth about three blocks away from where they had just experienced their skirmish. It was where Haji thought he had had seen the speeding getaway car turn right, just seconds after it had left the travel agency building. They had assured Leem and Reela that they'd be extremely careful as they continued their search for Ben, and that they would join up with the first city police they might come across.

The police who had come to the travel agency shortly after Leem's phone call had interviewed the boys and then left with the body of the criminal. But they had assured them that more men would shortly be in the area and on the search. Reela and Leem had left as soon as the officers arrived, because of the meeting they had with the king. Leem thought it important to make sure Ali knew what was going on, so that he could possibly provide more assistance.

"How many times did Leem and Reela tell us to be careful?" Haji asked with a straight face.

"I counted six," Mafulla said. "And they said to stay together."

"But that doesn't seem efficient at all," Malik said.

"No, but it's what Reela and Leem wanted. It's the only thing that got them to agree with our continuing the search without them while they met the king."

"You know, staying together is actually a pretty broad concept," Malik suggested, adding, "it's even a bit vague and general."

Walid looked over at him and asked, "What do you mean?"

"Together could mean bunched close, within three feet of each other like we are now, or it could just mean in sight of each other."

"Yeah, it could mean that, too," Mafulla reflected.

"And that would be tactically superior to what we're doing now," Haji added.

"Absolutely," Malik said. "Now, any adversary could see with one glance that there are four of us all together."

"I get what you're saying," Mafulla remarked.

"Yeah, and the travel agency guy with the gun back there was surprised when you and Walid rushed in because he didn't know you were coming. He thought at first that it was just Haji and me—just the two of us that he had to deal with."

Haji then jumped in, saying, "Well, initially, he saw only you, and then I was able to surprise him, and then you guys surprised all of us."

"That's right. The element of surprise was important more than once," Malik pointed out. "And as long as we keep walking along together in the tightest interpretation of what Reela and Leem wanted, we're a highly visible bunch of idiots with no surprises left. And actually, we're not providing what they wanted, which is an extra level of safety for all of us. We're doing the opposite."

"That's a really good point," Walid said.

"Don't sound so surprised," Malik replied.

"But surprise is what you're wanting."

"Hardee-Har," Malik commented.

Mafulla said, "You sound like me talking to Walid."

"I think you're right," Walid explained to Malik, ignoring the remark of his best friend. "We should continue with our search in a more dispersed way, with a looser form of togetherness."

Haji spoke up and said, "How about me on the left side of the street, Malik on the right, and then you guys could also split up a block back and follow us."

"But we'll be looking in the same doors and alleys and windows that you do," Mafulla said.

"Yeah, but since when is a second look a bad idea?" Haji said.

"Actually, it's a super good idea," Mafulla said, as if he were stunned by such a simple notion.

"Ok. You sound just as surprised as Walid did a few seconds ago."

"Yeah. I didn't mean to. We're just used to it being only the two of us, and having only our own resources of insight and tactical brilliance to draw on," Mafulla explained, pointing to Walid and himself, wagging his finger back and forth. "It just takes some getting used to that you guys can come up with good ideas that we haven't had ourselves."

"So, then, get used to it," Malik said, with a smile, and pushed Mafulla good-naturedly. Mafulla pretended to have been shoved much harder, and dramatically stumbled and bent over.

But then suddenly, he said, "Guys!"

"What?" Walid replied.

"Is this ..." he reached down to the street to pick up something he just happened to glimpse when his eyes had gone down toward the ground, during his momentary dramatic rendering of a man being shoved hard. "Is this ... red yarn and fuzz, maybe from Ahira's scarf?"

The boys all stopped and looked at what Mafulla was now holding in his hand. "That's red wool, all right, red yarn and fuzz," Walid pronounced.

"I wonder if Ahira left it as a trail?"

"You mean, throwing it out of the car?"

"Maybe. Or it could be that he was taken out of the car here."

"But we've walked only a couple of miles, and there's no blue car around."

"Why do we have to assume they're staying all together like us, and tightly together, and with a highly visible and now easily identified blue car parked outside wherever one or two or more of them are?" Haji now had another very good point. And they all realized that instantly.

"You're right," Mafulla said. "I was just assuming we'd be looking for that car, and the men, in the same place, but that's not necessarily the way it'll play out, if they're thinking at all."

"Yeah, we have to stay a step ahead of them, reasoning it through," Haji added. "We've got to outsmart them trying to outsmart us."

"Ok, so, let's look around and see if there's any more red wool on the ground," Walid suggested. The boys spread out and went over every square foot of sidewalk and street around them, moving cautiously forward. Malik had walked a little faster than the others and was now about ten yards down the street at an intersecting alleyway.

"Hey," he whispered loudly and waved. "More red wool." He reached down and picked up something from the corner of the alley. He added, "Right here."

The others caught up with him and Walid nodded as he saw what was now in Malik's hand. "Go down the alley and look," he whispered. "Look for more."

As Malik walked slowly down the alley, eyes on the ground, Haji carefully followed him, but Walid and Mafulla stayed on the sidewalk at the end of the alley, looking around for anyone who might be able to spot them in their search. Within about twenty seconds, Malik waved urgently at the two of them and they hurried down the alley that, at this point, was deep in shadows.

"What?"

"Look."

"Oh! A bigger piece of wool, like part of a piece of fringe or something. And, what's that next to it?"

"I think … I'm not sure, but—oh, man—it could be … blood."

"Wait. Blood?"

"Yeah, look."

At that same time, but a few miles away, it seemed like a

normal day at one of the beautiful spots in the city that had been set aside for public enjoyment. A lady entered the busy park, where so many children were running and playing a short distance from her. There were mothers with babies and toddlers sitting in the grass, and several dogs accompanying their owners, out for some fresh air. The lady walked over to a bench and sat down, and then took out some breadcrumbs in a little bag to feed the birds that, immediately, started to fly around her and land at her feet.

A man approached from the opposite direction and took a seat on a bench identical to hers that backed up to it and faced a small artificial pond. "Are you learning anything that we can use?" he asked as he looked down at a book that he had carried with him and was now pretending to read.

"Yes. A lot, as we expected."

"Good. And you're gaining access?"

"Very soon. I believe ... to the palace itself."

"Excellent. The master will be pleased."

"I'm having to work very hard to make this happen and I'm glad I'm already reaping such astonishing results." She spoke like this to attempt to raise her standing in the eyes of this man and any others who would hear his report. It was actually all easier than she had even hoped, and to a tremendous degree, but she spoke deceptively, as if the exact opposite was true.

"Your hard work will pay off and be greatly rewarded," he said.

"Yes," she replied, and smiled into her bag of crumbs.

"Just remember, much depends on your role," he said. "We're all counting on you."

"I keep that in mind all the time," she said. "You can count on me."

"You'll be elevated above all women, Muriel," he said in a very low voice, imitating their master. And then he stood up and walked off.

At the El-Noor home, Khata was lying on her bed, trying to read her school assignment, but instead of succeeding in the effort, she was staring into space. She should feel so happy and satisfied and excited. Her mother had praised her and her new teacher ever since the party ended. But she felt strangely uneasy. She couldn't say why. It was wonderful, having the new piano and getting lessons from a famous musician who seemed to be so nice, but there was something else that she couldn't quite identify and that troubled her. It was something that lurked just under the pleasant surface of everything. She felt almost guilty about her uneasiness, and confused about it, but she couldn't manage to ignore it. Things weren't right. In fact, something was very wrong. She felt it, and she knew it, but she couldn't put her finger on what it was.

Some distance away, in the Grand Hotel suite, all eyes were now on the visitor from Spain. He said, "The key to finding Santiago in or around Cairo is something you'd never expect. There are several reasons why he usually lives in remote areas."

Hamid spoke up now and said, "For privacy, of course, and security."

"Yes, both those things are very important to him," the Spaniard agreed. "But there's one other aspect to him that's quite odd, to an exceptional degree. He apparently learned a few years ago that whenever he stays in a modern city, there's always an area around his dwelling place where electrical things won't work reliably."

"Oh?"

"Yes. It's strange. Lights will flicker, if they work at all. There will be problems with radios. It becomes disruptive to the point that you can trace where he is by seeing where these problems develop."

"It's his energy field," Masoon said, and Hamid nodded.

"He's ravenous for energy," Reela added.

"Yes?"

"My brother Shapur met him briefly, without knowing who he was, and felt drained of all his energy for days."

"Is that so?"

Reela replied, "I suspect the man is an energy thief, for one thing, and it could be that the sum total of his accumulated force interferes with other energy flows that are around him, or any-where near him."

"So, we should look around town for power outages and disruptions, and they can point us to where he is," the king concluded.

"That's correct, Your Majesty," their visitor said. "If he's in the city, this will be your sign. But it might be more fruitful to search for him outside the city limits. This problem of energy interference is one of the most important reasons he normally lives these days in remote places. His presence will always be, at most, a rumor in desolate areas. No one can confirm his location in that sort of setting through a reaction in electrical systems, and by interference with electric devices."

The king pondered this for a moment and said, "Well, you're right in thinking that this is unexpected, and likely something that might not have occurred to any of us as even a possibility. It can indeed be an important key for locating our adversary. I deeply appreciate your coming here to tell us these things."

"And there are more things, Your Majesty, a few more. And they could be vital for you to know."

"Please continue. We're all keen to hear them."

15

A Conversation

"Are you boys all right? I heard there was some serious excitement." The king said this to Walid and Mafulla as they walked into his private sitting room upstairs in the palace.

"Yes, sir, Your Majesty, we're fine," Walid answered right away.

"Utterly unscathed," Mafulla echoed, adding, "And more experienced than yesterday."

"Good. Please sit and tell me all about what happened."

They took turns in filling in the king on everything that had taken place, from the time they left the palace looking for Ben, to the intervention at the travel agency, and then with the search they continued on for the missing boys. They got all the way to the point of finding the traces of his scarf that Ahira had left as a trail.

"Your Majesty, it was the strangest thing," Mafulla said. "Ahira had pulled some bright red fibers of wool from his scarf when the boys were taken out of the car to be led to that building where they were eventually found. And he let the wool fall on the street for us to see, and then in the alley, and what's amazing is that we discovered any of it at all. They were such small pieces of fuzz and yarn."

"You were guided," the king said. "Your eyes were opened and directed."

"Yeah, I guess that's it," Mafulla replied, with a look of amazement. "And any wind would have just taken it all away."

"And then a struggle took place," Walid said. "Ahira told us later on that he was worried about being taken into the back of that building. He had a bad feeling about it. He feared that this time, they might not come out alive, so he fought his captives and was injured doing so."

"We saw his blood on the alley," Mafulla added. "Not a lot, but enough to know there had been a problem and that we were in the right place."

"I'm still a bit concerned that you went in by yourselves at that point, without additional backup," the king said. "I hope I'm not repeating myself too much on this particular matter of interest."

"Well, there were four of us, at the time we made the original decision, all junior Phi," Walid said. "We had Malik and Haji. We would have preferred to wait and summon the police, who should have been somewhere in the area, but we were afraid to waste any time, given the fact that we saw the blood. We didn't at that point know what had gone on, but the evidence suggested it was nothing good, and that maybe we didn't have a lot of time to act, or something worse would soon happen."

"Yeah, we felt an urge to do something right then," Mafulla said. "But I did run back to the street one more time to see if there was anything going on within sight that we should know about, or any city police passing by, and that's when I couldn't believe it that Kissa and Hasina were right there, walking together, a block away. I mean, ten seconds slower or faster in getting there, I would have missed seeing them."

"I wondered how they got involved," the king said. "I had heard about it earlier, but only that they were there."

Walid took over at this point. "They were going to meet Ara and Kit, not far away. They had no idea what was going on, or that we were anywhere nearby. Kissa told me later that she happened to look up at just the right moment to see Maffie, and he waved at her and made a Phi sign on his chest, so she would know that something was going on and they should come join us, but also that she should be quiet, fast, and careful."

Mafulla said, "Yeah, so at that point we had six junior Phi together. And there was a palace guard, trailing the girls."

Walid quickly added. "And that gave us even more confidence, because, you know what the girls can do."

"Yes, they have great power," the king said.

Mafulla continued, "And Hasina walked up to me and said, first thing, with no hesitation at all, 'There is something, or someone, in a nearby location. And help is needed.' I mean: she nailed it just like that. So I told both of them what was going on, and they joined me and Walid walking back down the alley. We asked their guard to stay at the street as a lookout and backup."

Walid explained, "That was when we sent Haji and Malik around to the front of the building with the gun Mafulla had."

"What was your plan?" the king asked.

"Well, I guess we really didn't have one, I hate to admit," Walid said. "We were sort of going on instinct at that point."

Mafulla then added, "When we finally got into the place, thanks to Kissa, which wasn't easy, since the building was locked up in a bunch of ways, we couldn't believe that the kidnappers were already gone, and that Ben and Ahira were just lying there on the floor by themselves, tied up and gagged."

Walid said, "Yeah, it was a relief to find them both alive, and so we got them out of there as fast as we could. We saw two city policemen within about three or four minutes and told them what had happened. And they helped make sure that we all got back safely."

"You mentioned that Kissa somehow helped you to get into the building," the king said.

"Yes, sir," Mafulla replied.

"What did she do?"

Walid answered, "She told me later that she just knew she was supposed to do a quick meditation thing, where she made her mind a total blank for several seconds and it just came to her that we should go to a certain smaller window, and so Mafulla did, and he tried it, and it wasn't locked."

"I see."

"It was the only window or door that was unlocked. The lock on it was actually broken. He got it open and squeezed in through it and then came around and opened the door for the rest of us."

"Sometimes, it pays to be lean, wiry, and agile," Mafulla with eyebrows fully aloft commented.

"Indeed," the king said. "I'm certainly glad it all went so well, and especially since you had such a tussle earlier on."

"Yeah, that was a little dicey," Mafulla said. "And, with that in mind, Your Majesty, I've been wanting to ask your opinion on something."

"Certainly. Ask anything, my friend."

"Ok. When we got Ben and Ahira untied and found out all that they had been through, I thought to myself: Things so easily might have gone very differently, and much worse. The kidnappers could have killed one or both of them. The guys working for Santiago could have just taken Ben out of our lives and away from his family forever, and caused so much grief and pain and sadness."

"Not forever," the king said, adding, "But yes, for a time what would indeed seem long to us as we went through it."

"Oh, right, sure, but for the rest of our stay in this world," Mafulla said.

"Yes, and the difference is crucial," the king explained.

"I guess I see that, Your Majesty, but for a bad guy to be able to change the course of many lives in this world for the full length of time we'll be here, however long that is—that's a pretty big deal. I mean, one guy with destructive intentions can do so much evil and cause so much pain. And it doesn't seem fair, because one man with good intentions—well, it just seems to take a whole lot more work to do any lasting good. It's far too easy to do permanent harm in the world. It seems completely unfair, like the world is put together so that it magnifies the harm of evil, but constrains the benefit of good."

"Those are indeed often the appearances," the king replied.

And Mafulla then almost dutifully said, "But appearances aren't always good guides to the underlying realities?"

"Yes, and you can fully believe that," the king explained, "and not just say it for my sake."

"I guess I'm wavering a little bit today, Your Majesty, I have to admit. I mean, everything turned out fine with rescuing Ben, and I'm glad. And Ahira wasn't too badly hurt, and will heal completely, and that's good, but we've been through so much, and other people go through so much more. In wars, lots of innocent people get killed—young mothers who aren't soldiers, and old men, and little kids, and it just doesn't seem fair at all. When the al-Khoum brothers launched their attack on the palace, sweet and innocent people were killed. I mean, where's the justice? One crazy idiot with a bomb can do damage in seconds that dozens of good doctors working for weeks and months and even years can't fix. It's the Humpty Dumpty Problem."

"The what?" Walid asked, looking at his friend.

"The Humpty Dumpty Problem, you know, from the old English nursery rhyme. Humpty is this innocent guy, if I remember right, who looks like a really good egg or something, and the famous nursery rhyme tells his story."

"Ok."

"Humpty Dumpty sat on a wall,
Humpty Dumpty had a great fall.
All the king's horses and all the king's men
Couldn't put Humpty together again."

Mafulla said, "Or something like that." And then he added, "Except in our version, it would probably be some warped miscreant named Santiago who unleashed a strange and mysterious force to shove poor Hump and all his friends and neighbors off the wall, crashing them to the ground below."

Walid couldn't help himself. He said, "Sorry to interrupt here, but Mafulla: Miscreant? Really? That's pretty impressive. I continue to be awed by your linguistic scope and facility."

"Thanks, man. I try. But, Your Majesty, my point is that, in the story, all the good guys who came to the rescue, working together, couldn't fix the damage. I mean, we teach kids this stuff when they're tiny. And the whole situation, well, it's totally unfair. The bad guys have an advantage. Goodness is so fragile, like poor Humpty."

The king smiled and said, "I know things often seem this way. But perhaps we need to think a little more deeply. Our overall worldview can help us to understand the particulars of life better than when we rely just on surface appearances, and it can help us to draw our conclusions with a great deal more wisdom. That's why we need a worldview, a big picture for life, with the qualities of truth and depth."

"Ok, I get what you're saying—at least, the general point," Mafulla admitted. "But, could you elaborate a bit on how it helps here, with this particular problem?"

"Certainly. We've spoken about the basic big picture for human life in the world many times before, but for the moment, I can tell we need to get it back into the forefront of your mind. Does this sound good?"

"Yes, please."

"All right. This is the picture. We live in a world of infinite complexity and surprise. Our sense experience doesn't always tell us the truth about the physical realities around us. And it often won't even touch the spiritual matters behind the physical. As Plato understood, we are souls, conscious spirits, and in this world we're living with some measure of confinement to biological bodies, for reasons that go far beyond what we can now know. But we can grasp that there are many aspects of the constraints and limitations of this world that help us to build our inner resources and, in particular, the strength and depth of our souls, individually and together."

"Could you say more about that?"

"Certainly. It's only in a world like this one that we could develop the attributes of courage and patience, and persistence, and forbearance, and fortitude and resilience. These are all strengths of the soul that it's better to have than to lack. They contribute to a certain depth and greatness of spirit. And consider this. Various difficulties in life are necessary so that we can cultivate authentic

sympathy with others, and real partnerships in a nobility of struggle, with the deep and distinctive interpersonal resonance that only
this produces, along with so many other positive and important
spiritual attributes whose value goes far beyond their responsive-
ness to the particular challenges and difficulties that elicited them.
These qualities make us who we are. And we couldn't possibly just
be given such characteristics. Their own essence would logically
prevent that. They have to be grown from within, freely, and in
response to serious problems. But then, their benefits, as I say, go
far beyond their originating context."

"Ok. I get that. Struggle gives us the chance to become strong
and good and virtuous—by how we freely choose to respond to
difficulty."

"Yes. And there's more. Our conscious minds in this life depend
to some extent on the proper functioning of our brains and our
physical senses. We understand this. When a man is in a building,
he needs windows to see out. Likewise, while we're in physical
bodies, we require our physical brains and our various senses for
experience of the external world. The physicality of our bodies,
in all its strange complexity, enables our experience in this world
while we're embodied, but it also greatly reduces, or restricts the
nature and range of potential experience."

Walid spoke up and asked, "Could you say a bit more about
that?"

"I can," the king replied. "While we're embodied here in this
world, our physicality makes possible certain sorts of experience or
connection with the world around us, but it also limits and even
distorts what's available for us in our perception. In fact, every facet
of embodiment, while enabling, is also either limiting, or potentially distorting. The fact that we have a small number of senses, and
not more, is limiting. The fact that the senses we have can access
only a narrow range of the objective signals available to us can be
both limiting and distorting. The fact that matters of health can
reduce or interfere with our ability to use our senses well must also
be considered. And, as you know, there are animals with senses that

we entirely lack, as well as other creatures whose sight, or smell, for example, is vastly more acute and accurate than ours."

"Like Kissa's dog, Shibby, who always amazes me," Walid commented.

"Yes. Then consider the fact that each of us is born into one particular family, with its perspectives and beliefs, and in one specific culture, and we initially learn the native language of that culture. And then perhaps at some point we acquire another language, which is just as bound and localized in its own resources. And even the additional languages and related conceptualities that could, in principle, expand the sphere of our awareness are learned and understood through the filters we already have in place."

"That's wild to think about, Your Majesty," Mafulla said.

"It is. And it's important to ponder. Some even call it the scandal of particularity. We desperately want universal access to truth and understanding. But we always start from a particular place that's not universal at all—or at least, so it seems. The cultural and linguistic thought structures that we grow up with both form and restrict our experience. They give us windows, but they also give us curtains and filters. They enable, and they block. There's just so much that we don't notice. We may be culturally trained not to pay any attention to even quite important things around us, and crucial aspects of our environment. Then, we filter what experience we do have through our current beliefs, true or false, and even our prior attitudes and emotions, regardless of how relevant or distorting they might be. Sometimes, we see what we want to see and are blind to what we emotionally can't acknowledge. At other times, we think we see what we most fear, and are unable to notice what we most need."

"We're pretty much a mess," Mafulla said.

"But a magnificent mess," Walid added.

"What's so magnificent about us?"

"I want to say 'look in the mirror' but I have to remember it's you I'm talking to. Think about what we read in Pascal the other day about the greatness and wretchedness of our condition.

We're infinite and we're tiny. We're strong and we're weak. The Two Powers define us."

"True. Ok. I get it."

"Sorry, Your Majesty," Walid said.

"Not at all. I like your citation of the great French scientist and mathematician. It's quite appropriate here. Pascal understood this."

"Thanks. But, please, continue what you were saying," Walid urged.

"Of course. So, let's suppose that all this that I've described is our reality for ultimately good and crucial reasons. Yet, as we simply go about our daily lives, we easily miss some of the most important truths about life itself."

"That makes sense," Mafulla said.

The king added, "And many of the truths that we easily miss, many that might be farthest from the domain of everyday experience in their origin, could be most crucial for interpreting that experience properly."

Walid and Mafulla were hanging on the king's words here. He continued. "There's a deep human tendency, at almost all times and places, and there's also some good evidence—however difficult it may be to gather and evaluate—to believe that, at physical death, the soul is freed from these worldly distortions and limitations, and can then know and experience purely and directly, in the fullness of its vast capacities. There's also reason to think that the next adventure awaiting us after death is wonderful far beyond our ability to imagine while we're in these bodies that we currently have. Everything here can be, somehow, a preparation for what's awaiting us there."

The king then paused and said, "So, with all that in mind, what's really the capability of an evil man? He can lead some vulnerable souls into evil. He can impede the spiritual growth of others. He can cause physical pain and severe emotional distress, at least, among the insufficiently enlightened. And that's certainly bad, indeed, but it's also the worst he can do. And it's equally counterbalanced by what a good man can do. A good man can lead many people into the ways of goodness, and can facilitate the spiritual growth of others. He can bring to other souls great good pleasure, and he can lift the spirits of those around him. There's at least a parity, or balance, so far, wouldn't you say?"

"Ok. But what about murderers, like the people we're up against?" Mafulla couldn't help but bring up again the thing that was bothering him the most.

"Yes. It's an important question. So now, I'll ask you to go with me one more step. What do most people think is the worst that the evil man can do? And what's his personal opinion? It's very different from what I just suggested. Seeking to cause the most terrible harm, in his own misguided and feeble view, and in the sadly most common viewpoint as well, the man led by evil may murder you, which means he may kill your body. And then, what horrible thing has he accomplished as a result of his ill intent?"

"You're dead?" Mafulla said.

"Yes. But what does that mean? The man has freed your soul to be and experience all that it can, in its most essential form. Some wisdom traditions suggest there will be a new body for the soul, but without the weaknesses and limitations of our bodies now. The man with evil intent has released a soul to return, across any dimensional barriers separating fundamental realities, to its ultimate homeland where it can flourish in ways that are impossible in this world of mere preparation. And the loved ones who are left behind, and so then subsequently have to live out their earthly sojourns without your ongoing continued physical presence, they will be reunited with you one day, forever to share with you that fuller existence that awaits us. And if they know that fact in this world, deep in their hearts as well as their minds, then the perspective it provides can temper their grief at your premature passing and comfort them with the solid hope and knowledge that it will take to get them through all those days when they will inevitably miss you here in this life. And then, that same wisdom can guide them also into those eternal spaces and times, so to speak, when the coming reunion will be complete and unending."

The king paused. And Mafulla spoke again. "Ok, I see now that I was misinterpreting the worst that a bad man can do. I was just giving voice to the common view. I get that. And I should know better at this point than to fall into that simplistic perspective. But, still, what about the apparent difficulty of doing great good in our world?"

"Not all good is difficult. Much of it is easy. A kind word, a positive gesture, a smile, a helping hand can have beneficial effects far beyond what you ever might imagine. And since the effects are in the souls of beings who are of infinite value and worth, any good is great good. Some benevolence, by contrast, does take hard work, I grant you. But hard work is itself often good for us. It builds us up into what we're capable of being. We're meant to be strong and powerful. Great ease doesn't create great souls. So even then, when the hard things are tackled and done, the good that results is magnified."

"Your answers, as always, amaze me, Your Majesty," Mafulla responded, and then he added, "Can I ask another question?"

The king laughed with pleasure and love. "Yes. Of course you can."

"I understand what you've just said about the evil man seeking to do someone great harm, but instead, despite his harmful intentions, he just sends that man into a better world, as a consequence of his fatal violence—into the next great adventure, as you often put it."

"Good. I'm glad it makes sense to you."

"But, well, then, why is murder wrong in the first place? Or suicide? I mean, if killing a human body just introduces the victim, so to speak, into a much better form of existence, however ugly the act itself may seem to be, then why is it condemned rather than … praised and encouraged? I mean: I know how crazy that sounds, but it seems to be a logical question to ask."

"Yes, it is. Unfortunately, most people in our world who do manage to believe the right things still often believe them for the wrong reasons. They think that murder is wrong because they assume it's a horrible thing to be taken out of this world. They mistakenly believe the great harm is done to the victim. But the real harm, and the deepest harm, is done to the perpetrator. People should understand that murder is wrong because it's against the intent and purpose of our creation. Some of the more profound philosophers and religious thinkers have grasped this well over the centuries. We have been put here in this world for a purpose—each of us. We need to do everything we can to fulfill our purpose and to allow and help others to fulfill theirs. Taking another person out of this world, through murder—or doing it to ourselves, through suicide—wrongly ends the possibility of living out those proper purposes in this lifetime."

"But what if someone claimed that this is his purpose—to transition others out of this world through random murderous killing?"

"He would be sadly and perversely wrong, to an extreme degree. No individual purpose can legitimately be at odds with the overarching intent and scheme of creation. No individual human purpose can be to forcibly remove another person from this world who was placed here, ultimately, by and through powers far beyond the scope of his or her own decision making, and for deep and powerful reasons that can never be fully grasped in this life. Once we're here, the reasons and causes that put us in this world have a claim on our respect and deference. And, perhaps apart from the rare situation of assisting someone who is in the worst sort of extreme and unremitting physical agony, or in certain other equally extraordinary circumstances, it's not our choice to make, to simply decide to take anyone from this world."

Walid now weighed in with a question: "How then can it ever be acceptable to defend yourself to the point of taking another's life, like in a situation of war, or in protecting yourself while fighting violent criminals, like we sometimes have to do?"

"Acceptable is a plain word and a concept that's here without solid spiritual weight," the king said with kindness. "Taking the life of an individual who has chosen a path of violence may become a tragic imperative if your act is necessary to save an innocent life, such as your own, or other such lives—the lives of souls who have not themselves turned against their ultimate purpose."

"An imperative?"

"Yes. It can be a tragic imperative, or actual duty, in certain rare circumstances."

"But how can that be, in light of what you've just said?"

"We're here in this phase of our existence, here in the physical world, for creative love and loving creation—for the loving, giving, creative enhancement of life, and not for its destruction."

"Well, that's what I mean."

"Stay with me for a moment."

"Ok."

"Any action that properly embodies love of the most extensive kind is right. Any action that contravenes the intents and requirements of love is wrong. And love seeks at its core to nurture and protect the innocent. That's the only motive that can ever justify and impel the tragedy of removing someone else from this world, and only under conditions where it's rationally necessary, when there's no available alternative. And we seek to live consistently with this insight in all our dealings with even the most challenging opponents."

"That makes sense," Walid said.

"Yeah, for me, too," Mafulla agreed.

"Good." The king continued. "Now, more could be said on this issue, but let's return for a moment to the core insight of the big picture. We're here in this world of limitations and scarcities and challenges to develop and flourish in community with others. We can do things together that we could not do apart. We become our best selves in loving harmony with others. A focus on individual desire and power, and a choice of violence for the sake of implementing one's own desires, rips asunder the larger fabric of community, and relationships that could otherwise flourish. Homicide is thus wrong for more than one reason, and deeply contrary to the overall intent of our existence. In addition, the suicide of a basically healthy person who is not enduring endless, nearly unbearable bodily pain and suffering that can't possibly ever be alleviated, or who is not soon surely and inevitably about to enter into such pain, is also wrong, and deeply so, for similar reasons. Such acts are completely contrary to the loving intent of our existence here. They are always misguided, and should be avoided as wrong. All our actions should be acts of love. That simple rule should be our highest guide. And our own love should first and foremost seek in all ways to respect the wishes and requirements of the greater love that put us here to live out our natural earthly lives to the best of our abilities."

At this point, the boys were deep in thought, listening and processing what they were hearing. The king then went on to say, "The taking of a life as an act of defense can be a tragic moral imperative when no other way is available for stopping a misguided soul from inflicting severe violence and pain and even death on others. An unnatural death, inflicted on purpose, is always against the natural order of things. But the intent behind the act will be what magnifies or mitigates its damage to the doer of the deed. Taking the life of another human being is always an act with inwardly heavy consequences, and should be avoided if at all possible. But when it's required, it's more than acceptable, or merely permissible. It can be morally demanded and right and yet, paradoxically, because of this, forgivable at the same time."

"I thought that forgiveness only has to do with wrongs," Walid said.

"And with a certain range of grievous necessities," the king explained.

"This is a lot to get your head around," Mafulla responded.

"Yes, that's a primary reason why the great moral traditions have issued simple commands rather than lengthy explanations and rationales. Everyone can do the right thing on most occasions, or at least avoid doing the worst wrong things as a pattern of action. Not everyone in this world may be able to understand exactly why what is right is right, and also why what is wrong is wrong. But in the next world, I believe, it will be completely clear, for all and to all."

"I see," Walid replied.

The king poured himself some more tea and said, "There's another thought that's relevant to our discussion of right and wrong."

"And, Your Majesty, what's that?" Mafulla, as usual, was eager to hear more. He even added, "I'm keen to learn whatever you can share with us today."

"First, would either of you like some tea?"

"No, I'm fine, Your Majesty," Walid said.

"Me, too," Mafulla answered.

"Ok. So I'll continue." The king took another sip from his cup and said, "Throughout history, many men have sought to portray morally neutral things, and also trivial things, and—worse yet—even truly wonderful things as wrong and forbidden, just because of their own need for power and control, or on account of their fears, or due to an inner ambivalence and regrettable uneasiness with their own desires. Unfortunately, sincere people in many religious traditions have been guilty of this, but the truly spiritual souls within these traditions seem to do much better at getting it right. This long and unfortunate practice of overextending the borders of wrong, or sin, or evil has more than one negative effect. It actually undermines true morality, which is always about love and kindness and compassion. True goodness is all about those positive imperatives that improve us all; and any negative prohibitions that are also a part of the picture must be justified by what's positive."

"One more question, please, if it's Ok," Walid said.

"Certainly."

"You just now mentioned the truly spiritual soul. As long as we're being so philosophical: What is it to be a spiritual person, really? What is spirituality? And how does it relate to the good that love seeks to attain?"

"Ah, once again," Mafulla said with a grin, "you display some basic counting problems. Those are three questions, my arithmetically challenged friend. But I point that out, of course, only in the spirit of love and compassionate kindness."

Walid smiled and said, "Ok, three questions. I got carried away, once I was asking. But the real question is simple. What is spirituality?"

"That's easy," the king answered. "Spirituality is all about depth and connectedness."

"What do you mean?"

"The truly spiritual person sees beneath surface appearances and experiences things more deeply. He or she, in addition, brings depth where it's needed. The spiritual person also appreciates connections, and creates positive connections wherever they're needed and should exist—through both understanding the ultimate unity of all things, and creating new forms of unity within this shattered world of surface experience and the messiness of free will."

"So spirituality is about depth and connectedness," Walid said.

"Yes. And above all, the spiritual person seeks deep harmony, an ultimate form of connectedness: harmony within his or her own soul; harmony with other men and women; harmony with the greater realm of nature; and harmony with the source of all that is."

"And what's exactly the relationship of this to goodness?"

"The source of goodness is love. And love is the deepest impulse and action of the spirit. The natural modality of the soul is love. That's its intended way of being, both in its most fundamental existence, and here in the world. And it's precisely love that best discovers depth, endows depth, and forms and enhances connection. Love is the center of all. And when I use the concept of love, I'm not thinking of the many counterfeits and pretenders to the name, but the real thing."

"Boy, I wish Malik and Haji were with us right now to hear your answers," Walid said. "And, of course, Kissa and Hasina."

"Me, too," Mafulla added.

"Well, it's now your job to convey these ideas to them. The student must become a teacher, in order to learn and know at the highest level. We are at our peak as learners when we work to be great teachers."

"Wow, that's deep, too," Mafulla said.

The king smiled. "I'm glad we had the chance to talk of such things. We've all been far too busy lately, and I miss our philosophical talks."

"Well, you are the philosopher-king, for sure," Mafulla said.

"Thank you, Mafulla. But now, switching gears just a bit before we adjourn our meeting together, I have a few things to tell you about our problematic Juan Santiago."

"Something new?" Walid asked.

"Yes, and very interesting indeed."

Not far away, at the El-Noor house, there were wonderful aromas in the air. A door opened and closed.

"Mom? Can we talk for a minute?" Khata had just come in from outside. Her mother was just starting to prepare the family dinner and had a sauce on the stove.

"Of course, honey, come in. Do you mind if I work on dinner a little while we talk, or should I take a break?"

"You can keep working. I'll help."

"Good. Could you chop these vegetables?"

"Sure." Khata came around to the table where her mother was working and, taking a knife in hand, began to cut up the onions and celery stalks that were on a large plate. She had seen the process many times and had helped out often.

"Now, what's on your mind?"

"It's something a little strange," Khata answered.

"That's fine. Strange is my specialty. Tell me all about it," Rama responded with a kind smile. "Oh, and could you hand me that bowl?"

"Sure, mom," Khata replied and, passing her mother the bowl, she said, "It's about Muriel."

"Ok. What about her?"

"It's weird. She acts really nice to me, and she's obviously a great musician, and anyone would be really lucky to have someone like her as a teacher."

"Yes?"

"I don't know. I just felt really strange during the lesson, like something was wrong, something I couldn't identify."

"Well, most people, when they first start lessons in a new skilled activity or art, they feel a bit of what's called performance anxiety, a natural worry about not being good enough. And learning anything new always gets you out of the areas where you're most comfortable. But outside the cocoon of comfort is where we grow."

"Yeah, I understand that."

"Do you think that could be all you felt?"

Khata was quiet for a few seconds and only the sounds of her chopping and Rama's stirring a pot punctuated the otherwise near silence of the room. "I don't think that's it. I just have a strong sense that something's wrong. And I don't know what it is. I feel a crazy need to protect myself, or to be defensive, if that makes any sense, but I don't know against what."

"Have you been feeling like this generally, or just around Muriel?"

"Just around her."

"Has she said anything in particular that could worry you at all?"

"No, nothing I can remember."

"Has she done anything that made you uncomfortable, like when I had to go to the store and leave you two alone?"

"No, not really. It's not something she's said or done, and that's what makes this so strange. It's almost like I'm reacting to something she is, and I can't make a whole lot of sense out of that feeling."

"Really?"

"Yeah. It's like: Is there something going on in her life or in her willingness to teach me that I don't know about, and that's in some way bad, or even a threat? I just don't know and I hate to talk about anyone like that, even the way I'm doing it now with you, and please don't say anything to her about what I'm telling you. It's just because you're my mom and I can tell you whatever I'm feeling, even if I can't make much sense of it."

"Don't worry. I won't breathe a word of what you're telling me," Rama reassured her. She put down the long spoon she was using to stir and looked at her daughter. "You're sure you don't feel this in any other context, around anyone else, but just Muriel?"

"Yeah, I'm sure I haven't felt anything at all like this around anyone else, or in any other situation. It's so different."

"The reason I ask is that, sometimes, girls your age, and even boys, since you're all going through so many changes in your bodies, you can get unusual surges of feelings, emotions, and thoughts that are not familiar. And that will change, too. It's just a stage of growth. But it doesn't sound to me like that's what's going on at all."

"Well, I've never been fourteen before, so I wouldn't know. But I've been pretty much the same normal me in everything else. Well, maybe I've been a little more ready to cry, you know, to tear up at sad things, or to get excited about good things, but nothing at all like this. It's just a weird feeling that something's wrong, and maybe even dangerous in some way."

"I'm glad you're telling me. It may be nothing except an unusual manifestation of your time of life, or it may be your instincts, or an intuition about something. Let me talk to your father about it later, and see if he has any insight that could help us to understand what might be going on."

"Should … should I continue the lessons?"

"Oh. It's that bad?"

"Yeah, I think so."

"We have nearly a week until your next session. Do your practice, all the musical homework you've been assigned, and prepare like you're going to have the next lesson, but we'll talk about this some more and decide what's best. I don't want you to be uncomfortable. Lessons with a master like Muriel—well, it's a very unusual opportunity. But your peace of mind is the most important thing. Let me think more about this and talk to your dad when he gets home."

"Thanks, Mom."

"I'm glad we had this conversation."

"Me, too."

"Now, let's get those veggies finished and into the pot."

16

THE BIG DAY

KHALID STOOD FOR A MOMENT IN SILENCE, GAZING OUT THE window, and said: "To sum up, then, Victor Frankenstein lived by many of the keys to success identified by the great practical philosophers. He was a brilliant and well educated man who had a clear goal, a strong confidence in his ability to attain that goal, and a well focused concentration on what it would take to realize his dream. He showed a stubborn consistency as he worked toward the realization of that dream, and he clearly had an emotional commitment to his vision. But he'd never taken the time to think through the implications of what he was trying to accomplish. 'What will be the consequences of attaining this goal?' He never asked that simple question. Another good one would have been, 'What could go wrong?' And, in addition, as you saw in the book, Mr. Frankenstein acted in many ways contrary to good character in the manner he pursued his goal, and later on, in how he chose to deal with the various implications of its attainment."

Khalid glanced around the class for a second and said, "It's also easy to see that, despite Frankenstein's fixation on what he wanted to create, on the object of what was his driving obsession, he didn't really enjoy the process of working toward his goal. He couldn't take pleasure in it. There were many things he had to do in its pursuit that he found distasteful and even repulsive. And that alone should have given him pause. But he continued to rush headlong into what would turn out to be a disaster. And when it happened, he handled the process of dealing with it terribly. He ran from his own mistakes, and so compounded the problems. The result was that he created and released into the world a monster he couldn't control. And that's why this little book by Mary Shelley is one of literature's great cautionary tales about what aspirations we should nurture and what goals we should pursue. It's a good warning about how not to live."

The boys were listening closely. A couple of them nodded their heads in understanding. "Well, then," Khalid concluded, "I think that's enough for today."

His students all looked surprised. Jabari said, "Really?"

Their teacher smiled and went on: "We're going to be ending class a bit early, in plenty of time for the special event that will be starting in just a little while." He looked at his watch and said, "Hoda will be doing the same thing about now for the girls' class as well. It's King Ali's birthday, of course, and as you know, we're all invited to the party. I appreciate that some of you are even planning to help with the festivities. So I wanted you to have a little extra time to get over to where the celebration's going to take place, out behind the palace on the grounds near where the king's cars and ceremonial horses are kept." With various expressions of enthusiasm and gladness, the boys started picking up their things and getting ready to leave.

But then Khalid added, "Let's just make sure that we don't get so caught up in all the guy stuff with the sports being offered that the girls feel left out. In all ways, be considerate of the other guests and don't let your competitive spirit get out of control. As your teacher, it's my duty to remind you that your first job is to be a gentleman and a suitable representative of the palace, where it's my pleasure also to represent our joint enterprise of education and character. Today, like always, I'm sure that you'll make me proud. Unlike Frankenstein, remember: Character first, and then a capacity to enjoy the process. Now, go get ready to have some fun, and I'll see you down there."

Almost all the boys at once started talking to each other as they finished gathering up their books and papers, and some began to walk toward the door. "Thanks, Khalid," were words heard from a number of them as they made their way across the room. "See you down there" also echoed throughout the noisy group.

Walid and Mafulla were walking by his desk and Khalid said, "Walid, could you stick around for a couple of minutes? You can meet Mafulla in less than five."

"Sure, no problem," Walid said.

"I'll wait for you out in the hall," Mafulla suggested.

Walid replied, "Why don't you instead go on down to Hoda's and let Kissa know I'll be there in a couple of minutes?"

"Sure. Good idea. See you down there."

As Mafulla then walked out with Bafur and Set, Walid said to his teacher, "What's up?"

Khalid responded by digging down into his old, beat up briefcase and rummaging around for a minute. He pulled out several pieces of paper and handed them to the prince and said, "Look over the first page here and tell me what you think."

"Oh, Ok," Walid responded. He stood at the desk and began to read the document as the last of the boys left the room. Malik looked back and called out, "See you soon!" Walid looked up and waved to him and then continued to read.

Ten or fifteen seconds passed. Without taking his eyes off the page, he said, "This sounds pretty amazing."

"That's because it is."

"So, this scholarship allows a few of us from our part of the world to go to Oxford University in England, all expenses paid," Walid said.

"Yes, and from other parts of the world, as well. But, in the case of wealthy families, or royalty, the main point isn't the money, but the intellectual prestige that attaches to the scholarship, and the doors that will open wide for a student because of it. When you arrive as a representative of this program, you get the best tutors, the most advanced circle of friends, and really the most incredible boost to your own hopes and ambitions. You'll meet the people who'll be running other countries around the world one day and leading the businesses that cross national borders. You'll get to know students who in later years will be among the very top in their fields, whatever those areas might be, and all around the globe."

"That sounds great," Walid said. "Is this how you got to Oxford, in your own time?"

"It is. I came from a fairly humble background. But I did very well in school and then, because of this scholarship, at Oxford. And so, as a result, I'm on a committee to help select, every few years, who will be representing our part of the world on the scholarship, and so, who's going to be having this great educational experience."

"Wow, that's a lot of responsibility."

"It is. And that's why I'm showing this to you."

"What do you mean?"

"I'd like to offer you the opportunity of being the person, two years from now, who goes on this great adventure, matriculating at Oxford, spending at least a couple of years in the libraries of rainy old England, and then finally coming back to help run the kingdom with that sort of an education, with those experiences, and those connections around the world, in your personal repertoire."

"Me?"

"Yes, you."

"But, what about the duties I've already assumed for the king?"

"I'm sure arrangements can be made. Oxford is a unique institution. Your time there will benefit the kingdom for the rest of your life."

"What about all my friends?"

"You can come back to visit during the long academic breaks. The palace can afford the travel. And there are several times throughout the year when that would be possible. Sometimes, though, you might want to go off with another prince or member of a governing family to stay with them and see what politics and life are like in their nations. Some may invite you to go skiing in Switzerland or boating off the coast of Italy or Greece. There are wealthy French citizens attending Oxford who could have you as a guest at some of the most beautiful beaches in the world. You'd be able to enjoy experiences that most people can only dream of. Plus, you'd be training yourself for a rich and full life of the mind, as well as for great service to the people of our kingdom."

"Oh, man. This is a lot to think about."

"Yes, it is."

"But what about, I mean, there are some other things."

Khalid said, "Hoda came to Oxford with me."

"Really?"

"Yes, she did. Think about it. Talk it over with the king and Mafulla and, of course, with … anyone else you'd need to speak to about it."

"How long would I have to make a decision?"

"By the end of the academic year would be great. Sooner would be even better. But there's no rush."

"Oh, Ok. That's a good amount of time."

"I really think you're the man for the challenge."

"I'm honored, Khalid. I really am. I had no idea about all this."

"It changed my life. It lifted me to a whole new level of experience. It also got me to Yale for graduate school. It gave me some of the best friends of my life. It made me realize that I am, as the philosopher Diogenes once said, a citizen of the world. And, most of all, it provided me with a sense of nearly endless possibilities for my life. Plus, it played a role in getting me the position I have here at the palace."

"So, why did you decide to come and teach us, of all things? I mean, those beaches in France could have snagged you, right? Or you could have stayed in America, where so many people go for the opportunities. And yet, here you are."

Khalid smiled. "I love Egypt. It's a distinctive land. It's an important place in the human adventure. And I know what the king has in mind for our society. I wanted to have the chance to educate the future leaders of our nation at your age, when I can make a big difference. By being here and doing what I do every day, I'm helping already in the eventual transition we'll make, one day, to a full and robust democracy, which I know you and the king both want. Also, I have the time to think about things that really matter and write articles that are read all over the world by people in my field. And I'm at work on a book that I think could make a major contribution. But you students are the most fun and important piece of the puzzle to me."

"That's pretty incredible, and at the same time, it makes a lot of sense."

"Yes. There are certainly days when I think, you know, I could be skiing in the Alps right now, or lounging on a yacht in the clear blue waters of the Mediterranean, or holding a seminar at Harvard or Cambridge, or back in New Haven at Yale, or on a beautiful campus I've heard about in a place called Chapel Hill. But then it always comes to me that I'm doing exactly what I want to do, where I want to do it, and with the students I most want to have. Hoda can be with Kissa during the school day, and I can be with you and Mafulla, which, of course, isn't exactly the same thing, but it's interesting, to say the least. The result of it all is that, unlike poor Frankenstein and his immensely wretched creature, I'm a very happy man."

"That's so cool," Walid said.

"And the scholarship to Oxford is primarily what made it possible for me to choose my own destiny, thenceforth, and carve out the life that I want to live. So, think hard on this issue, and about this opportunity."

"I will."

"No pressure, I promise. Whatever you decide will be fine. And I mean that. Each of us has our own path. But just think about it."

"I will, seriously."

"Good. Now, go join your friends. I'll be there soon."

"Thanks again."

Walid walked down the hall with his head filled full of thoughts about Oxford University and its great past, and all the amazing people he could meet there. And then, within about thirty seconds, he saw some of the very best people he had met here—Mafulla, Hasina, and, of course, Kissa—standing together and talking.

"Whoa! You girls look great!" Walid said, as he approached.

"What about me?" Mafulla protested, and was promptly ignored.

Kissa smiled and responded, "Madame Alexander's finest!" Hasina did a fashion twirl as Kissa asked, "You like the new looks?"

"Oh, yeah," Walid replied. "You're both stunning today, pretty for the party to the max: sporty, yet elegant; current, yet classic."

"Yeah, I was just telling them how good they both look, once I could speak again," Mafulla said.

"You're so sweet," Hasina said, and patted him softly on the arm.

Mafulla grinned at her and then turned back to his friend. "What took you so long? I've had all this beauty to myself! It's far too much!"

"Oh, nothing to report," Walid answered. "Just some stuff Khalid wanted to talk about involving some academic possibilities and opportunities for study in the future. Nothing urgent in the present."

"Oh, Ok. So, I was just telling the extra lovely Hasina and Kissa about all the stuff we've got planned for this afternoon. And I think they're getting really excited about seeing our bocce ball skills, and maybe even our yet-to-be-tapped but almost inevitable badminton prowess."

"Ha!" Hasina laughed and said, "We'll see about that! I think the two of us should challenge you boys to a badminton match. You might be surprised."

"Ooooo," Mafulla said. "Somebody must be ready to achieve new levels of personal humility."

"Yeah, and he's Walid's best friend," Hasina said.

"Nice one, Hassi," Kissa commented.

"Yeah, impressive," Walid added. He turned to the confident man and said, "If I were you, I wouldn't provoke either of the ladies about their athletic prowess. You might be sorry."

"That's why you're the prince," Hasina said to Walid. "Wisely thought and well stated."

"Oh, yeah?" Mafulla said, going into a modified version of his muscle man pose. "Wait till you see this magnificent, well tuned physique in action today. Any opponents will beg for mercy."

"I'm almost ready to beg for quiet," Hasina replied, with no expression on her face.

"Ha! Another good one!" Kissa said with a smile. Then she added, "Why don't we go down to the party now? That is, Mafulla, if you can manage to drag all those heavy muscles the entire way."

"Hardee-Har, Har," he replied.

"Don't worry. He has other strong ones, auxiliary muscles, to carry the specially heavy ones, so there's no cause for concern," Walid explained, adding, "But you can never be sure, so maybe we should go down together, in case he needs help on the stairs, you know, if one of the truly massive muscles was to throw him off balance."

"Keep it up," Mafulla said.

"We're messing with you because we love you," Hasina reassured him, and that made the muscle man blush just a bit as he turned to Walid and did his double eyebrow jump.

"Yeah, well," Walid said. "I'm messing with you because you're a mess."

The prince and Kissa then led the way to the stairs and down to the first floor. Kissa wanted to know how Ben was doing since the kidnapping incident. Walid gave her a full report. He seemed fine. Kids can be incredibly resilient. They can bounce back from almost anything. It seems to be nature's way, a blessing to the young in a rough and tumble world. And Walid reminded her that Ben used to live mostly on the streets with some pretty tough characters, so those guys who took him were nothing he hadn't seen before. But

Leem also had a friend, a psychologist, who had begun talking with Ben to make sure he could process the experience in a healthy way. Ahira, on the other hand, still seemed a little shook up. The psychologist was going to help him, too. And already, Ibrahim and Leem were doing all they could to help ease his nerves about the whole thing, and were assuring him that guys like that don't tend to try the same thing twice. It didn't work once, so they simply assume it wouldn't work again. And they make other plans for their criminal mischief.

Ibrahim, in particular, was doing his best to convince Ahira that he had already experienced his big lifetime brush with danger, and that it was all most likely to be completely behind him now. He emphasized that the kidnappers had no particular reason to go after him at all. He had just been in the wrong place at the wrong time. And he reassured his friend that there would be some palace security now watching the school and the apartment and even keeping an eye on Ahira's place until this was over. He'd actually now be the safest he had ever been. And all of what Ibrahim was saying did seem to have some positive effect. Ahira had calmed down a lot since the day of their discovery and rescue. And the two of them were hanging out after work even more than usual. So, having been filled in on all these details, Walid was confident that Ahira would soon be back to normal like Ben.

Kissa and Hasina both said they were glad to hear all this. They had been talking about what the emotional toll of an experience like that could be for boys like Ben and even Ahira who weren't trained in what to do and how to handle such difficult situations. It was good that a psychologist was helping them with their feelings in the aftermath of what they had gone through.

Kissa then brought up another subject that had been on her mind recently. She said, "Something just came to mind. Have you guys heard about Khata's new piano and the lessons she's getting?"

"Yeah," Mafulla answered right away. "My aunt Muriel's moved to town from Alexandria, and mom's so excited about it, and she's Khata's new piano teacher."

"Is this the aunt who lived in Alexandria for so long?" Walid asked.

"Yep, that's her. And now she and her husband had to move to town for some sort of business reason, I think, and she's going to be getting involved in the local music community. But her first job here is to teach Khata music theory and piano performance."

"Wow, she's sort of famous, isn't she?" Hasina asked. "I've heard my mom mention her."

"Yeah, she's pretty well known in music circles, and throughout Alexandria. She's even performed in a lot of other countries. She's got major talent," Mafulla answered. And then he added, "We haven't seen her much over the years. I think it's made mom a little sad. So now maybe we'll have lots of family time to get to know her and her husband better."

"Good," Kissa said. "Maybe also we can get Khata to play us something soon!"

By that time, they were going out the back entrance of the palace and down the wide exterior stairs. "Wow, check it out over there!" Mafulla said. "It looks like everything's ready for the party." At a distance, they could all see several tables beautifully set up for a buffet that was going to be served later on in the afternoon. There were lots of colorful decorations everywhere. It was quite a festive sight. Back to the side of the royal garages, in the big open field, there were two badminton nets in place, with courts laid out, side by side, for the upcoming games. There were also two areas for bocce ball, and plenty of room for other things. A variety of athletic equipment could be seen off to the side in one part of the field. There must have been twenty men and women hurrying around, finishing various aspects of the party set-up and making final preparations for the guests who would be arriving soon.

Just as they were almost halfway to the party area, they heard a loud whistle and turned around. "Hey, Prince! Hi everybody!" It was Jabari, followed by Set and Bafur.

"Hey, guys!" Walid called back and held up to wait for them. "Jabari! You've got the uke!"

"Yeah, I brought it in this morning and stored it. Royal birthdays always call for the best in creative musical entertainment."

Mafulla said, "Well, now we know this is going to be a truly top-notch party. What are you going to play?"

"I'm starting off with some original material, then moving into a few old favorites, to get everybody in tune and inspired before the Happy Birthday song."

"Everybody?" Walid smiled and patted Set on the back as he said this.

"Ok, Ok, I'm not the best singer," Set admitted. "But I'll try to rise to the occasion, or the proper key, as the case may be."

"What have you been up to, lately, man?" Walid asked Set.

"A lot of reading," he replied.

"About?"

"Well, you know, since we were doing *Frankenstein* in class, I decided to add a little background research into philosophical ideas that might shed some light on the main themes of the book."

"Really?" Mafulla said. "Extra reading?"

"Yeah."

"For extra credit?"

"No, just for the extra understanding it might provide."

"Jeepers. That's very impressive, young man," Mafulla commented. "Keep it up. If we could just get more of the guys to be like you and put in those extra hours in the library, then I'd have all the playing fields of the palace to myself, and I could practice my distinctive athletic moves all afternoon long, day after day."

"And then you'd likely be at the bottom of the class, rather than near the top," Walid said.

"Yeah. Good point," Mafulla conceded. "A strong body and a strong mind, that's the goal. Balance is key."

"I do try to get in some exercise every day," Set said, "but I have to admit that I log more library hours than the average guy."

"Which is one of the reasons you're far above average," Walid said.

"I just hope one day I can do the stuff that I'm doing now, but in a university with great resources," Set said, almost wistfully.

"Sure. Why not? You sound like you're not sure," Walid responded.

"Well, my dad's income will pay for college here in Cairo, but I'm not sure how much philosophy they have available right now."

"You're pretty much Mr. Do-It-Yourself, anyway," Mafulla said.

"That's true. I'm sure I can find a way to pursue and practice the love of wisdom, wherever I might be."

"But, right now, Mr. Philosopher, you're at the location for a party, so find a way to have some fun," Kissa said to him.

"I play, therefore I am," Set said.

"Nice! Good play on the master play-maker, Descartes," Mafulla said and added, "The pronunciation of his name, you know, 'day-cart,' always makes me wonder if there's such a thing as a night-cart."

"A what?" Hasina said.

"A night-cart, a carriage in which to sleep and, perchance, to dream."

"Like Descartes, with a little Hamlet stirred in, " Set said. "You're historical."

"Ha! Very good! I thank you," Mafulla replied.

"Why was a mention of dreaming like Descartes?" Kissa asked.

Set explained, "He wondered how he could prove that he wasn't dreaming all the time, and that we weren't all likewise in slumber, mistaken that we were awake, but life's really all a dream."

"Oh! Maybe I've heard dad talk about that," Kissa replied.

Bafur then said, "I dream of food all the time. And otherwise, all I think about is 'I eat therefore I am … always full, and yet still strangely hungry.' So when do we start?" In response, everyone laughed.

"Soon enough, they'll have out some snacks, on a day-cart, or more likely a day-table, I think," Walid answered. "But then, after we do games and stuff, they're planning a great buffet dinner."

"Yeah, I could smell the aromas from the kitchen throughout the palace on my way down here." Bafur sniffed the air and turned his head as soon as he had said this.

"You're like a hunting dog with your nose," Jabari commented.

"Yeah, except it's not short, round, inky black, and wet—fortunately," Bafur replied.

"Awww, I think you'd look cute with a little doggie nose," Hasina said, adding, "I'd pat you on the head and give you a treat."

"Well then, Woof! Woof!" Bafur said, and held out his hands like begging paws, while shaking his whole body in imitation of an over enthusiastic, wagging dog.

"Down boy!" Mafulla laughed. "There will be no head patting or treat giving on my watch."

"Speaking of your watch," Jabari said, "what time is it?"

"Almost time for the party to start, going on 1:55 here in the PM."

"Hey, there come the girls," Kissa said, looking over Walid's shoulder.

'Wait, that's ... my aunt Muriel, walking beside Khata," Mafulla said. "I wonder what she's doing here today, coming to the king's birthday party? She ... doesn't even know the king ... I'm pretty sure."

"Huh," Walid said. "Well, she's certainly welcome. Any relative of yours, I'm always at least relatively happy to see."

"Not bad." Mafulla grinned and lightly punched his friend in the arm.

The boys hadn't noticed it yet, but a grand piano had been placed in an open bay of the royal garage, in a space closest to where the festivities would be taking place and only about fifty feet from the buffet tables. Khata's mother, Rama, had spoken with Shamilar, and through her help, Bhati had arranged for Muriel to be invited to play some background music for the occasion. The Alexandrian was thrilled. She believed that this was the best thing that could possibly happen at this point, for her, the mission she was on, and her master. She was now so close to gaining the access and information that would be important for her to obtain.

17

BIRTHDAY WISHES

CABLES AND TELEGRAMS AND NOTES OF VARIOUS KINDS with positive birthday wishes for the king had been arriving all day. There were messages left by telephone as well. Bancom had brought in some of them, and others had been carried up from the communications center by several of his assistants. There were big bags of well wishes from citizens throughout the kingdom, as well as personal greetings and celebratory cards from around the world. Kular received and sorted them, and periodically took them in to the king's sitting room and placed them on the large desk there, organizing them into categorized stacks—some from heads of state, others from top diplomats, leaders of international companies, and old friends and admirers from many nations. You would never guess from the sheer volume of mail, or from the postmarks and return addresses on so many of these missives, that the intended recipient was a man who for decades, and until relatively recently, had lived in a small house in a little village on the edge of the desert in a remote part of Egypt.

This outpouring of affection and good will was an eloquent testimony to the man and to the mission that he had so faithfully embraced throughout his life. It was also a powerful manifestation of how one person with a vision can make a huge difference. The work of many years, seemingly with only small effects along the way, can come to a spectacular culmination that changes everything. But such a result is typically possible only for the patient and persistent individual who will continue to do the right things day after day with a calm faith that those efforts can eventually pay off well, and far beyond the apparent impact of the little daily endeavors that quietly added up.

The additive arithmetic of positive value is always astonishing, however often you've seen its operation and summation. There's even a mysterious multiplication effect underway in any enterprise of goodness, kindness, and justice. But precisely the opposite plays out for those with contrary motives and intentions, despite any temporary surface appearances to the contrary. The king was right. The fabric of reality supports a noble quest, however difficult it might be, and brings ignoble adventures to an inevitably unproductive end. The explicit aims of those who pursue evil most typically fade from view like a desert mirage. The efforts of the good bring lasting results.

With the changing of the guard at the front palace gate, a lone officer, now relieved of duty for the day, walked into the palace with an envelope in his hand. He headed straight for the guard offices and gathering room. Seeing the man he was looking for, he said, "Naqid, I have something for you from the front gate."

"What do you have?" Naqid replied, as he turned toward the man.

"A messenger left this with me ten minutes ago," he said, and handed Naqid the envelope.

"Thank you."

"You're welcome," the soldier said and turned to walk off.

"Oh, Iban," Naqid called out after him.

"Yes, sir," the man replied, turning around and stopping where he was.

"If you'd like, you might enjoy coming by the king's party this afternoon, out back, behind the palace."

"Thanks, that would be great, but I'm not on duty for the rest of the day," the man replied.

"No, no, not as a guard, not as part of your duty, but as a guest, an honored guest."

"Really?"

"Yes, I've invited a couple of the other men also, who, like you, have served the king especially well. They'll be off duty, also. I just thought the three of you might find it a fun and relaxing time."

"I'm … I'm truly honored, Naqid. I don't know what to say."

"I hope you can make it for at least part of the time."

"Yes, definitely," the man replied with a big smile. "Thank you so much."

"It's my pleasure. See you down there."

"Are you … Are you sure it's Ok with the king?"

"Yes! He'll be very happy to see you there. Plus, there will be some great food waiting for you."

The soldier laughed, saluted his boss, and then turned and walked down to the main break room for a change of clothing in the locker area, off from the back. He felt a special sense of being appreciated as he made his way toward the rest of this great day.

Naqid looked at the envelope. It was addressed to "Mr. Naqid Bustani, Director of Palace Security," and it was marked 'Urgent.' He turned it over. There was no return address. He opened one end of it. There seemed to be another envelope inside, of nicer, heavy ecru stationary. This one was addressed, in beautiful, elaborate calligraphy: "To King Ali Shabeezar, The Soon-To-Be-Late Monarch of Egypt." Naqid turned it over. There was something written where a return address would normally be found. It simply said, on three lines: "Juan Osvaldo Santiago, Almost Everywhere, Cairo, Egypt."

Naqid now felt that it was his job to open this envelope as well, and carefully. He first took it into his office and called on one of his top guards to come and stand at the door. He placed the envelope onto the desk in the middle of the room and sat in a chair beside it. Cautiously, he used a linen handkerchief to hold the envelope, and a letter opener to slit it open across the top. He then squeezed it gently to open it up so that he could look down into it. There seemed to be nothing inside except a letter on matching paper. He then pulled it out and unfolded it. He thought to himself, "Good. No spiders."

The paper had written on it, in black ink, and in a fancy though not calligraphic script, the words: "Happy Birthday, King Shabeezar! May you enjoy this, your last one. And, please savor every remaining minute of your life on earth as well. There are fewer of them than you might think. Signed—Best Wishes, Your Final Adversary and Expert Guide to the Next World, Juan Osvaldo Santiago."

Naqid stared at the message for no more than five seconds and then walked over to his associate, saying, "Go find Masoon or Hamid as soon as possible and say that I need a conversation immediately. There's a new threat against the king. I'll simultaneously go to Bancom and see if he can contact either of them by radio or phone. Also, I need as many extra guards as we can have posted around the party area, and within minutes."

"Yes, sir," the guard said and began to walk away.

"Oh, one more thing," Naqid said. The man stopped and turned around. "As many of the extra men as possible should change into gardening and maintenance clothing, if the outfits are easily available, but all should be fully armed. If there are no such uniforms around, have them put on their normal street clothes."

Across town, Shapur and Shamilar Adi were at home, dressing for the garden party. Sammi and Sasha were at a neighbor's house. She was a kind older woman who had volunteered to get the little ones ready for the king's birthday celebration while their parents dressed and wrapped Ali's small present at home. Shapur would retrieve the children when they were ready to go. They also expected Reela any minute. And the palace was sending a car for them all shortly. They had turned the shop over to their most trusted employee for the afternoon, and they were both eagerly looking forward to the big birthday bash.

"It was such a good idea to make it an outside event today," Shamilar said as she looked into the mirror and fussed with her hair. "It's a nice temperature and not at all windy. The kids will enjoy themselves so much more than they would have in a stuffy, formal indoor party."

"It should be a lot of fun," Shapur said from the other room.

"Yes, indeed. I know our little ones will love seeing their brother."

Shapur had just sat down. He was silent for a second and then added, "I was looking forward to some bocce ball and badminton this afternoon, but … I'm not feeling all that well since we've been home. The dizziness and exhaustion … are starting to come back."

"Oh, my. Are you all right?" Shamilar appeared in the doorway.

"Maybe I just need to lie down for a few minutes until the car arrives. That's always helped in the past. For the last few days, I've felt much better, but it's hit me pretty hard since we arrived back home from the shop. Actually, it's gotten bad in just the last few minutes."

"How exactly do you feel?"

"I'm a bit nauseous, and my head is starting to feel a little woozy."

Shamilar walked over to the chair and said, "Dear man, let me help you into the bedroom and get you more comfortable. You do need to lie down. You should rest. We don't have to go at all. We can stay home and send our apologies and the king's gift later."

She reached for his arm, and he stood slowly and said, right away, "No, no, no. You should go. I wouldn't want you to miss this for anything. You and Reela can represent the family, along with Mafulla, if I need to stay here. The children can go with you or will be fine staying with Izira while you're gone. I'm sure I just need to take a break and relax for a while."

"You're sweet, but I wouldn't think of leaving you here alone, feeling so bad," Shamilar said, as she walked him into the bedroom. "Now, lie down and take it easy."

"Ok."

She sat and felt his forehead. "You seem to have a bit of a fever. Your arm felt warm and now your head seems even warmer."

"I'm sure it's just the exhaustion. You know how I am sometimes when I'm overly tired. And it's been a busy morning."

"I know. But you feel almost hot to the touch."

"Yes. It suddenly seems stuffy in here."

"Let me get you some water and a cool cloth." Shapur nodded slightly and closed his eyes. Shamilar watched him for a few seconds more and then stood up to fetch the water and cloth. But as soon as she got to the kitchen, there was a fairly loud knocking at the front door.

"Reela? Is that you? Come in," she called out toward the front. When there was no answer, she put down the bath cloth she had in her hand and walked to the door. Opening it, she saw no one. She stepped out a few feet. "Reela?" A strong gust of wind surprised her and she shielded her eyes from the burst of blinding sand that stung her skin. In a few seconds, when the sudden wind had subsided, she walked around to the corner and looked along the side of the house. But she saw nothing there. "Reela?" At that instant, she had a very strange feeling. And then, behind her, she heard a noise and jumped, from being startled. "Oh!"

"Sorry, Shamilar!" Reela said.

"Oh my goodness! You nearly scared me to death!"

"I'm so sorry! I didn't mean to frighten you. I thought I saw someone at the back of the house when I first arrived and knocked. I went around to check and walked the whole perimeter, but I wasn't able to find anyone or anything unusual. It was almost like I caught a glimpse of a fast moving shadow. But it was hard to see anything at all for a moment in that blast of wind that came out of nowhere."

"Yes. It blinded me completely for a second with badly stinging sand. I'm sorry to be so jumpy," Shamilar said.

"No, please, don't feel sorry in the least for any anxiety you may be experiencing. There's good reason. We should all be extra cautious in our daily lives. There are some wicked people in town right now, and they have an unfortunate interest in anyone who's linked in any way to the palace."

"Is Mafulla all right?" she asked.

"Yes, he's completely fine," Reela assured her. "And he's in the strongly protective environment of the palace. He couldn't be safer. I'm more concerned for you and Shapur."

"He's not feeling well, I'm afraid," she responded.

"Why? What's wrong?"

"He had a fever a few minutes ago and complained of nausea and lightheadedness—dizziness, he said."

"Where is he now?"

"I took him to the bed and went into the kitchen to get him some cool water and a cold cloth, and that's when I heard your knock."

"Let's go inside. You get the water and cloth and I'll look in on him, first thing."

They went through the door and Shamilar headed straight for the kitchen. Reela walked toward the back bedroom. Not more than ten seconds passed, and maybe less, when she heard his voice, with a tone of true urgency. "Shamilar! Come here quickly!"

"What is it?" She hurried at a fast pace toward the bedroom, and as she entered the door, Reela looked up at her from a seated position on the side of the bed.

"He's unresponsive," Reela said, with both shock and concern.

"What do you mean?"

"I can't get a response to anything I say or do. I've shaken him softly and held his face, but he won't wake up."

Shamilar looked stricken, and put her hands to her mouth and said, "Is he?"

"He's breathing, but it's very shallow. He's unconscious. He may be in a light coma of some sort."

"Oh, no. What can we do?"

"When's the palace car coming?"

"Any minute now."

"Get ready then. We're going to take him straight to the new university hospital, the big one nearby."

"Do you think he'll be all right?"

"I don't know. I hope so. I have no idea what the problem is. It's very strange. Has he come into contact with any unusual substance or sick person in the past few days, or had anything different to eat?"

"No, not at all. There's nothing out of the ordinary that's happened recently, since at least the time that strange Osvaldo man spoke with him and he came down right afterwards with symptoms similar to what he was reporting earlier, the same exhaustion, nausea, and dizziness. But he hasn't experienced anything nearly this severe. And he was better, almost totally normal for the past few days. I wish that awful man had never come to our shop!"

"I wish I could have found him by now and learned what he did to Shapur. I wonder."

"What?"

"Nothing."

"My poor, sweet husband," Shamilar said, and stroked his head.

"He's in some trouble right now, apparently," Reela commented. "But if we can get him to the hospital quickly, there's surely something they can do to treat him and stabilize him."

"Wait. I think I hear another knock at the door," Shamilar said.

"The palace driver?"

"Yes, it must be the driver of our car. I'll run to get him. You can stay with Shapur."

Upstairs in the palace, Hoda was in her classroom, putting together some materials for the next day's class. She was about to leave and walk down the hall to get Khalid and go out to the party. But first, something sparked her attention. She abruptly looked up from the papers in front of her and scanned the room, and then glanced out the window across from her. She stood up quickly and walked over to the window and peered out. Nothing. But a troubling sensation rose up in her soul. Something was happening. That's all she knew. Something was on the move. She took a deep, cleansing breath and made herself relax. But underneath that effective action, there was a crystalline focus that had been ignited in her heart. She walked out the door and down the hall, leaving her paperwork as it was on the desk. Entering Khalid's classroom, where he was sitting and reading a thick book, she said, "We need to go."

He was pondering something, and was deep into a line of thought the book's author was presenting. Hoda's voice came to him as from a great distance. He looked up and said, "What was that?"

"Sorry, dear. We need to go down now."

"Is it time already?"

"Not quite, by the official schedule, but I just had a strange sensation that somewhere in town, somewhere nearby, something important has happened, or is happening, and as a result, I'm on alert, and I feel like we need to be with the children."

"What do you mean? Is something bad going on?"

"I don't know what it is, but yes, something has happened to someone we care about. I'm not clear on it yet, but I feel like I'm on high alert, or, at least, an unusual level of focused concentration for a problem or a challenge that's not right in front of me."

Khalid stood up and said, "That sounds pretty serious."

"I wish I knew what it is," Hoda replied and let out a deep breath. "But it's not immediate family. I do sense that."

"Ok, that's good. So, I guess I'm ready," Khalid said, as he put a bookmark in the text he had been reading, and set it on top of his desk. "Let's go down."

"Thank you."

"But, you know, if anything truly scary happens here this afternoon, I'm depending on you and Kissa and all your superhero friends." Khalid managed a weak smile, and in response, so did Hoda.

"Yes," she said, simply.

"I mean, I can engage any adversary with superior reasoning—make no mistake about that—and I'm decently fit, but when certain things happen, I have to yield to my betters, at least in these matters, as well as perhaps, I must admit, several other domains."

"I can't imagine that anything will take place here. There are far too many of us around. With this sort of concentration of Phi, there's something like a shield, almost like a force field. But, then again, you never know. I'm sure our little girl will gladly join me in dropkicking any villain across the Nile who even thinks about bothering you."

"I appreciate that. But, remember, if Aristotelian logic will get the job done, or a stab of Kierkegaardian wit, or even a caustic tone of mere Oxonian disdain, the two of you can simply stand aside and watch the fireworks."

She actually laughed. "Oxonian disdain. You sound more and more like Mafulla. But it's very reassuring, what you have in your vast philosophic arsenal. I'd much prefer that sort of display, that variety of fireworks, in case any kind at all might be needed. Now, let's go."

In his small apartment not very far from the palace, Leem Hadad was sitting on the sofa in the front room. Young Ben came through the inner doorway and said, "Shouldn't we get going? We don't want to be late for the party!"

"Ibrahim will be here any minute."

"I wish he'd hurry," Ben said.

"We'll get there in plenty of time," Leem assured the boy with a smile. And at very moment, as if summoned, Ibrahim came quickly through the outer front door.

"Great! We can go!" Ben shouted.

"Yes! And, hello to you, too! I'm well, thank you. I hope you are. But, just a second," Ibrahim joked in reply. "There's something I have to tell Uncle Leem."

"Awww."

"I'll be quick. It'll just take a minute."

"What is it, my boy?" Leem asked.

"I found the musicians!"

"You did?"

"Yes!"

"Where are they?"

"In a flat near the university."

"How did you track them down?"

"It's kind of a long and complicated story that Ben will not want me telling right now, but some leads panned out. They've been hunkered down in that apartment most of the time since they disappeared from the Foxtrot Club where they were playing."

"Was it near where they were living when they disappeared?"

"No, that's the strange part. They were a couple of miles away in a real dump of a place. But, apparently, the day they were overheard talking about Santiago, they moved into the new place that none of the other guys in the band had heard about. Some of their musician buddies tried to find them at the old location and were told simply that they'd disappeared. The landlord didn't know where they had gone. And now, what I discovered is that they had moved into this much nicer place—still small, but in a high-end, elegant building, in a place they could never afford on what they make performing."

"Oh, is that so?"

"Yes, and I'm confident that we can find them there and question them about Santiago's location."

"You have no reason to think they're going anywhere any time soon?"

"No. I talked to a neighbor. He said they rarely go out and have few visitors. And there's no indication that they have a clue I've found their new place. I think we can take our time, go to the party, enjoy ourselves, and visit there tomorrow, preferably with some backup."

"Uncle Leem, can we all go to the party now?" Ben asked, sheepishly.

"Yes. Yes, certainly. We can go now," Leem replied with a smile.

"All right!" The boy exclaimed.

Turning to Ibrahim, Leem said, "Do you need to change first, or freshen up?"

"No, I'm ready!"

"Yay! Then, let's go." Ben actually started bouncing up and down.

Leem stood up and said, "Ok, but something feels strange to me and I have no idea why. I wish I knew what it is that's suddenly bothering me. It's odd. But I suppose it's nothing."

"Are you sure?" Ibrahim said, with a look of concern.

"No," Leem replied, thoughtfully. "Actually, I'm not sure at all.

But I have no idea what it is. Maybe it's nothing more than some old leftover hummus I had for lunch. It tasted Ok. But I should have tossed it out. Let's not worry about it right now. Let's just be off!"

"Good!" Ben said. "Let's go!"

They had no idea that they were less than five seconds from coming across a clear manifestation of what was troubling Leem, and it had nothing to do with old hummus.

18

THE PARTY

NAQID QUICKLY SAW THE KING IN HIS OFFICE. THEY TALKED for no more than four or five minutes. Ali was curious, but didn't seem much concerned about the news. The letter was just another piece of the puzzle that was developing. Still, the head of palace guards had the king's full approval for extra security to be placed around the party. There would also be special escorts for the young people present and a few of the other guests when they were ready to leave the festivities later on and return to their homes.

Masoon was scheduled to arrive any minute now to walk with the king and Kular down to the party. Bancom had contacted him by radio and briefed him about the note left at the gate. On the one hand, this new note could be just another example of distracting bluster, part of a mere game simply meant to get into people's heads. On the other hand, it could signal something serious, some form of imminent danger. Masoon knew he had to be prepared for either alternative.

Out on the grounds, the crowd had grown. Darwishi, the king's head chauffeur and director of the royal motor pool, was absolutely delighted to have been put in charge of the games. He began the afternoon's activities by asking Walid and Mafulla where they would like to start, and at the same time, both said: "Badminton!"

Handing them the rackets and the birdie, Dar briefly went over how the game is played and scored. The boys then asked if Kissa and Hasina could also join them—if doubles would be allowed—and he fetched two more rackets right away for the ladies. Just as they took up their positions on both sides of the net, a game of bocce ball started up nearby with Malik and Haji against Bafur and Jabari, and some of the girls set up a bocce competition of their own nearby on a second court.

There were several younger palace kids running around and rolling painted metal wagon hoops in front of them, a game of "rolo wheels," they called it, and a few older brothers and sisters were playing a card game of some sort at two tables that had been set up for that purpose in the shade. Another palace driver was helping a few youngsters to get kites up into the air, thanks to a gentle breeze that was perfect for the activity. And already, a large group of men had gathered around the two sets of horseshoe pits that had been prepared for this popular contest of accuracy in throwing, or "pitching," as it was often called.

The children of many palace workers had come with their parents for the party, and there was quite a buzz of activity, conversation, and laughter all around, along with shouts of victory or defeat and friendly taunts that could be heard from the different playing fields. A pickup soccer game, or as they called it, football, was also going on. And over to one side, at the far end of the large field, there was even an archery setup where a few administrators and several palace guards were engaged in a friendly competition. Every couple of minutes, a loud burst of laughter could be heard coming from their direction.

After reviewing the rules once more, aloud, Hasina asked for a few minutes of warming up before the real badminton play began. "Ok, you start for us," Mafulla said, and pointed to her.

She walked to the back of the court and looked over at Mafulla. "Wait. Do you hit overhand or underhand? Darwishi didn't say."

"Whichever you like," Mafulla answered. "Just don't show off by knocking it through the clouds."

"Very funny." Hasina held the birdie in her left hand and the racket in her right, a bit lower down, with its face flat and parallel to the ground. She had just ruled out even trying an overhead serve. She estimated that it would be the best approach for avoiding the embarrassment of a miss with her swing—Mafulla would never let her forget it—if she could see both the birdie and the strings. So, pulling the racket down, she dropped the birdie to where the racket face had been and swung it back up into position, solidly hitting the white, feathered cone, tipped with light red rubber, high over the net.

"Whoa!" Both boys exclaimed at her shot, almost forgetting to move toward the birdie to return it. Walid remembered just in time, and practically dove across the court, shoving his racket low to get it under the birdie just inches before it would have hit the ground, but not with enough force to arc it back over the net. The poor bird flew right into the strings of the net and dropped to the ground.

"Yaaaay!" the girls both yelled out in celebration. "Girl power!" Hasina said, with a big smile on her face.

"Man, you should have had that one!" Mafulla told Walid with a laugh.

"Yeah, since I was the only one who moved!" Walid replied, smiling.

"Hey, I was busy calculating the trajectory of her shot and the wind direction and speed before doing anything unproductive, like, I don't know, hitting it into the net."

"Well, good job," Walid said.

"You guys better wake up over there," Kissa called out. "Hassi, serve again. One to nothing!"

"Wait. Aren't we just practicing?" Mafulla said.

"No, I really don't think I'll need practice after all," Hasina replied. "One to zero. Get ready."

"But that's hardly …"

"It's Ok," Walid interrupted his friend to say. "Let the ladies have that one. We'll continue to play." He then turned to the girls and said, "So, we've spotted you a point."

"Too bad you couldn't spot the birdie in time," Kissa said with a huge grin. She turned to Hasina and said, "Go ahead and let the boys spot us a second point, as well, in their own special way." Hasina laughed and got ready to serve again.

"Yeah, right!" Mafulla said and, backing up just a little, he began to sway back and forth in readiness. He also started mumbling, "Birdie, birdie, birdie, come to papa! Birdie, birdie, birdie!"

Pop! Hasina hit this second serve low over the top of the net and it arced down immediately into the ground. Mafulla, unfortunately, was swaying to his left when the birdie came flying to his right. He couldn't reverse his balance quickly enough to get to it and almost fell in the effort. Walid, from his vantage point and moving in the direction of the action, watched the birdie once more hit the ground well within the boundaries on their side of the net. He said, "Oh, no!"

"Ha! Two! Two to nothing!" Hasina shouted, as Kissa cheered again.

"Jeepers," Mafulla said. "Jeepers."

Walid said, "Hey, watch it come off her racket and start to move in the right direction long before it crosses over the net. That was my mistake. I waited too late to move."

"Ok, Ok. Good idea."

"Get on the ball over there," Hasina said. "Make it at least interesting. We're going to feel terrible about beating you so badly."

"Hey, you don't know that you're the victims right now of a highly effective strategy to puff up overconfidence on your part."

The girls laughed and Hasina said, "Oh, yeah?"

"Yeah. Pride goes before a fall."

"Where then does humiliation go, after a fall? We need you to tell us! Or we could just wait to see the answer after the next serve."

"Enough!" Walid laughed. "Serve again. We're ready now."

"I guess you're as ready as you'll ever be," Hasina said, and glanced over at Kissa while she took her serving position once more. Bing! She hit the birdie hard and it sang as it touched the strings of the racket. This one was high and long. Mafulla backed up and was momentarily blinded by the sun as he searched the sky. The birdie somehow hit the ground.

"Out!" Walid shouted with great satisfaction.

"Out?" Hasina asked.

"Yeah, by two or three inches. You don't know your own power," he said.

"Good thing," Mafulla called out. "I was about to show you the return of your life."

"Yes, it would have been the return of my life, since I haven't seen one yet, and life is passing us by as we wait."

"Hardee-Har."

"Our serve," Walid announced.

"Yeah, change of serve, and it's still two to nothing," Kissa reminded them all as Walid went over to pick up the birdie and toss it to Mafulla. But before doing that, he glanced over at his friend and noticed that he suddenly looked different.

"Wait. There's something wrong," Mafulla said.

"Yeah, your skill level and performance so far," Hasina said.

"No, no, something really serious," he replied. The girls got quiet right away and looked at him. Walid stopped in his tracks and held on to the birdie.

"What is it?" Walid asked.

"I don't know. But it may be bad."

"Time out," Walid said with his hand up, looking at the girls, and they all moved closer to the net, still staring at their friend.

"Has anyone seen my family?" Mafulla suddenly asked.

"Not me," Walid said.

"No," Hasina said, "Not yet."

"There are so many people here today, maybe we just haven't spotted them yet," Kissa offered.

"They would have come over," Mafulla said.

Walid thought for a second and said, "Yeah, if they were here and saw us. But the king has guards offering a tour of the first floor of the palace for people when they first get here. Maybe they're inside, doing that."

"Yeah, maybe," Mafulla answered. "Where's Darwishi?"

"Over at the bocce ball court," Walid said.

Mafulla, still holding his racket, walked off their own court and toward where the other boys were playing bocce ball. "Darwishi? Dar?"

"Yes, yes, Mafulla, what can I do for you?" Darwishi said. "Is there a question about the rules?"

"No, but about something else."

"What is it?"

"My family—mom and dad and the kids and uncle Reela—I haven't seen them here yet, and they should be here by now. Have you noticed them around anywhere?"

"No, I can't say that I have."

"Is there any way you could send someone around the grounds and into the palace to find out whether they're here yet?"

"Of course, if you'd like."

"Yes. It's important."

"I'll get on it."

"Great. Could you do that right away?"

"Certainly."

"And, if they're here, have them come to the badminton court as soon as they can."

"And if they're not here yet?" Darwishi asked.

"Then, I'd like to know that as quickly as possible."

"We'll have an answer for you within ten minutes or less, I'm sure," Darwishi said. He turned back to Malik and the others playing bocce and said, "Boys, continue on. I'll check in on you later."

Haji at that point came over and walked up to Mafulla, as Darwishi was striding off in the direction of his office. "What's wrong, man? You look strange."

"I feel strange. We were playing badminton just now and I suddenly had a very odd feeling like there's something wrong, but I don't know what it is. And then I realized I hadn't seen my family yet, and they're supposed to be here."

"Oh, Ok," Haji said. "Let us know if we can do anything for you, anything at all to help."

"You bet," Mafulla said. "But maybe it's nothing. I'll get you guys if something's up."

"All for one," Haji said, and for a few seconds he watched Mafulla walk back toward the badminton court. And then he returned to the bocce action, now feeling a little odd himself.

Walid met Mafulla halfway back, and so did the girls. They had put their rackets down on the court. Mafulla walked up to them, and said, "Dar's going to go look for the family now."

"Good," Walid said.

Then Mafulla added, "I can't figure it out. I feel like something's wrong, something's going on, but I've got nothing specific, no vision or even an inkling to tell me what, and that's sort of unusual."

"Well, you're right," Walid replied. "Whenever you get a warning about something, it tends to be pretty specific and vivid."

Just then, Naqid walked up. "Excuse me, Prince, and everyone, but I need a moment with you, Your Highness."

"Sure, Naqid, what's up?" Walid asked, and then added, "You can say anything in front of all of us."

"Absolutely," Mafulla said, and glanced at the girls.

The head of palace guards looked around and nearly whispered, "Another threatening letter addressed to the king was just left at the main gate, less than an hour ago, suggesting that he has little time left on this earth."

"Santiago, of course?" Walid asked.

"Yes. That's how it was signed."

"Any details?"

"No, none at all, like usual. It could be nothing, again like usual, or it could signal some new threat. We're just being extra cautious. Additional security is around the party, mostly in plain clothes, and we'll be escorting everyone home later on, after the festivities are over."

"How does the king feel about it?"

"He seems unconcerned, but still approved the extra security when I showed him the note and requested more men around the party. He seems to agree that we should be careful."

"Ok, thanks for the information, Naqid."

"Your Highness," Naqid said and bowed, and turned to leave.

Kissa looked at Mafulla and said, "Maybe that's it."

"Yeah, that could be it," Mafulla agreed.

"And it would have really nothing in particular to do with your family," she added. "Well, at least no more than any other family here today."

"True."

Walid said, "How … do you feel now?"

"Ok, I guess. Still a little bit weird, but Ok."

"Should we play more or go check out what's going on around here, and maybe do our part to find your family?"

"We can play, at least until we hear something from Darwishi. We can play. I'm Ok. I won't lay down my racket while I'm being temporarily vanquished. We can quit … when we're ahead." And of course, he gave the famous double eyebrow jump.

"Oh, yeah, like that's going to happen," Hasina said.

Just then, they heard what sounded like applause from the distance, back toward the palace, and the sound grew by the second. The king had appeared outside, with Kular and Masoon right behind him. He had a big smile on his face, and was nodding and waving to the crowd that now greeted him so enthusiastically.

A short distance away, Ibrahim Hadad opened the door to their apartment and held it for Leem and Ben to go out first. Leem right away noticed an envelope lying flat on the doorstep and bent down to pick it up. "What's this?"

"I didn't see it there earlier," Ibrahim said.

"Who's writing us?" Ben asked.

"I have no idea," Leem answered as he began to tear it open. It was addressed on the front with the words, "To My Good Friends."

Leem unfolded a beautiful piece of expensive stationary and read aloud. "To My Good Friends: I call you this because of the useful role you're already playing in helping me to execute my plans. Those plans will be complete soon. But now, you should go enjoy the big party and say your goodbyes to the celebrant, who will be leaving us soon. Then again, you'll be lucky if you don't depart with him. Relish for now the hours you have together. Sincerely, Juan Osvaldo Santiago."

Leem looked up at Ibrahim. "What in the world does this mean?"

"I have no idea, uncle, but look," Ibrahim said, pointing to the side of the door. There was a red 'X' painted on the wall. "What's this?"

"I have no clue. This man has marked us—our home—for some reason. And this was done in just the last few minutes while we've been inside." Leem moved toward the mark and pointed and said, "Look here, the paint's wet."

"I bet this is why you had your strange feeling," Ibrahim said.

"Yes."

"What's going on?" Ben said.

"I'm not sure, son, but nothing for you to worry about," Leem answered with kindness, masking his deep concern over the content of the message and the mark of paint on the house.

At the Adi home, Shamilar had just walked quickly up to the front door, having heard what sounded like a knock, and expecting the king's driver to be there. She and Reela desperately needed transportation for Shapur, to take him to the university hospital as soon as possible. He was on the bed, unconscious, unresponsive, and breathing in only a very shallow way. His pulse had also dropped and grown a bit faint to Reela's touch. His condition seemed to be getting worse by the minute.

Shamilar swung the door open, and again no one was there. But a white envelope was on the ground, inches from the doorway. It was addressed simply, "To My Friends." Shamilar bent down to pick it up and heard the wind blow once more, just a single gust, but powerful against the house. She had to hold tight to the envelope to keep it from flying away. Something about the situation didn't feel right. She stepped back into the house while ripping open the missive. She unfolded the paper within, and began to read a short, perplexing message.

"To My Friends: I need you to be helpful to me, and you're going to be very helpful. I have plans that will be complete soon. It's too bad that you can't go to the big party today and say your goodbyes to the celebrant, who'll be leaving us soon. I'm also sorry that he'll be preceded in his departure. But for this, I have my reasons. Relish for now the short time that remains. Sincerely, Juan Osvaldo Santiago."

Shamilar walked quickly back toward the bedroom. "Reela, someone just left an envelope on the threshold at the front door, and this strange note was inside. When I reached down to pick it up, there was a sudden gust of wind, and it almost flew away from my hand." Reela reached out for the note and read it through.

"Very odd. Wait here," he said. "I need to go look at where it was left."

Shamilar sat down on the side of the bed as Reela left the room. She gently picked up Shapur's hand and right away thought how cool it felt, almost cold, to the touch. "Oh my dear husband," she whispered. "Stay with us. Please be all right and stay with us for a long time."

In no more than thirty seconds, Reela was back, but now with another man. He said, "This is the king's driver. He'll take us all to the hospital right away. I saw him as soon as I opened the door, and I asked him to follow me to get Shapur."

The man nodded and said, "Hello, Mrs. Adi. I'm sorry for what you're going through with the sudden turn of events. I'm at your service."

"Oh, thank you for coming, and for being here to help my poor husband."

"What seems to be wrong?"

"We don't actually know. He's fallen unconscious, into a coma or something, and desperately needs to get to the hospital."

"Yes, ma'am. We'll carry him to the car right away." The man bent down and with Reela's help got Shapur into an upright position, supporting his limp figure under both his arms, and walking him slowly to the front door. Shamilar opened the door and held it as they passed through and continued on to the car.

"Let me get my bag. I'll be right there," she called after them. But just as she turned back toward the doorway, she gasped. "Reela! Someone's painted a red 'X' on our door frame!"

Reela had just laid his brother down gently in the car, and turning back toward the house said, "What?"

"Look!" Shamilar pointed to the bright red paint.

"I didn't step outside or see that earlier," he said, as he walked back toward the door.

"I noticed it when I arrived," the driver said, "but I didn't know what to think about it."

"Someone's marked the house, for whatever reason," Reela said.

"Can … we get the paint off?" Shamilar asked.

"Yes, but not now, not in the limited time we may have. Shapur's health is much more important."

"Yes, of course," Shamilar said.

"We need to leave it where it is now and get going, as quickly as possible."

"Start the car. I'll be with you in less than half a minute," she said.

Reela turned toward the car, spoke with the driver again, and got into the back seat with his brother. Shamilar then quickly came out with her purse and walked to them at a brisk pace.

"Hurry!" the driver called out. "He's just stopped breathing!"

"What?" Shamilar exclaimed as she got into the front passenger's seat, closed the door, and then looked into the back, to see Reela on top of Shapur, administering hard pushes onto his chest.

The car started off and raced down the street in the direction of its destination. "Your husband turned gray and then very blue, quite suddenly," the driver said. "He gasped loudly for air, and then stopped breathing."

19

RING TOSS

KING ALI'S ARRIVAL OF COURSE HAD CREATED A VERY BIG and happy stir in the crowd of people attending his official birthday party, even after all the applause had died down. And he was now greeting everyone, asking about their children, commending them on the work they were doing for the kingdom, and just generally making all his visitors feel valued and welcomed to the festivities. He walked from group to group with a big smile and a hearty word of friendship for everyone he saw. Within a few minutes, he had decided to visit all the games, one by one, to see how people were enjoying the fun options that had been set up for them on this beautiful afternoon.

First up was ring toss, where some younger children were having a great time throwing rubber rings around wooden sticks. One boy in particular, who couldn't have been more than five or six years old, had an uncanny ability to get a ringer on almost every throw. The king discreetly asked about him and heard he was Ara's little brother, the son of a man who worked in economic forecasting for the kingdom. The king also learned his name, which made him smile because it meant wisdom, a great thing for a boy. "Alim!" The king called out, and he quickly turned around. "You're doing an excellent job!"

"Thank you, sir," Alim said with a big smile.

"You're all doing a fine job today!" The king spoke now to the entire group of youngsters who were engaged in the game. "I grant you all the title for the day of Chief Kingdom Ring Tossers! Now, please, carry on!" His gaze lingered on Alim for a moment more, as he noticed the young man pick up several rings from the ground and hand them to a smaller boy. Ali took note of this, and turned to walk over to the bocce ball courts that weren't far away.

At this point, some of the older adults were playing bocce and having a great time of it. The king lingered for a few minutes, watching and enjoying the friendly give-and-take among the players. He thought to himself again what a good idea this outdoor celebration had been.

At the horseshoe pits now, Haji was having quite a run of ringers and leaners. No one else could come close to his dominance of the game. His shoes flew to the targeted iron stake. Clang! Clang! The metal sang as each shoe hit its mark. Malik was clearly second best today. He had his share of ringers and leaners, too, but his throws seemed most often to drop onto Haji's or just land right next to them.

"What magic have you put into your shoes?" Malik asked after one spectacular high throw that Haji made drop into a perfect ringer.

"The only magic in my shoes is me!" Haji replied with a laugh.

"Very funny," Malik said. "But just a second." He walked down to the stake and picked up the most recently thrown shoe, noticing something strange right away. Bafur's father, Bashir, was standing nearby and watching the games as he munched on a large pastry of some sort. Malik walked up to him and said, "Excuse me, sir, but have you ever thrown a horseshoe?"

"Not many times in my life," Bashir said. "Certainly not the way you boys are throwing today, which is very impressive indeed."

"Thank you for the kind words. The breeze is blowing well for us, I think. But I hope you can help me with a quick experiment."

"Sure! What can I do for you?"

"Could you make just one throw of this shoe? I believe my friend Haji here has a special shoe for his throws. I want to see what happens when someone else tosses it."

"Yes. I can do that. I can't promise any accuracy, but I'll try." Bashir turned to Bafur and said, "Son, can you hold my treat while I do this?"

"Yes, father, certainly."

"No tasting."

"Are you sure?"

"Yes," he laughed. You're taking temporary stewardship of the item only. You're the trusted protector of the pastry."

"Ok." The boy grinned. "If you say so. It sounds like you may be giving me an important role."

"Yes, it is an important role. And stewardship is about careful preservation."

"Ha!" Bafur laughed. "Your roll is safe with me, for a time."

"Ok, then."

Malik handed Bashir the horseshoe, and the man walked up to the closest stake, took careful aim at a distance, and tossed it down toward the far stake. It fell a good ten or twelve inches short of the mark. "Oh! See! I'm so out of practice!"

"Not at all! That was quite normal for a first toss. It was even well above normal. Haji! Go get the shoe and bring it back." Malik turned toward Bashir and said, "Would you make one more throw? Just for me to see what results?"

"Sure, one more is no problem. Maybe I'll be better this time."

Haji trotted back with the shoe and started to hand it to Bashir. "Wait," Malik said. "Indulge me for a second, if you would, my friend."

"What?" Haji said.

"Stand next to Bafur's dad, aim up as if you're going to throw, with your full normal focus, and then do a practice swing, and give it immediately to Bashir to throw instead." Malik turned to the man and said, "And, sir, when Haji gives you the shoe, please, if you would be so kind, throw it down toward the opposing stake as quickly as you can, with no hesitation."

Bashir laughed and said, "I can do that."

"Good!"

Bashir then added, "Perhaps it's best to have someone else do my aiming for me!"

Malik laughed. "Ok. This is strange," Haji said with a smile.

"It's a scientific experiment! Indulge me," Malik replied.

So, Haji stood next to Bashir and eyeballed the stake in front of him, concentrating his aim, and then took a smooth practice swing. But instead of throwing, he handed the iron shoe instantly to Bashir who, as requested and with no delay threw it toward the target. Clang!

"It's a ringer!" Malik shouted! "Great throw!"

"Oh, my goodness! Oh, me!" Bashir squinted down field and said, "It looks like you're right! I got a ringer! That's a first! A first ever!"

Malik now jogged down to retrieve the shoe, and stood for a second looking at it. He reached over and picked it up with his right hand, and made some movement toward it with his left. Jogging back to Bashir, who was now accepting the congratulations of his son and other bystanders, he seemed to be switching the shoe and something else from one hand to the other. Then, reaching out with his right hand, he said, "I believe you accidently threw more than one thing."

"My ring?" Bashir looked shocked. "That's my old ring!" He looked down at his throwing hand to notice for the first time a bare finger when he customarily wore an old family ring, recently resized to be a bit larger for him. "How in the world did this happen?"

"The shoe must have somehow clipped the ring, and they both went flying, due to the sheer strength of your throw," Malik suggested.

"Oh, my goodness! I have a good deal more power in my arm than I realized," Bashir said and laughed.

"Yes, and it's no wonder your son is a strong one as well," Haji said.

Bashir beamed, and so did Bafur standing nearby. "My ring must have been a little loose. I think I noticed that earlier today."

"I'm glad we found it!" Malik said.

"So am I!"

Malik smiled and replied, "Thanks again for helping in my little experiment. It seems that my friend's horseshoes are normal. You threw once short, then once perfectly. Haji's consistency today could be just a testimony to his great skills, or else, temporary luck."

"Well, I'm happy to have been of help!" Bashir said. "Maybe now that I'm warmed up with a sense of hand and eye coordination, I should go down and have a turn at bocce ball." He looked over at Bafur and said, "Son, I can take that pastry off your hands now. Thank you for holding it."

"I got so excited at seeing your ringer, I almost forgot and ate it!" Bafur said, and everyone laughed as he handed it back to his dad.

"I'll be over at the bocce court," Bashir said to him. "You might want to place some bets, now that I have the hot hand."

"Yeah, I'll split the winnings and treat you to dinner!" Bafur said. There were more laughs as father and son walked off with a smile and a wave. Then Malik motioned for Haji to come close. They walked a bit over to the side, away from everyone else.

Malik said, "The ring was stuck to the horseshoe."

"What?"

"The ring was stuck to the shoe and I had to pull it off."

"What do you mean?"

"Have you noticed that my horseshoes often drop onto yours, right on them?"

"Yeah, a few times."

"And many are up against yours, touching?"

"Yeah?"

"You're magnetizing the shoes when you throw them."

"What?"

"You're sending some sort of charge through the shoes and it magnetizes them to fall onto the iron stake. And then, if I throw quickly afterwards, they pull my shoes onto them or up against them, to be touching."

"No way."

"Yep. That's what's happening."

"How?"

"You tell me."

"I have no idea."

"It's gotta be related to that thing you do, you know, the way you can heat up metal?"

"You think?"

"I know."

"Boy, that's sort of not fair. I mean: I have an advantage. That gives me an unfair advantage."

"No joke."

"I'm not trying to cheat."

"I know. You would never do that on purpose."

"But when I walk down to pick up my shoes, they don't seem to be magnetized. They don't stick to the stake or to the other shoes, even those that are up against them or on top of them."

"It's a temporary effect. It lasts just long enough and then sort of dissipates."

"What do you mean?"

"That's why, when I handed Bashir the shoe, he missed the stake. When you brought it and held it and did your practice swing, and then handed it to him, it was still charged, and it pulled off his ring and bang, he had a ringer, in two senses of the word."

"Adult ring toss," Haji said.

"Yeah."

"Maybe we should go do some archery," Haji suggested with a smile.

"That'll be fair," Malik agreed. "Unless you have some power over arrows, too."

"I really truly didn't mean to cheat."

"I know. You just have skills beyond what you realize."

"Strange, bizarre, weird, and different skills," Haji said.

"All true, to fit your personality beautifully." Haji pretended to be offended. "I couldn't resist," Malik explained, as his magnetic friend acted like he was going to choke him.

Leem Hadad, Ibrahim, and Ben had just arrived at the palace. Leem asked around for Naqid and finally spotted him at the north end of the grounds behind the big building, conferring with a colleague. He told Ibrahim and Ben to go ahead down to the games, and that he would join them in a few minutes. Naqid saw Leem coming his way and wrapped up his conversation to greet him. "Leem! Good to see you," Naqid said, as he walked toward the detective.

"Good to see you, as well, my friend" Leem replied. "I have something I need to show you." They met and shook hands and Leem took a paper from his pocket. "This was left outside our door right before we came here. And there was a mark of red paint on the door frame of the place, a red 'X' that had been put there."

"Really?"

"Yes, it's all very strange."

Naqid read the note and said, "Well, this is similar to one we received not long ago, earlier today."

"Indeed?"

"Yes, and I've put lots of extra security into place because of it."

"Good. What do you make of it?"

"It could be a bluff or it could be a credible threat," Naqid replied. "Of course, there's no way at this point of knowing which."

"This is quite a character we're dealing with," Leem commented. "He seems as mad as he is bad—a bit of a crazy man."

"I completely agree. We're not dealing with a normal sensibility here. It's altogether unclear what this fellow wants, but his threats are becoming constant and tiresome."

"Well, I'll keep my eyes wide open today," Leem assured his friend and colleague.

"Thanks, Leem. We have a lot of guards around in civilian clothing. But it's good to have a partner with your experience here on a day like this. Let me know if you see or hear anything at all that's out of the ordinary."

"I will." The two men shook hands again, and Leem walked down toward where the festivities were underway.

The palace car was barreling through town at a high rate of

speed. Shamilar was beside herself with worry, fear, and near panic. "Please keep him alive!" she said to Reela, who was working hard with chest compressions on his brother, to force air in and out of his lungs. He was also augmenting this with puffs of air into Shapur's open mouth. He had put a handkerchief over his brother's lips after having poked a hole in it, and was puffing through the hole, in the way he had been taught, many years ago during his service to the kingdom.

"I've had to do this before, twice, and both times it worked," Reela said to her, "So please, don't worry. I know what I'm doing. If we can get there soon, the doctors will help."

"Oh, my, goodness," she exclaimed. "Oh, my." She looked over at the driver and said, "Please hurry as fast as you safely can."

"Yes, ma'am," he replied as he turned the wheel and barely made it around a corner. Other cars, a couple of trucks, and several donkey carts were getting out of their way as quickly as they could. Some were yelling and cursing at what they assumed to be simply reckless driving. Others recognized the palace car and realized that there must be some sort of emergency going on.

The hospital was at this point only a few blocks away. Shapur's color wasn't as bad as it had been at the house when his breathing first stopped, but it wasn't good, either. And what made it all in a sense even worse was that Mafulla had no idea that any of this was going on. There was some sort of cloak of interference over the entirety of the proceedings. The boy's normal ability to discern any events connected with the wellbeing of his family had been blocked effectively enough so that he had no clear sense of what was going on with his father and mother right now. And this was something he'd ordinarily have seen because of his particular cluster of Phi skills.

"Hold on!" the driver said to Reela and Shamilar as he whipped the car off the road and into a drive at the front of the hospital, slamming on the brakes to bring them to as quick a stop as he could. He blew the car's horn. "I'll run in and get help!" he said as he jumped out and took off for the front door of the building.

Within less than half a minute, several hospital staff members had arrived at the car and loaded Shapur onto a gurney to rush him inside. Reela was doing what he could to keep up his life saving efforts as he walked beside his brother. Shamilar followed along, helped by a comforting nurse, but she was mostly in shock at this point and cocooned in a daze of unreality about what was going on and how it might end. Everything around her was a blur. Her inner thoughts seemed to be stuck in molasses, or quicksand. She could barely answer the many questions that people were asking her. But the kind nurse with her kept a light grip on her arm and guided her along into the busy building with soft and reassuring words.

Inside the hospital, things were happening fast and loudly, as various nurses and doctors shouted orders and information to each other above the clanging din of equipment being moved around and put into place. Shamilar was standing now a few feet away from where they had her husband positioned and were working frantically to save him from whatever had cut off his natural ability to breathe. Reela stood close by and answered questions from one of the doctors. One younger physician was continuing the resuscitation efforts while another used a stethoscope to check Shapur's heart and lungs.

After a couple of minutes, the doctor with the stethoscope shouted, "We've lost the heartbeat!" and another doctor began preparing a stimulant that they could use to seek to restore it. The first man slapped the unconscious Shapur on the cheek four quick times and shouted, "Come back! Come back to us, friend!"

Reela rushed over to where Shamilar stood. "My dear, it's best for us to get out of the way right now and let the doctors work. They know what they're doing. They need their space. Come with me. Let's give them more room."

"But … what's going on?" she asked.

"He's having a new difficulty. Often things get worse before they get better. But don't fear. Be of good faith. Say a prayer for our sweet man and come, let's stand outside in the hallway. They'll tell us when he's better and we can see him."

"Are you sure?"

"Yes. Come with me." Reela took her arm and gently led her out of the room and into the adjoining hallway and then down thirty or forty feet to a bench where they could sit, just barely out of earshot from where the frantic actions on the part of several staff were now taking place all around Shapur.

In the room, the doctors were trying everything they could think to do. "He's gone," one of them said.

"Not yet," another protested.

"No, he's gone. It's been a full minute with no pulse, no heart-beat. We've lost him."

"Stand to the side. Keep watch on the time." An older doctor bent over Shapur and said to him, "My friend, you're going to come back to us. You're needed still. It's not yet your time. You're a young man." All during this one-sided conversation, the experienced physician was pushing firmly on Shapur's chest and releasing. He turned to a nurse and said, "Make sure this doesn't collapse under us," as he climbed onto the bed with Shapur and began his work with a new intensity.

The nurse quickly slid a short table under the side of the bed to support them. "A minute and a half," the younger doctor announced.

"Bring the stimulant," the older man barked out. "Administer it now!"

"Perhaps you should let him go," a nurse said. "It may be that his time has indeed come, earlier than we'd otherwise expect."

"No!" The doctor working on Shapur practically growled out his curt reply. He was now sweating profusely, as drops fell from the end of his nose onto his patient's neck and chin. "There's no reason for this to be happening! Come back to us!" He spoke to Shapur with great feeling and kept working hard.

"Two minutes," the young doctor said. Another physician came into the room and saw what was going on and remarked to the senior doctor, "Ahmed, let me try."

"What?"

"Let me try. You need a break. I can tell."

"Ok, all right, prepare to take over. Position yourself to my right. I need to think. On my count of three: One, two, three!" And on that word, the younger physician, a man in his forties, slid to his left and mounted the bed, taking over the resuscitation efforts as his more senior colleague climbed down again.

The older doctor wiped his face with a cloth from a nearby table, and said, "The man is too young for this. And there's no discernible cause. Bring his body back to him. Don't give up on it. This makes no sense. We have to prevail."

"Two and a half minutes." Everyone in the room, on hearing that announcement, knew that their opportunity to save the patient was quickly dwindling.

"His wife needs him," the older doctor said by way of encouragement to his colleague who was now striving to make the stopped heart beat again. "He likely has children who need him. Is there anything?"

"Check for me!" The younger doctor said to the senior nurse, who was standing by with a stethoscope.

She quickly moved into position and placed the instrument where it needed to be in order to detect any cardiac activity. She listened. And she concentrated. Then she spoke. "No, there's still nothing," she said.

"Check again!"

There was silence from her for maybe twenty seconds, and then she said, "I'm sorry. I'm so very sorry. There's no sign."

"Three minutes!"

At this point, the newly arrived physician who was working so hard paused and looked at Shapur. His skin had changed color to a pallid grey tone again and had lost all signs of life. His open eyes stared sightlessly at the ceiling. Along with those eyes, his gaping mouth announced by its slack unresponsiveness that he was gone.

"Again!" the elder doctor commanded.

"Yes." His less senior colleague immediately went back to work, but now with no hope in his own heart for success. He was just going through the motions at this point and giving the head physician all he needed to be able to walk down the hall in a few minutes and say to the widow, with a clear conscience, "We did everything we could. I'm so sorry." At this point, he felt it was a noble but empty effort.

"Four minutes." The youngest doctor in the room announced this without lifting his eyes from the face of his watch. He had been present at too many deaths already in his short career, but still each one gave him a dry mouth, and a strange heaviness in his spirit. He could never disengage fully, the way he had been taught he should.

The effort continued in relative silence, apart from low rustles of cloth and a few grunts of effort. The seconds dragged by, as if reluctant to take everyone in the room to the destination they had all dreaded. The patient was indeed far too young for this to have happened. It was a mystery.

"Approaching five minutes."

"Enough." The senior doctor put his hand on his colleague's back. "It's enough. You've done your best. We all have. It's over. Our friend has left us and gone to the next world."

The younger man ceased his efforts at that moment. "I'm sorry, sir. I'm very sorry."

"Yes. We all are. Please, cover the body. I'll go tell his wife."

The youngest man in the room, the one counting the time, suddenly said, "Wait. I just noticed something."

"What?" The older man stopped and turned around.

"His ring—his wedding ring. His wife will want it." The man bent down and slipped the ring from Shapur's finger and tossed it toward his senior colleague.

"What are you doing?" The head physician looked shocked as he opened his hand and caught the ring.

"Getting you the …"

"Never treat a patient with that disrespect!"

"But, I was just …"

"Your thought was good, but your actions don't show the

respect that should be in your heart. Don't throw such a thing. Don't toss it. You should have handed it to me gently, with kindness and respect for the poor man, and for his wife."

"I'm so sorry. I didn't think. I meant no offense."

"You're young. You'll learn. You did right to notice it and get it to me. That was kind. Just, next time, please, no throwing of personal effects."

"Yes, Doctor. You're right, of course."

"You can remove the body after I've talked with his wife and the other gentleman. May this good man rest in peace."

20

DEEP DARKNESS

JUAN OSVALDO SANTIAGO WAS A MAN OF TRULY IMPRESSIVE abilities and quite unusual powers. But they had limits. He could interfere with all modes of knowing, up to an extent. He could cloak his activities and their consequences to a surprising degree. But at a certain point, his efforts broke down. They reached a wall they could not surmount.

As long as Shapur Adi had been alive on the earth, living in a physical body, there were things that a man like Santiago could do to him, and around him, while keeping information and awareness from the people closest to him. That's why Mafulla had not known, unlike in the past, that there was something seriously wrong with his dad. Shapur's sudden illness did affect Mafulla in a sort of undefined way. He felt strange, but there were no specifics in his heart or mind. He didn't know the reason for his unease. He wondered where his parents and the kids were, but had not fully connected the moderate mystery of their whereabouts with his foreboding sensations. They could have been delayed getting to the party for any number of harmless reasons. Work somehow interfered and made them late. Or maybe something with the kids had slowed them down. It wouldn't be the first time that Sammi or Sasha had spilled juice or food on a nice outfit of clothes moments before they were to leave the house for a special occasion. Shamilar would have to go into overdrive to remedy the problem and get them all to their destination.

Mafulla had made himself not worry, and had done everything he could to immerse himself in the many activities of the birthday party. Hasina was being very funny. And Kissa and Walid were keeping him well distracted. But now and then, he felt deep down a sense that something might be wrong. It wasn't strong enough to demand his complete attention. But it nudged him and nagged at him every few minutes.

At this point, Mafulla was with Walid, Hasina, and Kissa on the archery range that had been set up at the far end of the large main field. Hasina had just done some impressive shooting, clustering five arrows in the bulls-eye, grouped so close that they were actually touching each other. Mafulla was up next. He took the first arrow out of the quiver, notched it up on the bow, and aimed. But at that moment, he heard his father's voice, as words in his mind. "Son, I need you now."

He lowered the bow and said to his friends, "My dad needs me right now."

Walid said, "How do you know?"

"I just heard his voice. He said he needs me."

"Do you know where he is?"

"No, but I have to find out right away."

"We'll come with you."

"Ok."

They all put down their bows and arrows, and indicated to a waiting group that they could take over. Walid quickly apologized to them for leaving arrows in the target, explaining that they had an urgent need to take care of something. Mafulla then led them at a stride toward the garage offices, looking left and right along the way for Darwishi. He saw him near the main office talking to another driver.

"Darwishi!" Mafulla called out.

"Mafulla! I was just coming to get you," Darwishi said and stepped toward the group with the other driver beside him.

"Why?" Mafulla asked as they drew closer.

"You know our driver, Rahib?"

"Yeah. Hi, Rahib."

"Mafulla," Rahib said. "I'm sorry. I have some bad news."

"What is it?"

"I went to pick up your family for the party, and your father had been having trouble breathing."

"What?"

"When I got to the house, your dad was unconscious and your uncle Reela and your mother were taking care of him, and they asked me to get them all to the hospital as soon as I could. I dropped them off there in the care of the hospital staff and drove here as fast as I could make it back, in order to let you know."

"Is he … Ok?" Mafulla asked, still stunned by the news.

"Well, Reela was helping him to breathe when we got there and then the doctors took over. I can take you to him right now, if you'd like."

"Yes, and my friends will come, too."

"Very good. Please follow me to the car."

As they walked quickly toward the north part of the field near the side entrance to the palace grounds, Hasina put her hand on Mafulla's arm and said, "I hope your dad's going to be Ok."

"Thanks, Hasina. He somehow spoke to me in my mind a couple of minutes ago and so, as of then, he must have been Ok, however in need he still might be."

"You would know if something was badly wrong," Walid said by way of encouragement.

"I guess I would," Mafulla replied. "I've been having some sort of a strange feeling come and go for a while, without knowing what it was or what it meant. But you're right. In all past circumstances, whenever there's been a truly bad situation, I've seen it vividly. I've known in detail what was going on. This time, I've had none of that, and I guess it's a good sign."

"I'm sure your dad will be Ok," Kissa said, although she wasn't really sure at all, but she did want to encourage her friend. And she hoped mightily that he was safe, whatever could be going on.

At that point, they reached the car and got into it quickly. Rahib started the engine and pulled off down the drive and through the gate, passing the guard stand with a wave and turning onto the main avenue that would take them toward their destination. At this point, none of the Phi in the car knew what they'd face when they arrived at the hospital, but with every passing minute, each of them was beginning to have a sense of the seriousness of what might be awaiting them, however vague and ill-defined that sense still was.

Darwishi, meanwhile, had gone to tell the king what Rahib had reported, and Ali had Masoon go and find Hamid and ask him to get to the hospital as soon as he could. The king then cleared his mind for ten seconds and focused intensely on the situation. As a result, he knew right away what was happening. He saw Hoda and Khalid close by and asked Kular to bring Hoda over for a moment.

She appeared within a few seconds and Ali briefly explained the situation as he understood it, and requested that she accompany Hamid to the hospital immediately, if that was possible for her. She wholeheartedly agreed, and then spoke to Khalid quickly before following Darwishi across the lawn to meet Hamid at a waiting car.

The conversation in the car was serious and focused. Dar told the senior Phi everything Rahib had reported. When Shapur had been dropped off with Reela and Shamilar, he'd been in severe physical distress, unconscious, and unresponsive. The situation, Hoda and Hamid both realized, was grave. They didn't know exactly what they'd confront when they arrived, but Hoda had an inkling that they might already be too late to use their considerable powers to save their friend Mafulla's fine and loving father.

Rahib Nasula was doing his best to drive both quickly and safely to their destination. Given the young people entrusted to his care, he was going a bit slower than Darwishi, who soon caught up with him, and followed him closely the rest of the way. Both cars pulled up to the hospital at the same time, and everyone leaped out and walked at a fast stride toward the door.

On approaching the first staff member just inside the building, Mafulla said, "Shapur Adi is my father. He's in treatment here, just brought in with an emergency. Where is he, please?"

"I'm not sure," the staff member said, but just then, Mafulla spotted his mother down the hallway, seated on a bench. "Oh, I can see my mother." He walked quickly in her direction, followed now by his friends, and Hoda and Hamid.

"Mom!" Mafulla called out.

Shamilar looked up and said, "Oh! My son! I'm so sorry!"

"What? What's happened?"

Reela said, "The doctor just told us a minute or two ago. They said they lost your dad in the emergency room."

"What do you mean? Where is he? How could they lose him?"

"No. I mean he's gone. His heart stopped beating. He passed from this earth." On hearing Reela's words, Shamilar began to sob.

"What?" Mafulla's mind nearly went blank. He had seen his dad very recently and he was fine. There had been problems of exhaustion and such for a while after he had apparently met Juan Santiago, but lately, he'd recovered and was back to his old healthy self. He had seemed fine.

Reela took a deep breath. "His heart stopped and they couldn't restart it. They did their best."

"I … don't … understand."

Hasina and Kissa stood right behind Mafulla and both had their hands over their mouths in total shock to hear what Reela was saying. They still processed it more immediately than Mafulla could. He was just swimming in the mental void that had just been created, treading water, trying to keep his head up and breathe. His thoughts were all slowed down, and gummed up, and seemed nearly unable to move.

Reela reached out and put his hand on Mafulla's shoulder. His voice then seemed to come from a distance. "Your dad's time had apparently come, for whatever reason. His body stopped working, and his spirit left."

"But he was fine."

"Yes. He was fine and healthy, we all thought. But the contact with Santiago must have had more of an impact than we realized."

"I'll kill Santiago."

"We all feel that way, my boy. Your father was a very good man—the best."

Shamilar looked up at Mafulla and said, "Please, come here and let me hug you." He instantly walked over to her, overcoming his shock and disbelief, and sat down and put his arms around his mother.

"I'm so sorry, mom. It's such a shock I can hardy think."

Walid spoke to Reela: "Where is he?"

"What's that?"

"Where's the body?"

"It's inside the room down the hall, Prince, to the right," Reela said, as he pointed the way.

Walid began walking in that direction, without even having a reason to do so, at least consciously. He got to the door of the room where the doctors had worked on Shapur and turned in to the room itself. There were four people in there with the body: the older doctor who had returned to the room, his slightly younger colleague, and the youngest physician, just out of internship, along with one senior nurse. Shapur's corpse was covered with a sheet and lying on the bed in the midst of them all. Two of the doctors were busy filling out paperwork. The third was just staring into space. The nurse was on her knees, beside the bed, praying for the soul of this man she didn't know, and for his family who had just been left behind.

Walid stopped and simply looked. There was his best friend's father, under a sheet, dead and gone. Or, at least, that's where his physical body was. Walid felt a wave of intense sadness, then, oddly, a second wave of equally intense interest. Something had happened here, something of immense consequence. Walid instinctively, or intuitively, looked around the room, checking for windows, doors, and details. He gazed at the nurse on her knees, praying. His eyes then returned to look at Shapur's body, covered entirely by the sheet. He suddenly felt a strange sense of connection or union with Mafulla's dad, in his spirit, and it was in the next moment as if his own spirit was reaching out beyond an invisible dividing wall. The moment seemed to stretch out slowly, and the room felt like the center of something big that had happened, or that was then happening, or that soon would be about to happen. Walid's mind was nearly blank.

He instinctively walked forward, all the way to the bed. He brushed past two of the doctors and gently touched the sheet over the head of his best friend's father and then put both his hands on the places where Shapur's temples would be, focusing all his energy on whatever he was supposed to do here, maybe somehow conveying vitality or care from somewhere deep inside him and into this form—communicating the essence of life, proper function, love, aspiration, compassion, and all that's involved in being fully human. He didn't understand his impulse at all, or know exactly what he was supposed to do, but it was as if he was just meant to be here and make contact and allow whatever was to happen to somehow come about through him, or with him present.

Walid then for a moment almost thought he was going to pass out. There was a sudden wave of dizziness overwhelming him. He felt a huge surge of something seem to move through him and as if it was going into Shapur's body. His arms tingled and then ached. His head felt like it was going to explode, and then the surge subsided. His own heart was racing. He struggled to calm himself and be empty, and serve as a vessel to convey whatever it was his role to pass on at this moment. He stood still. And he stepped back and looked around the room again. Then, the strangest thing anyone might imagine transpired.

There was a loud noise of indeterminate origin or nature. It was sharp and sudden. But it was so unexpected that it was gone before anyone in the room could pay sufficient attention to it to be able to think or say right away what it was. They all heard it. And everyone looked up. The sheet over Shapur had moved, ever so slightly.

"What?" The senior physician actually dropped his pen.

"Look!" the youngest doctor in the room said, the one who had been the timekeeper. He pointed.

"At what?" The middle-aged physician asked.

"The sheet moved! That was something—a gasp, or a cough!"

"No. It's impossible."

All the doctors rushed to the top of the sheet. The senior physician pulled it back. Shapur was still and inert, just as they had seen his face when he was pronounced dead. And then suddenly he, or his body, jerked in some sort of spasm and appeared to gasp noisily for a second intake of air, like a loud, explosive snore. "Nurse!"

She had already stood up. "What is it?"

"I don't know," the old doctor said, in astonishment. "Bring me your ..."

"He's breathing!" the younger associate said.

"Praise God!" The nurse exclaimed.

Now, again, Shapur clearly coughed. He sucked in air with the most noise Walid had ever heard when someone breathed. He coughed a second time, and rattled loudly with another breath. His body jerked and shuddered. His abdomen rose up off the hard bed and fell back down. A trickle of saliva streamed from the right corner of his mouth. There was something like a faint groan that continued for a couple of seconds. Then, everyone heard, "What? What? Oh! Oh!" These words came from his mouth.

The older doctor was stunned. The man spoke? The man who was long gone had spoken words. He then blinked his eyes two or three times, but barely. He slightly turned his head. Walid bent down and stared at his eyes. In a moment, they had gone from dead to alive. In that evanescent instant, his flesh, the skin on his face and neck, had been completely transformed from dead back to living. Walid had never seen or even heard of anything like this. Neither had anyone in the room, despite all their medical experience and deathbed sojourns. All the doctors instinctively stepped back at first in reaction to this uncanny thing, as a thrill of fear and wonder crawled across the skin of their bodies and made two of them gasp a deep breath before their professional concern could take over once more. This was far beyond anything they knew or expected or even considered remotely possible. It was just physically impossible, and it was happening right in front of them.

"It's a miracle," the nurse said softly and with reverence.

Walid felt a moment of dizziness again and fought to recover. He turned. "Mafulla! Shamilar! Reela!" He shouted as loudly as he could toward the hallway he had just walked down. He moved toward the door to shout again. "He's back! He's back! Your father's back!" At this point, the prince was in the doorway and facing down the hall, yelling out the good news.

Everyone down by the bench and on it was now looking up, in a new wave of stunned shock and disbelief at what they might be hearing. Walid stepped toward them and repeated his message. "He's back! Shapur's come back to life! He's back! Come quickly! Now!"

Mafulla just bolted and ran down the hallway, momentarily forgetting everyone else. Reela offered his hand to Shamilar, who rose slowly, in total confusion and said to him, "What did he say?"

"He says that Shapur is back, and that he's alive!" Reela exclaimed.

"How can it be?" Shamilar asked.

"We don't know, but the prince says we have him back!" Reela gently pulled her up off the bench and led her down the hallway, with Hasina and Kissa following close behind.

Kissa looked at Hasina. Their eyes met in a brief, intense gaze. But no words were spoken as they continued down the hall at a brisk walk.

Walid was back at the head of the bed. "Mr. Adi, you're all right now. You're in the hospital and you're Ok. We're all here for you."

"Walid. Walid, my boy," he said in a groggy voice. "The things, the things I've seen!"

"Mafulla's here, too," Walid said, just as his friend got to the bedside.

"My son!" Shapur said.

"Dad! You're Ok!" Mafulla exclaimed.

"Better. Much better than Ok," he said. "Much better."

"What do you mean?" Mafulla asked.

"The things I've seen just now—the beautiful, wonderful things!"

"But the doctors said you were gone, that your heart had stopped and that we had lost you. And we couldn't believe it."

"Yes, I was gone but not lost. I was found." He paused and said again, "I was found."

"What happened?"

Shapur was then silent for maybe five seconds. He stared straight at his son, and then looked around slowly. Hamid and Hoda slipped into the room at this moment and stood quietly, joining the others in listening for what next might be revealed. The man who was gone now smiled weakly and said, "I think I passed out at home, on my bed, and then I was unconscious for a while. I can't remember exactly when it happened. It's like I was asleep. I saw and heard nothing." He spoke now in a low voice, but one of excitement. And after that sentence, he gasped a few more times for air.

"Yes, that's what they told me," Mafulla replied.

"But then I woke up, and it was so strange. I was looking down at my body, and my brother was working on it—on my body— and trying to get it to function properly, to breathe. We were in a car. Or, what I was seeing was taking place in a car."

"You woke up during that?" Now, Reela was asking the question, from right behind Mafulla.

"I think so." Shamilar had moved over to the other side of the bed and had taken hold of Shapur's hand.

"My wife. I love you."

"I love you so much, Shapur! I can't believe I have you back."

"Yes, it seems that I'm back, for now, from an adventure in the next world, the home land."

"Please stay with me."

"I will. I think I will."

"Shapur, you say that you awoke in the car?" Reela asked again, a bit puzzled by what he'd just heard.

"Yes, my brother. Somehow, I saw everything you did for me. I thank you for it. I awoke to see it. I was … I'm sorry that this sounds strange … I was not in my body when I came to, but I was … above it, and above you, looking down, and watching your hard efforts for me."

"You were above me?"

"Yes, in some way. I was above you, and seeing through the roof of the car. I know I sound like a crazy man, but this is what I saw. And we got to the hospital and I was watching, and I wasn't worried, and then it happened—the most amazing thing."

"What happened?"

"I saw a great light at a distance, and it suddenly grew dark between me and the light, and I felt a pull toward it, and then I felt like I was moving to it. I was somehow moving in its direction."

The senior doctor suddenly spoke up and said, "Should you be speaking now, dear man? Shouldn't you just get some rest for the moment?"

"I'm fine. Thank you," Shapur said quietly, in answer to the voice of the man he couldn't at the moment see. "I'm a bit groggy but I'm fine and I have to tell you this. I have to tell you all."

"What, is it, brother?" Reela reached out to touch his arm. "What do you want to tell us?"

"I traveled some distance, or so it seemed. My soul was moving. And it was I, the person speaking to you now, my inner self, my spirit. And then, somehow, I entered a place of tremendous beauty beyond my imagination. It was like a vast garden with bright grass and water, and in the distance, rolling hills and mountains, and I was there but also floating above the scene. And there were beings of light, sparkling, and brilliant, and there was an engulfing warm glow coming upon, and even from, everything. And I felt like I was filled with love and care and kindness, as if all of it too was coming from all around me, emanating from everywhere around me and through me and even inside me. And it was erasing walls between me and the other things and the beings near me. I was still me—but somehow also inside them, and they in me. There was no inner separation or distance."

He paused for a moment, and said, "And it was then that my mother met me, bless her soul—my mother, my dear, dear mother."

"You saw grandma?" Mafulla spontaneously spoke up.

"Yes. She was a young woman again and she glowed with light, and I felt like she was smiling. And she greeted me and made me feel so deeply welcome, even more so than I had already felt. And I asked without a bodily voice, 'Mother! Where am I, Mother?'

And she said, again, without sounds, 'You are where we come from and go to and have our place forever, our eternal home filled and overflowing with love and blessings.' I heard her words as if they were thoughts, beautiful thoughts that came to me with gentle power."

As Shapur said this, a tear ran down his cheek. "And it was wonderful beyond any words, amazing beyond what I can even think to say. There were colors, colors everywhere more intense and bright and brilliant than I've ever seen. And the light was everywhere, and it was soothing and uplifting and I was floating in comfort and love. And my mother led me toward a far place. She somehow guided me, and the words came into my soul, 'Just to let you see it now, from a distance,' and we flew and we flew and it felt so free and then what I saw amazed me even more."

"What was it?" Mafulla again couldn't help but ask.

Shapur took a deep breath and let it out. "It's impossible to say, my son. It overwhelms me. There are no adequate words. But it was a dazzling darkness that cloaked an infinite light. It was magnificent beyond my imagination. It was a concentration of no light and all light somehow at once. It was the source of all illumination not itself illuminated but illuminating all around it with energy that goes beyond anything you can think or feel or grasp, and ... with love—an endless, limitless, powerful love that by its very nature makes all things possible. It declares and creates and manifests universes and galaxies and planets and souls and worlds beyond anything we can know. And it does so in an endless eternal act of play—serious, loving, extravagant, deep creative play. I felt all that in seeing and sensing what I did. And we are all intended and needed and wanted and supported and we're all important—each of us—we're eternally valuable, because of this source, our source, this vibrant center of all being, or what's wrapped deep within it, behind it, under it, above it, throughout it and … somehow … also everywhere deep within all else. Words are just not enough."

He paused and looked into Shamilar's eyes, and then Mafulla's. "I wanted to enter that deep source of light. It seemed to be where I belong. Everything within me nearly ached to enter it fully—not just to see it, but also to be in it, and with it, and through it. And, in that moment, I felt knowledge pouring into me, not in words or thoughts or sentences, but like water gushing into a cup and making the cup bigger as it filled it, and then filling it more. I was expanding with a knowledge of all things and a deep understanding, and the wisdom that we merely glimpse here as if in bits and pieces, but it was full there and I was so full, and my being was enveloping all that I should and could ever know."

"What happened then?" Mafulla could barely speak the words.

"That was when I felt a tug back to this world, a sense that I was needed back here, and that it was not yet my time to enter fully into the entirety of that wonderful richness, the vast wealth of the spirit that awaits us all. And my mother smiled on me again, and another being approached, and it was my father! My father! And I felt his strength and a new, full wisdom. And he helped me to reconcile myself to turning around, away from the deep source of light everlasting, and then … then I was awake again here—in this body again, and yet my eyes were blind and my ears were deaf, and I felt a stab of pain and then soreness everywhere. And my body sucked in air, and a mist appeared and began to clear and then I saw Walid. And … here I am. Here I am, back from the great adventure."

The room was silent for a moment. Then the senior doctor spoke. "That was remarkable, simply remarkable. I've heard things, many things before, but not all that. It's extraordinary. God be praised. It's a blessing to us all, a great blessing."

Shamilar lifted Shapur's hand in hers and with tears of joy streaming down her face, she said, "You're here now, my husband, my Shapur, here with me, and Mafulla, and our friends. And we're so glad you're back. We're so glad."

He gently squeezed his wife's hand, and turned again to look at Mafulla and then at Walid. He said, "I think I know where the enemy of the king is, the man who did his best just now to kill me, and to keep you all from knowing. I can see what he is doing this very moment. I see him as vividly as if he were here with us in this room."

"You know where he is?" Walid asked.

"Yes, in some way, I do. I do now. He did this to me. He made my heart and my body stop. He's alone responsible for what happened to me. He was outside our home. He sought to harm me, and you, and the family. He means to harm many people."

"He did this to you?" Mafulla asked.

"Yes. He thought he knew what he was doing. He meant me great harm. He meant to inflict much pain on you all. But he had no idea what would result. I met joy and knowledge. And now, he can't escape from my sight. And it's time to stop him," Shapur said.

"How?" Walid asked.

"I'll tell you," he said.

21

THE UNEXPECTED JOURNEY

THE OLD LADY FROM DROMEDA BEGAN TO COME OUT OF A sound slumber. Meskhenet Maayuf opened her eyes. Half asleep, she said, "Sab? Is that you?"

"Yes, good wife of mine, but it's also more than just me. It's your morning coffee and breakfast."

"It's what?"

"Breakfast in bed for you today, my fine lady."

She rolled over and squinted toward the flap of the tent. Faint light from a nearby fire flickered across the desert sand.

"Why are you bringing me breakfast in bed, so to speak?"

"Yesterday was a long day of travel, and I know you've not been sleeping well recently. I had a good, solid sleep all night long, and so I decided, as a token of my ongoing, undying love and deep esteem, that I'll act as your personal butler this morning. I've had the cook fix you something extra special."

"You're so funny."

"The coffee's hot, and the meal is, too. Here, sit up. I'll put something behind your back to prop you up." Sab did as he said, and then handed his wife the small metal plate and a utensil. He smiled in the thinning darkness and said, "Eat and enjoy your tasty repast."

She sampled it and said, "Um. This is good. My compliments to the chef."

"I'll tell him later."

"Remind me how far we are from Cairo," she asked. "Did you say two days?"

"That's about right. Today we arrive at El-Wadi, and then tomorrow we leave the camels and get into a truck that the Alexandrians are providing for us. By tomorrow evening, we should be there."

"I'm weary of travel."

"Yes, I am, too. But we need to see the king, and soon."

"Of course, it's most urgent. Has Zet continued to read the book?"

"He has."

"And his opinion's unchanged?"

"It's even stronger. He says he's more certain than ever that Ali needs to see it immediately."

"I'm glad we can accompany him to the seat of power."

"I think it's important. He couldn't have come all this way insufficiently protected."

"He would have had the Alexandrians."

"Yes, and they're powerful protectors. They could defeat any ordinary attackers, and even certain others. But it's better that there be no attack of any sort. The stakes are too high for us to have stayed home and merely hoped for the best."

"You're right, my husband."

"This could be our last trip across the desert. And I mean, of course, to include in that description our return—if everything goes well."

"Yes. We never know."

"It's quite an experience, being out in the great expanse."

"Yes, it is. It always has been."

"It's hard but also beautiful."

"Such is life."

"True, so true."

The elderly lady sat silently enjoying her food for a moment. And her husband was also quiet for a time beside her. "Did you see the dog this morning?" she asked.

"Yes. The men love his company. He's by the fire."

"Is he still Ok?"

"He seems fine—the same. He's adapted to travel quite well. I have to admit that I'm a bit surprised at how much he seems to like it. He actually appears to enjoy himself."

"It's amazing to me that we got him to lie on the small pallet and allow himself to be pulled across the sand."

"I think he knows he couldn't limp all the way from our village to the capital."

She laughed and said, "You think he knows such things?"

"He knows more than we realize. That's my strong feeling."

"You've always had a deep communion with him."

"Yes, he's a great blessing to me."

"He seems to feel the same about you."

"It could just be my table scraps and tummy rubs," Sab joked.

"Funny man."

"Then again, he could be attracted to my sense of humor."

"I've never heard him laugh at one of your jokes."

"No, that's true. He keeps his mirth to himself most of the time. But I can tell that sometimes, on the inside, he's completely cracking up at something I said."

"Silly old man." She laughed.

"No, no, in the next life, if he's given full voice, I wager he'll be able to repeat all the most hilarious one-liners he's ever heard me utter. And then, dear wife, we'll hear him laugh, loudly and long."

"I hope you're right," she replied. And they ate in silence for a few seconds.

"He may even howl with laughter."

"No more silliness this early," she chided him with kindness.

"As you wish."

"He's a good dog." She couldn't help but smile.

"He has the joy." Sab said.

"Yes, I agree. He has the joy. No doubt about that," Meskhenet replied.

"And he's a part of our joy," Sab added.

"Yes, he is."

At that moment, the animal under discussion appeared at the door of the tent. They heard his breathing before they could detect his shadowed outline against the waning darkness and crackling firelight some distance away outside. Then, a bit of tail wagging against the tent fabric officially announced his arrival. Thump, thump, thump.

"Gimpy! Come in, please," Sab said. And the animal obedient-ly wagged his way over to Meskhenet, where he politely smelled her plate, but from a respectful distance of a few inches.

"Have you eaten yet?" she asked him.

The tail wagged harder. And there may have been a faint whine.

"I'll take that as a no, or at least as an indication of … not enough."

"I'll get him something," Sab said. "I'll be right back."

"Wait. Would you mind bringing me some more coffee? It's good today."

"Not a problem, madam. Your wish is my most important concern and task."

Across the sand, in Cairo, it was the start of a new school day. Everyone was seated and ready. "So, how did you like the party?" Khalid smiled and looked around the classroom, as he put his old briefcase down on the desk.

"Awesome!" Jabari said, right away.

"Really great!" Set said, and then added, "Jabari's playing was a fun part of it."

"Yeah, I'm not surprised. It's always super," Mafulla replied. "I'm just sorry I had to leave early, but it was a big family emer-gency that seemed really, really bad for a while, and then it mirac-ulously turned out fine, and in some ways much better than fine."

"I was so glad to hear that," Khalid said. "Hoda filled me in last night." At this point, Khalid looked at the other boys and said, "Mafulla's dad had something like a very serious heart attack as he prepared to come to the party, and he was rushed to the hos-pital in great distress, but after a big scare, he managed to bounce back onto the path of what looks like an extraordinarily fast and complete recovery. It was a very great relief in the end, a genuine turnaround."

"Oh, man," several of the boys then said at about the same time, adding various words like "Glad he's Ok." And "Good to hear he's recovering."

"Haji said, "I'm sorry he had to go through all that, man, and your whole family, too. We wondered what had happened to you. I'm just relieved that it turned out Ok."

"Thanks," Mafulla replied, simply.

Khalid then asked, "How was your dad later in the evening, after Hoda left the hospital?"

"Tired but good," Mafulla said. "Thanks for asking. Walid and I crashed at the hospital for the night, in case dad needed anything. He was in good spirits this morning, and actually walked around the room almost like normal. He just said his chest is really sore, from a lot of people pushing on it. I think they're sending him home some time before lunch. I wish we hadn't had to leave the party before the main food was served and Jabari played. But, you know, you can't schedule emergencies."

"No, you can't," Khalid agreed. "Emergencies rarely respect the flow of our normal lives. They have a way of surprising us. They rearrange things with a power almost like a strong gravitational force. They pull everything else around them out of place and scramble our plans. You responded as you had to, and I'm so glad you were able to be there with your father when the situation apparently turned around. But I do wish you had also been able to experience the dinner that was brought out after you had to leave."

"The king actually sent some of the food to us, later on," Mafulla explained.

"Oh, good," Khalid said.

"All the food was just amazing!" Bafur exclaimed. "I felt like I had died and gone to heaven! Oh. Sorry, Mafulla. I shouldn't joke that way."

"No problem," Mafulla said as his thoughts momentarily went back to what his father had told them all.

"Thanks. I just mean that the food was so spectacular! And there was so much of it," he said in a voice of astonishment.

"The games were all great, too," Malik commented. "I mean, in addition to all the food."

"Yeah, I think we played every single game, except what was set aside for the smaller kids," Haji said.

"Khalid?" Set suddenly looked concerned about something.

"Yes, Set?"

"Could I ask Mafulla a question?"

"Now?"

"Yeah."

"About?"

"His dad and what happened."

"Mafulla, is that Ok with you?"

"Yeah, sure. No problem." He turned to his classmate. "What is it, man?"

Set looked back at Khalid and then at Mafulla. "I don't quite know how to say this. But I was reading the other day about ... death and life stuff and ... I was just wondering, when ... your dad had his problem like a heart attack, did he just go unconscious like in deep sleep, or did he experience anything? I don't know if you guys talked about this, but I was just wondering. I don't want to pry into something that's none of my business, but I'm really interested in this question, from a philosophical point of view and, you know, genuine curiosity."

"No, that's Ok, it's not prying at all," Mafulla said. "And, as a matter of fact, dad's heart was stopped for a long time. The doctors said he was ... actually dead. And that was really tough and, you know, pretty traumatic for all of us. But then he came back, and when he popped awake, he was excited and talking, and he described some pretty amazing things he said he had experienced."

"Really?"

"Yeah, and he saw and described some of the stuff that was happening around him and to him when he was supposed to be unconscious—and even when they said he was dead. He described it all at first from a perspective of hovering above his body. And everything he said about what he saw going on in the car on the way to the hospital, and once he got there, all the medical stuff, turned out to be true, and people were shocked that he could know it. And then he talked about a bright light and moving or flying or something toward it, and seeing a totally beautiful place and meeting his mother and father, and they were young again, and then he saw something really strange and amazing from a distance, and knew he had to come back, and that it wasn't yet his time to go all the way into the love and kindness and support and what he called the source of all things."

"Wow," Set said in a low voice.

"Yeah, wow," Jabari said, thinking back on the somewhat similar experience he had when he fell into the Nile River on a trip the class had taken some time back. But he otherwise remained quiet now and just intensely interested in what Mafulla had described.

Haji looked puzzled. "You mean, his body was in the hospital, but his mind or soul or something was moving, traveling, through space, away from his body?"

"Yeah, maybe through space, at first, or something really like it, and then through dimensions or something and across a border and … into somewhere else. I know it sounds strange."

Khalid spoke up at this point and commented, "As a matter of fact, there are many ancient reports and beliefs about such death, or near death, experiences."

"Really?" Bafur said.

"Yes. There's an ancient tradition of texts and burial markings often known loosely and collectively as *The Egyptian Book of the Dead*. There's also something very roughly like it in Tibet, again, several different texts known together in a popular way as *The Tibetan Book of the Dead*. In all these ancient documents, there are indications of light and travel and beautiful places after earthly death."

"So, people must have died and come back and talked of such things," Haji said.

"Like my dad," Mafulla commented.

"Yeah, like your dad," Haji agreed.

"Yes. Some think that these books resulted from the stories of those who had themselves crossed the line between life and death and then, improbably, returned. Others speculate that some of the stories, or accounts, that have come down to us also result from revelations to living people who have not experienced any separation of soul and body through death but who, in deep meditative states, somehow accessed these things, and then talked or wrote about them."

"But the people who had the experience, like Mafulla's dad, actually went to heaven and came back?" Bafur asked.

"Well, they seem to have gone somewhere beautiful and loving, and then to have come back," Khalid cautioned, adding, "at least, in their experiences."

"But the somewhere would have to be heaven, wouldn't it?" Jabari spoke up and said.

"Perhaps, heaven," Khalid said.

"But, what else could it be?" Jabari asked, perplexed.

"Another stage along the way to the ultimate destination," Khalid suggested. "But maybe not yet fully there. An anteroom, or a transitional place, maybe."

"What do you mean?"

"Remember when we went to Alexandria, as a class trip?"

"Sure."

"Well, we walked over to the motor pool, and then rode in cars. We crossed town and arrived at the dock. Then we got on a boat. We were on the Nile for a while."

"Or … in it," Set said, looking at Jabari, and the smaller boy nodded his head and gave a silly thumbs-up.

"Yes. And then we got to the docks in Alexandria. And finally, we were in the city itself. And then, last of all, we got to the hotel. So, it could be that our existence is a bit like that. It's a journey, an unexpected adventure that takes us through many stages, to many places. Our life now on earth is one of those stages, one of those places. And there are other places, or dimensions, or stages beyond this one, and perhaps others beyond those, and others."

"So, which one is heaven? When do we actually get to heaven?" Jabari asked.

"We don't at present know with certainty. Perhaps we can't, at this stage. It could be that what comes next is a part of heaven, already, the outlying borders of paradise. There are some who suggest that heaven is not just one big place, or one simple state of being, but rather many. It could be that what we experience after death is an intermediate phase, not still here and not yet there, or by contrast it could be that, at the very moment of earthly death, we're already setting foot, so to speak, in the heavenly realm, but just the arrival area—a bit like when you come to the palace, and you go through a main door and are, depending on the door, in one or another large entrance hall at first. You don't step through the front door straight into the king's private room—or into the dining room, Bafur." Khalid smiled and said, "In the palace, there are many rooms."

"Oh, man!" Jabari said.

"What?" Set turned and asked him.

"I suddenly realized, from what Khalid just said: What if you die and go through a spiritual door into the palace of heaven, and it looks beautiful and great. And then you move through the first entrance hall, and the next thing you know, you're in a place that looks sort of familiar, way too familiar, and it's the afterlife version of ... this classroom! And there's getting ready to be a big, big exam that goes on ... forever!"

Everyone laughed. And even Khalid smiled. "Or—Oh, man! Someone, not to mention names, is giving a really long homework assignment, or, worse yet, everlasting homework assignments!"

The boys really liked this one. Khalid said, "Always a comedian."

"And the jokes are, obviously ... divine," Jabari said, to continued chuckles, whereupon he did his best version of Mafulla's double eyebrow jump and got an even bigger laugh.

"How we go from the cosmic mysteries and the deepest issues

into mere silliness always amazes me," Khalid said. "But, for some reason, just as strange, I approve."

"If there aren't jokes in heaven, I'm staging a protest," Jabari said, "a funny protest with silly songs to make my point. I'm taking the uke." Khalid just shook his head.

"I'm sorry, guys. I have to joke a little," Jabari said, looking around at his classmates. But, you know, what happened to me in the river on the way to Alexandria—well, I had some stuff go on and, I mean, I experienced some of what Mafulla was talking about, and it was wild, and great, and amazing. I didn't have as much happen, but there was a light, and it felt so good. It was by far the best experience I ever had. And the next thing I knew, I was sort of throwing up water and coughing, and lying on my back on the barge and trying to figure out what had happened."

"Yeah, that was scary," Bafur said. "It was awful when you fell in the water, and when they got you out and you looked really dead."

"Yeah, totally," Haji said. "Not just partially. But all the way."

"But what came between falling in and getting out was pretty strange and wonderful, at the same time."

"Would you want to experience that again?" Haji asked.

"In one sense, yeah, the good parts, but in another sense—not any time soon," Jabari answered. "Not until I'm supposed to. I mean: I sort of understand that it's not for now, but for later. You shouldn't rush it and go for the experience before it comes to you. That would be bad."

Elsewhere in the palace, Bancom had just entered the king's private sitting room to bring him the news that had crackled through the radio from the military outpost at El-Wadi.

The king thanked his chief communications officer and, as Bancom left, he decided to take a few moments to enter into a deeper mental state of open-ness and connection, and reach out to his old friends, Sab and Meskhenet Maayuf.

At this point, they were on their camels, crossing the mid-morning sand, and were well on their way to El-Wadi. Sab turned to his wife and shouted over the breeze in their ears, "He knows."

"What did you say?"

"He knows. Ali knows."

"Yes. And that's good."

22

WALKING HOME

THE KING HAD SENT A PALACE GUARD TO ASK HODA IF SHE could come to his sitting room for a meeting after school. He had also dispatched another man to find Layla with the same request. Hamid and Masoon would be there as well.

Hoda walked into Kular's office, where Layla now was sitting and having a cup of tea. "Layla! You're already here."

"Hi, Hoda! Yes, I was close by when the king's message got to me."

Just then, Kular came out from the inner doorway that opened into the sitting room. "Oh, hello, Hoda! The king will be right with you and Layla. He's almost done with his prior meeting. It shouldn't be but a few more minutes. He appreciates your being here at such short notice."

"Never a problem," Hoda said, adding, "You're looking quite well and vigorous, if I may say so, Kular."

"I thank you, young lady. I think the work suits me, and so does the food!" He said this while rubbing his stomach.

"Well, you do keep in good shape, as well," Hoda replied.

"Yes, I do what I can. Father Time tries his best to make it difficult, but I've learned something important that I try to share with others whenever I can."

"What's that?"

"Nothing great is ever easy."

"That's the truth," Hoda said.

Kular commented, "The most important things can be the hardest."

Layla added, "You're so right about that. I'm working on a charitable event to be held in three months, and it's the hardest thing to plan I've ever attempted. But if it all comes together, it could be one of the most beneficial initiatives ever launched in the kingdom."

Kular then nodded. "I believe it was the ancient writer Horace who famously said, 'The greater the difficulty the greater the glory.' And I'm convinced that the glory comes in working through the difficulty, even before and distinct from any success we might have with it."

"That's a wise perspective," Layla responded.

"Thanks. I gain a lot from the ancients. Horace is so insightful in his poems. I especially love the *Odes*."

"And his *Epistles* are full of wisdom as well," Hoda added to the mix.

"Indeed!" Kular then turned back to Layla and said, "So, this event you're putting on: What's the cause that's being supported?"

"Education, and especially the preparation of young women for active lives of citizenship," Layla replied. "I think our future depends on it."

"I agree wholeheartedly." Kular said.

Hoda remarked, "Throughout far too much of the human adventure, education hasn't been valued enough, and even where decent educations were available, it was normally for half the population, which makes no sense at all. We need all our young people prepared for active and productive lives, as well as for the rich inner life that only a good education can spark fully."

"Hear, hear!" Layla replied, and Kular actually clapped. "We should have you come and speak to the group," she suggested. "I don't know why that never crossed my mind before."

"Well, I'd love to help out," Hoda offered.

"Let me do some more of the planning, and I'll give you the details," Layla said.

"Good. I'm ready, willing, and able."

Kular excused himself for a moment to run down the hall and get something for the king. Layla asked her friend, "What are Khalid and Kissa up to, on this fine afternoon?"

"Khalid has a few things to grade, and then the two of them are going to walk home with the lovely Hasina, I believe."

"Good. I thought she might be going home with Kissa today, but I wasn't sure."

"They have some tricky homework, and I think they want to tackle it together," Hoda explained.

"Well, you'd be the one to know about that, for sure," Layla laughed.

"I'm a relentless task master," Hoda said, playing along. "But, the greater the difficulty ..."

"The greater the glory!" Layla laughed, adding, "And you're preparing our young ladies well for the many glories of their future."

"I'm certainly working hard for that result."

Layla suddenly looked serious. "Do you know why the king wants to see us today?"

"It's probably about what went on last night at the hospital."

"I couldn't believe it when Hasina got back with the news of everything that had happened. Our poor friends! What an ordeal!"

Across the second floor of the palace, in Khalid's office, Kissa and Hasina were throwing a rubber ball back and forth, in variously strange and gymnastic ways—under a leg, behind the back, arching it overhead and backwards. "Hey, Dad, how much longer?" Kissa called out to Khalid, who was still hunched over a paper, making some marks on it with his pen.

"Soon. Close," he replied, adding, "Not long."

"That's your last one?"

"Last one."

She turned to Hasina and grinned and said in a lower voice, "He's monosyllabic when he's concentrating."

"I heard that."

"He said, monosyllabically," Kissa commented with a funny face, and made Hasina laugh.

"Shh!"

The girls both grimaced and went back to their game in relative silence. And their moves became even more acrobatic.

Not four minutes had passed when there was a rustling of papers being gathered and pushed into a briefcase and Khalid announced, "All finished. Ready to go?"

"Yeah! We have lots of homework to do, thanks to your lovely wife," Kissa said.

"Good!" Khalid replied.

"Good?"

"Yes, it's important to keep yourself exercised intellectually, and not just in class, but also throughout the day," he explained.

"Well, we're going to be so exercised on this assignment that I think we'll be intellectually sore for a week. I can already feel my mental muscles tightening up and all my conceptual tendons are aching badly. Ouch."

"I'll pretend I know what that means," Khalid responded, and then said, "So, if your mental muscles and tendons can take it, let's go home."

Kissa grabbed her book bag and Hasina picked hers up off the floor and they followed Khalid out the door, down the hall, down the stairs, and over to the palace guardroom, where Khalid immediately spotted a guard he knew well. "Omari!"

"Hi Khalid, and ladies," Omari said.

"Hi Omari!" Kissa and Hasina said at the same time."

"Look," Khalid said, "Hoda's in a meeting with the king, and I know that normally one or another of you fine top guards is supposed to accompany us home, under such conditions as we're in these days."

"Yes, indeed, and I'm ready right now," Omari answered.

"That's great. But I was thinking, you know, it's just a short walk home, and we've had no particular reason to suppose that we face any particular problem—I mean, the family—at this point."

"The king's pretty cautious," Omari said.

Khalid replied, "Ok. You're right. I just didn't want to take you away from any important work you might have."

"This is my most important work," he smiled.

"Good point. We should have you accompany us, then."

"Great. Let's go."

The two gentlemen led the way back down the hall, chatting about their respective days. Omari also asked the girls a couple of questions along the way and they entertained him with some funny answers. They were walking briskly down the halls, and then, ultimately, out the side door of the palace, where a pleasant temperature was awaiting them, along with a slight breeze. Hasina took a deep breath and said, "I feel like I've been inside all day!"

"You have been!" Kissa reminded her.

"Oh, yeah, true. That makes the escape even more blissful, the sun on my face, the air in my hair!"

"You could make advertisements for skipping school," Kissa said in a voice of admiration.

"I heard that! Don't even say such a thing!" Khalid replied in mock horror. "That would be like telling people to skip some of the best of life!"

"Oh, my!" Kissa said, and made Omari laugh.

Hasina looked at her friend and said, "I guess once you become a teacher, it sort of messes with an important part of your brain." And then she added, for Khalid's sake, "But I mean that with all due respect, sir."

"Ha. Ha." Khalid responded. "Your respect is duly noted with what's left of my messed up brain."

Hasina then said, "I guess you could enjoy the sun and fresh air without skipping school, if you did all your intellectual work outside on nice days."

Kissa interrupted, "Don't get him started or you'll hear a long lecture on the ancient peripatetic philosophers who did exactly that."

Khalid said, "From the Greek word that meant walking around."

"See? Ok, Dad, we've already learned enough for one day. Mom made sure of it."

Khalid laughed. "All right, all right." At this point, they had passed out through the side palace gate and were on the sidewalk of the main road headed toward their neighborhood.

After a minute or two, Hasina nearly whispered to her friend, "I need to ask you something."

Kissa looked at her for a second and said, "Dad, and Omari, we're going to slow down for a second and walk a little farther behind you, for some private girl talk, if that's Ok, for just a minute or two."

"Oh, Ok," Khalid replied.

"Sure, that's fine," Omari said, and glanced back. Hasina and Kissa both slowed their mutual pace just a touch and began to fall back a bit, while the men walked on ahead, talking.

Kissa said, "What's up?"

Hasina made a face and said, "I think my hair looks bad recently. It's sort of awful."

"What do you mean?"

"You don't know?"

"No, not at all."

"You're just being kind. Look at it. It's limp and seems … even a little greasy."

"No! That's not true at all. It looks normal to me. It has a nice shine."

"Look more closely." They slowed down a little more. Kissa peered carefully at her friend's long hair, lifting a few strands for examination.

"Ok … it's maybe not quite as shimmery and bouncy as usual. But it still looks great," Kissa said.

"You see? I knew it," Hasina lamented. "I have no idea what's causing the problem. I wash it and brush it like normal, but it's just … misbehaving for some reason."

"Do you think you've had a spell put on you by the evil Santiago? Has he gone that far?"

"Very funny!" Hasina replied. "Then, we'd have to stop him fast."

"Yeah, but it's probably not him. You know what they say about girls our age," Kissa reminded her friend.

"What? That we're suddenly attracting male attention like magnets, whether we want to or not?" Hasina replied.

"No, silly. Well, that too, but I meant that our bodies are changing in many ways at our present age, and sometimes the chemistry of it all goes a little haywire for a short time, and you get blemishes or irritability or … limp hair."

"I'd rather be just irritable." Kissa laughed at that, and then Hasina continued, "I mean: I'm already a little irritated about the bad hair. I'd take irritability alone any day."

"That's funny. But, yeah, I know what you mean. Still, it really isn't a big deal, Hassi. I mean, if you hadn't asked me to stare, I wouldn't have noticed a thing different, and I'm sure Mafulla hasn't."

"You don't think?"

"No. Boys are mostly oblivious to the small stuff, to the subtle details that we often work so hard to get right. And yet, the overall effects of all the little things add up and grab their unconscious minds, and their hearts, it seems. But, when one thing gets strange for a while, they'll never notice, or even care if they did. You're a total package, brains and beauty and bravery and … girl brawn."

"Ha! Thanks. I guess you're right—I mean about it's being no big deal and Mafulla probably not even noticing."

"And if he did, by some reverse miracle, notice anything different, he'd likely think it was cute, or endearing, or something."

"Ok, you've officially cheered me up. Thanks, friend."

"You're welcome, friend."

Khalid and Omari had stopped for a moment at the street corner up ahead of the girls, almost in sight of the house. And Khalid thanked their guard again for joining them in the walk home, assuring him that everything was Ok at this point and that he could go back to the palace after a fine job of escorting them safely along.

"You're sure you don't want me to go all the way to the house, and enter it first, and have a look around?" Omari asked.

"No, That's not necessary at all. It's always locked up tight while we're away," Khalid responded.

The girls, seeing them in conversation, had slowed down and then also stopped, to continue to talk more privately. They were now nearly the length of a full city block back from the men, and Omari had continued to glance at them, occasionally. From where they stood, he could be seen smiling and nodding and then turning to walk back in their direction. As he approached, Kissa smiled and said, "That's it? We're on our own now? No more strong guard?"

"Your dad says I've done enough, and that the house is locked up like a fortress. So he officially released me to go back. Everything seems quiet this afternoon."

"Oh, Ok," Kissa replied.

"I was supposed to meet Amon in about ten minutes any way, so, if you two are also fine with it, I'm off."

"Thanks Omari! It's fine and dandy," Kissa said. "Say hi to Amon."

"Will do."

And Hasina said, "Thanks for coming along. We'll see you soon."

Khalid, meanwhile, had started up walking again, and had fully turned the corner onto their street. The girls were still pretty far back and at first didn't notice him walking on, as they continued to talk. Omari had actually begun to jog back toward the palace and was getting farther away. No one had a clue as to what was soon to happen. And that was strange. In fact, it was almost as strange as the impending events themselves would be.

Khalid was lost in his own thoughts at that point, and hadn't even looked back or thought of waiting for the girls. And, as he made his way a little farther down their street and then glanced up ahead toward home, he noticed to his surprise that there were two men just coming around the corner of the house and walking toward the front door. It looked like they were maintenance men or house painters, and he couldn't remember hearing Hoda talk about scheduling any work. But then, she often hired various people for small jobs around the house and didn't mention it to him.

He didn't recognize the men, but nothing about their appearance or presence worried him. To go greet them sooner and offer any help they might need, he quickened his pace, squinting ahead to make out what exactly the two of them might be doing. And as he drew closer, he could see that the taller of the men was at the front door with a paintbrush and a small can and was already dipping the brush in. Then, to his great surprise, he saw the man make a bright red diagonal mark on the side of the doorpost, moving from upper left to lower right. And now he reversed the motion, moving his hand and the brush from upper right to lower left. The result was something that Khalid could just barely make out from this distance—a small red 'X' painted beside the door. That was extremely odd and more than a little confusing to see.

"Hey! Hello! Excuse me!" Khalid shouted toward the men as he increased the speed of his stride. He had just raised his right hand to motion to them. The smaller man standing back from the door and watching his colleague with the brush turned and saw him coming. He also held up his hand in what seemed for a moment to be a greeting, and then it turned into a nearly universal signal to stop. Then his hand dropped forward, with his fingers pointed toward Khalid. And that puzzled him completely. "I'm Khalid El-Bay, the owner." He barely got the last word out before things turned bizarre.

The air around him suddenly felt like it had changed consistency. There's no other way to say it. What had just been nearly intangible seemed instantly to have the thickness and weight of dense syrup. Gravity tripled its hold. All the energy felt like it had left Khalid's body. He went from dramatically slowing down to now feeling like it would be impossible to move forward. His legs buckled and he dropped slowly to the ground, on his knees and hands. He was completely stunned and slightly panicked, because he had no idea what was going on. His first thought was that maybe he was having a stroke or a seizure. But then, he couldn't think at all. He was now looking at the ground, as his body tried to support itself and not fall flat.

"Dad!" Kissa had just turned the corner. She saw him on the ground and, shocked, began to run in his direction, at first not even looking up toward their house. "Dad!"

"What?" Hasina now also saw Khalid face down on the ground and then looked up and noticed the men at the house. She mentally registered the small man with his hand raised in a strange way. And she knew in that instant that they were up against something that had to be stopped quickly. She called out to her friend, "Kissa! The house! Go serious Hoda-Phi! Now! Now!"

Kissa glanced up as she ran toward her father and saw the little man with a terribly ugly expression on his face and his hand raised toward Khalid. At that instant and without any delaying interval of conscious thought, she responded to Hasina's words with the most fiercely aggressive attempt she had ever experienced to draw on the great energy beyond her and channel it with force into that man's head, the man who was apparently trying to harm or even kill her father.

He instantly cried out in pain and surprise and staggered. And then he shifted his gaze and hand gesture toward Kissa. She felt, as a result, a wave of something she didn't expect.

At the palace, Hoda and Layla had just walked into the king's sitting room, as Kular held the door open for them. When Hoda entered, her expression was very serious and her first words to the king were, "Kissa and Hasina and Khalid are at this instant under some form of attack. There's power involved. Join with me to help them."

"Yes," Layla said. "I can see them: Khalid's on the ground. There are two men at your house, Hoda. One is pointing his hand. He's brought Khalid down in a sort of temporary paralysis, and has now just turned on Kissa. The girls are already fighting back."

The king stood up from his chair and walked toward them. He took Hoda's right hand and Layla's left, and the two ladies held hands as well. In that circle, they mentally left the room and traveled to a space ten feet in front of the small man and created a wall. And right then, Kissa felt a cessation of the force that she had just experienced. The onrush of power suddenly vanished, as if it was blocked entirely or snuffed out. She and Hasina then both walked boldly toward the small man, who at this point looked totally bewildered.

King Ali, Hoda, and Layla then began systematically to shut down the power this man had directed toward Khalid and had sought to use against the girls. Hadrat Anami, the most senior honorary status Santiago to his peers, who was often referred to as "The Second Santiago," had never felt anything like what he now experienced. His body went cold. An extraordinarily painful and icy explosion of arctic water seemed to fill his body and soul and stab him everywhere with a thousand sharp jagged shards of frozen misery. His lungs felt like he was drowning. He was seized with fear and ripped with agony, and then his mind went blank. His long cultivated spiritual force was stripped away from his core so quickly that he couldn't understand or even clearly realize what was happening.

The problem for this wickedly deluded man was that long years of training in perverse spirituality had penetrated his core, and the power now being extracted from him by force was too tightly integrated into his soul for him to be able to survive its elimination. He gasped and contorted, his body twisting, and then he let out one terrible, strangulated, and muted scream as he collapsed to the ground, much like Khalid just had, but with greater force. His body could not catch itself. He fell face down and his entire torso jerked in spasms while his arms and legs violently twitched.

At this point, King Ali pulled back. But Hoda continued on, as did Layla, for another few seconds. Anami's heart quivered and then stopped. The entire neural system supporting his soul's sojourn on this earth was shut down. His spirit, such as it had come to be, was wrenched out of the corpse that now lay on the ground in front of the two young ladies who were witnessing this in the flesh. And they knew in an instant whose power was at work.

The man with the paintbrush had dropped it onto the ground as he watched with confusion and then horror. He could not believe what was happening to his boss, a man he feared greatly and served slavishly. To protect himself, he reached toward his belt and pulled out a small revolver. Swinging it up to take aim at the girls, he was immediately stunned by a large military knife tearing into his abdomen before he could level and fire the weapon. He doubled over in a stab of searing pain and fell.

Kissa turned back to her father, rushing to his aid. He was on his knees, with his forehead touching the ground, and still had not spoken. "Dad! Dad! Are you Ok?"

Hasina had now reached the painter and, bending down, pulled her knife out from him, wiping it quickly twice on his coat and twisting around to double-check the small man who was still on the ground and make sure that no more defensive measures would be needed. He was dead. They both were. She had not wanted that result at all with this other man, but she felt she had no choice. It was likely the only thing that would have stopped him. She had intuitively known that nothing but drastic action would work. When she reached down and touched the painter to check for a pulse, his flesh made her shudder in disgust and pity, and sadness, mixed together with relief.

"Is your dad all right?" she called out to Kissa.

"I don't know, yet," Kissa said. "Come quickly."

Hasina rushed over to her side, where she already had her hands on Khalid's head. "Help me, Hassi," Kissa implored. Hasina placed her hands as well on Khalid and they both prayed and opened their spirits, and allowed healing grace to enter them and flow forth into the man they both cared about so much. They stayed there, motionless, for thirty seconds or more, with a total concentration beyond anything they had experienced before, until Khalid groaned loudly.

He mumbled, "What happened?" His head was still down, but his voice now became moderately strong and clear. "What … happened to me?"

"Daddy, you're Ok! You're going to be Ok."

"But what happened? There were men at the house and I called out to them. And then I couldn't walk, and I couldn't even stand, and all my energy left me. I was paralyzed, and losing all my conscious awareness. What did they do to me?"

"We're not sure, but one of the men had strange power and attacked you with it. And we saw what was happening, and we retaliated to stop him, and I think we did, for a moment, but then he sent a force of some kind toward us. And then a much greater power intervened. It was mom and Layla and the king, I could tell. And they took him apart, and shut down all his powers, and he couldn't survive it."

"Are they here?"

"Not physically. They're in the palace, I think, but they knew what we needed, and they acted."

"And the other guy was going to start shooting and I had to stop him," Hasina said. "I didn't want to do what I did, but I had no time for anything else, and I don't think anything else would have worked."

"What?" Khalid asked.

"They're both dead now. The men who were harming you are both gone now and can't hurt you any more."

"Are there others?"

"I don't think so, not here."

Khalid slowly struggled to rise, and he sat up and said, "Why were they putting red paint on our house?"

"I don't know," Kissa said, "but it's been happening to other people who also know the king, to their houses." At this point, Hasina lifted her hands off Khalid. As he had been speaking, she had moved her hands from his head to his right arm and was making only light contact, and then realized that she could withdraw her touch. That instant, Kissa said to her, "Hassi, go see if there's a note of any kind, either on the ground, or in the possession of the men. There have always been notes where there were red 'X' marks on doorways."

As Hasina walked toward the house with her back toward Kissa and Khalid, there were suddenly two shadows near the two of them, behind them. Before Kissa could see or hear them, because of her concentration on her father, Malik and Haji had appeared just twenty feet away. Malik called out, "Kissa, what in the world just happened here? What's wrong?"

And before she could answer, Haji said, "Are you guys Ok?"

"Oh! Malik. Haji. Good. We're Ok."

"What happened?"

"Yeah, what's going on?"

"We were just walking home and those two men on the ground near the door were here already and doing something to our house. And dad was walking ahead of us and called out to question them and the small man began to hurt him with some sort of power, through his mind and with a hand gesture. And dad fell and Hassi and I saw what was going on, and we acted with our hearts and minds to stop the man. And we did, but he fought back. And then we felt the king and mom and Layla intervene from a distance—they're in the king's sitting room, I think, in the palace right now—and the man with the power just died. The life was somehow ripped out of him. Then the other guy was going to shoot us and Hassi stopped him."

Malik looked at Hasina. "What did you do?"

"My knife. I didn't want to, but I had to—no other choice. It was in my bag like usual. I stopped him with it."

"It's Ok," Haji said. "It was necessary. You did what you had to do. The king calls it a tragic necessity."

Malik walked quickly over to the tall man and Haji approached the shorter of the two. "They're both gone," Hasina said. "Would you guys walk around the house and check to make sure there aren't any others nearby?"

"Sure," Malik said, and added, "Did you have a Phi escort home?"

"Omari, but dad told him to go back to the palace right before we got up to the house, when everything looked fine."

"Oh."

"Go look around the back."

"Sure," Haji answered, and both the boys jogged around the house, Malik to the right, and Haji to the left.

"There's a key under a blue pot at the back door. Go inside too, after you check outside," Kissa called out to them. "Give it a full sweep. Look carefully."

"Will do!"

Kissa helped her father stand up. He felt a little strange at first, but that passed quickly and he got his bearings and looked all around. He spoke to Kissa and said, "He stopped my brain before I could engage him … with superior reasoning."

"Dad! Don't be funny now!"

"I'm just glad that two of my favorite superheroes were with me to save the day."

"Yeah, well, we had help."

"It sounds like you stopped him before help intervened."

"True, but that might not have lasted long, not with this guy. He was pretty strong."

"It lasted as long as it needed to."

"Good point."

Hasina picked up something from where the tall man was on the ground and waved it in the air. "Got it! An envelope!" she said. "It was in the guy's pocket."

"Another one of those stupid notes," Kissa concluded.

"What notes?" Khalid asked.

"Leem Hadad got one, Mafulla's parents got one, and the king has gotten a couple. They're notes of warning and harassment from a bad character named Juan Santiago."

"Hoda's mentioned him to me. Was it Santiago just now who attacked me?"

"Unlikely," Kissa said. "But indirectly, yeah. The guy who went after you was probably one of his close followers, and I would guess, one of his top guys. We've had to deal with a few of his men before."

"Oh."

Hasina said, "Kissa, should I open the note?"

"Yes, please." she replied.

"What does it say?" Khalid asked.

Hasina ripped it open, pulled out a piece of paper, and unfolded it slowly. She stared at it for a couple of seconds and said, "Well, this is different."

23

VISITORS

KULAR KNOCKED ON THE DOOR AND CRACKED IT OPEN. "YOU have visitors, Your Majesty."

"Yes, thank you, Kular! I was expecting them. Please, send them in."

The king's butler held the door open wide, and Meskhenet Maayuf came walking into the room with a big smile. Ali broke protocol and stood up to greet her with a broad smile of his own. Sab and then Zet Noni followed her through the door, and Zet was clearly looking all around, amazed, taking everything in.

"Greetings, my friends!" The king beamed his welcome. "Come in! Come in!"

"I like your new house," Meskhenet said to the king. "Very fancy."

The king laughed and said, "Thank you, my dear, though it's not exactly new. However, it is relatively new to me."

"It's a bit more room than the place you had in Dromeda," she said with a big smile.

"And the food's much better than I could fix for myself, back at home," he said.

"I'm sure that's an understatement," she laughed.

"And greetings to you, Sab! Hello there, Zet!"

"Your Majesty," Sab said with a smile and a deep bow.

"Hi Ali, I mean, King Ali, I mean, Your Majesty," Zet said, and looked a bit flustered. He did a quick bow for good measure and when he straightened up, he saw that the king was smiling at him and nodding.

Sab added, "Oh, and please may I officially convey the greetings of the entire village?"

"Yes, you may," the king replied. "And do let them know of my continued great fondness for all of them, as well."

"Indeed!" Sab responded. "You're highly thought of there, you know, by both people and animals."

"And speaking of animals," the king said.

"Yes, he's with us here in Cairo, and had a marvelous trip!"

Ali laughed and said, "Good! Good! Now, please, have a seat." He gestured to a large sofa and some chairs and added, "Make yourself comfortable anywhere you'd like."

Again, breaking protocol because these were his oldest friends, the king made sure they were all seated before taking his own chair. Kular was still standing right inside the door. The king called the butler over and made full introductions, and greetings were exchanged all around. Then he said, "Kular, my friend, would you bring in some tea and treats for our visitors?"

"Yes, Your Majesty! Right away," he replied.

The king looked at Sab with great kindness in his face and said, simply, "I knew you were coming."

"Yes, I felt it," he replied.

"So did I," Meskhenet added and then tacked onto her words the phrase, "Your Majesty."

"But I admit I don't know why. It could be something about a book, a very old book."

"Yes," Sab said. "You're too good. We can't get anything at all by you. I was going to pretend that we're here on a long needed vacation and spontaneous sightseeing expedition."

"Oh, my husband!" Meskhenet sighed. Looking at the king, she said, "Tell me. Are all men like this?"

"Just the really good ones," he replied.

"I see." Meskhenet laughed and Sab cleared his throat a bit loudly. She then merely shook her head.

The king continued, playing along, "And, as you know, there are indeed many wonderful sights to see all over town, while you're all here, vacationing."

Sab looked over at his wife and said, "See? Even the king keeps his sense of humor, and in such times as these."

"You're two peas in a pod," she said.

"Thank you, my dear," Ali said with a smile and a nod. And then he turned back to Sab. "So, what about the book? Is it a travel guide to the most famous tourist traps in Cairo, with helpful tips on overpriced hotels and restaurants?"

"Oh, don't I wish!" Sab said, as Meskhenet continued to shake her head. "Actually, now that I think of it, a guide to the best hotels and restaurants in the desert would have been useful on the way here. And a section on desert entertainment would help."

"It would be a very short book," the king said with a straight face.

"Yes, apparently so," Sab agreed. "And … there was only one real terrestrial sight available along the way."

"Indeed?"

"Sand."

Zet laughed out loud at this. The king smiled again and replied, "Oh, yes, and it's a sight of great antiquity, carefully and meticulously preserved all these centuries—every grain. We really should have official sightseeing guides posted along the way on signs, as sources of information for travelers. But it would hardly be worth the cost for them to say only, 'Behold, The Sand!' and 'Sand Ahead,' and "More Sand," and other such expressions of the entirely obvious."

Sab laughed. "You two, cut it out," Meskhenet said with plenty of amusement hiding behind her tone.

The king chuckled, as did Sab and Zet, and he said, "Ok, Ok, we should get down to whatever more serious business is at hand."

Sab turned to the younger man with them and said, "Zet, why don't you tell the king the reason for our journey?"

"Yes, of course," Zet said. He shifted on the sofa and explained, "Ok, Your Majesty: A book arrived in the post a little more than two weeks ago for one of the store's former customers, a man who worked with that Santiago fellow. He had ordered it through us from a rare book dealer in London. A long time had passed, and you came and chased those guys out of the area, which has been a great relief to us all, by the way. And everyone continues to feel very grateful for that," Zet added. "But then, the book arrived long after the customer had gone, and I didn't know what to do with it. So, I began to look it over."

"What's the book?" the king asked.

"*Spiritual Power, Force, and Warfare*," Zet answered. "It's by a man named Manchu Leeko. Here it is. " He reached into a bag he was carrying and pulled out the old volume and rose up and, after a step or two, leaned forward and handed it to the king, before returning to his seat.

"I haven't heard of this before," the king replied, as he took it from Zet and began to examine it, glancing at the spine and then at the front cover, which was elaborately engraved.

"It was apparently first published in 1697 in London," Zet said. "What we have here seems to be the third edition."

"What do you make of it?" the king asked, as he opened the cover and turned to the table of contents. "And why do you think our adversaries ordered it?"

"It's a book of occult knowledge, or at least occult lore," Zet said. "It struck me right away as very strange. The parts I've read carefully go into great detail to depict the world as a battlefield between traditional moral concerns and what the author calls 'true power,' and he takes it as his task to point out the path of victory to those who choose the side of power against goodness. And that seems to describe our foe."

"I see."

Kular at that point quietly entered the room again and placed down trays of tea and cakes and other snack items and made his way silently back out. The king gestured to the food and said, "Please help yourselves. Now, Zet, what sorts of things are in the book?"

"There are odd spells and incantations, and recipes for mental and spiritual access to forms of force that he claims goodness would never embrace."

"Oh, my." The king sighed.

"I showed it to Sab and Meskhenet and, within a day, they told me that it's likely something you'd want to see, right away."

"Yes, they were correct, as always."

Sab then spoke up and said, "We suspect that Santiago had heard about this book or read about it, and had felt that it would be helpful to his cause. I've now read it through, as well, and I knew right away that some of the things in it would give you major clues as to who this man, Santiago, might be, deep down, and what he's up to, ultimately. I suspect he's been using a few of its techniques already, and so must know of them from some other source. But the book appears to be a big compendium of methods for men like him. "

"It is a big one."

"Yes, it's nearly four hundred pages of mystical techniques and advice on psychological and spiritual conflict."

Meskhenet then said, "When it came into our home, I began to have visions of this Santiago seeking to harm people who are in some way close to you, and I knew we had to come here and bring you the book ourselves."

"Whom was he seeking to harm, in your visions?"

"First, two boys about Walid's age that I didn't know, then the two young girls who were on the recent trip—Walid's friend Kissa, and Mafulla's friend Hasina. Then, he went after Mafulla's father, and shortly after that, Kissa's father. It seemed to me, in the visions, that he was unsuccessful in each case, from what I could detect."

"All that has indeed happened, and very recently."

"Is everyone all right?"

"Yes. Fortunately, in each attack you just identified, either the man himself, or whatever associate might have been involved in the violence, was indeed thwarted. Were there any others?"

"Yes, I'm afraid so. Your brother Rumi is in grave danger, as well as his wonderful wife, Bhati."

"He and Bhati are at a medical conference in Alexandria."

"He should be warned."

The king asked, "What have you seen Santiago try to do?"

"Well, it's different. With the two boys, he was seeking information, and he sent followers to torture them, question them, get what he wanted, and then kill them."

"Yes. The prince and Mafulla stopped the men."

"I'm glad. And then, after that one use of guns and knives and ropes by ordinary followers, every subsequent effort to harm someone in your life has involved one of his top disciples or Santiago himself, and has taken the form of mental force, with the use of a spiritual power to injure and to attempt to kill."

"Correct, and in each case, it broadcast itself to us. We knew in time to stop it, except for the incident with Mafulla's father, which we now believe to have involved the original Santiago, successfully cloaking for once the intended harmful actions. That plan proceeded and brought apparent death, but for only a short time. The dear departed one was, in that case, returned to us, and with a power to see his attacker, wherever he might be."

Sab responded to this by saying: "That's very interesting. But you said that this involved the original Santiago? What do you mean by the word 'original' here?"

"He's honored several of his top disciples with his name, and has paid other people in town to adopt it, in order to confuse our search for him. So there are many Santiagos on the loose, many copies and fakes, but only one original."

"I see."

Meskhenet said, "He's finally come to realize that you have great power. He has no idea how great. But he also has unusual power. I sense that even his top followers have a degree of this power. They are even fairly advanced."

"Yes."

"But he's frustrated that each aggressive use of spiritual resources by a disciple somehow announces itself in such a way as to bring immediate and effective countermeasures. So, I believe he has in mind for Rumi and Bhati something more purely physical."

"What exactly did you see?"

"Guns. Two guns. And they'll be wielded by two men with no real spiritual development whatsoever."

"Early-stage followers of his?"

"No. I don't think so. Not even that degree of association."

"Hired guns?"

"Yes. That's what I feel. Hoodlums. Street thugs, brutes really, paid assassins—they'll be two men who'd do anything for money. But they have no spiritual power, or even much mental engagement. They'll be almost like machines or—I hate to say it—even poisonous insects stinging something that happens to be in their way. He's chosen men whose minds have dimmed to nearly that degree. They'll not operate on the level where you have your most keen awareness."

The king picked up the thought, saying, "I see. So their actions would not broadcast themselves in such a way that we would definitely know, and could respond, within the realm of the mind and spirit."

"Yes, I think that's his plan, and I believe it's already to some extent underway. The man is a clever adversary."

"When is this going to happen? When will Rumi and Bhati be confronted?"

"I'm not sure—perhaps within a few days, or less. It's not immediately imminent, I think. It's not today. It may not be tomorrow. I can't tell. But I feel it's going to take place soon, and that it's going to be hard to anticipate beforehand because of the different means employed."

"Why is he doing this?"

"He seeks to undermine you. He's enraged at what you did to stop his major scheme of self-empowerment, the unusual plan he had for using all the animals he was collecting. He thinks you robbed him of his rightful avenue to greater power and that you now must pay in several ways."

"That's what I've suspected about all that's been going on. Of course, we've been using many resources looking for him so that we can stop any further crimes on his part. But his cloaking abilities seem to have effectively thwarted our search, up until now."

"You say that someone who died and came back to life can see where he is?"

"Yes, in a sense. It's the father of Walid's best friend. He now seems to have occasional flashes of vision as to what might be a circle of ten or twelve feet around the man, and sometimes more. So he can tell whether Santiago is standing on sand, or on a city street, or is inside a tent or a building, but not too much more than that. He has a hazy sense of the man's location, but it's not very precise. Still, it's quite helpful in allowing us to avoid false directions of pursuit."

"Good. The man needs to be found soon and stopped."

"Yes."

"I should also tell you this, which you may already have realized. He has no ambition to take your place in the kingdom. He would've been content for you to stay in your position and eventually answer to him, were it not for the unforgivable sin he thinks you've committed against him. No one can ever be allowed to believe that he, the great Santiago, can be thwarted. No one can dare go against him."

"I see."

"In his mind, you've committed the unforgiveable sin. And now, he must get even. He needs his revenge. And it's become a major distraction for him. He's obsessed. He keenly wishes for someone else to serve in your place. He doesn't really care who it is. His only requirement is that the king of Egypt ultimately be his servant, and of course, that the national monarch not be you."

"Well, one thing at a time," the king responded. "We need to warn Rumi." He stood up, and so did everyone else. He gestured to them and said, "Please, sit and have a snack. I'll be right back."

Dr. Rumi Shabeezar and his wife Bhati had a comfortable suite of rooms at the Palace Hotel in Alexandria, where a large regional convention of physicians was meeting. Paki Alexander, one of the senior palace guards who had been chosen by Masoon to accompany them, because of his relative seniority among the intermediate Phi, was staying in a room next to theirs for both security and support. A few military men who were stationed in Alexandria, along with one local Phi, were also being of service to him, as needed. It was the second day of meetings. Rumi had just left the main meeting room for the daily luncheon break. As he walked across the lobby of the hotel, a man approached him.

"Dr. Shabeezar? Doctor! Hello, there! Nazreel Hasbalam." The man extended his hand and the two of them shook. "I enjoyed your talk yesterday on village care in remote locations. I've tried to do something like what you suggested and it's worked wondrously."

"Oh? Where's your clinic? Are you from around here?" Rumi asked the man.

"No. My wife and I are just visitors to Alexandria, like you. She's off at the tourist sites today, as many of the wives are. My clinic is to the south of Cairo, due south and far down, near the famed latitude, the Tropic of Cancer," Hasbalam replied, with a smile and a shrug. "It's a small village where professional medical care had long been needed. I grew up nearby, the son of a merchant and, after my training, I decided to open a general practice like the one you described."

"How has it been?"

"It was a struggle at first, as you can imagine. There was no one to help. And the people are so poor. But I persisted and the clinic has grown. I have one junior colleague now and that's made a tremendous difference for the better."

"Excellent."

"We're not on a major route of commerce such as your home village—was it … Dromeda?"

"Yes, you remember well."

"Thank you. We don't have quite the population, or the itinerant need that your village has experienced, due to all the travelers who pass by, but there was no one at all before our clinic, no skilled medical help for more than fifty miles in any given direction, and sometimes a hundred."

"Well then, you've made a big difference, I'd imagine."

"Yes, I've been able to help a lot, after I was able to get the people who didn't already know me to trust me and submit to some of the less pleasant techniques of modern medicine."

"I know what you mean."

"Our immediate tools and procedures might cause pain, or to some degree discomfort, or even unease over the short run, but many of them do help to secure the existence of a long run for the patient."

"Indeed. And yet, as you suggest, the sales pitch is often difficult, as it takes people far beyond what they know and what makes them comfortable. It's much easier to recite an incantation than to take an injection or swallow some unpleasant medicine every day."

"Well said. We do often have to work hard to sell people on what they need—which is, on the surface, so counter-intuitive."

"Yes, but we learn quickly that there's a big difference between needing something, knowing you need it, and actually wanting it enough to choose it."

"Again, very well said. You, my dear sir, are every bit as much a philosopher as a physician."

Rumi laughed and responded, "Thank you. But I think Hippocrates would be more pleased with my daily routine and typical thoughts than Socrates ever would."

"No worries! That man was impossible to please!" Hasbalam said, and they both laughed. He thought for a second, looked at his watch, and asked, "Do you have plans for lunch?"

"Oh, I promised my wife to come up and have lunch with her."

"I see. Are the two of you, by any chance, free for dinner?"

"We might indeed be. I'll check with her to make sure she hasn't made any other plans. Will you be back down in the afternoon session?"

"Yes! I wouldn't miss it. The speaker is supposed to be a world expert on tropical and sub-tropical diseases."

"Good. I'll see you then and maybe we can make dinner plans," Rumi said.

"It would be a pleasure to meet your wife and continue our conversation."

"Yes, indeed."

"I won't hold you up any longer at present. See you at the next session."

"Good. See you then," Rumi said, and with a nod, turned and made his way to the elevator with a light and untroubled spirit. He had no idea what was soon to come.

And in Cairo, trouble was also on the way. Since her recent opportunity to play the piano at Ali's birthday party, as well as to meet so many people who worked with the king, Muriel al-Baki had felt very confident about her ability to impress her master. She had made a list of everyone she'd met, their jobs, and any personal details she'd been able to learn about them. She knew some of their schedules and even the locations of their homes. All this information had been revealed in what appeared to be casual conversation, but Muriel was always digging hard for the sorts of details that she knew Santiago wanted and could use. And she had a prodigious memory for whatever she learned. Desire can be a great fuel for attention and remembrance. Her part-time job as Khata's piano teacher was already paying off far more extravagantly than she ever could have imagined or even hoped.

But she didn't yet have all the information she wanted to present to Santiago. So she planned to drop by the El-Noor home on some excuse or other and ask a few carefully contrived questions. She had already provided a good bit of information a week earlier, at a clandestine meeting with the master's assistant across town, but wanted to hold off on her report about the party until she had been able to tie up a bit more detail on some of the participants.

As it turned out, when Muriel arrived at the El-Noor home, Khata was not around, and she thought to herself right away that this was good. She could now spend all her attention on getting the extra information she wanted. Rama had connections, and Muriel believed she could be talked into revealing almost anything. She had her trust. And that could be manipulated well. Because of this, she was sure that she would be able to discover everything she was seeking. She still had no clear idea how it was going to be used by Santiago. But all of that was about to be revealed.

24

A Special Gathering

The king had scheduled a closed-door meeting to last for three hours. In attendance were Masoon, Hamid, Omari, Amon, Hoda, Layla, Kissa, Hasina, Walid, Mafulla, and for the first time in such an important setting, Malik and Haji. Two of their recent visitors, Sab and Meskhenet Maayuf, were also present for the duration of the session, and their participation made a big difference. The king referred to the gathering as a "multi-mind" working group. He had spoken to Walid and Mafulla on several occasions about what he called "collective consciousness" or "collaborative concentration" as a high level activity that could uniquely take place in such a setting. Mafulla liked to call it a "mind-mesh" but Walid would often joke that, with him involved, it could often turn into a mind mess, producing mind mush.

The basic idea was simple. Bring together a group of well disposed, talented, diverse, and smart people—between two and twenty, ideally, although sometimes more could be accommodated—pose them a problem that requires a highly creative solution, and then encourage their candid and free flowing interaction over the problem. The king also understood something deep about this distinctive process. You can't replicate the elevation of thought that can result in such a group by any means other than face-to-face conversation. You can't do it by correspondence or telephone, or with transmissions over the radio, or by any other means. Clearly, many forms of creative and productive collaboration can take place through any mode of communication. But one thing was clear to Ali. There's a special kind of thought that can arise only when people are physically present with each other, spiritually attuned, and mentally engaged.

The king believed that our embodiment in this world is no accident, and no incidental aspect of our existence. The physical dimension of our lives, here and now, matters. Even for the most spiritual or mental of activities, embodiment must be respected. Bodily propinquity creates a matrix for creative thinking that's unique. Physical presence has no close substitute. There's an engagement and an energy arising from the most basic form of personal proximity that can't be produced in any other way. The king often called this "The Proximity Principle." And its insight often guided his decisions.

Socrates philosophized on the streets of Athens and at dinner parties with other individuals and groups of people, rather than just retreating into an isolated place where he could have enjoyed quiet solitude and an uninterrupted time to think. This was likely the reason. It's no coincidence that the greatest flourishing of philosophical thought in human history was to be found in ancient Athens, where many creative thinkers knew each other personally and talked together, daily, and face-to-face. The renaissance artists of Florence provided another vivid example of this. So did the Royal Society in England, with its far-reaching group impact on early modern science. The cluster of individuals in America who were known as "the Founding Fathers" produced a roiling cauldron of new and powerful political thought and commitment that's unparalleled. And they did much of their best work in person, talking together. Even when there were conflicts or disagreements, the possibility of working things out seemed to be enhanced greatly by the factor of physical presence.

Another example of this phenomenon would be the array of

painters, sculptors, and writers working in Paris between the late nineteenth century and the early decades of the twentieth. Many more such cases could also be cited. Camaraderie, fellowship, friendly association, and the conversation made possible by physical presence can cause something to happen in a communal way that could never be replicated by people as individuals working in isolation and thinking merely within the confines of their own minds. We certainly all need private time. But without lively interaction with like minded others as well, the greatest things don't happen.

There is an old and often cited proverb, frequently used by the king and echoed by others in the palace: As iron sharpens iron, so one man sharpens another. And the same principle holds, of course, for women, and across genders. The truth of this is seen on sporting teams, in military units, occasionally within neighborhoods, and in families. It can be found in modern business, and in the various arts and professions. A proper form of interpersonal stimulation leads to a greater level of excellence through what we might think of as combinatorial creativity, and of course this crosses all matters of gender as it transcends age, or race, or geographical origin. Peak human greatness requires community.

This was a chief reason that Hamid and Masoon most often worked out together, rather than mainly doing their individual exercises alone. They made each other better. It was also one of the insights that led the king, early on, to invite Mafulla to live at the palace in close companionship with the prince. It was one of the reasons that Walid's father, Rumi, liked to go to medical conferences. The conversations that would take place there, sometimes even in casual settings, could spark major creative leaps and novel, important ideas. The interaction could also, at the same time, generate the inspiration or motivation to put those ideas into action, along with building a network of new partnerships that alone could bring great new things into the world.

Everyone thought of the king as a genius and as extraordinarily wise. He clearly was both of these things. And he was smart enough to know his limits. So he always sought to involve others in thinking through a major problem in creative new ways. He often huddled with advisors and cabinet ministers to take on the challenges of the kingdom and develop new ways to improve life for the citizens of Egypt. He regularly talked with his brother, Rumi, and with Bhati. And he shared much more than most sovereigns would with the two young people closest around him, Walid and Mafulla. He believed that in many voices, wisdom can be found. The more insightful advisors he could involve on an issue of importance, the more certain he could be that all facets of the situation would be recognized and all avenues of effective action identified.

This meeting was devoted to the challenge of Juan Osvaldo Santiago and how it could be dealt with most effectively. All known facts were laid out, including some new and crucial information that had been provided by Mafulla's father after his unexpected brush with death, along with the surprising content of the note that had just been discovered at the El-Bay home. There was also a close discussion of the many hints to be found in the old book that had recently been brought to the palace from Dromeda.

"So, here's the latest news," the king said. "Our good friend Shapur Adi clearly saw Santiago in what appears to be a desert setting with two other men, although there may have been more nearby, and his location seemed as if it was miles outside of town. There were at least three tents in the area. And Shapur is convinced that we can soon find the spot. He's also confident that he can track most of Santiago's movements, wherever he goes, although his visions seem to encompass only the man himself and typically, at most, several feet on either side of him, rather than including some grand sweep of his overall surroundings. On occasion, he's seen a bit more. He has a more typically episodic vision of the man that seems to be a real-time view, but a narrow and limited one. And I believe that, despite its limitations, it will be of real use to us."

"This is an ability that came back with him from the next world," Hamid said.

"Yes. It's almost as if it's some form of cosmic payback for Santiago's murderous intentions toward him. And it may be crucial for us," the king replied. "But we can return to this in a minute. First, I want to read all of you the note that was just discovered at the El-Bay home after the attack this afternoon." The king reached into a folder and pulled out a piece of paper. "The message is quite different from the others we have received in the past. Here's all that it says." The king then read the words: "The piano teacher is one of us. Signed, Juan O. Santiago." Now, what do you make of that?"

Walid spoke up right away. "That's just too strange." He turned to his best friend and said, "Mafulla, it's your aunt Muriel. This can't possibly be true, right? So, why would Santiago write it?"

"Well, speaking the truth doesn't seem to be high up on his list of priorities, in any case," Mafulla said.

"Good point. But why would he write this, in particular, to us, and presumably plan to leave it at Kissa's house—if it's just another falsehood? I mean: Why this particular claim, of all possible false claims he could make?"

Hasina said, "Maybe he's trying to turn us against each other with a new suspicion, hoping that it will result in actions on our part that can be a diversion and weaken us."

Kissa asked, "But then, why would he pick someone who isn't in this room? Why someone who's new to town? He could have chosen a lot better if his aim is to turn us against each other."

Layla spoke up and said, "And why would he think for a second that we'd believe him?"

"Maybe he doesn't," Mafulla replied. "But he still introduces a doubt into our minds by writing this and having his men deliver the letter."

Walid said, "And yet surely, the claim has to be false."

Amon replied, "But then, if it's false, how in the world would Santiago know anything about Muriel and her work with Khata? They had nothing to do with the trip to Dromeda, and Muriel hasn't even lived here for a long time. He'd surely know nothing at all about her."

Walid then said, "Good point. Actually, it's a very good point. He'd need many more eyes around town than it's reasonable to suppose he'd have. But even so, why would he pick her to make this claim about? And on the other hand, what's the chance of its being true? It just doesn't make any sense that she'd be involved with this guy."

"What do you mean, Prince? Why not?" Amon asked.

"Well, first, there's no connection between anything she does and what we know of him."

"Not so far as we're aware," Omari said, "but there's still much that we don't know."

"Ok," Walid replied, "I grant you that. But I mean: if this crazy claim were true, if Mafulla's aunt was in some way working for Santiago, then why would Santiago himself tell us?"

"Well, did he in fact tell us?" Hasina asked.

"What are you suggesting? I don't' understand."

Hasina seemed like she had just experienced a breakthrough idea. She looked at various faces around the room and then said, "The letter was with the two guys who were killed. It was signed 'Juan O. Santiago.' Right?"

"Yeah. So?" Walid seemed a little puzzled but also curious.

Hasina went on. "The other recent letters were signed 'Juan Osvaldo Santiago'—the full name, or at least that's what I've heard."

"You're right," the king replied.

"Ok," Walid said.

"So ... I'm thinking that maybe the fake Santiago who attacked Khalid wrote and signed this one maybe for his own reasons, and then didn't sign the name as it had been signed on the previous occasions."

"What do you mean?"

"It's likely that fake Santiagos sometimes write these notes anyway, presenting them as from their leader. The handwriting has differed a bit, across notes. But they were surely told what to say. It could be that some of the previous notes left by others were even dictated. And maybe this time, this fake Santiago decided not to write what he had been told to say, but to send his own message."

"I still don't get it." Walid looked genuinely perplexed.

"Maybe this time, he wrote just what he wanted to write. Maybe this message didn't come from the real Santiago at all, in any way."

"I'm not following you, yet, either," Mafulla admitted. "Say more."

Hasina said, "Ok, suppose that Fake Santiago, Short Version, worked for the real Santiago and was a top follower. And then Santiago—the original Santiago—brings in Muriel to work for him, for whatever reason. Sorry, Mafulla. But I'm just running with a hypothesis here."

"It's Ok," Mafulla said.

"And she's talented and smart and a great musician, plus, she's an attractive lady, even a bit glamorous. Maybe the original Santiago is even attracted to her, as a man might be to someone like her."

"Ok."

"And imagine she does a great job at what she's been told to do."

"Like giving piano lessons to Khata?"

"Or something else here in town that the lessons are covering, or cloaking. Maybe she's getting better secret assignments than Short Santiago and becoming closer to the original Santiago, and is now the big man's favorite. Plus, she's got her own skills. Mom told us about her being Phi, right?"

"Yeah?"

"Well, maybe Short Santiago got jealous. He's been hiring all these unworthy people all over town to take on a name that he worked so hard to get, and he's even having to pay them to do it, and that's really demeaning to him—dispiriting, discouraging, and everything."

Kissa spoke up and said, "Ok. I get it. And then this already powerful, impressive woman comes in and gains special favor with the boss, and, as a result, Short Santiago's pushed even more to the margin, into the shadows, and he gets really mad—I mean extra furious—and he decides to expose her, to get rid of her, for his own purposes."

"But," Malik asked, "wouldn't the real Santiago kill him for that?"

Now Mafulla entered into the reasoning and said, "Well, sure, if he knew. But, maybe Short Santiago thought he could keep it quiet, you know, completely secret."

Omari spoke up and said, "So, maybe he had another message he was supposed to deliver, probably a normal, taunting one, and he wrote this one instead and thought he was going to get away with it. And he either forgot how the other ones were signed, or signed this one in a slightly different way on purpose, to let us know that something new was going on with it, but while still maintaining deniability with his boss, in case he was caught."

Walid at that point scratched his head and said, "Well, fellow detectives, you've just spun a pretty interesting tale about Muriel and the bad guys that … could be true. And that's pretty disturbing, if it is, because she's been all around, and at the king's party."

Mafulla sighed aloud and let out a deep breath and said, "Yeah, unfortunately, you might be right. From what we know, they've both traveled a lot, Muriel and Santiago. They could have met somewhere, I guess. But why in the world would he recruit a musician into his group in the first place? And why would she, a member of my extended family and a Phi, think for a second about joining him, of all people?"

"Good questions," Hoda said. "But Farouk al-Khoum had been Phi and went bad because of his need for huge success and power, remember?"

"All too well."

"Overwhelming ambition or greed for something can do it."

Haji said, "And, Muriel's pretty famous, already. Maybe she got a taste of worldly importance, and wants more money or power or status or something, and Santiago lured her into his stuff with lofty promises."

Kissa said, "She's certainly Shamilar's sister, but it's not like she's been hanging around with the rest of the family and absorbing all the Adi goodness, day-to-day. You guys mostly lost touch with her a long time ago, right?"

"Yeah. For years," Mafulla said.

"Then she suddenly appears here in Cairo, right when all this other Santiago stuff's going on." Kissa was tapping her index finger on the table as she said this.

"I hadn't thought about it like that," Mafulla admitted.

"I hadn't either," Walid said. "Maybe we should."

"Geez," Mafulla said, and made a face. "This could be bad. What do you think we should do?"

Ali said, "Proceed quickly but surreptitiously, and with great caution. We need to learn more soon."

Hoda asked, "So, do you think we should let Muriel keep doing whatever she's doing and just monitor her closely?"

"For now, I think so," the king responded. "On my request, Layla recruited her some time ago to visit with Khata and interview the young lady for possible Phi status."

Kissa looked over at Hasina, and Hassi gave her a small thumbs-up. Both were pleased to hear this.

"I sure didn't ask her to move here," Layla said. "I thought that maybe she'd visit and drop by Khata's home a couple of times and give some musical encouragement and a couple of lessons. It didn't even enter my mind that she'd relocate with her husband to Cairo, and even to Khata's neighborhood."

"No, and that was a surprise to all of us," the king said.

"Do you," Layla wondered aloud, "suspect now that she came here, leading us on to think it was for what we asked her to do, but it's really in service to something that Santiago wants?"

"That could be," Hoda concluded. "And Short Santiago got so mad that he gave the game away, hoping to get Muriel out of the picture."

"We still don't yet know exactly what the game is," the king reminded everyone. "We need to find out what Muriel might be doing and why."

"Boy," Mafulla said, "this is really going to upset mom a lot."

"She shouldn't be told yet that any of this is suspected," Hoda said.

"Not at all," Layla emphasized. And then she said, "We could be wrong. There's no need to alarm your mother at this stage."

"Oh, Ok. That makes sense."

The king asked, "Did Muriel come to the hospital to see your dad, Mafulla?"

"She did."

"Was there anything strange about her visit?"

"Well, now that you ask, yeah, I think there was something a bit odd."

"Could you elaborate?"

"She seemed to be more interested in who had been in to visit before her than in how dad was doing. I mean: she asked about him, right away, but then she asked a lot more questions about other people."

"I see," the king said and thought for a moment. Then he continued. "I believe that some of us now need to make ourselves more available to Muriel than might otherwise happen in the natural course of things, and see if we can lure her into revealing in any way what she might be doing. She could still be innocent of anything sinister, and we need to remember that. But if she in no way imagines that we suspect her, she may ask something or say something that will give us an important hint as to what might be going on."

There was agreement all around to this suggestion, and then the king went into a few of the details learned from a look at the book that had been brought to town by Zet and his older friends. Sab kicked in a few thoughts now and then, and his wife Meskhenet made some extremely astute observations. The king then asked for ideas about their ultimate adversary's most likely next move, as well as on what actions they should take now. Lots of possibilities were envisioned and tactics were developed for handling various potential outcomes. Everyone contributed. No one was silent.

It was a thoroughly impressive meeting of the minds, and those present were able to accomplish more in a short period of time than the younger people there would ever have imagined possible. What amazed Walid the most was that the oldest people in the room, Sab and Meskhenet, their current visitors from across the kingdom, had voiced some of the deepest insights during the three hours they had talked together. At first, both Walid and Mafulla had been hesitant to say certain things in their presence— any remark involving a mention of Phi, or suggestions that would make sense only with a background of knowledge about Phi. The huge surprise that surfaced after just about fifteen minutes was that these two elderly people were among the most senior members of Phi in the entire kingdom, and maybe the world. They were regarded with the utmost respect by the other senior Phi in the room, both for their experience and the extent of their insight. Walid could not have been more stunned, at first, when this was initially revealed. And yet, after a few moments of thought, the otherwise unexpected information made sense of a hundred little things that he had noticed about his old neighbors during his years of growing up in Dromeda.

The king had explained the need to provide extra security for Walid's parents while they were away from the palace at the medical conference, but without alarming Walid too much about the danger that might present itself. He made some suggestions and they all formulated a plan. And in that connection, Sab finally gave them all a more complete account of the book that they had brought the king and what it might mean for understanding and defeating Santiago. He also made lots of references to other books and historical figures whose behaviors might shed light on their current adversary. It amazed all the young people present how much he knew. A few of them took extensive notes on the points he made, and as a result of his report, everyone felt much more of a sense of who their mysterious enemy really is, and what he might be doing.

When the meeting ended, many of those present stayed around to talk, one-on-one, or in small clusters. Walid and Mafulla had offered to go with Omari and Amon the next morning up to Alexandria, very early on the first train out, to augment the security for Rumi and Bhati that was already being provided by their friend Paki. That way, Walid's parents could leave the conference there in greater safety and they could all get back to the palace before the king initiated any large scale movement against Santiago.

On the way out of the king's sitting room, Malik and Haji walked along with their friends, the Viper and the Storm. Haji said, "Mafulla, I just had a thought."

"That sounds like major news. Should we call the newspaper?"

"Funny man," Haji replied with a smile, and stopped walking. "Yeah, go call the paper and tell them to get your obituary ready, in case you decide to keep it up with the friendly insult humor."

"Oh. I'm sorry," Mafulla said and stopped. And the others did, as well.

"Yeah?"

Mafulla then grimaced and said, "I didn't mean it as an insult at all. I was just making a lame joke."

"It's Ok," Haji replied. "Walid told me not long ago that when you're a little nervous, you make bad jokes—and we're all a little nervous about Santiago."

"Oh, he told you that, did he?"

"Yeah, he did, and you're going to view any joke at my expense as especially bad when I tell you what my thought is."

"Oh," Mafulla said, and added, "Not to be repeating myself."

"Hey, it's Ok. I've already forgiven you. Just don't keep it up with comments that sound like digs. All right? But you can still feel bad if you'd like, when you hear me out. In fact, I highly recommend it."

"Oh, Jeez. Ok. I'm totally, absolutely, one hundred percent sorry."

"Good. Now. My thought was sparked by the idea that, you know, since your dad has fortunately recovered from whatever Santiago did to him, our bad guy has now been thwarted once again in an attack. And this wasn't one of his followers being refused his intended result. This was, from what we can suppose, the man himself."

"Yeah, true."

"Well, he's surely even more frustrated now and mad and maybe almost humiliated that he can't really kill any of us ... so far."

"That's probably right."

"How then do we know that he won't try it again? Especially this time, when he's got his own warped sense of honor and power to defend."

"Man, that's insightful. Why haven't I thought of that?"

"Maybe you were too busy figuring out ways to make me the butt of a joke."

"Ok, Ok, I said I'm sorry and I am. Really. I didn't mean it. I grovel at your superior feet. And they're quite impressive. You're awesome."

"I know you didn't mean anything bad. And I appreciate the groveling, however brief. It's over. But the question is, what's your dad's level of protection now?"

"Reela's with him a lot and he's pretty strong and, for the present, the Sakat brothers are staying closer than usual."

"That's good, but how about Phi protection?"

"Everybody's doing other stuff, I guess."

"And so it looks like we're just assuming that Santiago won't try the exact same thing twice," Walid said.

"Yeah, that's my point," Haji said. "I think it's bad to make big assumptions when a lot's at stake. Remember what Khalid once taught us. I think Mafulla's dad needs some level of Phi protection."

"I'm not doing anything," Malik said. "I could stay with him."

"I don't have another assignment either," Haji added. "And that's why I brought this up. I could sit with him while you're gone to Alexandria."

"Wait. I shouldn't expect other people to take care of my own father," Mafulla said.

Anticipating what he might be thinking, Walid suggested, "Hey, Maffie, why don't you stay here."

"What?"

"Don't go with me tomorrow. Your dad may need you. My dad's got lots of security. We're just adding on an extra layer."

"But you shouldn't have to go up alone," Mafulla said.

"I'll be with Omari and Amon, and Paki's there already," Walid said.

Malik turned to his own best friend and said, "Hey, here's an idea, Haji. Why doesn't one of us go with Walid, and the other one stay to help with Mafulla and his dad? We'd be cross-partnering, but it's still all League of Crime Fighters."

"International," Mafulla said.

"Yeah, International."

"Sounds good to me," Haji said.

"It's not a bad idea," Walid conceded. "What do you think, Maffie?"

"You wouldn't mind my not going along to Alexandria?"

"No, not at all. I'm one of the people here suggesting it."

"We normally fight these things together."

"Yeah, but your dad needs you and my dad may need me, and they're inconveniently in different cities."

"You're right."

"So, this one time, we can divide to conquer—and there may likely be no fighting at all for either of us."

"Ok, if you're sure."

"I am."

"Who goes on the away team, and who stays on the home team?" Malik asked.

"Flip a coin," Mafulla said.

"Ok. Who's got a coin?" Walid asked. Nobody spoke. "Oh, good, here we are, the rich boys' club. Nobody has a single coin of any denomination, however small?"

"Ha!" Mafulla laughed and said, "We're rich in spirit." And then he added, "There's still a way. Malik and Haji, put your hands behind your backs and each of you pick a number between one and ten and put out that many fingers. Either the highest or the lowest will stay with me. You pick your number and keep it hidden and then I'll decide secretly whether it's high or low that stays here, and I'll tell Walid without you hearing me. And then we'll look at your fingers and he'll announce the winner."

"If there's a tie?" Haji asked.

"Ok, if there's a tie, we'll do it again and nobody can repeat what they first picked, and so on, until we get a result."

"That sounds fair."

"Good. So, now, choose your number. Put out that number of fingers behind you. Keep your hands behind your backs." Mafulla moved over and whispered something to Walid.

Walid then said, "Show your hands."

Malik showed two fingers sticking out, Haji four.

Walid announced, "Mafulla said that the low number goes with me, and the high number stays here—his rule."

"Correct," Mafulla said. "So Malik, you go to Alexandria on the train early in the morning, and Haji, you sleep a little later, go by school briefly to tell Khalid what's going on, get our assigned work, and then come over to my family's house."

"Which of us won? Which of us has the better deal?" Haji asked.

And Malik said, "Yeah, who lost? Who has the tough assignment, the less desirable duty?"

"I guess we'll find out those answers soon enough," Walid said.

And he was right. But none of the boys had any idea how the answers would appear, or that the tough assignment would turn out to be one of the worst in the entire history of Phi duties, ever.

25

MISCOMMUNICATION

REELA WALKED UP TO LEEM AND HANDED HIM THE MORNING edition of *The Kingdom Daily News*. "Have you seen the paper yet?"

"No, let me have a look."

He said, "I think you'll like it."

Leem looked down at the front page. The headline, in nice big bold letters, was, "Juan Osvaldo Santiago: Criminal, Thief, Lowlife."

He laughed. "Oh, this is good." And then he began to read aloud.

"It seems that our fair city is suddenly full of people with the name 'Juan Osvaldo Santiago.' You may have met one of them recently. In our research, we've come across quite a few. And those we have met all have two things in common: First, they're introducing themselves with a fake name that they have been recently paid to adopt. And second, they've taken money for this strange duty from one of the most despicable and disgusting criminals of our day."

Leem looked up and said, "Oh I like this—despicable and disgusting." Then he continued to read.

"Many people throughout the city were greatly affected by the rash of animal abductions a short time ago. The population was perplexed and pet owners were terrorized, never knowing when their beloved animals might disappear. The criminal behind it all was a man from birth named Juan Osvaldo Santiago. He was living in the western part of the kingdom until recently, having fled here from Spain."

Leem commented again, "Fled here—that's very nice. He'll hate that." And then he returned to his reading aloud. "But now, he has relocated to our fair city, one step ahead of the law, and is planning much worse nightmares for our citizens to endure. If you have recently met anyone by this name, beware. It could be one of his top henchmen, who, oddly, also share his ruined name, as a sort of perverse prize conveyed to them because of their criminal expertise, or it could be nothing more than a poor local sap taking on the name for money. It could possibly even be the pathetic evil wretch himself." Leem laughed out loud and went on.

"Sources tell us that the original Juan Osvaldo Santiago is paying men in town to adopt and share his name for six months, to make it harder for the local police to find him or track his movements. The more people using this name in Cairo, the more difficult it will be to locate the perpetrator of this deception, the crass deviant himself. He's using this cloak of confusion to allow him to plot new schemes against the kingdom that will make life miserable for many of us in the days to come, unless he's quickly apprehended." Leem nodded his approval. "This is good."

And he couldn't help but laugh out loud again when he got to the middle of the next sentence. "Various sources who know the man well have described him as a ridiculously egotistical, shrunken little lizard, a foul smelling, neurotic and pathetic coward with delusions of grandeur, and plenty of money to spend—cash embezzled from his terribly deceived family back in his homeland. The real Juan Osvaldo Santiago is said to be uneducated, uncultured, and a completely uncivilized oaf in all ways. After a string of embarrassing failures in business and politics, he has escaped to Cairo, our sources tell us, to organize gang activity and make money the only way he knows how—by stealing it. But he must be stopped." Leem laughed again.

Reela said, "I knew you'd enjoy this."

"Wait. Let me finish." He continued.

"With this in mind, the Chief of the Cairo Police has declared a two day amnesty for anyone who has received money to bear this name. You can come in to your local police station, turn over any false identification you've been given, and resume the use of your birth name without penalty. You can even keep whatever money you've been paid. The police are also offering a small reward, in addition, for anyone who comes forward in the next forty-eight hour period. After this brief time of merciful amnesty, anyone bearing the name will be arrested and held on charges of interfering with a police investigation, or worse. All who are found will also be severely questioned after the short period of amnesty ends."

He looked up at Reela and said, "This is just perfect."

"I thought you'd like it."

"Let me read the last paragraph." Leem squinted and continued.

"One of his hired men recently described the real Juan Osvaldo Santiago to us like this: 'He's lower than the most offensive camel dung. He's worse than an irritating insect. He's scum pretending to be something important. He should be tossed out of Egypt like the trash he is.' When asked why he worked for a man that he so despised, this associate said, 'He fooled me like he fools many, and now I'm in too deep. If I tried to quit, he'd kill me.' The Chief of Police assures us that this is not true for any of the citizens who have taken on his name for pay in the strange ruse that has been going on recently. So, please, if you have received money to pretend to have this name, or know someone who has, take advantage of this short window of grace to visit the local police station, briefly explain your involvement, and receive both the city's thanks and a reward."

Leem put down the paper and shook his head. "Wow. That's very good, indeed. They printed the entire story that we concocted as if it was theirs, and even added several great flourishes to make it even better. How did you get it to happen so quickly?"

"I convinced the publisher that it was almost entirely true, as much as any story in a major paper typically is, but with just a touch of artistic license, and that it would serve a beneficial purpose in getting this man into custody as soon as possible. Plus, the fellow owed me a very big favor. I once saved his life. That helped."

"Oh, my. Well, I'm glad you're on our team. The mix of truth and exaggeration in the piece is perfect and should enrage Santiago quite nicely, and offend him enough, I would imagine, to get him to do something really stupid."

"That's the plan."

"Yes. I just wish I could see his face when he reads this. I hope the king is pleased."

"He is. But of course, as you know, he always regrets the use of artifice or deception of any kind. And yet, he realizes the stakes we face with this character, and suspects that this little ruse will work like a charm. I took a chance and told him about it only after we had launched it. He understood and even laughed aloud like you and shook his head, when I showed the printed version to him a little while ago. I think he thoroughly enjoyed it, despite his qualms."

In a neighborhood not too far away, Khata's mother Rama El-Noor brought in a beautiful tea set and placed in on the table in front of her visitor, Muriel al-Baki. She sat across from her and said, "So, how did you enjoy your visit to the palace and the king's birthday party?"

"Oh, it was a great treat and a real delight," Muriel said. "What a fun occasion! Thank you so much for getting me the coveted invitation!"

"It was my pleasure," Rama said. "You played beautifully, as always."

"You're so sweet." Muriel smiled, and then added, "I'm just sorry I never got a chance to actually enter the palace itself."

"No? I'm surprised. I thought for sure that you'd take advantage of the tour being offered for all visitors."

"That was my plan, but due to my role in the festivities and the time commitments surrounding it, we didn't have an opportunity when I arrived, and by the end of my duties, the tour was no longer offered."

"What a shame!"

"It was a real disappointment."

"I'm sorry you didn't get a peek inside. I had asked that they give you an arrival time that would allow for the tour before you had to start playing. There must have been some sort of miscommunication. I knew you'd love to see the interiors. The Golden Palace is such a highpoint of Egyptian architecture and interior design. Plus, there are many treasures in it, and such beauty everywhere."

As Rama handed her a teacup Muriel said, "I've heard that there are many items of great worth in the palace, and even storied things of ancient legend housed in it."

"Yes, of course, we also have the museum, with its extensive holdings, but I'm sure the king keeps closer to his own protection many things of value that are dear to his heart."

"I was wondering about that," Muriel said.

"Oh?"

"Yes. Are there private collections in the palace that aren't available on tours like the one given at the party?"

"Yes, I'm sure there are things in the king's personal quarters that never go on broader display."

"Where in the palace does the king actually live?"

"On the second floor, on the side opposite the classrooms where Khata's a student—on the other wing, but not a great distance away."

"I didn't realize that the king lives in any sense close to the palace school rooms."

"Well, not that close, but on the same floor of the palace."

"I see."

"But ... there's a secret that very few know." Rama lowered her voice.

"Oh? Would it be wrong for a newcomer like me to be a little bit curious?" Muriel smiled conspiratorially and put the fingers of her left hand over her mouth.

Rama slowly put down her cup and sat perfectly quiet for a moment, as if listening to make sure they were still alone in the house. She then leaned in toward her guest and said, "I just heard that the king stores some of his greatest treasures, a few items of myth and legend, in the basement of the palace, if you can believe it, in an ordinary storage room, almost in plain sight."

"No."

"Yes." Rama laughed and said, "I've even heard that the door of the room where these things are kept is marked with a sign that says, 'Royal Family Clutter.' Can you believe it? The king can be such a wit. And these secret items are said to be so immensely valuable not because of their monetary worth, necessarily, but due to some sort of ancient power, whatever that means."

"Oh, my goodness." Muriel felt almost dizzy to be hearing such revelations, knowing how valuable this information would be to her master. "Royal Family Clutter?"

"Yes! Of all things!"

"Do you … have any idea what's there?"

"No, I'm afraid that no one beyond the royal family, and perhaps a few other top advisors, is even allowed to know. We're now talking about the deepest secrets and most precious things of the kingdom."

Muriel felt a tingle all over to be in possession of such information. Her mouth was suddenly dry, and she then remembered to pick up her teacup and take a sip. "Well, this is all so fascinating. I had no idea I'd learn some new secrets today! I'd just wanted to drop by and thank you again for my invitation to the party. It was a wonderful experience, even without a peek inside the famous palace."

"Again, it was my pleasure. And I'm sure something can be arranged to get you in for that peek."

"That would be truly marvelous."

"By the way, Khata's been preparing well for the next lesson." Rama deliberately spoke in these ambiguous terms, as a sort of enjoyable miscommunication, for the sake of toying with her guest.

"I'm not surprised at all. She's as diligent as she is talented."

"Thank you for your kind words, and for the way you've been encouraging her."

"It's my true delight and satisfaction. I see great things ahead for our relationship and its results."

"Marvelous! Oh, I must ask: Do you have time for some hot biscuits? I've been baking some for Khata, and there are a few extras. They'll be ready in a minute."

"That's so nice! I wish I could stay longer. But thank you for the offer! I'm sure they're delicious."

"You have to run?"

"Yes, unfortunately. I do enjoy our visits, and your home is always so lovely. But I have an upcoming appointment to dash off to. You know how it is for the newly relocated. There's always something to do."

"I'm sure."

"I just wanted to pop in. And I'm so glad we could talk."

"I am, too."

The early train to Alexandria was clicking along the tracks. The boys and their two older friends had all gotten a little extra sleep since it pulled away from the station. They weren't overly concerned about the mission they were on. After all, Santiago had tried to kill several friends of the monarchy in recent days, but to no avail. They would just go straight to the hotel where the medical conference was being held, fetch Walid's parents, hustle them back to the train station, and take the next train out, back to the capital city. It would be a six Phi mission once they got to the hotel, and that alone was comforting. Plus, they would have some military support and a senior Alexandrian Phi escorting them back to the rail station for the trip home. There was even an additional reassurance that the people who might be planning an attack on Rumi were not particularly intelligent or in possession of any serious power. The protection detail should all be back in the palace with everyone safe by dinnertime.

The hours passed as if blown along by a stiff wind. "Prince! Malik! We're here."

"What?"

"We're pulling into the Alexandria station!"

"Oh, man," Walid said while opening his eyes wide and

stretching. "I needed that." He yawned really big. Within a second, Malik did, too.

"Don't!" Omari said. "You're going to make me …" and then he yawned as well, very noisily.

"Did you guys get any sleep?" Walid asked the two older Phi.

"We took turns," Omari said. "Someone had to be watchful."

Amon nodded his head toward Omari and said, "He snored so loudly I thought he was going to wake up everyone in the train, and even throughout several villages along the way."

"Ha!" Walid laughed. "I must have really been out! I didn't hear anything."

"One thunderous snort was so gigantic, I was worried it might derail us."

"Stop it," Omari said. "You snore, too, but like an old lady." Both Walid and Malik had to laugh at that.

"I may snore, yes, but if I do, it's only like a healthy normal man," Amon replied.

Omari laughed. "Oh, is that right?"

"It's you who snore like a big and terribly sick camel in a massively large cave. The engineer didn't even have to use his horn to let people know we were coming."

It went on like that for a couple more minutes. Walid had heard such banter between friends before, especially during his long trip to his home village, between a couple of older men, and it always made him smile. Then, in a very short time, the train came to a stop, the four of them got off, and a waiting car took them to the Palace Hotel, where the conference was still underway. Paki met them at the front door.

"Where's Rumi?" Omari asked, right away.

"He's in a session. Four soldiers guard the doors, with two at each entrance. Our senior Phi friend from here in town is in the room and close to him."

"Have you seen any suspicious individuals in the hotel or in the broader area?"

"No, nothing. And since the king's message, we put some men in street clothes around the neighborhood as an early warning system."

"Ok, good," Omari said. "Amon, why don't you follow Paki to the conference hall where Rumi is, and I'll check on Bhati. She has two guards outside the suite, posted right after the king's phone call. At the close of the session downstairs, bring Rumi up to the room and we'll all have a quick lunch and then return to the train station."

"Sounds good."

"Walid, you and Malik can come with me."

"Ok."

Omari looked around for a moment and then asked Paki, "What's the room number upstairs?"

Paki stepped closer and lowered his voice. "424. Knock and say the name 'Kular.' That's the password."

Omari motioned for Walid and Malik to follow him. "Eyes and ears," he said and held up three fingers, then two, as they walked through the front door, passing by several bellmen, and crossed the lobby.

"Walid whispered to Malik, "Triple Double."

"Yeah, I got it."

"Ok. Good."

"This feels really different," Malik said in a soft voice, to Walid.

"You're right."

"You don't look much like Haji."

"Thank you," Walid said, just as a joke. Malik smiled for a moment, and then grew serious in his expression again.

Omari led them to the stairway rather than the elevator, and the three of them began the climb. They had just passed the door for the second floor when it opened behind them with a loud creak. All three stopped and reached for their belts where their weapons were concealed. A man came through the door and glared at them. He had a can of paint in one hand and a brush in the other and was on his way down. He was clearly just a hotel employee who, because of his work, couldn't ride on the elevator with guests.

When they got to the third floor landing, Omari motioned for them to stop. He opened the door and looked in, down the hallway, just to check. There was no one there except an older lady at the far end looking for something in a bag. He closed the door and began to walk again up the next flight of stairs toward the fourth floor. Malik thought he heard something behind them, down the stairway, and paused to look that way, but couldn't see anything. After a brief glance, he continued up, following Walid and Omari.

Their older associate opened the door on the fourth floor and walked through it. BANG! Walid heard the loud sound before he got to the door. So did Malik. Both pulled their guns instantly and Walid jumped through the doorway, dropping to the floor. Malik stayed close to the door's edge, aiming his revolver around it and down the hall in the direction of the noise. And then he peeked out to look. They were both shocked to see two men and a long painter's ladder that had just hit the wall hard as the men tried to maneuver it into position to get out of a room and down the hall to the stairway door. The two guns pointed at them scared the painters nearly to death, and they simultaneously dropped the ladder, making an even louder sound. Omari was beyond them when the men made their first noise and he turned quickly to see what had happened. One of the men shouted to Walid, "Don't shoot!" Three doors opened along the hallway. One man stuck his head out. Two other figures could be seen farther down at a distance.

Omari intervened quickly and said, "No problem. We're security. Everything's fine. Please take your ladder and clear the hallway. We're sorry for the sudden fright."

"You should be more careful!" The man protested and shook his head.

"Yes, and perhaps you, as well."

Two soldiers who had been sitting outside a door halfway down the hall had jumped up and were walking toward them rapidly with their weapons at the ready.

Omari saw them and held up his hand and said, "Kular! We're guards from the palace. You can stand down."

The man with the ladder who first spoke to Walid now said, "We could have been killed! You shouldn't wave guns at innocent men!" He was looking back and forth at Walid and Malik and then down to Omari.

Omari heard this and turned back to the man again and said, "We're sorry. There may be a dangerous criminal, or group of such people, in the hotel. We were too quick to react. Please accept our apology, and let us go about our task. We'll also let you get on with your work."

"Ok, fine, sure," the man replied. "Just be careful with your guns."

The other painter working with him simply shook his head and picked up his end of the ladder. He said, "Come on. Let's get out of here. They're waiting for us downstairs."

Walid and Malik replaced their weapons in their belts and each mumbled the word "Sorry" to the men as they walked by. Malik held the door open for them.

The three Phi then walked down toward Suite 424 and Omari spoke again to the two army guards who had been positioned outside the suite to protect Bhati, but he talked now in a lower voice. They nodded to him, then silently bowed to Walid, and returned to their chairs to sit back down. Omari knocked on the door and, with his mouth close by to the edge of it, again said the word, "Kular."

A slightly muffled response came from behind the wooden barrier. "What was that?"

"Kular," Omari said. Then he added, "Omari and others for Kular."

A latch was unlocked inside and the door nob turned, and the door opened a crack, and then a bit more. "Who is it?"

"Bhati? It's Omari with helpers."

"Oh! Omari! I'm so glad you're here." She opened the door wider and said, "Walid? Malik? Why did you two come, my son?"

"I wanted to help watch out for you and dad," Walid said, as he entered the door before Omari and hugged his mother.

"Well, then, where's Mafulla? You're normally inseparable," Bhati said, and then turned to the other boy. "It's good to see you, too, Malik. I'm just surprised that you're here with my son and not the ever present Mr. Mafulla Adi."

"He was going to come," Malik said, "but his dad just had a serious medical problem that was caused by Santiago."

"Yes, I heard! Is he all right now, fully recovered?"

Walid replied, "Yes, fortunately, he's come back to health fast and completely. Mafulla just thought he should stay behind as a part of the team watching Mr. Adi. You know, for his mother's comfort. And simply to be nearby at such a time."

"Well that's good. I wish we had been in Cairo for the king's birthday. Then, perhaps we could have been of help to Shapur and Shamilar."

"It's Ok. You had to be here. Mafulla was going to come with me today, but I encouraged him to stay with his dad. Haji and Malik then volunteered to help, and each of them picked a number and the winner got to come with me. The loser had to stay in town and help my almost-brother, the almost-duke, or earl, or whatever."

Malik smiled and said, "I like your characterization of our little game to decide who would do what. It feels good to be the winner!"

Walid laughed and said, "Great. Come on in and sit down and we'll visit with mom and get some food sent up here. I'm hungry and I'm sure Paki and Amon will be up with Dad shortly."

Bhati welcomed them all in and they talked for a few minutes, then Omari asked around about food preferences for the light lunch they would shortly enjoy together. Knowing what Amon and Paki would like and getting a suggestion from Bhati about Rumi, Omari decided to ask one of the two soldiers outside in the hall to go down to the kitchen, hand in their order, and wait to get the food. He wrote out a suggested list of things and gave it to the man, saying, "Please ask the chef to prepare these things as soon as he can, and come back when you have the food and drinks. If you can't carry it all, just ask for help from the kitchen or the bell stand."

As the man took the piece of paper and began to walk away, Omari added, "And, why don't you get something for yourselves as well? It can be our treat. You can both eat when you're back on duty here." He figured that the hallways were quiet enough now, and so one of the guards would be well used for such an errand. By sending one of them down for the food, he would be able to keep the family and Phi together in Bhati's suite of rooms, as a part of their security.

Within five minutes, there was a knock on the door. Omari walked over and said, "Who is it?"

"Kular."

"More please."

"Paki, Amon, and a friend."

Omari opened the door and the three of them came in. Walid walked over to hug his dad, and greetings were exchanged all around. Omari then explained to Rumi the whole story about why they had come and what the plan for the day now was. When they were finished talking about it all, he told Rumi, Paki, and Amon that they should have their food within probably half an hour, at the most. That would give them plenty of time to eat, get a couple of the now waiting cars back to the train station, and arrive home on schedule.

The suite was big: it had an entry hall, a large sitting room straight ahead from it, and a dining area off to the left side with a table large enough for eight. There were two enormous bedrooms and three bathrooms all together. Expansive views of the city were available through the tall, wide windows that ran along the outside wall of the main sitting room. Light was indirect at this time of the late morning and the interior furnishings of the room glowed in their gilded and jeweled tones. A discreet beige carpet cushioned their steps.

Bhati invited everyone to sit and be comfortable while they talked and waited for lunch. Paki, Omari, and Amon sat on large stuffed chairs. Malik plopped down on the end of a beautiful sofa. Rumi pulled back a chair from the long dining table not far away, saying that after the morning conference session in formal, stiff chairs, he needed to use it to lean over for a minute and stretch out his lower back. Then, sufficiently stretched, he sat at the table. Bhati brought him tea from a small kitchen area off the dining space, and Walid sat down with him.

"I'm really sorry all this is going on, Dad," the prince said.

"Well, in the most general sense, I suppose it can't be helped," Rumi replied. "I knew long ago, and so did your mother, that a restoration of the monarchy to its proper lineage would put the family in a position where we'd most likely have to face things like this, or at least, circumstances of danger in some measure. And it's a real shame, since Ali is such a splendid king."

"Yes, he is," Walid agreed.

Rumi nodded and went on. "He's working so hard to prepare the kingdom for democracy and, eventually, an enlightened age of prosperity for most, if not all, under a benevolent rule by the people. How such a good man can attract terrible enemies is still one of the mysteries of life—to me, at least."

"I feel the same way," Walid replied. "It's hard to imagine that everyone wouldn't be won over by his character and vision for the future of our land."

"It's the price of freedom," Rumi said. "I mean, of course, in the philosophical sense of freedom, or free will, which underlies any real form of political freedom. Unless we're free in the deep metaphysical sense, and then an existential sense, we can never be truly free in a political sense. And that's why your uncle has dedicated his life to increasing the scope of our personal, existential freedom through better health and education, so that we can initiate new forms of political freedom with wonderful, positive consequences for our nation, and this entire area of the world. But the very nature of free will allows for wickedness and violence on the part of men who use that freedom badly and choose wrongly."

"Well said," Walid replied.

"I'm just sorry that you, at your age, are having to go through so much of this," Rumi said. "Think about it for a moment: Ari and Idi Falma, Farouk and Faraj al-Khoum, and a surrounding cast of bad characters in both those cases—and now we face what could be the very worst and craziest of them all, this Santiago maniac, who seems to be setting new standards for heinous behavior all the time."

"Yeah, it's truly gone from bad to worse, in terms of our enemies, ever since we got to the palace," Walid said. "It's almost like each of the challenges we've faced has prepared us for a worse one yet to come. I'd hate to try to imagine what's next."

"That's an interesting perspective, son," Rumi said. "Very insightful, indeed. When you're on the proper path, perhaps life is always like that. Each challenge prepares us for the next one. And they get bigger, so we can grow yet again, and even more. I have to say: Every time we sit and talk, I'm increasingly impressed at the wisdom and insight you're developing in your heart and mind."

"The fig doesn't fall far from the tree," Walid responded with a smile. And it was an interesting choice of words, almost in a deep, unconscious anticipation of what was going to happen in the next few minutes, to both the fig and the tree.

But, at the end of that sentence, Walid could hear Omari say, "Something was just slid under the door."

Paki got up to go look, and picked a folded note off the floor. He opened it and said, "This is from the manager. I'll read it. 'An urgent message just arrived from the palace, by telephone to the main office. Someone named Bancom said you should be notified immediately that there may be harming imposters in the area.' That's all it says, other than the manager's signature below the words."

"There may be harming imposters in the area," Omari repeated, with a quizzical look on his face. "What in the world does that mean?"

"It's a medical conference full of doctors," Rumi said. "Maybe Bancom has chosen his words carefully and is saying that not everyone in attendance at the sessions is a real physician, and that there are imposters among the attendees, people who are here to do harm, and not any form of good."

"Well, he would tell us this in such an abbreviated way only if he or someone thought these imposters might be Santiago's men," Omari commented.

"Yes, but the people we're watching out for were supposed to be street thugs, though, right?" Paki asked and then added, "We didn't expect anyone with the intellect or sophistication required for the convincing impersonation of a doctor."

Omari was puzzled as well, and had a question for Rumi. "You say Bancom has perhaps chosen his words carefully. Why the use of the word 'harming'?"

"Maybe it's a miscommunication," Walid suggested.

"What do you mean?"

"The manager could have misheard Bancom. Maybe he said 'charming' and was warning against charming imposters, and that could be imposters of any sort, like perhaps, people pretending to work here and appearing to be helpful and kind."

"That could be," Rumi said. "There are some quite charming people here on staff. But, what I had in mind immediately is that the oath all physicians take begins with the promise to do no harm. So by the phrase 'harming imposters,' Bancom could mean to allude to a fake doctor, an imposter of whom it could be said that he is doing harm, and, by choosing that word, 'harming,' he lets us know to suspect people pretending to be physicians, rather than others in the hotel, like bellmen or desk clerks, or such. And this way, he does so without telling the manager too much that he doesn't need to know."

"Wow, that would be like a code. But it makes sense," Walid said.

"I wish they had a phone here in the suite," Omari remarked.

Paki had a sudden thought and said, "If Rumi's right in this subtle interpretation of Bancom's words, then, since we won't be having any more contact with the conference or its attendees, the message effectively tells us that there's really nothing for us to worry about."

"Why didn't he just say that?" Walid asked.

"Well, he couldn't have known our current situation in all its details. He doesn't know that we have Rumi already away from the conference attendees. He's just offering us a generally helpful warning here, and we'll certainly heed what he says and be careful as we leave, with eyes on anyone who looks like a doctor."

Omari then asked Rumi: "Did any of the others here approach you in any way during the conference?"

"One man," he replied. "I've had many conversations with people while I've been here, in small groups, typically. But there was one man who sought me out between sessions and introduced himself. He was indeed quite charming and engaging. He invited Bhati and me both to dinner last night, but she had a bit of stomach discomfort, so we couldn't join him."

Omari looked over at her and said, "I'm sorry to hear about that, Bhati, but in light of this message, I'm glad the two of you were not able to go. Rumi, Tell me if you see the man anywhere near us when we leave."

"I will."

And with that, everyone in the suite now felt comfortable that they knew a bit more about the possible danger they might face. They had not been thinking along these lines at all. It struck them as a vitally important piece of information to have. And now, of course their way forward was clear: Carefully avoid anyone who looks like a legitimate conference attendee, and they'd likely avoid any trouble. They could easily do this and complete their mission without incident. Every one of them inwardly relaxed a little with this thought.

They didn't have a clue that their comfort was itself based on a simple miscommunication of a different sort, or that it was going to be as short lived as at least one or more of them.

26

Lunch Arrives

The king had a meeting in his sitting room with Layla and Hamid. Layla briefed him on the recent conversation between Rama and Muriel. After the working group session, the king had asked her to visit Khata's mother and let her know, gently, that their piano teacher might be involved in some unpleasant and even traitorous activity. When she first heard this, Rama was shocked and amazed at the fact that her daughter had felt suspicions, and she told Layla right away about Khata's troubled feelings regarding Muriel. As far as Layla was concerned, that pretty much sealed the deal on Khata being invited into Phi. But she would still have to tell the king and, unless things proceeded more quickly than she expected, she would likely have to at least go through the motions of speaking with Muriel about what she had determined in her time with the girl. Otherwise, the piano teacher might become suspicious and grow more guarded.

Rama was a woman of great inner strength and confidence. So, once she heard the entire story and had been assured of Khata's safety in all ways, she volunteered to do her part to snare Muriel into a trap. Layla had made some suggestions, and it was those ideas that guided her when the newcomer had recently visited.

While Layla was reporting all this to the king, Kular knocked on the door and, opening it, said, "Your Majesty, lunch has arrived for the three of you. Do you want it in the dining room?"

"Yes, thank you so much, Kular. We should be in momentarily."

He turned back to Layla and said, "From what you've told me, it sounds like Santiago must indeed be looking for something, as we had suspected, some sort of treasure, or item of legend, that he thinks may be found within the palace."

"Yes, Your Majesty," Layla replied. "We know it's The Ring of Phi, The Stone of Giza, or The Book of Phi."

"The man is always searching for extra power, it seems," Hamid said in response.

"Yes, and any one of those items could certainly give him that," the king replied.

"He really puzzles me," Hamid then commented.

"What do you mean?" Layla asked.

"Well, here he is, sending out a spy to gather information, and for what? Does he plan to storm the palace? Where's his army? The criminals we've dealt with in the past had much more extensive networks of armed associates and hired troublemakers. Shapur has seen him, with that new capacity for remote viewing, but only in the company of a few people. What in the world is this man thinking?"

"Maybe he's not thinking it through very carefully," Layla suggested. "Anyone in the grip of a destructive passion like hot anger, hatred, a lust for power, or a desire for revenge can't typically think well or straight. The emotion is always twisting their minds."

"That's right," the king said, nodding. "This man's greatest strength may be his passionate intensity, and of course, as these things usually go, it could also be his greatest weakness. Badly negative emotions or attitudes boosted by extreme intensity can derail almost any enterprise."

"So true," Hamid said. "And, by contrast, as we know, positive intensity of the right sort, a proper passion aligned ethically to a noble cause, can somehow be both hot and cool at the same time. The elevated aspiration or cause that inspires can also direct and properly regulate the mind that harbors it."

"Yes," The king said. "When sound values govern positive intensity with a noble enthusiasm, great things can happen. This man, unfortunately, seems to have none of that in his soul at present."

"The scope of his cause does not exceed his own ego. That's his main problem," Layla commented.

The king suddenly made a gesture, as if requesting quiet for a moment, and paused for a few seconds, apparently listening into the silence, and he looked very serious. He said, "I think we should take a minute and, within our hearts and minds, ask for support and assistance for our friends in Alexandria. Then, we can take the time to relocate to the dining room and have our lunch. Please, join with me in thinking of our friends and any needs they may have."

Mafulla and Haji were sitting in the front room of the Adi home, doing their assignments in silence for the moment. Shapur was resting in the back room, protesting to Reela that he felt fine and needed to check the shop. Shamilar was coming in, now and then, and reminding him of what the doctor had insisted. He needed to rest for at least a few more days before going back to work, or even visiting the store. As the senior doctor had put it: "Mr. Adi, you're not getting over a cold, but your own recent death. It's a bit different." That at least made him laugh.

Reela was a perfect audience for Shapur in this condition, and the two men were talking about the whole situation—what was known and what wasn't, what might happen next and might not, and how they could take specific small actions to protect the family better. Reela had also asked Shapur to repeat the entire story again about his vivid and compelling experiences while apparently unconscious, and then deceased. The brothers shared moments of wonder, a few big laughs, and some reminiscences of their childhoods. The morning had gone well, despite the patient's underlying frustration over the fact that things were not yet completely back to normal. He didn't enjoy prolonged inactivity, even in the comfort of his own home.

The Sakat brothers were at this point sitting outside the house on guard duty. Another guard was minding their shop and keeping an eye on the Adi store, in Shapur's absence. Badar was reading a detective novel, and Mumar was whittling away at some wood with a small knife. Shamilar had spent some time sitting with them and chatting, on and off throughout the morning, and she was making sure they were well supplied with tea and snacks. The king had arranged to have some lunch sent over, and he would do the same for dinner, to feed everyone who was there. Ali considered Shapur and Shamilar at this point to be like extended family.

Following a few hints that had been provided by Shapur's new mental ability to view Santiago's immediate surroundings, the king had directed Masoon and Hamid to organize some small search parties to comb the nearby desert and locate the man. Shapur didn't see Santiago all the time, but mostly when he focused hard on him. And even this was not always effective. The visions came and went more unpredictably as time passed, even when he made a strong effort to concentrate on their enemy. And then, when he was successful, he couldn't usually see far beyond the man himself, only a short distance in any direction around him, and anything else beyond that was a blur, or not in the picture at all. Nonetheless, Santiago seemed to be in a desert environment most of the time, or at least outside the city.

Their recent guest from the foreign intelligence service in Spain had apparently been right in his prediction that the monster would not stay in the city itself, or near the electrical grid where his strange personal interference might spark the sort of attention and inquiries that could compromise his privacy and position. And there was no reason from Shapur's visions to think that Santiago had a large group of men with him. But much was yet unclear. Masoon was out searching at the moment. Hamid also had other groups out, but he was personally taking a break to have a special meeting with the king.

Badar Sakat put down the book he had been reading and said to his brother, "You know, from what Shapur's told us, there's no reason to think the adversary is anywhere near us."

Mumar replied, "That's right, but he's been sending people to do much of his dirty work, and we have no idea where all of them are."

"Also true, and a good point," Badar conceded.

Just at that moment, a truck came around the corner, slowed in its approach, and pulled up to the house. Badar stood up. It was a standard military vehicle with two men inside. Mumar turned toward the open door of the house and said, in a strong voice, "We have some company arriving." Reela heard him and excused himself for a moment from Shapur's room, and walked toward the door. He then stopped and looked out a window.

"Who is it?" he inquired.

"Military truck," Mumar answered.

"Be cautious. Ask for the password," Reela reminded him.

As the driver began to open his door, Mumar stood up beside his brother and held up his hand, saying loudly, "Password, Please!"

"What?"

"Password! We need your password." As Mumar repeated himself, Badar slowly reached toward his gun.

"Oh, sorry! It's 'Kular'!" At that point, Reela was at the door along with the Sakat brothers and had heard the answer, and it was correct.

"Ok, then," Mumar replied. "Thanks for coming. You may approach."

"Lunch has arrived!" the driver shouted out, with a smile.

"Lunch? An entire truck this size for lunch?" Badar asked, as he walked forward.

"The king apparently thinks you're very hungry," the soldier replied. "We actually have lunch and dinner for you in the back. If we could have help unloading it all, we could get back for our next assignment more quickly."

"No problem," Reela said, as he walked forward toward the vehicle with Badar and Mumar. They went straight to the back and lifted the canvas flaps and were amazed at the amount of food that awaited them. "Incredible! This could feed us for a week!"

Within ten minutes, it was all unloaded and taken to the kitchen area where Mumar and Reela helped Shamilar sort it out, while Badar stayed on guard out front. And then, in no more than five more minutes, Mumar was bringing his brother a heaping plate of food, while also carrying his own out front.

"Oh, my! A feast indeed!" Badar exclaimed.

"Yes, this should get us through the afternoon quite nicely," Mumar replied.

"I would say so!"

"The fried cheese is amazing. You have to try it." He held out the plate to his brother and pointed.

Badar replied, "I don't need convincing. It looks great!"

Reela was right behind Mumar with additional tea for them, which he put down on a small table next to where they had been sitting all morning.

"Thanks," Badar said. "Can you join us for lunch?"

"I'd love to, but I'd better get back inside with my own poor brother, who's so sick and tired of being housebound."

"How's he feeling?" Mumar asked.

"The same, completely normal," Reela answered. "That's what makes it so hard for him to be confined to the house. We should get word to the doctor soon, and perhaps he can lift the restrictions on Shapur's activities before he drives Shamilar and me crazy and we are the ones who need a doctor." They all laughed.

"Reela, by the way," Badar said, "Have you heard anything about the results of the article in the newspaper?"

"Yes, indeed I have. You know, Leem Hadad wrote it, at least the first draft, and I made a few additions and had it put into the paper, and it's worked marvelously well. Fifteen men have turned themselves in as paid Santiagos, and so we now have their additional information. That's fifteen more than we already knew about."

"Wow, that's a lot."

"And they were living and working in various parts of town."

"The details they've provided should clarify the picture considerably, I would imagine," Mumar said.

"Yes, we've interviewed each of them extensively, built up a profile of what they've told us, and we know a good deal more now than we did before the article. It was all Leem's idea, by the way, and I think it was a stroke of genius."

"I bet it made Santiago boiling mad."

"Yes, indeed, " Reela laughed. "I certainly hope so. That was a major part of its intent, as well. Now, we can wait for him to trip himself up, as a result."

"Oh! The hummus is also especially good today," Badar exclaimed. "There's some spice I don't know. Here, try some on the pita."

In the hotel suite in Alexandria, Walid looked down at his Reverso watch. "Shouldn't lunch have arrived by now?"

Omari said, "Yes, you're right. Someone should go check on it. We can't be late for the train."

"I'll go," Amon offered. And with Paki and Omari's agreement, he left the suite, heading for the kitchen downstairs, this time by means of the elevator. Bhati began packing the last of the things she didn't already have in her bags and then, about five minutes later, she emerged from the master bedroom to say to the room generally, "Boys, Amon should be back any minute now with lunch, so I think you'd better all freshen up and wash your hands."

Omari responded, "Good idea!"

She smiled and reminded them, "There are three bathrooms with soap and fresh towels in each." Then she said," I'll get the table ready for us while you men all clean up." Everyone acted on her suggestion right away, and as Omari went into one bathroom, Paki made his way to a second one, and Walid gestured for Malik to go first back into the third available room.

When the last bathroom door closed, at nearly that moment, there was a knock on the outer door to the suite. Rumi was closest to it, and so, turning in its direction, he said, "Yes?"

The name 'Kular' was said from the hallway, and so he stepped forward to open the door. Bhati had walked over toward Walid from the dining table and was going to ask his help with moving some flowers off the table to make more room for all the food. The prince was at the moment standing near the big windows in the main sitting area, straight back from the door to the suite, looking out. But at the knock, he had turned slightly, to see his dad go open the door. And then he looked over at his mother, who had just said, "Walid?"

The next instant was crammed full of the sort of thing you can never see coming. Whether this is a fortunate or unfortunate fact about life is up for discussion. The initial flurry of the unexpected, happening at rapid, mega-speed, quickly flipped the temporal switch on the flow of experience for everyone in the room and, after a first frantic instant packed with perplexity and confusion, it gave way to that slowed and stretched fullness of time that Walid had experienced on several occasions in the past year.

Rumi turned the door nob and gently began to pull the door open, but that movement was suddenly accelerated with explosive force, as the door was slammed inward by two men storming into the room, guns out, searching rapidly for their intended victim. Rumi had been forced backwards and sideways and was knocked to the floor by the hard concussive push of the door. Walid turned back quickly enough to see the two intruders, both in military clothing, scanning the room and showing an expression of recognition when they glimpsed Bhati not far from her son. As soon as Walid registered their faces and actions, he knew what was about to happen and began to move to put himself between them and his mother. His movement preceded the next motion of their arms, as they began to raise and aim their guns at her.

The prince was determined to protect her and take the bullets that in the next split second would be meant for and, in fact, long planned for her and intended to leave her dead on the spot. There was no room in his consciousness during this first reaction to reach for his own gun. It was almost as if he had forgotten there was one stuck down in his belt. His only instinct at the moment was to shield his mother from these men and what they intended to do.

The two intruders had their eyes locked on Bhati, and so didn't immediately notice the fact that, a bit off to their right, Walid was on the move to intervene. Their peripheral vision may have picked it up, but they'd had their orders drummed into them to the extent that they were paying no attention to anyone else in the room but the one woman—the woman, the woman, she was the target. They were to shoot her and get out as quickly as they could. That was what they had been paid, and paid lavishly, to do.

As Walid threw his body between their guns and his mother and they began to squeeze their triggers, he suddenly remembered his own weapon. But it was too late to prevent what was about to happen. Some things can't be stopped

Omari had not heard the sound of the door being forced open and Rumi falling to the floor because he was in the bathroom that was attached to the master bedroom, farthest back from the entry. At the time it happened, he also had water loudly running in his sink and was bending over and splashing it onto his face. Malik had thought he heard some noise, but didn't make anything of it, since he was also closed into a small room with running water, and what he heard could have been almost anything. Walid and Rumi could be rearranging furniture for the meal, or it could be many other things. Because he had no expectations of imminent danger, his interpretive framework didn't allow him to feel any alarm or even curiosity at the fairly faint bumping noises he heard.

But Paki was different. From the first loud sound of the men coming into the room and pushing Rumi down, something he could hear above his own ablations, though barely, it took him exactly three seconds to interpret it, suspect some version of what was indeed happening, grab his weapon, open the door of the bathroom, and emerge from it, coming around a corner with his face dripping wet. But the seconds that had passed by now were too many for him to get into a position where he could stop what was about to happen.

As the shots rang out, a blur of movement took the shooters by surprise. Walid had come in front of his mother to take the bullets meant for her, but he in turn had been supplanted by someone who was bound to let neither of them suffer this harm. Some other figure had leaped over a chair and jumped between Walid and the guns.

At that irreversible juncture of time and action, King Ali, sitting in his dining room in the palace, suddenly knew what had happened and he said aloud in a sad but measured voice, "We have … failed." He took a deep breath and let it out and said, "A sudden and violent death has at this moment come to one of our own. God bless his soul."

Hamid looked stricken and gazed up at him and said, beyond all considerations of decorum and formality, "Ali."

Masoon suddenly stopped his horse five miles from the outskirts of town and dismounted. He then motioned for his men to hold up where they were. The wind whistled through the silence of their stillness. He seemed to be listening, but was in reality feeling what had just occurred.

Hoda was sitting in her office during the lunch hour, and felt as if a block of ice had formed in her stomach. Kissa, having a bite of lunch outside on a bench in the sun, experienced a strong shiver. Hasina, sitting on the ground a few feet away, looked at her and said in a voice of alarm, simply, "What is it? What's happened?"

In his father's house, Mafulla put down the cup of tea that he had been lifting up to sip from, and he looked around the room, searching throughout his immediate context for something, anything, that could explain what he'd just had rush through him. He stood up and said, "Haji, what just happened?"

"I don't know, but I felt it, too," the boy replied with a look of great concern on his face. "Something really bad."

Sab Maayuf reached for the hand of his wife Meskhenet and held it and gave it a small squeeze while saying, almost under his breath, "Greater love has no man than this."

"It's true," she replied, as tears welled up in her eyes. "It's the deepest and most powerful truth."

The king had made sure to send The Stone of Giza with the rescue party that he had directed to go to Alexandria and retrieve

Rumi and Bhati. He gave it to Omari who then, as the senior and lead member of the team being sent, apart from the obvious status of the prince, decided to entrust this powerful object to Amon. The king's intent was that if something unfortunate were to happen in Alexandria, they would have with them the best and most powerful medicinal antidote imaginable, and that it would be available to them to use instantly, in order to mitigate anything that might require this most potent remedy.

But at the moment, in the midst of the crucial possibility for which the king had sought to prepare, the stone was in Amon's pocket and he was locked in a freezer in the hotel's kitchen. He had just minutes before been badly deceived.

When he'd arrived downstairs to check on the food they had ordered for lunch, a man dressed as a member of the kitchen staff had asked him to help get something from the freezer, something that he said was needed for the completion of the meal order. In his typical, friendly way, Amon had followed the man into the big, nearly room-sized unit, like those used by most large restaurants and hotel kitchens. Once inside it, the man had said, "Just a moment, I have to grab something for our use," and had turned and, within two or three quick steps, had shut the door on Amon from the outside, locking it securely, and turning off the interior light. The door was made of thick steel. Amon was now standing in the dark and the cold, realizing instantly what had happened to him, and there were no obvious options for him to use to gain freedom. So, he was stuck and completely out of commission for the time he was needed the most.

His first thought when he heard the click of the lock was that he should have given the stone in his pocket to Omari or Paki before he left to check on the food. Some legitimate member of the large kitchen staff was sure to come and open the door eventually. But Amon had no idea when this would happen. And so, he was sidelined with the stone. The kitchen staff imposter and the army imposter who initially had taken the order downstairs from the suite had then both made their way to the service elevator and back up to the fourth floor where their third confederate awaited them, and where their awful job was to be done.

Bancom's earlier telephone call to the hotel manager, conveying an urgent message to his friends, had meant to warn of the possibility of "army imposters," not "harming imposters," or "charming imposters." And this simple misunderstanding caused by a crackling phone line had directed everyone's attention toward the wrong people, away from the real dangers they faced. But not even Bancom had suspected from the scant evidence he had about the possibilities in play that a member of the kitchen staff would also be kidnapped and replaced by a man whose fake credentials and elaborate story had gotten him in as a substitute. Santiago had sought to leave nothing to chance, and had put more than one plan in place that would lead to the same result.

The men the monster hired had not known, of course, that anyone would come down to check on food, or that the man who did come down would be hiding anything in his possession that was the most desirable item to have available in a situation of battle. They had no idea that locking Amon into the freezer had neutralized not only him, but also a medicinal stone of legendary power. There was a man in the kitchen only in case the royal visitors were to give instructions to bring food to their suite, or if the kitchen might be able to send up some food as a purported gift from the manager of the hotel. But the man there had also been given instructions to be alert and to improvise with any opportunity that might be presented. A strong poison had been at the ready.

Using false written orders, the hired assassins dressed as Egyptian military had managed to deceive and replace the real soldiers stationed as guards outside the room only a short time before the rescue party had arrived from Cairo and told them of their intention to leave soon with Rumi and Bhati. The man in the kitchen had been positioned earlier in the day, at the opening of work, and was eager to do whatever he could to get a potential extra payment from the wealthy individual who had hired him as a backup assassin. And the primary plan had been to act at dinner-time, or later in the evening.

But now that Rumi and Bhati were set to leave the hotel before the end of the conference, and had conveyed that to the disguised adversaries on guard duty, those men knew they had to move quickly. And so, when one of them had been sent down to the kitchen with the order for lunch and a request to bring back the food when it was ready, he had merely nodded at his colleague outside the room and held up one finger, meaning to wait. Once he had gotten to the kitchen and found his confederate there, they had taken the opportunity with whispered comments to hatch a simple plan that they hoped would work. They were in a bit of a panic that they now had waited too long to attempt what they'd been paid to do. And poison couldn't be used, because they didn't know which order was the woman's, and their strict orders were to seek to kill only her. They worried that their target might be too well protected now with additional resources. And they had few options remaining than just to go in, guns blazing, and see if that could get the job done without getting killed in the attempt. The element of surprise was their only hope. Once back up at the room, two of the men had gone in, and one of them had stayed in position to ward off any assistance that might arrive after the gunfire began.

When they had made it back up to the suite, the two gunmen, now knowing the password, successfully got through the door, as planned, and had indeed sighted Bhati quickly. The woman was to be shot. Anyone else was expendable, but not to be targeted if at all possible. They should survive and live, the rest of them, to suffer the loss and the grief. That was the plan and the whole point of this. It was to be a focused strike. That was Santiago's order. The first two bullets had been fired before Paki appeared in the room, gun up and shooting back at the intruders. One other revolver was also in use a split second later, adding to the thunderous noise in what suddenly seemed to be a tightly enclosed space for a major gun battle.

When Walid thought he was a mere millisecond from a bullet or two ripping through the middle of his body, he had instinctively shut his eyes against the impending experience. And as he fell, he heard his mother scream out. He hit the floor hard and realized to his surprise and confusion that he had felt nothing from a gunshot wound or anything else except the floor. And at that moment he opened his eyes once more, quickly looking around to see what had just happened, as he instinctively raised himself up on one arm and scrambled to get into a defensive or offensive position, whatever was now needed.

It took him a full second by the clock, and much longer in the flow of recognition, to make out exactly what he was seeing. Two intruders already lay dead on the floor, but there was a third body on the carpet as well, splayed out, arms and legs arrayed in an unnatural position, unmoving, and bleeding heavily.

Walid seemed to be suspended between two eternities, caught in a delayed, frozen moment. And his mental state became thick and almost impenetrable as he first thought he recognized the clothing of the third victim on the floor before an identity or name or relationship could dare come into his mind, which had suddenly grown slow and cold and almost distant. Everything in him preferred to be far away from this scene, rather than present to take the responsibility to identify fully and name what had just happened, and who, in addition to the enemy, now lay dead in front of him.

27

A Big Sacrifice

At least ten gunshots had nearly deafened everyone in the room. The one enemy outside the door quickly fled when he heard the loud exchange, fearing for his life under the onslaught of what was clearly superior firepower. His backup role had been forgotten and tossed aside in panic. He would deal with the consequences later, he told himself, or avoid them completely if he could. He clearly didn't know Santiago, or that any avoidance of consequences now would be impossible. So he ran.

He fled down the hall toward the stairwell as fast as he could, and flew through the door there in such a frantic state that he almost fell down the first flight of stairs. Only his handgrip on the bannister saved him. By the time he got halfway down the entire stairway, at the landing for the second floor, still descending at a reckless speed, he felt a brief wave of something almost like relief, despite the continued throbbing of his heartbeat in his head.

The moment his left foot rose off the landing to make contact with the last flight of interior stairs that now stood between him and escape, he heard the door open loudly below him, at the first floor. It was Amon, followed by three soldiers who had found him and released him from the kitchen's freezer, all armed. Despite his shock at this sight, he somehow got off a first shot, but just barely, and the bullet went straight toward Amon's right shoulder. But Phi skill instantly kicked in, and the palace guard twisted slightly, just in time to evade contact. The bullet nicked the cloth on his arm, but completely missed any flesh. A second later, Amon and two of the soldiers had returned fire at the man, and they didn't miss. He crumpled and fell and rolled down five steps and now lay dying on the stairs.

Amon leaped over his body and continued to run upward, followed by two of the other men, while the third disarmed their victim where he lay. Up past the second floor, to the third floor, they were taking the stairs two at a time, as fast as they could. Amon burst through the door at the fourth floor landing and paused momentarily to check the hall for any other adversaries. Seeing none, he then ran full speed toward the now unguarded suite.

Less than two minutes earlier, the only human sound that had pierced the air of Suite 424 at the Palace Hotel after the thunderous fusillade of gunfire had just taken place was the single scream that had been ripped from deep within Bhati Shabeezar's heart. It was filling her son's brain as he hit the floor and opened his eyes to see what had happened.

The second that Walid saw three figures on the floor, he jerked his head around to look at his mother for signs of injury, since his whole attention and effort had been to shield her from the bullets that had been deliberately directed at her. He saw no sign of blood or injury, but the utter shock on her face gave him an inner chill of fear and momentary panic, as he then quickly turned back around to the room. Paki was checking the two intruders, the bodies closest to the door, for any sign of life. Omari was practically diving toward the third body, as Malik instinctively ran toward the door with a gun he'd been given, mindful of the fact that there might be more adversaries in the hall.

Halfway down that hall at a full-out run, Amon suddenly saw a gun and then a hand and an arm and now the first part of a figure emerge from the door of the suite. He aimed his weapon, finger on the trigger and yelled out, "Halt! Drop your weapon!" as he himself came to a sudden stop in a shooting crouch, ready to take down the gunman.

"Amon! It's me, Malik!" the boy shouted. "Come quick!"

Amon recognized him then instantly and continued jogging toward the door. "What happened?"

"Shooters!" Malik replied tersely.

Amon preceded him through the door and into the sitting room where the unexpected and dreaded scene was playing out. The two gunmen were dead. Paki was picking up their weapons and tossing them across the carpet, as he simultaneously scrambled toward where Omari was working furiously over a figure on the floor. The ripping of cloth could be heard, and Omari said "No!"

Walid saw and consciously realized through the fog that had descended on his brain that it was his father, Rumi, lying still, unmoving, in a large pool of his own blood.

Amon said, "I have The Stone!" and shoved his hand into his pocket, pulling out a cloth bag and fumbling fast to open it and hand this last hope to Paki, who had turned to receive it from him.

"The Stone!" Bhati exclaimed. "The Stone of Giza! We're saved! My Rumi's saved!"

Paki grabbed Omari's shoulder and said, "Take it, brother! Put it into Rumi's hand!" Omari didn't reply or move in response, and Paki was stunned by this, and confused, and then he reached down and over to Rumi's hand himself and placed the brilliant green emerald into his palm and pressed his fingers around it.

"It's too late," Omari said to him, in a voice of disbelief.

"What?" Paki couldn't understand what he was hearing.

"It's too late."

"What do you mean?"

"He's gone."

"It's The Stone! The Stone of Giza! Surely …"

"It's too late. Our … Rumi … is gone." Omari repeated, with no emotion in his voice whatsoever. "There's no one here for it to help." Then the silence was, for a second or two, dense and thick.

Omari turned to where Walid was now standing and looking

on, and said, "Prince, I'm sorry. I have no words. There's nothing we can do."

"Why? Omari, why do you say this?" Walid asked, in shock. "It's The Stone of Giza! It can bring him back! It can heal him and bring him back to us!"

"No. He was shot in the heart and the head and his soul was sent away that moment, and this … can't be healed. There are no stable structures or processes left that it can enhance or augment."

"But anything …"

"No, not anything. Not this."

"Mafulla's dad came back."

"His body was somehow still a vehicle. It could support his life."

"The Stone can dramatically heal."

"Not everything. Not when the spirit's already gone and the body's torn apart in this way. Not in this way. Mafulla's dad didn't have The Stone bring him back, and he didn't come back to this."

"But."

"He was pulled back to a body that was capable of functioning."

"But I."

"Not even you, now."

Amon interrupted to say, "I was too late. It's my fault. They tricked me and locked me up. I should have been here. I had it with me."

"No. No, I don't think that, even two or three seconds after these wounds, it could have helped. He was gone instantly, as soon as the bullets did their work. We couldn't have gotten to him fast enough even if we'd been standing beside him with our stone."

Amon said, "We should have given him The Stone as soon as we got here."

"Yes. Maybe we should have. But we couldn't have known that. I've never heard of it's being used that way."

"But."

"And perhaps, even then, there would have been too much catastrophic damage. It's not a deflector shield or a barrier. I don't know that it can prevent harm."

"But, Dad," Walid said and went over and knelt down and touched his father's arm, directing his gaze away from the awful wounds.

Bhati had her hands over her mouth and streams of tears ran down her face, flowing across both cheeks. And at that moment, she put her hand on a chair to steady herself and began to say, "My husband, my love, my Rumi." And with all the strength she could summon, she took a step, and then another, and then a third and a fourth and knelt beside Walid and touched Rumi's arm, and she began to sob softly. She reached out to the side of his head, and started to smooth his hair down. Her movements were slow and almost without thought. She stroked his head and cried and her throat seemed to close up as her eyes swelled even more full of tears, and she was unable to think beyond this moment and this man who had been her husband and companion and her friend for all these years. And here he was, or was not. Here was his body, but not with his soul. Where was he now? Where had he gone? How could she look on and touch this body that had always been the dwelling of his spirit, and know that he was no longer here? "Oh, my dear, dear, man." She sobbed.

Walid then began to cry and put his hand on her arm, and then he reached over to hug her. And Paki and Omari and Amon and Malik were without words, as each of their souls was cut deep by the sharp jagged edge of a grief that they had not been prepared to feel on this day. The danger had been real, but still in some way remote and even abstract. They were doing their jobs like they normally did. And they always prevailed. They had always some-how prevailed. There was no thought or worry or concern that this would ever happen today. Not this. They had come so that it could not happen, and would not happen, and now they were in the presence of their terrible failure to stop it. There were moments, quick fleeting moments, where all this weighed on them, but without words, without conscious thoughts, without any vehicle of expression or articulation apart from the nearly suffocating gut realization of the enormity and finality of what had happened. They had to make themselves breathe.

The loving husband of Bhati, the devoted father of Walid, the dedicated physician and friend to the poor, the brother of the king, this unique and respected and admired and loved man had just been taken from them for no good reason. For the rest of their lives on earth, they would have to live with a huge empty hole in their spirits and in their daily experience. There would be no more Rumi to turn to for advice, wise counsel, inspiration, or comfort. His voice would not be heard in the palace. His warm presence would no longer enhance the room or the hallway, or wherever his work might take him in Cairo or throughout the kingdom as a whole. His laugh would not echo through the hallways. His jokes would come no more.

There was silence in the room now, aside from the low sobs of Rumi's sudden widow, the good wife and mother who with his help had raised in all the best ways a prince and future king. Even time seemed to bow deeply in grief, unable to move at its normal pace to the next moment and the one after that.

"I'm so sorry," Amon said, to the room generally, but especially to Bhati and Walid. "I'm so very, deeply sorry." Malik walked up to him and put his arm across his shoulders and with his left hand grabbed Amon's left arm and squeezed it.

Omari said to him, "We all are. This is not your fault. We all failed today." He then looked at Walid. "I ... don't know what to say, Prince."

Paki added, "We completely failed you. We've failed your mother, and your father, and our king."

"No," Walid said. "No, you did your best."

"It wasn't good enough," Omari said.

"It didn't stop what, apparently, couldn't have been stopped," Walid replied. "You have to let it go. We all have to somehow let it go. I just don't know how. Dad was a hero. He gave himself. He sacrificed his life right here to save mine, and my mother's."

"You threw your body in front of hers to save her," Paki said. "I saw you move with courage and no fear. And then I saw a glimpse of him do the same for you. Rumi acted to save you, Prince, and you, Bhati. His great love commanded his sacrifice, and he gave his life willingly, quickly, and decisively, to save you both. And he was the only one of us who succeeded today."

Walid struggled hard to swallow, and said, "It should have been me." He was silent for maybe five seconds and then let out a deep breath and said, "His sacrifice ... will be honored." The prince fought to control his voice. He said, "His love will go on."

In the palace, around the table, all was quiet. "Ali," Hamid repeated. "What's happened?"

The king momentarily put his head in his hands. He then raised his face and said, "It's my brother. It's Rumi." A single tear began to run down his cheek. "Two men stormed the suite in the hotel and tried to kill Bhati. It all came to me just now in a flash. Walid threw himself in front of his mother, and Rumi put himself in front of his son."

Hamid said, "Is Rumi?"

"He's gone. Rumi's dead."

"But, what about The Stone?"

"It was late getting to him, but there was already too much damage in the attack itself, to his brain and heart. He was gone in the instant. He couldn't be brought back. He's elsewhere now. Bless him forever."

Layla said, "And the others?"

"Unharmed, bodily, but dashed down and crushed in their spirits. I can feel their hurt and helplessness."

Hamid flashed with anger. "We need to stop this man, now!"

The king replied, "We need to show this man another way."

"But, Your Majesty, he's pure evil."

"He's a man far down a path of evil, but he's a man."

Hamid took a deep breath and let it out, and nodded slowly. "Yes. Yes, I know you're right."

At the Adi house, Mafulla walked to the front door and looked out. He suddenly knew. "Haji!" He turned to his friend, who was at that point rising from his seat. "It's Walid's dad."

"What?"

"Walid's dad—he's ... gone."

"What do you mean?"

Mafulla felt an icy cold sensation throughout his soul. He could hardly think. He said, "He's left our world. Walid's dad has left. Someone shot him and no one there could protect him or save him."

"Did you see it?"

"In a flash, some of it. I felt it before I could see any of it, but then the flash came. I could sense that he wasn't the target, but that he died protecting the target."

"Who?"

"Walid's mom."

"Is she?"

"She's safe, but in shock."

"You know that he's dead?"

"Yes."

"But they have The Stone."

"I know. And yet, for some reason, it can't bring him back."

"Your dad came back."

"Yes, thankfully. But this is different. Poor Walid. Poor Bhati."

"Is Walid Ok?"

"He's physically untouched. But no. He's far from Ok."

"What should we do? Should we go to the palace?"

"I don't know. We're still on duty here. Something might happen here. I would hesitate to leave."

"Ask Reela what we should do."

"Good idea. I'll ask Reela." Mafulla still felt like he was in a mental fog with the realization of what had just happened to his best friend's father, who seemed almost like a second uncle to him. He stood for a moment more, collecting himself and stabilizing his emotions, and then he walked into the back room where Reela was with Shapur.

At the palace in Cairo, the school day was just past its midpoint. The girls had all come back into the classroom after their lunch break and were taking their seats. Hoda was sitting at her desk. She had just become aware of what had happened. And as soon as the realization came to her, she felt a sharp wave of lamentation in her soul, then something almost like a protest, and then a flood of guilt that she had not been in Alexandria to stop this thing. But on the heels of these feelings and thoughts was a strong realization that she was exactly where she was supposed to be right now, and doing what she was supposed to be doing, and that it was not her place to feel guilty or angry or distraught at the thing she was not able to prevent. Her inner grief and surge of keen protest had quickly been followed by a sense of inner acceptance. Her job today would be one of love and comfort and support, beginning now, but especially needed, and to be expressed, when Bhati and Walid came home from this terrible time in Alexandria. She would have her work to do.

At the moment, she knew that she had to talk with three of her students. So, she asked the class to read the first five pages of the third chapter in the book they were going to discuss next, and write a quick reflection on that passage, while she had to see three of them outside of the room for a few minutes. Then she asked Kissa, Hasina, and Khata to follow her outside, explaining to the others that they would be back within ten to fifteen minutes, at most, and probably sooner. Ara was being left in charge as room captain, Hoda said. She should collect the essays when they were done, and if the four of them weren't yet back at that point, she should begin to read them aloud for discussion.

Hoda then asked the three girls to follow her into her office a short distance down the hall, and when they arrived there, she closed the door softly and said, "Would you all take seats for a minute? I have some very sad news."

"What's happened, mom?" Kissa asked, right away. "I felt something big, something serious that's happened. Is Walid Ok?"

"Yes, dear. Walid's safe."

"I felt something, too," Hasina said, in a very soft voice and with an expression of great concern.

"Mafulla's safe, too." Then she looked at Khata and said, "So are Haji and Malik."

Khata said, "What's going on? I had the oddest, worst feeling a few minutes ago, and I didn't know why, and it hit me so hard. It feels like something disappeared, and that friends of ours are suffering in some way, like they're feeling shock and confusion and really bad sadness and terrible grief. But: Why? What is it? What's happened?"

Hoda said, "Khata, I know that you have a rare gift to feel the feelings of others and to know, at times, when something important or big, or difficult is happening to a friend."

"Yes."

"Kissa and Hasina have this ability, too."

"I ... didn't know that," Khata said, in surprise, as she looked at her two classmates.

"Yeah," Kissa said.

"It's good sometimes, and it's tough sometimes," Hasina said.

"But how?"

"We can talk about the how later," Hoda replied, gently. "There's a lot to tell. But for now, I need to focus on what you've all just been feeling and let you know what I've realized about it."

"Ok," Khata said, as tears welled up in her eyes and she didn't understand why.

"There's been an incident in Alexandria," Hoda began. "The king had reason to believe that an enemy of the palace, Juan Osvaldo Santiago, would send men to attempt to kill one of our friends there."

"Who?" Kissa asked.

"The king had been told that his brother Rumi was in danger," she explained. "He's been at a medical conference at the Palace Hotel in Alexandria for the past couple of days with Bhati, and as soon as the king learned that he might be under a threat, he sent Omari and Amon to go get him and bring him safely back. And Walid and Mafulla volunteered to join them."

"Mafulla's there?" Hasina asked.

"Actually, no. In the end, Malik offered to take his place on the trip, so Mafulla could stay behind with his father who is, as you know, recovering from an attack himself. So, Walid and Malik made the trip, and Haji stayed behind to help Mafulla at his his home, his family's home today."

"Oh."

"But what I have to tell you now is still very difficult."

"Is Rumi Ok?"

"Walid and Malik are there, as I said, and are unharmed. It turns out that the assassins who were sent to kill a friend of the king were actually told to shoot Walid's mother, not his father."

"Oh, no," Kissa said.

"And they tried to do as they were told," Hoda continued.

"Is she?"

"She was not hit. They failed in their assignment. Walid jumped in front of her to save her."

"No! But you said," Kissa looked shocked beyond words.

"Yes, I did. He's untouched."

"But ... how?"

"His father dashed in front of him and saved both Walid and Bhati from the guns of the assassins."

"Was he badly hurt?"

"I'm afraid that our brave and loving friend is gone."

"What?"

"Rumi sacrificed his life for his family."

Kissa gasped and her hands went to her face, and so did Hasina's. Khata sat in shock with her hands in her lap. Tears were now rolling down her face, as she felt not only her own grief, but the grief of the others who meant so much to her.

"But, mom, Doctor Rumi had serious protection," Kissa said.

"Yes, but as it turned out, the precise circumstances prevented any other outcome."

"But didn't they have?"

"Nothing could help, in the situation."

"What about the shooters?"

"The two of them, and an accomplice, are all dead at the scene."

After a few seconds, Kissa said, "Should you ... tell the other girls in our class?"

"We need to wait a few minutes, until a phone call or cable would have had time to arrive at the palace. I can't reveal my knowledge of this to anyone right now but you, and I must ask that you not let anyone know I told you these things before any of the modern communication devices could have brought the information to us here in the palace. But official word should arrive any minute now."

Khata looked puzzled and said, "I don't understand. How did you know all this, if there's been no communication of it yet?"

Hoda took a deep breath and replied in a voice of great kindness, "I'll explain it all later. I'll just say now that it's a little bit like the way you know some things that are strange to know, but it's more vivid and complete. For the time being, I just need to ask for your promise that you won't talk about this aspect of the situation with anyone other than the three of us."

"Ok," she said, softly and still tearfully.

"The three of us share the abilities you have, the rare abilities that you've felt throughout your life so far."

"You do?"

"Yes, and we've developed them. In particular, I've spent most of my life honing and expanding those abilities, as well as others."

"You have?"

"Yes. And on occasion, I can see something vividly and in great detail that's happening at a distance, and I can even peer into minds and hearts to learn secrets that have not yet been expressed. That's how I'm able to tell you girls this, now."

"You can do all that?"

"Yes. Not all the time, but most often when it's needed." Hoda got up out of her desk chair and walked around to Khata and put her hand on the girl's shoulder. "We'll talk more about this later. You have wonderful gifts that I can help you develop. But we must keep quiet about that now. It's best not to share this with anyone else, yet."

"Ok."

"No one else at all. I'll speak with your mother about it later."

"Ok."

"But, Mom, how can we go back to class after what you've just told us?" Kissa asked, tears rolling down her cheeks, as well.

Hoda took a deep breath. "You can't. You won't have to. In less than five minutes, I'll go tell the girls, and we'll all say a prayer for Bhati and Walid. In fact, we should begin that now, deep in our hearts. And we'll postpone our formal reading discussion that had been planned for this afternoon. We can do it later. We'll just provide support for everyone who needs it and conversation for anyone who wants it after they hear the sad news. And then we'll allow the girls to do whatever they might feel a need to do. You can all stay in the classroom or go to the library, or walk outside. Or we can contact a parent for guidance, if that's needed." She paused a moment and added, "I should go now, and try to do what's best for the girls as they deal with this knowledge."

"The man who did this," Hasina said, "Santiago: What will he do next?"

28

The Return Trip

Someone had brought three copies of *The Kingdom Daily News* to the small camp in the desert. And as a result of the front-page article anonymously written by Leem Hadad and placed in the paper by Reela Adi, Juan Osvaldo Santiago was completely enraged. He was insulted, offended, and livid beyond words at what had been written about him. It's safe to say that he had never been so angry in his life. He had just crumpled up his copy of the paper and then torn it into shreds, shouting insults at the idiots responsible for this vile trash, as he put it. He was pacing and spitting at the sand in his fit of temper as he hurled abuse toward the pathetic unworthy fools who had said and written such idiotic things about him. Who were they? They were all mindless vermin! They had no knowledge of him at all. They were incapable of recognizing true greatness! He went on and on, and the men with him had never witnessed such an extended display of fury spinning out of control. The article was having its intended effect.

It had been a very short time since Santiago had last slipped surreptitiously into the city to engage in the wickedness that had caused Mafulla's father such trauma. He had not intended to return to Cairo anytime soon, but rather wait until he had a fully developed plan to gain access to the object he most wanted. An assistant had just met with Muriel al-Baki to hear her latest information relevant to this, and he was due into camp any time now to make a full report on what had been learned. That information would be crucial in developing a final strategy for what he wanted to accomplish.

In one sense, his plan was all going quickly, much faster than could reasonably have been expected. But in another sense, it couldn't possibly go fast enough. Santiago had no patience for anything that resisted his will. And to know that Shapur Adi had recovered from his full, murderous assault was a huge blow to his considerable ego. And it was greatly perplexing. That, alone, was a terrible frustration and humiliation, but now this absurd newspaper article had taken the damage over the top. He was losing any semblance of rationality about the situation. He felt he should return to the city sooner than he had imagined. Even if he could just kill someone at the stupid newspaper, and perhaps some palace guards, that would help him vent the roiling emotions inside and would suitably alarm the king and his minions. It would be a great follow up to Alexandria, assuming that the plan there worked as intended. He, Juan Osvaldo Santiago, was not to be trifled with. He would have his revenge now, for it all, for everything. These were the thoughts that ran through his mind, when he was able to think at all, in his continuing rage.

But it was at this precise moment that the strangest thing happened. As he was pacing randomly, hurling curses at "all these morons" and the monarchy and mankind generally, while tattered shreds of newsprint were flying through the air and bouncing off the hot sand, borne aloft by the swirling desert breezes, a scene suddenly flashed into his head. There it was. The attack had happened. And in that moment, he registered the fact that the mother of the prince had been spared. Before his callously shriveled heart could even begin to rage anew at this additional affront, he saw the father of the prince dead and reasoned that suitable shock and grief were spreading, as a result. He didn't understand for a moment that Phi would react differently to a death, even to the death of a greatly loved man, than what he had hoped. Their grief would be bounded with wisdom and hope. Their suffering would be contained and ultimately mitigated by the sense they had of what's to come. He would not be causing the depth and duration of agony that he had so deeply desired to inflict.

But he was oblivious to all that and now said, barely above a whisper, "Finally." This was not the specific death he had wanted, but at this point, it was nearly as good for his purposes. He felt a sense of great relief and accomplishment.

That turned things around for Santiago considerably. He almost enjoyed a jolt of satisfaction and inner celebration. But that couldn't totally efface what he had just been feeling, and so he was harboring now a growing storm of contrary emotions. There was a thrilling exhilaration at the murder of an important foe, and at the resultant misery it would surely spread. And yet, layered around this and undergirding his mindset, there was still a sense of umbrage, and a nearly demonic rage at the reckless and vile aspersions that had been cast on his history and public image by those he considered so unworthy of an opinion at all.

"Osvaldo!" he called out to one of his top followers who was at the moment sitting in a small group near one of the tents. Three men actually turned and looked at Santiago, but his now pointing finger showed which of them he was addressing, and the man stood up and responded immediately, taking a step or two toward the leader.

"Yes, Master!"

"We'll return to town shortly."

"As you wish!"

"Choose two of the men with some degree of power."

"Yes, right away. When do we leave?"

"Within the hour, if possible. Make preparations."

"Yes, sir, immediately."

The monster of legend wiped his hand over his mouth and set his determination anew to go and create some gratifying havoc among those who had dared to resist him in his ineluctable march to ascendency, and then were so idiotic as to heap ridicule on him, in addition. Everyone must pay, he thought to himself. And then he added, in a mumble to the air, "Yes. Yes. Everyone will pay dearly. And then they'll know."

Walid and his mother had spent some time together in quiet communion near the lifeless body of their loved one. Someone had gotten their Alexandrian Phi friend and the captain of the guard from downstairs. And there were now ten soldiers in and around the suite, watching over the area, protecting the guests from any further possible attack, and making arrangements to get everyone, along with the body of the king's brother, back to Cairo on the next train out. The train would be held as long as needed. Phone calls had already been made. As stunned as everyone had been, an air of acceptance had already begun to settle over all. And the most advanced guard among them was now convinced that they needed to get on their way back home.

Paki came over to Walid and his mother and said, "Prince and Bhati, I'm sorry to interrupt your time together, but everything has been prepared for us to leave and get you back to Cairo, along with … Rumi."

"Ok, Paki, thanks," Walid said. And then he added, "This is all so strange, so unreal. It's as if we've passed through a warp in time and space. Everything's changed because of one big change."

"Yes, Prince, I know what you mean."

"Mom, are you Ok to leave with me now?"

"What of Rumi?"

Omari had just walked up, and he said, "We'll take care of everything. Don't worry about any of it. We've already made preparations, and he'll … accompany us on the train. We'll have a special car."

"Does the king know?"

"Yes. He does. He'll be awaiting our return."

Bhati nodded. At the palace, word of the attack was spreading. The news, of course, shocked everyone in the girls' class. They all knew and liked Walid's father. He had always been kind to each of them, with an unusual grace that flowed from a spirit of love and concern. He was not just someone they knew, but someone they all felt attached to in a very personal way.

After telling the girls, and making sure they were all right, Hoda went down the hall and knocked on Khalid's classroom door. A few seconds later, he opened the door and looked at her quizzically. She said, "I have some terribly bad news for you and the boys."

"What is it?" he nearly whispered. He felt a jolt of worried anticipation.

"Walid's father, Rumi, has been killed in Alexandria."

"Killed?"

"Murdered."

"But." Khalid looked surprised and even perplexed.

"If I could come in and tell everyone at once, I can get back to my girls sooner. They're all dealing with the news right now."

"Oh, yes, sure, I understand. Please, come in."

Hoda stepped through the doorway. "Boys," Khalid said, and the few members of the class who were in attendance looked up from the test they had been taking and were nearly finished answering. "Hoda has something to tell you and it's some very bad news for us all."

"Are the guys Ok?" Jabari asked right away.

"Yes, your classmates are all fine." Khalid looked to Hoda, who nodded in agreement.

"Good," Set replied.

Hoda then said, "I don't know an easy way to tell you this, but a short while ago, today, our friend Walid's father, Rumi, was shot and killed in Alexandria."

"What?" Bafur said aloud, in a voice of real shock.

Hoda took a breath and continued. "Assassins had been sent to shoot and kill Walid's mother, but when they attacked, Walid jumped in front of her to save her life. And at that same moment, Rumi got in front of both of them, sacrificing his own life to preserve theirs."

"Oh, man," Set said.

"Is Walid?"

"Walid was unharmed, bodily. But it's been very hard for him to go through this, and for your classmate, Malik, who was also with them today. They're dealing with a terribly traumatic situation, but as well as anyone could possibly expect to do so."

"Oh. Gee," Jabari said. He knew that Hoda had some sort of ability to help people in difficulties, through prayer or meditation or something, but he had no idea what she could or could not do. He looked at her intently at this point and said, slowly, "And, nothing could be done about Rumi's … injuries?"

"No, Jabari, I'm so sorry to say. Nothing. They were too severe and extensive."

"Wow."

"They'll be coming back this afternoon, late. We should all seek, in whatever ways we can, to be of support and comfort to the prince and his mother during this especially hard time."

Khalid had sat on the edge of his desk. "Is there anything in particular that you can think of for us to do before they return?"

"Nothing that occurs to me right now."

"Ok, well, we should let you get back to your class, as we all deal with this news the best we can." Hoda nodded and slipped back through the door and walked down the hall to her girls.

Khalid, Jabari, Set, and Bafur all sat for a moment in silence. "This is really terrible," Jabari said. "I mean—after Mafulla also nearly lost his dad, and now this." His voice trailed off.

"Who would murder one of Walid's parents?" Set asked. "How could anyone have anything against either of them? They're just really nice people who spend all their time doing good things."

"Well, I suspect it's the work of this man named Juan Santiago," Khalid observed.

"Oh?"

"He's the person who was behind all the animal disappearances a while ago, and Walid and his parents were with the group that stopped him from doing any more of that. Santiago had been living near their old village, and had to flee when they went looking for him. He's apparently still angry and resentful of what they did to stop him, and wants revenge. He seems to feel that if he can hurt anyone connected in any way with the king, he will get at least a part of the satisfaction he seeks. Until he's found and captured, we're all under a measure of threat from him."

The boys sat for a moment absorbing this information. "Who is this guy, really?" Bafur asked. "I saw the newspaper article."

"A man originally from Spain," Khalid answered. "He's apparently traveled the world in quest of some sort of spiritual power, but not for appropriate and moral uses."

"Why, then?" Set asked.

"He's working to attain his own dominance and hegemony over other people. He seems to be a man who had a difficult childhood and felt excluded and humiliated by other kids at the time. And now he's set against the world. He only wants to control and harm others and prove himself to be strong, and to be what he thinks of as great."

"Ambition out of control, untethered from proper values," Set offered. He then added, "It's a classic recipe for disaster."

"Yes," Khalid replied, impressed with the boy's insight. "Well said."

After a moment of silence, Jabari spoke up. "I can't imagine what it feels like to suddenly lose your father like that. I mean, at our age. You sort of assume that your dad will always be there for you. And death is just so final."

"Yeah," Set agreed. "It must feel really sad and strange and awful. And shocking."

Jabari added, "And scary. Really scary."

"Yeah, that too."

"And Walid's dad had worked his whole life to learn and develop skills and become a doctor and be the best doctor and person he could be, so that he could help others, and he did help a lot of people all his life and, just like that, this jerk Santiago takes it all away."

"You're right. He didn't just take one person out of the world, but he eliminated every good deed Rumi would have done if he had been able to continue to live a full and productive life. Lots of people won't have the doctor and friend and helper they could have had," Set said.

"And the king has lost his only brother," Bafur added.

Jabari picked up this thought, saying, "The king's parents are long gone, and he doesn't have a queen or a sister, and he has no sons or daughters, and now his closest family member, his brother, has been taken away from him. I wonder what it's going to be like for him."

"The king is strong and wise," Khalid said. "He'll probably be able to deal with it better than anyone else could. I'm sure he'll be a great support and shield for Walid's mother, and for our good friend and classmate through this difficult time."

Then Jabari said, "My mom always bakes something when there's a death in a friend's family. She'll want to do it for Walid and his mom and the king, I bet. But, it seems kind of silly in this case, with the huge palace kitchen always supplying food, no matter what happens."

"Let her do what she wants and feels called to do," Khalid said. "The grieving family will appreciate it, and it might make her feel better to have something she can create with love to show her support and comfort. It's her way. Food can have meaning far beyond its physical nature. A cake is not just a cake. Where it comes from and why it was prepared can make all the difference. Those affected can benefit from your mother's skill and care."

"You're right," Jabari said. "We all feel sort of helpless, and like there's something we wish we could do."

On the train home from Alexandria now, Malik was sitting next to Walid. They had both been quiet for a while. Then Malik spoke up, but in a low voice. He said, "You know, if Mafulla had come instead of me, you two together might have been able to stop those guys."

"What?"

"You and Mafulla—the Viper and the Storm—you two seem

to have a pretty incredible partnership and a great track record. And maybe if you had been together today, with Mafulla backing you up instead of me, then the two of you could have taken down those guys before they did anything."

"No, man. You were there. You saw how fast it all happened. I mean, I was in the same room with them and I couldn't do anything to stop it. They came in too fast and caught us by surprise, and I was too far away from them, standing where I was. If Mafulla had been there, he would have likely been just as far away, or in the bathroom like you guys were, washing up."

"Yeah, but I'm just not as advanced yet as you two, I think."

"It's not your fault at all," Walid said. "Don't think that for a second. We had plenty of older and more advanced Phi on the job, and it still happened. Omari's incredible. So is Paki. He's super advanced. And Amon is as tough and smart as almost anybody. And together, they couldn't stop it."

"True. But."

"Some things are just going to happen, I guess. Maybe some things just can't be prevented."

Malik let out a big breath. "Well, at least thanks for saying that, man. I've been really worried that having me as your backup just wasn't good enough."

"I'm not just saying it. You took part in shooting those guys, right?"

"Yeah, but too late."

"Not too late to keep them from killing mom and me. I forgot for a few seconds that I even had a gun. And I ended up on the floor. Just think what they could have done if you hadn't helped to bring them down."

"Ok, that makes me feel a little bit better. Thanks."

"Sure."

"Not that it ever feels good to shoot somebody, and especially if they die. I wish they could have been stopped some other way."

"Yeah, but you did the only thing that could be done, and I'm here because of what you and my dad and the other guys did."

"Thanks, man, really. But … here you are helping me to feel better, and it should be the other way around."

"Well, there's not really anything that anyone can say to make what happened any easier for me to deal with. I just have to make myself remember what I already know and draw on it."

Malik turned and looked at his friend. And Walid went on. "I know it was … a transition for dad, a big new adventure that started right away. Hopefully, he didn't even feel any pain, just a freedom of release. I know what it's like to get really, really hurt. Either the lights go out for a bit and you feel nothing, or you sort of float out of your body and you feel nothing. It's only later, if you survive, that whatever damage your body got hurts like crazy. With the stuff that happened to dad today, he probably escaped the pain and suffering part and went right into … the really interesting part."

"It's just crazy that bad guys get to decide like that who gets to live and who doesn't."

"That's free will," Walid said. "If everyone was prevented from doing anything bad, we wouldn't really be free. And like the king told me recently, it's not as if they've done anything really bad to my father. They tried to kill at least one of us and damage the others for life with grief. I'm sure that's what their intent was. But if we're right in our beliefs about what comes next—and what happened to Mafulla's dad in the hospital just really confirms it all, in my view—then my dad's living more fully and freely right now, and is likely saturated with more knowledge and joy and love and other good stuff than he could've gotten the normal way, living with us for decades more. Mom and I just have to hang in there and remember this and know, at some point, that we'll be reunited with him. I mean: What those guys did was evil and wrong, in itself, but they couldn't hurt dad or us the way they wanted to. They don't have that power. Nobody does."

"Yeah—well said, man. I believe all that, too, but it helped just now to hear you say it the way you have," Malik replied. "So, there you go again, helping me."

"Hey, that's what I do," Walid said. "Don't worry about it. And I want you to know: It's been a good thing from the start to have you here on the trip. You've helped in lots of ways. I'm glad you came. I'm just sorry you had to see what we all saw and, you know, have such a truly tough day." Walid took a deep breath and added, "I guess Haji won the contest after all, since he ... missed all this."

Malik instantly said, "No, Walid, sorry to disagree, man, but I'm the winner. Just to be in the presence of such bravery, such strength and courage—that's given me something forever. It was, obviously, scary and hard and sad beyond words, but I think I'll be a better person for the rest of my life because of going through all this with you. Thanks for bringing me, and for what you did today, you know, to help save your mother's life. You would have done the same for your dad or for me. I know that for sure. You showed me something really important." Walid just nodded and took a deep breath in response.

Amon and Paki came around with a variety of food that had been packed up by the hotel staff. No one was hungry, but most of them tried to nibble on something just to give their bodies, hearts, and minds more strength for the journey, and for the inner healing they all needed, and for whatever would await them when they got home. Bhati was sitting with Omari and said, "I feel Ali with us. I have ever since the moment it happened. He's giving us support and strength. He's helping, as he always does."

"Yeah, I'm sure he knew right away what happened and what we would need because of it, and that he's done everything within his power to reach out to us."

"He's a man of great strength and compassion."

"He has more strength and compassion than I can really imagine," Omari added in agreement. "And it's always there for the needs of others. That's his work in the world."

"Just like Rumi," Bhati said, and her eyes glistened again. "Just like his brother ... my dear husband."

"That's right," Omari agreed. "Their brotherhood has always

shined forth in many ways. I know their mother was so proud of them."

"She was. And they admired and respected her to the utmost."

"I'm sure."

"She knew what it would take to prepare them for their journeys, from the earliest days. She did everything to make sure they would have the lives they deserved, and that would benefit all of us around them. Both of her boys grew strong and wise and have made a tremendous mark in this world."

"I'm confident they'll do the same in the next world," Omari said. "She's probably already welcomed him and, in companionship with her husband, his legendary father, is even now preparing him for the great things yet to come."

"Do you think we'll have such opportunities in the next stage, chances to do more and to be more?" Bhati asked.

"Yes. Actually, I do. All of this has not been preparing us for nothing, or for one long, endless vacation. I think we're being equipped for amazing things. But what they might involve, we're unable now even to imagine. I suspect that the next stage will be even more interesting than this one, and without most of the, unfortunately, necessary turmoil and trouble we have here, as a part of our education."

"We can hope," Bhati said.

"Hope is healthy," Omari replied.

"Yes, it is," she agreed, adding, "I certainly hope the worst is over with this horrible man, Santiago."

Omari took a deep breath and let it out and said, "I suppose we'll find out soon enough.'

29

THE PALACE

MURIEL HAD MET AGAIN WITH THE MYSTERY MAN WHOSE real name she still didn't know. She'd been instructed simply to call him Osvaldo and she did so, but with a bitter distaste for it, since she felt so close to the real Osvaldo. It bothered her that she couldn't speak to the master directly during this assignment. But she understood that he needed to keep his distance at present, and she followed his orders in hopes of her proper reward. She reported to the intermediary all she had learned from her time with Rama, and her words were well received. The man praised her even more highly than he had before and left their meeting spot quickly to take her information back to the secret desert camp as soon as he could. As it turned out, he arrived at the campsite a good distance outside town right before Santiago left to take his top three followers into the city.

The master listened to the report and grew even more excited about his trip into Cairo, which could now serve multiple purposes. He and his most advanced disciples chose fast horses and began their short journey toward the next chapter of their terrible revenge.

One of the men, however, an individual named Miguel Abad, was beginning to resent and doubt everything that was going on with Santiago, despite his personally advanced development and favored status. In the length of time he had been with the master, he had seen many things that confused him, and some that repulsed him. As they rode toward the city, he started rehearsing in his mind all the grievances that had built up in his heart. "Santiago," he thought to himself: "Who is he really? He insists on being called 'The Master,' and yet, what has he mastered? He's certainly mastered some esoteric spiritual knowledge and skills, and he's obviously mastered the other men, his seemingly loyal followers. But he has no mastery over his own emotions, or his ambitions, or his thoughts." All of this, and a lot more in the same vein was running through Abad's head as the four men now crossed an initial long stretch of sand and moved toward the nearest small road.

Miguel had learned enough about spiritual things outside of Santiago's teachings to know that this so-proclaimed master was trespassing and poaching on territory that was not rightfully his. His encroachments into the spiritual realm were at odds with what he had come to see as the most fundamental nature of spirituality. Santiago sought to strip off the power elements for his own use and leave behind the moral foundations of it all. Miguel had been attracted at first to the man's brashness and lofty rhetoric about what the world needs. And then he had been sufficiently enticed and lulled into acquiescence by promises of greatness that he had long ignored the small warning signs and feelings of ambivalence that continued to crop up in his heart. Like all men, he was a master of self-deception and rationalization, and had long deceived himself, as Santiago had sought to deceive him. In fact, he had been living proof for years that no one else can fool us unless we are willing first to fool ourselves. And that's how we become fools, indeed.

Deep down, Miguel knew that there was instability in his teacher, and basic untrustworthiness, but he had long masked this knowledge from himself, pretending that everything was fine and that the glories of their collaborative triumph in the future would make all things right. But the thefts of the animals had deeply bothered him. And now, many things cumulatively had been troubling him about the current mission of revenge they seemed to be pursuing. Where was this taking them? What was the outcome to be? How would any of this benefit the followers who had entrusted their lives to this man who now ultimately seemed to care about no life other than his own? What would it matter for the good of the world and the ascendency of spirit?

The trip into town was long enough that Abad was able to ponder all these things deeply and without interruption. The small and trivial straw that was about to take the camel down, as it's said, was this recent unpleasant business about paying ordinary and unworthy people to take on the name that he had worked so hard to earn. They would adopt the name, all right, but only for cash. What had he been given to take it on? The name was supposed to be such an honor that it would, in itself, compensate and reward him for all that he had sacrificed and fought to accomplish. It was bad enough to be chased out of Dromeda and to have led a gypsy existence since then, and now in old desert tents so close to the comforts and enjoyments of a city. But this name business had been the biggest humiliation, no matter what Santiago said to justify it.

Miguel was still going along, and to all outward appearances seemed loyal. But inwardly, he was experiencing a combination of doubt, anger, and a growing sense of rebellion against what he had been caught up in. His own inner resources had been developed enough that he was now able to entertain these thoughts in his heart without Santiago sensing them at all. That was an ironic aspect of all this. A younger, immature, less developed follower harboring doubts or anger toward the master would have been found out instantly and dealt with severely. Only a highly advanced disciple, by contrast, a person more fully inducted into the depths of the enterprise, could reach such a point of near rebellion without anything's being known or even suspected, precisely because of his serious knowledge and skills. Abad could now masterfully cloak his thoughts and feelings, even from Santiago himself. This was, of course, just another instance of the ancient truth that with power comes possibility.

All this was running through the mind of Miguel Abad as the

four men made their way in the direction of the city, toward a first destination, and then on to whatever else Santiago had envisioned for them. He rarely shared his plans in advance. He expected blind loyalty and simple obedience instead. He said it helped them to be comfortable with the unknown. He often spoke of partnership and collaboration, and even community, but never actually practiced any of it. He would simply say whatever it took to manipulate others in accordance with his own desires. And of course, he wasn't alone in approaching life that way. We see this path of ego as a common pursuit in the world.

One of the men at this point moved his horse up beside Miguel's and said to him, "You seem to be deep in thought, my friend. What's on your mind today?"

"Nothing, really," he answered. "Nothing at all, and yet everything. I was just taking the chance to meditate and ponder the mysteries as we ride." The man looked impressed and nodded and moved away. Miguel was indeed advanced, and seemed to be an older soul than most. His words were to be respected.

Near the opposite edge of Cairo, the king was now at the train station with several friends, including Hamid and Layla, along with a large contingent of palace guards and Egyptian military, when the train from Alexandria appeared down the tracks at a distance. Kissa and Mafulla were standing right beside the king. Masoon's son Haji was slightly behind them and remaining silent as the train approached the station. Hoda had offered to stay at the Adi home and supervise the guards there while also offering, in effect, the only real prevention against the possibility of another severe attack against Mafulla's dad.

Ali was waiting on the platform right beside the reserved train car when Bhati stepped off, escorted by Omari. She walked straight to the king, and he hugged her tightly. She buried herself in his embrace and sobbed for a few moments. He then spoke to her briefly, and she nodded her appreciation, and they hugged again. Paki stepped off the train, and then Walid and Malik appeared. Kissa could not contain herself. She ran to Walid and burst into tears as she reached for him. Malik moved past them and briefly put his hand on Walid's back, as the prince and Kissa embraced. Mafulla and Hasina were standing together as they watched their friends. He took her hand and they both felt an inward fluttering of sympathy and sadness and loss, as they held in their hearts what earlier they were told had happened.

Within five minutes, all the friends present had hugged Bhati and Walid and had spoken to them. As Amon then took charge of having Rumi's body transported to the palace, the rest of them got into waiting cars for the short drive back. Even the air seemed thick and heavy with sadness for the loss of that one bright light in their lives.

Just looking into Kissa's eyes made Walid tear up again, but at the same time, he experienced a great, wordless comfort as her spirit reached out to him. It suddenly occurred to him that he was the man now, in the direct lineage of his immediate family. His father was gone. His grandfather had long been gone. And back through the generations, they were all now depending on him in a distinctive way for the family's proper work in the world. It could have been a difficult thought, with a nearly oppressive sense of responsibility, but it wasn't. It was simply his turn. And he embraced the thought. With Kissa next to him in the king's car, Walid felt oddly calm, and in a way that he could never fully say or even quite define, he felt ready for his new role in things. He still had his dear mother, and that was so good. And he had his wonderful uncle, Ali, to rely on for advice and help. But he was the man now in his immediate family, and one of the two on whom Bhati would rely unconditionally. Walid, in his youth, and Ali, at his age, would be her main bulwarks and support from now on.

We all need a structure of emotional support in our lives. Most often, this is provided by family and friends and, sometimes, even by the more casual acquaintances where we work or live or go to school. When a major part of this structure is taken away, we have to make adjustments. There's an uncertainty at first, and an anxiety about what this will be like, and whether we can move forward with courage, as we know we should. The king had lost his dear brother, a constant encouragement and confidant for almost all of his life. Walid had lost his father, because of whom he came into this world and learned and grew and felt protected and helped and loved. Now, what had seemed like life itself was revealed with a new vividness to be just a passing phase or stage of life—as all are, ultimately. Each of the surviving family members would walk the path forward from this day on without this dependable and strong companion physically present.

The king was prepared. He was always prepared. And so was Walid, even though he didn't especially feel like it until this moment when he looked into Kissa's eyes. He knew now, though, because he realized in a deep way that he had been given and would be provided with all the support and belief and strength that he would need in his life. And this was what he would rely on for the challenges and the adventures to come. He could almost feel his spirit rising into his new role with a confidence he would not have anticipated.

And, of course, there was also Mafulla—and Hasina, and so many others, but especially Mafulla. When they got back to the palace and had sat with the king for over two hours to decompress and tell their stories and hear his loving wisdom about everything that had happened and that might yet come about, they all had a meal together. And, afterwards, Walid and Mafulla enjoyed some time alone to talk at length. Walid later told Kissa that it was, maybe, the most important conversation of his life. And she knew enough of his many talks with the king to understand the significance of a statement like that. He and Mafulla had become, deeply, brothers of the spirit.

Throughout their one-on-one time together that evening, Mafulla had helped Walid remember at a more fundamental level all they knew that could shed some sort of light on his father's death and bring comfort and hope. And, to a greater extend than he would ever have expected, this helped him to cope and let go emotionally, and even begin to reconcile himself to the tremendous loss he had just experienced. It also helped him to turn again in his heart and mind to face in a more positive way the future that awaited them all.

The king now was having a brief time alone, in quiet meditation. Bhati was with Layla and Hamid, and was greatly comforted by their presence and words, and their love for her. Hoda had sent a moving note and they could feel that she was with them all in spirit. Her love was a powerful support.

With the permission of Kular, Bancom opened the door and haltingly stuck his head into the doorway of the king's sitting room. He said, softly, "Your Majesty?"

"Yes?"

"I'm so sorry to interrupt you at a time like this, but I have an important message that must be delivered right away."

The king took a deep cleansing breath and said, "Certainly. Come in, Bancom. You're always welcome here. What do you have for me? What's the message?"

"Mumar Sakat just called in from the guard post near the Adi home where he's been temporarily working, as you know, and said that Shapur has told him Santiago is now on the move with three other men. I hope that makes sense. He may be coming into the city very soon."

"Please let Masoon know."

"Yes, Your Majesty, right away."

"Thank you for coming in. I'm glad you brought me this information."

"I'm … terribly sorry about Rumi," Bancom said. "We all loved him, and greatly admired him, as you know."

"Yes. Thank you, my friend. He knew of your great esteem and valued it highly. He'll prepare the way for us all to follow him some day. I'm sure of that. He'll be awaiting us."

Bancom nodded and bowed and quietly left the room. Down the hall, there was a knock on Walid's door.

"Who is it?"

"Zet."

"Zet?"

"Yes."

"Come in."

"Hey, Walid. Oh, hi, Mafulla."

Both boys greeted their visitor. Walid was lying on his bed and Mafulla was on the floor, propped up against a dresser.

"Walid, man, I'm so sorry about what's happened."

"Thanks, Zet. It was bad. But I'm still here because of what he did."

"Yeah, I heard."

"Come on in and sit down with us," Walid said.

"Oh, Ok. Are you sure?"

"Yeah, we've just been talking, and we're pretty much talked out—I mean, about deep life and death stuff."

"I bet."

"So, get our minds on something else and tell us what you've been doing for the past couple of days. We haven't seen you."

"Well, I've just been mainly sightseeing—you know, around Cairo."

Mafulla said, "What sights have you seen?"

"Lots: The Nile, down at the docks, the government buildings, the shops, the big marketplace—Mafulla, your family's great shop—the beautiful houses in the exclusive neighborhoods, and some really big ones, bigger than any private homes I've ever seen before. And then there was my favorite thing of all, other than the Adi Shop, of course: the National Museum of History. It's huge."

"I'm glad you saw the shop," Mafulla said. "I hope everyone was nice to you. My parents haven't been around there much since my father's health scare."

"Yeah, the people working there were very kind to me. I introduced myself as one of your friends from across the desert and they treated me like … a prince—or at least a duke or something."

Walid smiled for the first time. "Good," Mafulla said.

"So, what did you think of the museum?" Walid asked.

"It's awesome."

"Ok, enough already with the ridiculous amount of tedious detail," Walid replied. "Just give us the big picture."

Mafulla was glad to hear his friend sort of joking. It was a good sign of his inner resilience.

Zet was at first surprised and then halfway suppressed a grin and said, "Well, Ok. Sure. I can simplify it all. I started of course with all the Egyptian stuff, which seemed appropriate. It's amazing what's in our history. I saw great photographs of the pyramids, and some scale models, and the Sphinx—which is sort of spooky. That whole part of the country must be wild."

"Yeah, it is."

"And then I examined all the artifacts on display and imagined what it must have been like to live all those hundreds and thousands of years ago."

"Back before there were even any camels," Mafulla said.

"Really?"

"No, I'm just kidding."

"Oh. Good joke, then. You had me fooled for a second there." Zet scratched his head and looked amused. "I thought, how would people get around on the desert?"

"Yeah, it would be a problem. So, what was your favorite thing you saw?"

"Um. Actually, I loved the room of Greek stuff."

"Yeah? I've never been in there," Walid said.

"No? I figured you'd likely seen everything in the whole giant museum."

"Well, we've been on a quick tour, and I've seen the room, basically. I mean I looked into the room and sort of glanced around, but I didn't have time that day to go into it and really scrutinize what was in there."

"But I'm guessing the king has seen everything there," Zet said.

"No, I don't think the king has even had time to go to the museum at all since we've been in town."

"Really?"

"Yeah."

"How about you, Mafulla?"

"I was with Walid the day he went ... I mean, since I was a little kid."

"Oh?"

"When I was maybe six or seven, my parents took me there, but I don't remember that much, except a cute girl who was also with her parents."

"You remember the girl," Walid said.

"Yeah, but more importantly, I'm sure she remembers me."

"There you go." Walid said and made a face for Zet. And then he said to Mafulla, "I wonder if that could have been ... Hasina."

"Wow. No way. You think, maybe?"

"Who knows?"

"What if it was?"

"Stranger things have happened."

"It could have been a moment of historic destiny, right there in the museum of history."

The boys were silent for a few seconds, letting this sink in. And then Zet concluded, "So, maybe I've seen stuff here in town that not even you two and the king have seen."

"That's probably right."

"Very Cool."

"So, you say you really liked the Greek stuff?"

"Yeah, since, you know, I've never been to Greece, and apparently, when all the Roman guys were courting and romancing our famous Cleopatra, they'd give her stuff from Greece as well as from Rome. And even before then, her dad got some legendary Greek items as gifts from people."

"I didn't know that," Mafulla admitted.

"Yeah, I saw some weapons and small statues and some really amazing jewelry—for men as well as women. And the most incredible thing, of course, was the famous ring of legend."

"What do you mean?" Walid asked. "What famous ring?"

"The Ring of Gyges!"

"Guy Jeez?"

Zet exclaimed with a big look of surprise, "You didn't know that the museum has the Ring of Gyges?"

"Nope—not at all. What's the Ring of Gyges?" Walid asked.

Zet was stunned. He looked at Walid's best friend and said, "Mafulla, surely, as a native of Cairo, or a big reader, you've heard of the ring!"

He just looked puzzled and said, "No, I never have."

"I can't believe it. I just can't believe it. It's in your own museum and it's under thick glass and there's a written explanation all about it on the wall next to the display case. You're sure you haven't seen it or at least heard of it?"

"Yeah, I'm totally sure," Mafulla replied. "So, what's the deal about this ring?"

"The deal is that it's probably the most famous ring in all of history."

"Really?" Now Mafulla was getting interested. "What makes it so famous?"

"The … whole story about it! The myth! The legend! And—you never know—Maybe, even, the reality!"

"Ha!" Walid now actually laughed. And he said, "Again, my friend, you drown us in overwhelming detail from the outset. Slow down and pace yourself. Give us one specific piece of information at a time, to help us to absorb all this deluge of reportage."

Zet laughed and said, "Ok, Ok, Make fun of me."

"I love your enthusiasm, which is certainly contagious, but we'd also cherish a display of your knowledge at the present moment," Walid replied.

"So," Mafulla said, with emphasis, and gesturing imploringly with his hands, "What's the story about this ring?"

"Well, Ok, so, you know how things of legend and myth tend to be," Zet began. "You have to suspect that most of them are fake—just ordinary items that people have made up a story about, so they could feel important and get other people's attention or something, or so they can sell the thing for a lot of money, or give it as a gift that will really, super impress the gullible recipient, and especially, if it's an important person whose favor they're trying to curry."

"Yeah, yeah, we know," Mafulla said. "So, even if this ring is a fake, what's it a fake of? What … is … the … story? You're making us crazy here."

"Wait. First, let me make sure I get this right. You're not just messing with me? You really don't know the story of the Ring of Gyges?" Zet asked with apparent sincerity.

"Should I strangle our friend right now, or would you like to do the honors?" Walid asked Mafulla.

"No, let me. I'll be the one to … ring his neck," Mafulla said.

"Gee, I guess I could really use the ring about now," Zet commented, playfully and painfully drawing it all out.

"How could you use it?" Mafulla asked.

"Yeah! What would you use it to do?" Walid insisted.

"Oh, just to disappear and be invisible, of course," Zet said.

"What?" Both boys responded at once.

"It's the famous invisibility ring!" Zet exclaimed.

"What do you mean, invisibility ring?"

"The one first described to the world by no less a writer and authority on hidden truth than Plato himself! Plato! I'm sure you've heard of him: Student of Socrates, teacher of Aristotle, philosopher of the ages? Tell me if anything rings a bell here."

"We know who Plato is," Mafulla said. "And we've read some Plato. But where does he talk about an invisibility ring?"

"In his most famous book, the *Republic*."

"Oh, Ok. I haven't read that one, yet. And I've never heard of this ring. What did you call it?"

"The Ring of Gyges."

"How do you spell that?" Mafulla asked.

Walid said, "What difference does it make how you spell it?"

Ignoring Walid's protest, Zet looked over at Mafulla and named each letter for him, "G-y-g-e-s," and then he explained, "but you pronounce it as if the 'y' is a 'u-y' like in 'guy' and the second 'g' is a 'j' and the 'e' is a double 'e' and the 's' is a 'z'—like 'Guy-Jeez'—it's simple."

"Yeah, really, super simple," Mafulla said. And then he repeated it himself: "Guy-Jeez."

"That's it. The Ring of Gyges."

"Wait! Hold on!" Walid interrupted the two of them and asked, "You say it makes you … invisible?"

"Yeah, completely invisible. Imagine what a bad guy could do with that!" Zet exclaimed, without actually realizing at first how this comment connected up with what was going on in the kingdom and the city at the moment. But then, as soon as the statement was out of his mouth, he suddenly got it and made a face and said, "Uh, Oh."

"Yeah. Uh, Oh, but times about a thousand," Walid echoed, and Mafulla's mouth just fell open.

Zet said, "Mafulla, you look just like …"

"I know, a hungry camel."

Walid said, "But of course, it could always be a fake."

"Yeah, it could. But what if it isn't?"

"Oh, man."

What Walid and Mafulla both were really hungry for at the moment was more information. And it was a good thing they were so intensely curious. What they would learn in the next minutes was going to be a huge part of their ability to deal with a cascade of events that would soon arise and quickly get out of control, and result in something unimaginable.

30

A Famous Artifact

THE BOYS HAD ASKED ZET TO TELL THEM THE WHOLE STORY from the start, and he was eager to do so. He'd spent most of his time back in Dromeda reading alone in the small bookstore where he worked and now, thanks to the king, partly owned. He loved having someone to talk with about what he'd read, especially when it was something really interesting. And he had never had such a rapt audience as he did when he now began to answer Walid's insistent questions.

"Ok, so, Plato writes that Socrates and this guy Glaucon were having a disagreement over what morality or justice is, or what goodness is. I last read it a long time ago, so I'll do my best here on the details. But I think it was about why people act morally. Socrates said that it enhances your life to be good. Glaucon was arguing that people act in a moral way only as a necessary evil, believe it or not."

"What?" Mafulla said.

"Glaucon had a low, dismal view of human nature. He thought that people behave ethically or morally or even legally only when they think it's necessary in order to avoid punishment or disapproval, or to gain goodwill. And he believed that whenever anyone can truly get away with something that's generally deemed wrong or unjust, he'll likely do it, as long as he's convinced that he won't get caught."

"Strange. And interesting that someone would say that, but where does the ring come in?" Mafulla asked right away.

"Well, he tells a story."

"Who does?"

"Glaucon. He's trying to prove his point to Socrates, and tells a story."

"Why would he do that?" Mafulla asked.

"What?"

"Why would he tell a story?"

"Because stories are powerful. They're a great way to prove a point or to do philosophy."

"Oh, Ok."

Walid had to interrupt at this point and said, "Let the man go on!"

"Ok. Sorry. Go on."

"So Glaucon says to Socrates something like: 'Do you know that guy called Gyges of Lydia?' And Socrates answers, 'Yeah, I do.' And Glaucon says, 'Well, he had an ancestor a long time ago, a guy who was a shepherd. And one day back then, there was a huge storm and an earthquake and the ground shook terribly. And a big hole suddenly opens up in the pasture where the shepherd is walking around with his sheep. And he goes to look into the hole and actually gets down in it and finds a bunch of stuff, like old treasure that's been buried under the ground. And there's a gigantic fake horse, maybe made out of wood or something, and there's a door into it and inside the door—get this—there's a really big deceased guy wearing only a gold ring. So he's lying there totally naked except for a gold ring on his finger. And, yeah, I know, it's a strange setup to the story."

"A big deceased guy."

"Yeah, dead."

"I know what it means."

"Oh."

"And he's wearing only a ring?"

"Yeah. Apparently."

"Ok. So far, this is indeed a very strange story," Mafulla said.

"I agree. And it gets a lot stranger, really fast."

"Why would Plato make up such weird stuff?"

"Well, that's sort of going to be my point. Maybe he didn't."

"What do you mean?"

"Maybe it happened. You know what they say: Truth is stranger than fiction."

"All right. So. Keep going."

"Ok. And so the shepherd takes the ring off this guy's hand—off his big finger—and he puts it on, and for some reason that Glaucon doesn't explain, it fits the shepherd guy. Or at least, it fits well enough. And then, he goes to a gathering of other shepherds, where they're going to put together a report for the king of the land on, you know, how many sheep there are in the kingdom, or something. They're probably also discussing the storm and the earthquake. And at some point, our shepherd with the new ring twists it in some way towards his body and it makes him invisible."

"Right there? With the other shepherds around?" Mafulla looked dubious.

"Yeah, right there, and he just … disappears. And Plato says—I mean, Glaucon says to Socrates, but Plato is the one writing all this, of course—so Glaucon says that the other shepherds, and I can quote this: 'suddenly talk of him as if he's absent.' And I've got to tell you that I've never understood this part of the story at all."

"What do you mean? You fully get the part about the huge dead guy wearing only a ring, sitting in a fake horse in a hole in the ground, and the ring can make people invisible, but this part, the stuff about how the guys speak, trips you up a little bit." Mafulla was making a face.

"Well, Ok, but listen: When the man twists the ring and suddenly becomes invisible, why didn't the other guys just totally freak out and go running out of the meeting, screaming and crying out to the gods? A man they know well had been sitting there beside them like normal, but playing with a ring, and suddenly, poof, he vanishes? And we're told that the others merely talk of him as if he's not there."

"Yeah, that doesn't make a lot of sense," Mafulla said. "And it's in that way maybe even stranger than the other stuff."

"But, go on with the story," Walid urged him.

"Ok, I will, but first, and this may be important: Here's what I think. The ring makes our special shepherd invisible, but the other guys sitting right next to him or across from him don't go nuts and freak out in fear and shock and panic, right?"

"Sure, from what you just said," Mafulla replied.

"And they don't say, 'Whoa! What just happened?' either."

"Ok."

"So, the ring must have done two things, not just one."

"What do you mean? What else?" Walid now asked.

"It must have made him invisible, number one, and number two, what we're not told but that's sort of demanded by what we are told, the ring must have given the guys sitting there, the other shepherds, a sort of limited amnesia, a short term memory blank—so they forget that the suddenly vanished guy had been there at all and so, at worst, they speak of him as absent, in the words of Glaucon and Plato."

"Ok, that actually makes sense. So, we've got a ring that creates invisibility for the wearer and limited amnesia for other people who are close by." Mafulla wanted to keep track of all the major elements in the narrative.

"Yeah."

"So, as a result, after he vanishes, they're just sitting around saying, 'Too bad old Fat Fingers isn't here today. Wonder where he is?' and stuff like that. And nobody's stunned or panicked."

"Yeah, the amnesia hypothesis makes sense of all that, and of something else that's yet to come."

"All right then," Walid said. "Please proceed. Let's get to what's yet to come."

"Wait, I have a question," Mafulla said, and Walid made a face.

"Ask anything." Zet encouraged him.

"You said that it wasn't just putting on the ring that made the guy invisible, right?"

"Right, he had to twist it or turn it, or a part of it. That's not entirely clear."

"One twist?"

"That's what Glaucon makes it sound like, but I personally doubt it."

"Why?" Walid asked.

"Well there's a reason, but we'll get to that in a minute."

"Ok, so go on," Walid urged him.

"Well, all right, so this shepherd with the ring turns it or twists it maybe once or maybe three times or seven times or something and, poof, like magic, he's invisible."

"I like your sound effects," Mafulla said.

"What?"

"The poof, the sound of the disappearing—I like that."

"You do?"

"Yeah. It's much better than bang or click, or bam or sizzle or whiz, or especially pop or thud or kerchunk."

"Good. Thanks."

"Poof seems to do the job uniquely well for vanishing."

Walid took a deep breath and expelled it and said, in a tone of still friendly insistence, "Why don't we stop interrupting and commenting?"

"Ok, Ok. The interruptions will now go poof." Mafulla grinned at Zet and made a hand gesture, like he should go on, or continue.

Zet said, "So, after turning the ring, he looks down and realizes that he can't see himself. He can still feel his body and move and hold stuff, but he's completely invisible to normal sight. His clothes are invisible, and his entire body, and the ring, of course. He then turns the ring back in the other direction, Glaucon says, and he reappears. Then he does it again and vanishes again. He's making sure he isn't crazy. And still, nobody in this shepherd meeting is freaked out in the least. The guy is appearing and disappearing, popping in and out of existence, as far as they can tell, and nobody shouts out in surprise or alarm. And I can guarantee they hadn't seen anything like this before. That's why you really have to add the limited amnesia effect."

"That does make sense," Mafulla said. "I mean, as much as any of this does." He looked at Walid and said, "Sorry."

Zet continued, "And then he gets an idea. He's now sitting there visible again and he talks to the other guys like nothing's happened and he offers to go to the palace and take the king the report on the flocks that they're putting together in the meeting, and they all agree. He must be a persuasive guy. Because, for one thing, I'm guessing, who wouldn't want to see the king? Every guy there may have wanted to go, or at least some of them. But, I don't know, maybe it's a long journey, and maybe the king's a jerk, so it could be that he's only moderately persuasive. Actually, it might be that nobody else really wants to make the trip in the first place, because, I mean, who's going to look after the sheep for the guy who leaves? So maybe our guy is only a little persuasive. But in any case, the shepherd with the ring then makes the trip and goes to the palace and uses the ring and kills the king and becomes king himself."

"Wait. What? Why does he kill the king? How does he kill the king?" Walid asked in a voice of concern.

"Glaucon doesn't really say how. But the guy's invisible, so no one can see him do it."

"Oh, Ok," Walid said. "So how then did anyone know he did it?"

"He later told someone."

"Ok. But why would he do it in the first place?"

"I guess he wanted to be king, you know, for the perks and power."

"Oh."

"I forgot to add the fact that when he got to the palace, he first got friendly with the king's wife, Glaucon tells Socrates, and she ends up helping him and getting him the access he needs to kill the king."

"He got friendly with the king's wife?" Mafulla asked.

"Yeah. Romantically, I think."

"He just shows up, and the king's wife likes this guy right away and, he somehow gets her involved in what he wants to do?"

"Yeah."

"Right away? I mean, he just shows up and then, before you know it, he's in with the queen?"

"It seems so."

"And at the time, he's visible or invisible?"

"Hmm. I have to admit I don't know the answer to that one. Glaucon doesn't make that ... clear."

"Hey, 'clear' is a pretty good play on 'invisible.' Not bad," Mafulla had to comment.

"Thanks. I've always assumed that, at least when he's talking to the queen, he's most of the time visible. But he likely showed her the trick and she was very impressed."

"How was she impressed if she would have had limited amnesia?"

"Oh. Yeah. Ok, so maybe he was a persuasive guy after all and just told her what he could do and convinced her of it with words alone."

"Ok. But, there are some uncertainties or gaps in the story so far."

"True, and yet the point is that, by having the ring or using it, or describing it somehow, he gets super friendly with the queen and then with her help, he kills the king and takes over the whole kingdom and I think marries the queen."

"I still don't get one thing. Why would the queen suddenly team up with this messenger who's a shepherd she's likely never seen before?"

"I don't know. We've speculated already that he's maybe a good talker, and persuasive. And, I don't know, it could be that he was a real charmer and, I don't know, really good looking or something."

"Except when he was invisible."

"Yeah, except for when he put on the ring and turned it and did whatever else he did to make it work the magic."

"But, really. Why would the queen want to team up with this

guy who just shows up with a report on sheep, and help him to kill her husband? She doesn't really even know him at all!"

"I don't know. Plato doesn't say. But maybe he convinced her about the power of the ring and she thought 'Whoa, this is big,' and she wanted in on the long-term action it would make possible, too. She saw the potential. Maybe she didn't like the way the king treated her. You know, not every king is like Ali, for sure. In fact, I think it's clear from a study of history that our king's pretty rare. So, maybe she wanted to team up with a guy who had the power to do whatever he wanted, unseen, and she could share the power—or so, at least, that's what he made her believe, silver tongued devil that I guess he was. But, again, Plato doesn't go into all that."

"Why not? Why did a great writer like Plato tell a story that has so many unknowns in it?"

"Well, Plato, I mean, the reported teller of the tale, Glaucon, wasn't mainly narrating a great story in all its relevant details, but just quickly laying out the main aspects of the story to make a point."

"Which is?"

"Ok, get this. Glaucon said to Socrates at the conclusion of the story, basically: So here's my point. Take any man you think to be good and just and upright, and then take an unethical creep, and give each of these guys a ring like this to use, and pretty soon they'll both be doing the same stuff, the very same stuff, with impunity. They'll be thieves and double-crossers and liars and murderers, and basically they'll just do whatever it takes to get what they want, since they can go invisible and not be seen doing it. And also, they can't even be found out later because, you know, there can't be any real witnesses."

"Wait. I thought there was just one ring." Walid said, looking confused. "Where does a second ring come from?"

"No, there's just one in the actual story. The two-ring scenario was nothing more than a further thought experiment, for after the story. Glaucon's suggesting that every one of us would act in the ways we normally consider immoral if we could just get away with it, if we just had a magic ring, even the most apparently honorable and moral of people."

"Wow," Mafulla said. "That's pretty extreme and harsh."

"Yeah, or maybe, in other words, he's arguing that people actually behave well only because, otherwise, they'd be punished or shunned, since, without a ring, they can't guarantee that they won't be found out. And the upshot of his argument is that, in reality, there aren't any truly honorable and just people—just selfish, manipulative, self-serving people protecting themselves from any negative consequences."

Mafulla said, "So ... the suggestion is that everybody's actually bad, or corrupt, without any real morals, and the ring simply reveals it."

"Exactly."

"But, how do we know that it's not just a made-up story in the first place, and a hypothetical ring—you know, a ring that Glaucon's merely creating with the trappings of history, as itself a vivid thought experiment? You know, the ring and the entire story was simply an imaginative invention just to make his point. That would be the most natural thing to believe."

"Well, of course, and that is exactly what most people think. It's just a matter of story telling, creating a vivid parable or something to make a point. And here we are remembering it thousands of years later. So it was vivid enough to be really memorable."

"I don't agree at all with Glaucon, by the way," Walid said.

"What do you mean?" Mafulla asked.

"I don't think for a second that everybody's really like that."

"Oh. I don't either," Mafulla responded. "My dad would never act like that. The king would never do bad stuff just because he was invisible. Your dad was the same way. And your mom is. And my mom."

"Lots of people we know, in our families, and in our circle of friends, wouldn't exploit a ring like that," Walid said with a tone of great confidence.

"I happen to agree. I feel the same way," Zet said. "But it's still a pretty compelling thought experiment. And the question at issue can be posed much more modestly. And then it's really interesting: Would you act any differently at all if you could become invisible before your action, and people would have limited amnesia surrounding it, not remembering they had seen you come around and then vanish? Would you do anything while invisible that you wouldn't do normally?"

"You mean other than run around in hot weather naked as a yard dog to cool off?" Mafulla asked.

"Yeah, well, including that, but also other than that."

"Ok. It's really not a stupid or trivial question, when you put it in those terms," Mafulla said. "I'm pretty impressed."

"Yeah, that's why people are still talking about it, all these centuries later. The question is maybe a new avenue into deep self knowledge."

"So, let's get back to our original starting point here." Walid interrupted all this reflection by saying to Zet, "You saw a ring at the museum here that they're claiming is the actual Ring of Gyres that Plato wrote about?"

"Yeah.

"They actually say that?"

"That's what's written on the plaque on the wall beside it."

"Really?"

"Well, to be precise, they say on the written description that this ancient item has long been reported to be the legendary Ring of Gyges. That's how they put it. So, they're being careful and, you know, noncommittal. They're teasing us with it."

"But wait. If there really was such a ring and it was in Cairo, why wouldn't at least some people here have been trying to use it?"

"My guess is that people have tried in the past, and it didn't work, because they thought that all they had to do was put it on and turn it once, like it seems to say in Plato. But that's why there's got to be more to it than that. And they didn't know there was more to it, and so when they did a twist or a turn and stayed visible, they concluded that the ring doesn't work and that it's obviously just a fake, or that the story is after all simply made up—a fiction, a fable, and no more. But the ring is what it is, and it's presumably been handed down with this identification being credible enough to get the attention of some antiquities experts and historians, and so it ended up in the museum. I mean: it's not like it's in some two-bit carnival curiosity shop."

"When did it get into Egypt?"

"I think Cleopatra had it."

"You actually think someone gave it to Cleopatra?"

"Yeah, but first, let's suppose it's the authentic ring, and that it works if you know how to use it, Ok?"

"That's a big assumption, but for now, Ok."

"I really suspect that someone gave it to Cleopatra's dad and that she got hold of it and figured out how it works and how to use it."

Mafulla asked, "Why do you say that?"

"Well, there are these stories about her sneaking out of the palace at night, and I think her father had her pretty closely guarded when she was a young woman. He didn't want her hanging around with all the guys who were interested in her—you know, when she was our age or a little older. And then there are stories about her disappearing now and then a few years later to meet secretly with Julius Caesar, who really wanted to marry her. But a lot of her people disapproved of him and the Romans, and so she had to slip out unseen to visit with him. And how did she do that? Simple. The ring."

Mafulla said, "But I've heard she was ..."

Walid shot him a look and he quickly said, "Sneaky, just ... really clever ... and very sneaky."

"Maybe. But I think it could have been from using the ring," Zet opined.

Walid pondered this for a couple of seconds and said, "So, you think the ring you saw is really the one from Plato's story."

"It could be."

"And so, the story ring actually exists and has come down

through the centuries and has ended up in the Museum of History right here in Cairo. And you think that the people who have had access to it don't really believe it's magic, and so no one has ever stolen it or anything."

"Oh, I don't know. Like I said, maybe several people have tried to take and use the ring, but my guess is that they slipped it on as soon as they picked it up and they gave it the one turn mentioned in the Republic, and it didn't work, and that's going to happen only so many times before people wise up and start thinking that, Ok, obviously it's only a fake, and it's all just a legend without real merit, you know, a false but entertaining myth. And so, clearly, the tale of the Ring of Gyges was really nothing more than a made-up story that Glaucon told to make a point, or that Plato attributed to him, and nothing else."

"So then, why would our very serious museum have it on display?" Walid asked.

"I don't know—maybe just because of the legend itself and the provenance of it, or something."

"The what?"

"The historical chain of ownership—it must have been distinguished enough to, you know, impress the museum people at some point in the past. And, let's face it, a lot of people have got to think it's cool to have such a ring under glass here in Cairo. I'm sure it gets talked about, far and wide. It's likely a pretty big attraction, even though it's never attracted you two guys."

Walid then mused, "But if the people who have concluded it's a fake are wrong, and it is real, and if somebody bad got it and figured out how to use it, then there could be major trouble."

"Yeah. Major, major trouble," Zet said.

"What's the ring look like?" Mafulla now asked.

"It's basically round."

"Come on."

"Just kidding. It's really old looking and engraved or something. You should go see it."

"Hmm. Ok."

"We need to tell the king about this," Walid said.

"Yeah, right away," Mafulla agreed.

Some distance from town, it was now late and dark, aside from the light of the moon, and Santiago and his men were making their way down a dusty road that ran into the city from the northwest. They could finally see some lights up ahead of them. They had an ongoing arrangement with a stable on the edge of the marketplace. Their horses or camels could be put there and fed and watered, and the men could sleep in a building next door that was configured with small rooms and beds, and there was a single bathroom on each of its two floors, like a cheap hotel for transients and visitors.

Most people would think that a man like Santiago could never put up with these conditions, and find them despicably beneath him. But, oddly enough, his Spanish heritage kicked in when he first saw the place and, in its humble setting, he felt positively messianic, like Jesus of Nazareth as a baby, sleeping near the animals in a simple, rough outbuilding, a setting that made his inner sense of his own majesty even more impressive, by contrast. This is how the man actually thought of himself. All that his religious upbringing had managed to accomplish was to instill in him the beginnings of a sense of himself as divine, and the feeling within of a comparable superiority and mission, in his case, not for the good of people in the world, but for the universe at large which, he thought, in his heart of hearts, desperately needed someone like him in charge here on earth. He alone could be strong. He would be transformative.

There were rumblings in at least two parts of Europe at the moment that some other living individuals might harbor similar grandiose feelings and intentions. Santiago had already begun to look into the possibility that he might be able to work with one or more of them to advance his own cause with their help, and of course, ultimately at their expense. People were to be used. Power was to be gained.

When he and his men arrived at their first destination by the edge of the market, he told Miguel to stable the horses and see to their food and water while he and the others secured their basic sleeping accommodations for the night. In the morning, he said, there was important work to be done. The gross blasphemy in the newspaper could not be allowed to stand. Revenge was necessary and must be had quickly. He would give them something to write about, those few who might remain after his planned action—something that was true, because he would make it true in the light of the new day's sun.

"They'll see," he said to the men, and then he laughed, which was not at all customary for him, and he added, without explanation, "Or, more likely, not. But they'll suffer. And they'll die, as they should."

In the palace, Walid's parents Rumi and Bhati had shared a suite of rooms like those enjoyed by the king, but a bit smaller. They had an entry office that was usually staffed by an assistant, a large sitting room, their own dining area, two bedrooms and two baths, as well as a small additional office where Rumi had done much of the record keeping and other paperwork related to his medical interests and public health projects. He had also used that comfortable getaway as a reading room for his ongoing personal studies.

This evening, Layla, Hasina, and Kissa were staying with Bhati in her suite, to offer any comfort and support they could. It was to be a time of fellowship, sisterhood, and encouragement. Layla knew from her own experience long ago that it would take a while for the true enormity of the loss and its full impact to sink in. There was an unreality about these early days, when a bereaved spouse could almost feel as if their lost loved one had just stepped out of the room momentarily, or that they were simply away on a trip and would be returning soon. Finality and permanence are difficult things to feel and absorb and adjust to, in any full sense. They take a while. It's a transition that's actually never complete, and this is probably appropriate since, according to the world-view that both Rumi and Bhati held firmly in their minds and hearts, the separation of death was not truly final or permanent in a cosmic sense, but only in our earthy time frame, or for the rest of this stage in the overall journey.

We're never required to close the book completely on an intimate friendship or connection of the heart just because distance or disability or even death has come between us. Everything of lasting good, every act or bond of creative love in this world, will be transformed and enhanced and available in some other form in the next adventure. There is an eternality of goodness and love, an everlasting productivity of it that evil can't begin to approach. All the ladies who were gathered in Bhati's rooms on this evening were convinced of this, but they were not yet all at the same stage of understanding it deeply and having it wholly permeate their consciousness. This was something that would be helped along by the conversations of the evening.

An assistant butler had brought in a tray of tea and cookies for everyone. Layla rested beside Bhati on the sofa, with an arm hooked around hers, and the girls sat on two nearby chairs. Hasina had poured tea for each of them and she had put cookies on two small plates, gently placing one near the moms and the other between her and Kissa.

They had all been talking already for nearly three hours. And the worst of it, emotionally, was over, at least, for now. They had grieved together and cried a lot, and embraced and shared stories and reminisced. As a result of all the emotion and its expression, a gentle weariness had finally crept up on all of them. But their minds were still alert, as if the trauma of the day was keeping them watchful and wary in a subliminal way, despite their evident safety in the palace.

"What do you think this terrible Santiago is going to try next?" Bhati asked the ladies, generally.

"It's hard to say," Layla replied. "He seems so unpredictable. The only guarantee at this point is that it will be something despicable."

"Yeah," Hasina added, "if we knew what all his ultimate goals were, we might be able to do a better job of imagining possible scenarios. But aside from the obvious revenge activity that's going on—and who knows when he'll feel satisfied with that—we really don't have a clue what else, if anything, he might have in mind for the future."

Bhati took a deep breath and let it out and said, "Well, we do know that he's been on a lifelong quest for spiritual power, and that's not likely to stop."

"True," Hasina said.

"What else is there in the area that could give him power?" Kissa asked. "He tried the animals, and that was strange. What could he try next?"

"Well, there's the Sphinx and the pyramids, not far away," Hasina said. "They've been long rumored to be portals of power."

"Yeah," Kissa replied, "but if this guy's the monster of legend, he can't get near the Sphinx, for whatever reason. Remember?"

"That's true," Hasina reflected. "Mom, you told us that, right?"

"I did. It's a part of the legend, however unexplained and mysterious. He can't go near the Sphinx."

Hasina said, "And I suppose that, because of the power issue, it's a good thing he can't."

"Yes."

"So I guess he has to stay closer to Cairo and find something here."

Kissa said, "I think you're right."

"But, what would it be? Is he after a person with power, or some ancient artifact or religious item? What is here in town that could enhance his power?"

"Well," Layla replied, "Obviously The Book of Phi, The Ring of Phi, and The Stone of Giza all fit the bill pretty well, and could be on his dream shopping list."

"That's surely right," Hasina said. And she added, "But they're stored safely here in the palace. Right?"

"That's correct."

"Do you think he'll try to get his hands on one or all of those things?"

"If he knows about any of them, and—let's face it—they're all so legendary that, given his interests, he's probably heard tales of them for some time now. And I can't imagine that such a man wouldn't lust after these things and crave their possession, each of them."

"Do you think he knows they're in the palace?" Kissa asked.

"He's probably long suspected that, and our friend Rama has recently and usefully fanned the flames of that likely suspicion in her remarks to Muriel, which I'm sure he's heard by now."

"But how could a man like that ever hope to steal something that's so well protected? He doesn't have anything like an army, does he?"

"No, but as you know, he has strange power, even possibly great power, and that can be the equivalent of a small army, by itself."

"Yeah, I guess—which is a scary thought."

"How do you think he might plan to use that power to get something here in the palace?" Kissa asked.

"It's hard to imagine," Layla said. "But the book that our friends brought from Dromeda has a lot in it about deception. The king has let me look through it, and that theme caught my attention as I read. For all the talk about spiritual power, force, and warfare— the words and concepts in the title of the book that Santiago had ordered through the bookstore—there's much more in it about simple deception than you might imagine. And when you think about it, the misuse of power for selfish ends always involves many forms of deception. And then, one of the most frightening things about deception is that it's a major key to asymmetrical warfare."

"To what?" Kissa asked.

"To situations where one adversary, or a small group, has to fight a large power, or many enemies. Deception can be a force multiplier for the deceiver, and a force neutralizer on the side of the deceived. And so it can act to equalize a situation of initially great power inequality, such as the one Santiago faces by coming up against the king and our members of Phi, as well as the entire Egyptian military. He's up against some pretty extreme odds."

"And yet," Bhati interjected, "if he wields terrible power, deployed through masterful deception, he could be like the small deadly snake that takes down a large camel. Look at what he did today without any use of unusual spiritual power or force, but just with conventional means put into action through simple clever deception."

Hasina said, "So we'd really better be thinking through all the possibilities of attack on his part. Like, where would he strike next? And how could he do it? What forms of deception should we be on the lookout for? What should we be preparing to detect?"

"Yes," Layla agreed, and added, "I'm sure the king and Masoon and Hamid and others are already working hard on answers to these questions, as well."

"Mom, I've told Kissa something that I haven't told you yet," Hasina said.

"What' that?" Layla asked.

"After we got out of school today, but before we left the grounds, I saw Walid's friend, Ibrahim—you know, from Alexandria?"

"Yes."

"He was here at the palace and I said hello and told him the sad news about Rumi and he was really shocked to hear it, of course, and very sad. We talked for a few minutes about everything that's going on, and he got quiet for a moment and then told me that he and his friend Ahira had spent part of the afternoon yesterday taking Ben to the big art gallery nearby, and then to the Museum of History, which only Ahira had seen before."

"Yes?"

"And he said that, while he was in the museum, he got this really strange feeling of something wrong, or that something was going to happen, or that something there shouldn't be there. He said it was a confused feeling, but that it was almost like a foreboding, a nearly oppressive sense of foreboding, and he didn't say anything about it to Ahira or Ben, but instead made some sort of excuse to get them out of the room they were in."

"Which room was it?" Layla asked.

"He didn't say. But he said that the feeling he had was one of the worst inner sensations he's ever experienced, and, Mom, you know that there have been Phi in his family, serious Phi."

"You're right."

"So, maybe something's going to happen at the museum."

"Have you told anyone else about this yet?"

"Only Kissa."

"Yeah, only me," Kissa said.

"I think the king needs to hear about this, and of course, Walid and Mafulla, and Hamid and Masoon."

"It's kind of late," Hasina pointed out.

"Yes, of course, you're right."

"We could pass on what we know early tomorrow."

"Yes, in the morning, the very first thing in the morning, we'll get this information to the king," Layla said with a feeling of conviction, and almost urgency, and real insistence. Just in hearing the story, she had felt a twinge, a very small twinge, of what she immediately recognized that Ibrahim must have felt. And she knew it was significant. One thing she didn't know is how truly urgent this matter might be. Some terribly unfortunate things were set to happen very soon. And the museum would play a crucial role in them.

31

The Daily News

Mafulla, as usual, was up first. He walked down the hall and entered the breakfast room and happened to notice the newspapers lying on a side table, where they were normally put. His regular habit was to make a plate of food and pour some coffee before reaching over and grabbing up one or more of them and browsing the day's articles. But today was different. The morning's main headline that blared out across the front page of the top paper got his attention:

"Rumi Shabeezar, Member of Royal Family, Slain."

Just seeing that gave his stomach a jolt. He took a couple more steps over to it, picked up the paper, and while still standing began to read. The account was basically accurate, and attributed the violent act to "an enemy of the state, the criminal Juan Osvaldo Santiago, and his hired thugs." As Mafulla finished the article, he unfolded the paper and noticed a second large headline, right below the fold:

"Dire Threats Against Your *Kingdom Daily News*!"

"Really?" he thought to himself, and continued to read. "The editorial office of this newspaper has received in the past several hours some serious and credible threats against the lives and health of our employees, not just targeting top management, but also our editors, writers, photographers, printers, and even our dedicated delivery people. A few envelopes left near and inside our building were found to contain coldly threatening letters, all purporting to have been written by the criminal, Juan Osvaldo Santiago, the despicable street thug we profiled in yesterday's edition. When the threats were received, our publisher contacted the city police right away and they assured us that they would establish extra patrols around our place of business. There were even suggestions made that some active duty military would be posted throughout the neighborhood as an additional precaution, given the vital role that this paper plays in the life of the city and kingdom."

He read on. "We deplore these actions on the part of an apparently desperate and immoral man and ask our readers to be alert and watchful to any sign of treachery they may detect in our immediate environment. The truth will not be silenced. We will not be muzzled by those who would seek to do us harm. A free and open press is necessary for the maintenance of a civil society comprised of well-informed individuals. When the press is threatened, it is an attack against the very fabric of our nation. And no such threat, we assure our readers, will cause us to hesitate to print what we think the citizens of our kingdom need to know."

At that moment, Walid walked into the room. "What's up?"

"Look at this." Mafulla handed him the paper, pointing to the article.

Walid read the headline and said, "Really?"

"Read the whole thing."

"Ok." Walid stood there and silently went through the short article. "Man," he said. "This guy just will not quit."

"He's made plenty of idle threats."

"Against the king, yeah, so far. But he's done plenty of harm already, too."

"That's the truth."

"So," Walid said, "What do you make of this?"

"He's really mad about the article that Leem wrote and Uncle Reela had them run, and so I guess that's serving its purpose. I bet this threat's not idle at all."

"What do you think he'll do?"

"I don't know, but I sort of have a bad feeling that whatever he does is going to happen soon."

"Yeah, he likely knows that, after what he did to my father, the entire military is looking for him."

"Well, my dad has mentally seen him in a camp somewhere in the desert nearby. And if he plans to harm someone at the newspaper, I bet he'll come into town and do it himself."

"Why do you think that?"

"Because, he probably anticipated that an attack on your family would generate a widespread response and that he'd be hunted down. And even though he likely has no clue that my dad can see him, he's got to know that a camp of tents is easier to find smack in the middle of otherwise empty sand than one guy, or a few, in a big city full of people. So, whether he planted these threatening letters personally or not, my guess is that he's coming in to do the dirty work himself."

"That's a good point. You should tell the king that."

"Yeah, probably so. But you know the king—he's likely had the same thoughts."

"Still, to be sure."

"Ok."

"And we've also got to let him know the stuff Zet told us about the Ring of Gyges and the museum."

"That's true."

"Let's eat fast and go to see him right away. He's just working in his office this morning, I think, and this afternoon it'll be much harder to see him and talk. He has a lot of things to do to prepare for my dad's … you know, the service, tomorrow."

"You're right," Mafulla agreed, and he walked over to get a plate. "Let's get this show on the road."

Down the hall, Layla, Hasina, and Kissa were having their own breakfast in Bhati's suite and just finishing up. "We need to see the king," Layla reminded everyone.

"Definitely," Bhati said. "Give me a few minutes to put myself together."

"You don't have to go," Layla said. "We can take care of it."

"Are you sure?"

"Absolutely. Stay in this morning and rest. In fact, Kissa can hang out here with you. Hasina and I will go down and brief the king on the story she heard from Ibrahim, and on our other speculations from last night that might be useful for him to hear."

"Ok, that sounds good," Bhati said. "Kissa, is that all right with you?"

"Yes, absolutely," she answered. "We can just relax here and talk while Layla and Hassi go on the errand."

"All right, then," Bhati said to them all. "That's what we'll do."

Layla turned to Hasina and said, "Let's each just freshen up for a minute and then go see the king."

Within about fifteen minutes, they were at Kular's office. Looking in, Layla said, "Good morning, Kular."

"Oh, good morning, Layla."

"We have some important information for the king. May we see him for five minutes?"

"Yes, certainly. He's here working this morning in the sitting room. Let me tell him you're here."

"Thanks." As Kular then ducked through the inner door to the main room, Walid and Mafulla walked up, intending to head down to the office where the king often worked outside his private rooms.

Walid said, "Layla! Hi. Oh, Hey, Hasina. What are you guys doing?"

Layla said, "Hi Walid. We need to see the king for a minute." Mafulla appeared behind his friend and just smiled and did a little wave.

"Is he in here?"

"Yes, he is. Are you Ok this morning?"

Walid took a deep breath and let it out. "I guess so. I mean, as Ok as a person can be in the situation."

"Did you get some sleep?"

"Pretty solid. I was just so exhausted. How's mom?"

"We had an important time together last night. We talked and cried and talked some more, and I could tell that it really helped her. It helped the three of us, too."

"Where's Kissa?"

"She stayed with Bhati while we came down to talk to the king. Your mom seems peaceful today. But, still, we thought it would be good for her to relax and have some company while we ran our little errand."

Mafulla had been silent to this point. He was standing behind Walid, who was now in the doorway to Kular's office. He wanted to greet Hasina, but didn't want to interrupt Walid and Layla.

"What are you here to talk about with the king?" Walid asked, adding, "If it's not prying for me to ask."

"No, no, it's not prying at all."

Just then, Kular reappeared and said, "Sorry. Oh! Prince Walid! Mafulla! I didn't know you were also out here. I'm sorry for the delay. The king just had some instructions for me, regarding … this afternoon. He can see you now, ladies."

Walid said to Layla, "Is it Ok if we come in, too? We have a pretty urgent message for him."

"Surely," she replied. "It could be that we need to hear your message also, and that you need to hear ours."

"Good," Walid said, and motioned for the ladies to precede them into the king's rooms.

Ali was standing near the window with the newspaper in his hands when they all entered the room. "Good morning, Your Majesty," Layla said. Hasina smiled and did a quick little bow of her head.

"Layla, Hasina, come in!" the king responded. And then he spotted the boys and said, "Walid, Mafulla, good to see you both, as well."

The prince explained, "Layla said it was fine for us to come in with her and Hasina. We were here to see you, too, and we both have things to tell you, apparently, and she thought it might be good for us all to be in on the reports."

"Very nice. I agree. This is often a good idea," the king said. "But first, how's everyone feeling this morning?"

"I'm Ok," Walid replied.

"We're all doing about as well as could be expected," Layla said.

"Bhati?"

"She's strong and to a remarkable extent at peace, I believe. Our time with her last night was important, and this morning it's been clear that we've all crossed through a doorway of acceptance."

"Good."

"Kissa's keeping her company during our short visit to see you."

The king nodded his approval of this. "So, please, tell me what thoughts you have for me. I was just reading the news that the paper has provided for us all, this morning."

"Yeah, we saw that, too, Your Majesty," Mafulla said. "Santiago's threatening the newspaper and I think he's going to act soon. And maybe in person."

"Oh?"

"Yes, sir. But I'm forgetting: Ladies first, please," Mafulla said, and gestured in a gentlemanly way toward Layla and Hasina.

"Good. Before you start, please sit and be comfortable," the king said. He motioned for them to take chairs, and they all did.

Hasina quickly told the king about seeing Ibrahim and hearing about his visit to the Museum of History and the strong feeling he had in one particular room there, a foreboding of evil, or of something about to happen. Walid and Mafulla couldn't believe it, and the prince spoke up immediately and reported what Zet Noni had just told them the previous evening about the museum and the Ring of Gyges. Mafulla added some detail now and then about the story of the ring. The king expressed his surprise. And he told them that he had not yet been able to visit the museum since coming to Cairo, because of all his duties in this time of taking the reigns of the monarchy and dealing with so many problems the kingdom had been facing. He had no idea that there was such an item on exhibit there.

Mafulla then explained why he thought that these threats against the paper might signal that Santiago would soon come into the city, or even be here already, to make good the threats and carry them out himself. But just as he had made his point, Kular opened the door and said, "I'm sorry, Your Majesty, but Naqid is here with an urgent message."

"Send him in, please," Ali responded.

"Your Majesty," Naqid was saying as he walked through the door, "I'm so sorry to interrupt, everyone, but Bancom just got word of some strange events happening at the Museum of History."

The king said, "What's going on?" Mafulla and Walid looked at each other.

"Apparently, there's been a theft. One guard and a city policeman have just been killed, and there are very odd reports coming in that make little sense—something about unseen, invisible attackers."

"Has anyone been captured?"

"No, not yet, not that I know of," Naqid answered.

That very moment, Bancom came barging into the room himself, almost at a run and unannounced, as Kular stood at the open door, now holding it for him.

Slightly out of breath, he said, "Your Majesty! Everyone! Forgive me! Masoon and his men very early this morning found Santiago's encampment outside of town and there was a big battle."

"What happened?"

Bancom caught his breath and said, "There was fierce resistance, both a gun battle, and some other forms of violence, apparently. Masoon's second in command sent a messenger with a note that was radioed in, and in it he reported that everyone was killed."

"What do you mean, everyone?" The king stood, and all the others began to, but he quickly motioned with his hand for them to stay seated.

"Oh, I meant every one of the enemy! I'm sorry for misspeaking so badly, Majesty!"

"That's all right, Bancom. How many of the adversaries were killed?"

"Eighteen of them. And they were extremely well armed."

"Santiago was not among them?"

"No, Your Majesty, apparently not."

"I see. Were there casualties on our side?"

"Three wounded. One killed."

"Whom did we lose?"

"A younger man, apparently, from Luxor."

The king took a breath and let it out. He said in a low voice, "May his soul be blessed in all ways ... May all their souls be transformed and blessed." Then he said, "Now, Bancom, my friend, please send a message immediately to the outpost that we need Masoon and the men back as soon as possible. There are attacks going on in the city already. We think that Santiago may be here."

Walid spoke up and said, "Should Masoon go to the museum, or to the newspaper?"

"No, he should come here," the king replied, and then turned and said, "Bancom, tell Masoon to come straight to the palace and set up protection. Say to him the words, 'The true Ring of Gyges from ancient times may be in use.' He'll be surprised at first, and likely perplexed for a bit, but when he thinks more about it, he'll know what this means. He's read his Plato well."

Bancom was surprised to hear these words, because he, too, knew the Republic and the famous story. "Did you say the Ring of Gyges?"

"Yes."

A bit earlier that morning, the Museum of History had just opened its doors for the day. The first four visitors strolled together toward one room where the next stage of their destiny awaited them. Santiago had feigned politeness and friendliness to staff members when they arrived, as he had done initially with Mafulla's father. He had greeted the guards at the door and a few other workers within the museum when they entered and made their way through the main hall and the first set of exhibits. They walked by displays of coins that had been used in the kingdom throughout the entire history of Egypt, including Roman, Greek and various North African coins that were created of different materials. They passed many exhibits of ancient papyrus that held messages written in several languages. But they didn't do more than glance down at these fascinating and priceless treasures. They were men on a mission, and their attention had a single focus.

Santiago felt a flash within, a knowing, however vague, that something had happened and all had been lost in the desert. He had anticipated trouble. And he had worked hard to prepare his men for it, for two long days and nights. He was sure he had left his followers well defended. He had planned to use them for many of his schemes. But he realized in that moment that there was now to be no turning back, and no immediate reinforcements for his plans. There were others in Spain, but they would be of no help now. Power and military force beyond his expectation had taken away the only men who could have played any role in the coming events. He alone, with these three men he had selected, and a couple of confederates in town, would have to avenge all the others and move forward into the glorious future he had long envisioned. This flash of knowing simply served to enhance his determination and fortify his intent, while further fueling his bitter anger.

"There it is," Santiago said and walked over to the object he sought. The three other men gathered around him in such a way as to block a direct view of his actions from the sight of any museum guard who might walk by, but not in a manner that would seem too artificial. Standing, now, right in front of the ancient artifact he sought to obtain, he whispered, "Miguel."

"What?" the man answered in a likewise low and hushed voice.

"The hammer!" Santiago hissed. "Wake up! Give me what you have! Hand it to me!"

Two days of minimal and fitful sleep had affected all of Santiago's men, but especially Miguel. He said, "What?"

Santiago replied, "The hammer … in … your clothing, you imbecile!" He paused in a momentary flash of inner rage and mumbled the word, "Idiot!"

A surge of responsive anger coursed through the disciple as he heard these words and now suddenly remembered his task. He reached into his coat to retrieve a small hammer that he had slipped into the museum under his clothing. Then he handed it to Santiago without a word, and once again hid well his inner fury. He wanted to use the hammer on this man and not just give it to him for his own plans. But he restrained himself. This was not the time. It soon would come.

"Now," the master whispered, "I want the big noise on three. One, two, three!"

The other men, on cue, laughed loudly and began to clap as if Santiago had said something extremely funny and profound at the same time. One coughed. A guard looked in and saw what seemed to be unusual merriment in the presence of one of the exhibits and, odd as it was, he shrugged it off and thought nothing more of it. The laughter of children was often to be heard in the museum, but rarely that of grown men. Still, a witty remark, on occasion, could evoke such a response. Some men could be exceptionally loud and raucous, and especially tourists. The guard glanced in for a moment more and then moved on, as another visitor outside the room asked him a question. He had seen the four men all walk into the room moments earlier, but as he now peeked in again and noticed only three, he had no memory of what he had registered less than a minute before.

Two groups of school children had arrived in the building during just the last several minutes. And a few dozen foreign guests who had also come in were now bunched together in small, guided tours. They were variously walking and standing throughout the first floor of the large and well-used building. The general noise level in the front hall had been rising along with the numbers of new visitors.

That sound of sudden laughter and applause from the room of Greek Antiquities had, of course, been meant to mask the noise of the hammer being brought down sharply on the enclosure that held the precious ring. The glass was thick and the top of the transparent display case was locked securely. Only a swift hit with the hammer could crack and loosen the glass enough and allow Santiago to get his fingers into the still tight enclosure and fish out the ring, which he now expertly did. He immediately slipped it on his finger and performed precisely the right actions, turning it quickly several times, and in the right ways, as if he had practiced well for this moment.

In the blink of an eye, there were apparently just three men standing around the display, not four. But the hammer now strangely seemed to be hanging in midair. One of the other men, a follower named Carlos, said, "Oh! What's this?" For a couple of seconds, he was mentally off balance and had no idea where he was or why. None of them knew about the brief psychological impact the ring had on those it affected visually. But then, the image he saw of the hammer hanging mid-air touched a place deep in his mind. And he suddenly came back to himself, as if from out of a thick fog, and remembered what was going on. He said, "Please, sir, the hammer," and he reached out to get it and handed it back to Miguel. The disgruntled follower, in turn, was having his own problems. He looked surprised at first and yet took the tool that Carlos was handing him. In the initial moment, it meant nothing to him. It only confused him. But then it also made him remember where he was and what he was doing, and why this object had been floating in the air in the first place. It all began to come back to his mind, and so he slipped the tool into his pocket once more.

In the next moment, Miguel whispered to their leader, "I also need your knife! It's still a little bit visible!" The faded, barely detectable and blurry image of a knife then seemed to move up and over and through thin air toward him. He quickly grasped it by the handle and placed it in his belt, under his own coat.

He then nodded at Carlos and they moved away from the one man who could at present still be seen standing at the display case. As Santiago had instructed, they walked out of the room and down the open hall, toward another room near the back where they could see a guard sitting in a chair just outside the door. It was a guard station where the man or one of his colleagues was always to be found. This other room contained some of the more unusual and rare antiquities that were quite valuable, but that were recognized and appreciated primarily by historians and scholars. The room was located away from most of the other exhibits and their visitors. It was even a bit out of the way, and that was also part of the reason a museum guard was always placed there. And it was a rare form of seated service in such a setting, which anyone lucky enough to have the assignment always greatly appreciated.

While Miguel hung back a bit, Carlos approached the uniformed man to talk and asked him a question. As he began to give an answer, he suddenly reacted as if he were being choked from behind. His hands flew up to his neck, his face contorted, and a look of sheer terror crossed his features. He struggled in his seat and tried to stand but couldn't do so. Some unseen force was resisting him and holding him down. A muted gagging, or terrible straining sound was all the noise he could make as utter confusion matched his pain. And within seconds, he slumped down, strangled and dead in the chair.

A large marble column prevented anyone else in the museum's main hall from seeing any of this at the moment. So Carlos could take a couple of seconds and prop the guard up a bit with the help of Miguel, who quickly came to his assistance. And then the two of them could just walk away in the company of their unseen leader and be completely unsuspected of any foul play, with their first horrible experiment now complete, and in Santiago's mind, a success.

As these two now walked straight toward the front of the building, to get out as quickly as they could, but without drawing any attention to their haste, their master spontaneously decided to take a detour over to a second guard who was standing alone some distance away, leaning back on a wall. The invisible man balled up his fist and hit the guard as hard as he possibly could, right in the lower gut, and instantly doubled him up. With a loud grunt, the stunned older man fell to the floor and Santiago, smiling broadly, walked on.

Some nearby tourists had seen the guard suddenly double over and fall. And they immediately gave voice to hushed exclamations, as two members of their group rushed over to check on the man, whom they assumed must be having some sort of medical emergency. One visitor reached down and felt his pulse, and said, "My friend! Are you Ok? Are you all right?" He reached out and touched the man's arm and looked around for any help that might be available. Not seeing any other nearby guards, the man called out, "Can anyone help us?"

An armed city policeman happened to be in the building on his morning rounds through this part of the city and heard the man call out for assistance. Crossing the hall, he immediately ran to the guard's aid, passing right by the unseen attacker. But his presence on the scene as an officer of the kingdom along with his quick action caused Santiago to stop and turn around and walk back toward the stricken guard. He was tired of people resisting him and seeking to mitigate or reverse his chosen deeds.

As all the tourists had now stepped back and the policeman was bending over the man, asking what had happened, his service revolver was slipped quietly from its holster and cocked and discharged into him before anyone could notice the movement of the gun at all. The loud report of the shot rang out—BLAM! It absolutely stunned those nearby, nearly deafened them, panicked them all, and instantly drew everyone else's attention throughout the hall. Some saw the gun clatter to the floor as the policeman now also collapsed, bleeding profusely and groaning from his traumatic wound. But no one had any idea what had just happened.

Santiago was at this point standing a few feet away and enjoying immensely his little bit of cruel revenge and further experimentation, which only proved to him more fully that the ring was working perfectly, just as he had hoped it would. He was satisfied.

He turned to walk away, but then suddenly remembered some extremely valuable gold coins he had noticed near the front of the museum. As all the remaining guards dashed over toward their stunned colleague and the gravely injured policeman, he dodged them and stepped to the side. Looking around, he grabbed the small case housing the most rare coins. He then smashed it to the floor, broke the glass, and scattered all the gold pieces across an area right in front of him. He quickly bent over and scooped them all up into his hands. For a moment, a small boy not far away, whose teacher had made him crouch down at the sound of the gunshot, saw the case fall and shatter and the coins bounce around on the floor, rolling about. But then they seemed to gather themselves together and rise into the air, only to become blurry and clustered together, as if defying both gravity and the normal laws of sight.

But Santiago looked down and realized that, like the knife he had hidden earlier in his belt, these coins were still visible, though barely. With quick thinking, he reasoned that even though the cloth of his pockets wouldn't hide them, perhaps his hands would. So he reached back down into the pockets and grabbed them all and held them now in cupped and closed hands and, as he suspected, they disappeared almost completely from view, a small fortune in ancient treasure.

Miguel and Carlos, who were already outside the front door, had stopped when they heard the gunshot. They didn't know at first what to think. Had Santiago become visible again? Had he been shot? But, surely, he wouldn't let such a thing happen. He could think well on his feet, even invisible feet. So, what was it? Fortunately, their third confederate was now just a few seconds behind them in getting to the front entrance door. He had been the last one to leave the ring's empty display case, staying around to try to make sure that the theft was not discovered too soon, and so he had still been inside, walking toward the door when the shot rang out. Looking back, he saw that there was a policeman down. And with no obvious assailant in sight, he realized quickly what the master must have done.

No one else had been in the Greek Antiquities Room to notice the empty display case until right after this fourth man had left. But then, not twenty seconds later, a British tourist had walked up to the case and had seen to his surprise that there was nothing in it. Noting the description on the wall and reading of an invisibility ring, he at first suspected that this must be some sort of a joke—a ring that makes its wearer, and apparently itself, invisible. But then, he had thought better of the situation, or worse, as the case may be, since there's not typically a lot of joking around to be found in a serious history museum. And as he bent over to look closer, he saw lots of glass fragments and shards off to the side, showing that there had been a top on the display that was now shattered. He turned around and walked quickly out of the room to find a guard and ask about it.

He looked left and right and then saw the guard in the chair toward the back of the hall, sitting in a bit of an awkward position. The visitor walked up and spoke to him, but the guard was apparently asleep and unresponsive. He tried to wake him, at first with a word, and then he touched the man on the shoulder. At that, the guard's body slid down and fell out of the chair, inert on the floor.

"This guard has been injured!" the tourist yelled out. "Help! This man needs medical attention!" And just that second, the gunshot rang out in the hall.

But Santiago and his men were all soon outside the museum and its current chaos, and well on their way down the boulevard. He had now given Miguel the valuable coins for safekeeping. His mind was already elsewhere. He was on his way to go make the big statement of revenge that he was determined to bring to this city that now represented for him so much frustration. He didn't care how many people had to die for his act of vengeance and petty self-expression to take place. In fact, from his point of view, the more he had to kill, the better it would be.

The sheep he was going to eliminate, he thought to himself, did not deserve to live. They were unnecessary blights on the face of existence. They were mere irritants. Then, switching metaphors, he thought of them as dirty swine that enjoyed spitting in the face of greatness. He enjoyed switching the images in his mind to insult his inferiors in new ways—and sneered inwardly at those mangy, snarling, smelly dogs. It would be his pleasure to dispatch them, to rid the city and the world of them, and the sooner, the better. Then, and only then, he could go and take for himself the object he really wanted, and that he felt only he deserved. And now, he thought in his heart, no one could stop him from possessing it. Many more would probably have to die. And that was fine with him.

32

REVENGE AND POWER

SCHOOL HAD BEEN CANCELED FOR THE DAY. THE ENTIRE palace, along with the kingdom more broadly, was in mourning. Hamid had sent word to the Adi residence that Shapur and Shamilar and their two small children at home were most likely out of danger at this point, and so Hoda could rotate off duty there. She would be needed soon at the palace, instead. Shapur in turn conveyed a message back that, from what he could see, Santiago had traveled into the city with three men.

With his newfound ability to view the monster of legend, Mafulla's father had mentally been able to see a stable for camels, what looked like a cheap travelers' hotel, several street scenes, and what may have been parts of the Museum of History just this morning. But then something very odd happened, and the man at the focus of his episodic sightings seemed to disappear. Even more oddly, Shapur then began seeing, in bits and pieces, as if through Santiago's eyes, or at least from where they might be. It was all more than a little confusing. And there were some terrible sights. The visions were sporadic, and were mere short flashes of scenes, but they would likely still be helpful in the possible tracking of the man. The entire message of Shapur's most recent visions, with all their oddity, was conveyed to the king's nearest outpost, where it was quickly radioed in to the palace.

Within minutes, every member of Phi working closely with the king had been briefed on the unexpected turn of events at the museum, and what it might represent. Omari, Paki and Amon were already down in the palace guard readiness room, preparing for a special patrol near the newspaper's offices. They had been asked to dress in civilian clothing for the assignment, so they could blend in with the crowds on the street. They were going to be looking for Santiago and, of course, all the new information put a novel twist on their assignment. As Omari stuck a second revolver into his belt and made sure it was well hidden, he said to his friends, "So, Ok, let's go find this invisible, insidious, intolerable man."

Paki smiled and said, "I have great confidence in our ability to locate both the undesirable and the unseen. Fortunately for us, invisible isn't the same as undetectable."

"I certainly see what you're saying, even if I may never see what you're talking about," Amon replied with a measure of cleverness that got a smile from both of them. They had all, of course, grieved the loss of Rumi quite heavily. But they were each far enough into the life of Phi to realize when they had to put any sad or negative feelings behind them and equip themselves emotionally and mentally to do the job that was now theirs to accomplish. A use of humor often lightened the mood among Phi before a military action of any kind. That was one of the many reasons they had always admired Mafulla and his customary dose of Mafoolery. He had a habit of channeling any nervousness or concern, or anxiety into something positive, in a form that could help relax his friends, as well as his own spirit, boosting them all forward in a positive mood. Wit can have hidden power.

The three Phi made their way through several hallways to the back loading dock where they walked out of the palace, down some stairs, and over to a truck that looked like a commercial vehicle parked there to make a delivery of groceries to the palace kitchen. In it were three other men waiting for them. Omari greeted the man sitting on the passenger side of the front seat. "Captain al-Suki! I didn't know you were escorting us. I'm glad you're with us today."

"Yes, indeed, and I thank you. It's an honor, sir," al-Suki replied. "But please call me Rashid."

"As you wish, Rashid, and gladly." Omari smiled.

The captain said, "Ever since we had the good fortune to meet the prince, we've been assigned to several duties involving the palace."

"Yes. I've seen you around, now and then."

"It's always great. Like you, of course, we're in plain clothes today. And I have two of my most trusted men with me—Omar here, and Amin, who's in the back." Omar was behind the wheel and, as soon as Rashid mentioned their names, Amin came around to their side of the truck from the back of the vehicle.

"Amin! Omar! Good to see you both again," Paki now said, turning back and forth to the two of them. "It's reassuring to have three highly decorated warriors with us on this mission."

"Thank you, Paki. Good to see you all, as well," Amin said, as Omar smiled and nodded with a small wave of his hand. The two other Phi guards also added their own quick words of greeting. Then, the captain got down to business.

"You can load up in back and, as soon as Amin closes the doors, we'll be on our way," Rashid said.

"Thanks," Omari replied, and the three Phi guards went around to the back of the truck, opened it up, and climbed inside. The doors were then quickly shut from the outside, and within no more than a few seconds, the truck started up and began to move. It was only a short drive to the newspaper's offices. They were taking the truck mainly because it was quick and it contained, hidden in the back, more weapons and containers of ammunition, in case they were needed on the mission.

Only a few minutes later, the brakes squeaked and the truck slowed down, and then parked. The Phi waited, prepared to jump out. A few seconds afterwards, the back doors were opened.

"Thank you, my friend," Amon said to Amin, as he exited the truck.

"Do you realize," Paki commented, just as Rashid and Omar came around to join them, "that we have on this little mission Omar and Omari, as well as Amon and Amin?"

The men laughed and Rashid said, "Well, it sounds like a match made in heaven."

"As long as it wasn't made for heaven!" Omari replied and got a knowing chuckle out of all of them.

"No, my friend," Rashid said. "There's no cause for concern. The only travelers into the afterlife today will be our foes, and I'm not sure that heaven is the intended destination stamped on their tickets."

Amon then said, "We certainly do try to honor and save life, whenever we can, but with these characters we're hunting today, it's sadly not often possible."

"Yes, it's a terrible shame how people waste their talents and lives chasing the wrong things," Paki said. "And then, rather than allowing us to correct and reform them, they insist on a life-or-death battle."

With that, and a few more comments on the nature of their task, the men went over some last minute plans and split up. The soldiers were assigned to the inside of the building and the three Phi stayed outside. Omari, Paki, and Amon quickly found a bench with a good view of two sides of the building. On a third side, heavy construction was underway, making it less likely as an avenue of approach, and the fourth side adjoined another business. Two of them sat and one roamed about, on alert for anything that might seem odd.

They had expected Santiago to come into town and go straight to the newspaper in order to get his revenge, or make his dramatic statement of keen displeasure. His prior visit to the Museum of History had caught them by surprise. But it was now safe to reason from everything they knew about him that the newspaper office was his next destination. And the sides of the building the king's men could see were the ones he would naturally approach first, if he indeed came from the direction of the museum.

The streets were busy. This was a fairly well populated part of town during the business day. The sidewalks were getting almost crowded, and there was a great deal of low, ambient street noise added to the cacophony of the construction going on, as a large new brick structure was being put up next to the newspaper offices. It looked like some sort of an office building as well, a bit modern, but with a few more traditional touches added on. In the middle of all the activity swirling around, it was going to be difficult for the Phi to spot and identify their adversaries—three or more men they had never seen, among all these other people, as well as the man that they would likely not see. But they were trained to be watchful and aware in many ways. If even the wind blew differently, they would know.

Omari could hardly believe his eyes when he suddenly saw down the street the king's old friends who were visiting from the village of Dromeda, the elderly couple, Sab and Meskhenet Maayuf. They were walking along with, of all things, their frequent companion, Gimpy the dog, on a long leash. He was moving almost as slowly as they were, and with his small distinctive limp. Omari's first instinct was to go and warn them quickly about what might be getting ready to happen. But he realized that, since they were very senior Phi, he had other options. So he made his mind calm and did his best to send their way an alarm, a suggestion that they should probably go in another direction with their dog-walk. Things could become extremely dangerous at any time. In a sense, he was mentally waving them off, urging them to leave the immediate area because of trouble brewing.

But as soon as he began to project these thoughts, he seemed to sense, in response, a "Yes." It was just a simple yes. Not a "Yes, thank you, we'll do as you suggest," but only a yes. He was not at all sure what that meant. But the responsive thought came with a tone and feeling of comfortable assurance, so he didn't think more about it. A senior Phi can have his own knowledge.

A man was standing near the newspaper building, in front of a low knee-high wall, holding what looked like a copy of the day's paper. No one had noticed him or paid him any attention. And certainly, no one could suspect for a moment that next to him was a fully invisible man, now concentrating his thoughts and energies on someone inside the building: the editor of the very story the visible man was perusing once more.

In the newspaper's offices, at one desk among many others, a man about forty-five years old suddenly grimaced and dropped his pen. He muttered "Ow," and lifted a hand to his temple. "Oh!" Both hands now grabbed his head, his elbows planted on the desk. "Ow, Ow, Ow." He let out a loud groan, and the man at the next desk looked up and saw, to his shock and immediate horror, that a small dark stream of blood was trickling out the nose of his colleague, the city desk editor.

"Tarik! Are you all right?" What's the matter? Tarik!"

The man just groaned again in response and tried to stand. But as soon as he was upright, he bent over at the middle, holding his head, and then he gave a shout of sheer pain and collapsed onto the floor.

A voice rang out. "Someone get help! Call the hospital! Someone help us, please! It's Tarik! Something's wrong!" People began getting up from every occupied nearby desk to see what was the matter. And soon, another person could be heard crying out in agony, and then a third. There was mass confusion, as some of the other people turned here and there to offer help, but didn't know who needed it more, or what it was that they could do. Panic and perplexity began to spread.

The soldiers stationed inside the building down at one end saw the commotion from a distance and heard the shouting. "What's going on?" The captain asked Omar.

"I'm not sure, sir. I'll go see." Omar walked briskly toward the site of the problem, whatever it was. And then, within seconds, he was waving the captain and Amin over to where he was standing.

"What's happened?" he asked the nearest person.

"I don't know! The men were suddenly stricken with something! They're in pain and bleeding! We don't know what's going on!"

The captain was there now as well and was looking over one of the victims. The man was barely alive and his breathing was fast and shallow. Omar said, "What should we do?"

The captain replied, "Go to the main office. Use the phone.

Make a quick call to the hospital. Tell them we need help. Then call into the palace command post. Let them know what's happening. An assault of some kind has started. Be quick and come right back, in case you're needed here!"

Omar ran off. Rashid bent down again to check on the man lying at his feet. Someone nearby was crying. The captain felt for a pulse. He tried again. Then he let out a deep breath and said, to no one in particular, "We've lost him. He's gone."

"What?" Amin asked.

"The poor man has died," the captain said. "Go outside and tell our colleagues what's happening in here. Find them quickly. We need to stop whatever's being done."

Outside, Santiago was standing near the front door, beside his man who was gazing at the paper, now seated on the short wall. The master was in a state of high agitation. But, of course, no one could tell. He had succeeded in causing great pain to three men, and death now to one of them. But he was having trouble finishing off the other two. He couldn't understand it. He felt a void in his power or, more accurately, a limit closer to him than he had experienced in many years. He was being frustrated in the free use of his accumulated spiritual force. And it was confusing him immensely. Somehow, his intended conveyance of brute power, brain to brain, was not fully working as it should and, after the initial success, he could now suddenly feel his efforts falling short. "What's this?" he said, out loud, but in a vicious whisper.

"What?" his disciple asked, as he continued to look at the paper.

"Nothing," Santiago whispered, surprised to realize that he had spoken aloud. "I'll let you finish them now, the ones inside."

"Me?"

"Yes! Do it, this moment!" The man felt a knot in his stomach and a thrill of adrenalin throughout his body, with no understanding of why he was being given the task. "The three men," that same whisper from the nearby air explained. "One is dead. Take down the next two. It's your privilege, your honor. Do it."

The man with the paper blocked from his mind any further questions and began to concentrate with all his might. Santiago was trying to buy some time, when there was little time to be had, to figure out what he was experiencing and why a task that should be easy for him was suddenly elusive and even beyond his best efforts. He had never felt such a lack of effectiveness in an immediate use of force.

Inside the building, Captain al-Suki had just moved to another man, the global news editor, who had been writhing on the floor. The man cried out and went limp. "He's dead!" Someone nearby suddenly shouted, and there were screams in the room. Many people were now moving away from their stricken colleagues and rushing to leave the office and the building, not knowing what they might face next. They just wanted to get away from whatever was happening. The captain had bent down and checked and confirmed now that this second man, tremendously bloodied from his nose and ears and mouth, also had no pulse and was unmoving. He instinctively scanned the room, but saw nothing that could be connected with this.

"Get out!" Rashid shouted to the few people who were still near this second man and, some twenty or thirty feet away, a third co-worker in distress. "Everyone get out of the building quickly and stay clear of it. Now! Please! We're Egyptian Army! Leave quickly for your safety!" No one waited to be asked again. Only the captain stayed at the scene, as he moved toward the third man and saw his thrashing body jerk once, and then twice, and then also become limp and still.

Santiago had decided now to do something dramatic that did not involve spirit-to-spirit or brain-to-brain force. He would dig deep and create a massive shaking of the building, almost like a focused, limited earthquake. That would bring down the ceiling on the men he had already attacked, as well as on any others around them. He would not wait to see if his disciple's efforts had worked. He would take charge again and do this thing that only he could do.

And with all the strength, focus, and force within him, he acted to unleash the greater power from beyond him that he knew he could access, and direct it as a vast force of destruction to the building. But, beneath the strain and intensity of his consciousness, he was stunned to feel nothing else—no inflow of power, no outflow of force. Suddenly, he was nearly dizzy with perplexity and uncertainty, and a wave of something he had not experienced in many years, a sharp flutter of true fear. What was happening? What was wrong? A vortex of shock and worry and almost palpably thick anxiety knocked his callous spirit off kilter and slowed down his thoughts. He fought for clarity. Then he tried again. Nothing. He then battled a second and more forceful wave of fear that hit him hard. His knees felt weak.

Of course, no one could see the expression of shock and near terror that would otherwise be on his face. He looked all around as if that would allow him to find a solution for this unexpected problem. Miguel and the other man … what was his name? Santiago in his panic couldn't even remember for a moment the name of his other disciple sitting across the street with Miguel—wait—Carlos! Yes, Carlos! Miguel and Carlos must be summoned, but how?

The whisper again, this time with a tone of desperation in it that could be mistaken for mere emphasis and, as a matter of fact, was: "Get Miguel and Carlos! We must leave now! This work is done!"

"Master, they'll see me walk away and then they'll follow," he whispered back. "You told me earlier not to signal them in any way. It might arouse suspicions."

"Yes! Fine! It's best! You remember well. I was right. We must go quietly and at once!"

As he said this, people began to come running out of the building, and some were yelling, "Help! Help us!"

The crowds streaming by on the sidewalk were mostly perplexed at first. A few were alarmed, and many moved away or walked faster, with, of course, no idea of what was going on. A few stopped to ask what might be the matter. But the people passing by, for the most part, continued to move toward their various destinations.

Amin had come out another door moments earlier and had run

right over to Omari, Paki and Amon. "Something's been happening inside. People are being stricken and bloodied, and there's no assailant anywhere in sight."

"What are the symptoms?" Paki asked as the three of them rose from their bench.

"They grab their heads, they shout in pain, collapse, and bleed from the nose, mouth, and ears."

"Santiago must be here, or nearby." Omari spoke as he scanned the street, and especially the area closest to the building. The others were doing the same.

"Thanks for the alert," Paki said. "Go back and join your captain, in case anything else takes place inside. If nothing more happens in the next four or five minutes, all of you come back out and support us in our search."

The Phi saw nothing that helped. People were clustered in twos and threes and what might have been fours, walking here and there. It didn't help that there was a popular café across the street and many people were going in and out of it, as well. Some were now looking up in concern over what might be happening at the newspaper, where shouts could be heard. But in the crowded conditions, no one could make out what was happening, and most turned their attention back to their companions, or people at nearby tables who might be asking about all the commotion. Despite quick visual searches of the area, none of the Phi had really noticed the man who had just gotten up off the low wall where he had been sitting near the building. There were too many others around, walking by. He folded his paper and began to stroll in the direction of the Maayuf couple and their dog, now browsing at a newsstand, and still about half a city block away.

Within no more than twenty seconds, there was a sharp loud sound that broke through, and rose above, all the other ambient street noise and conversations. It was the unmistakable sound of a dog's single shrill bark that then transitioned into a long stretch of growling. And that in turn gave way to an extended outbreak of insistent yapping. Omari and Paki both immediately looked in its direction. Gimpy was going nuts and straining at his leash. The Phi guards both started walking toward him, not quite knowing why, but also not questioning their instincts. Other people were moving away from the dog as they walked by, allowing him a good bit of space. And some were giving the old couple disapproving looks for their apparent lack of control over the animal in such a public place. But the Phi were focused and stared right at him, as well as at the space and air directly in front of him, where his attention was fixed.

As a man walking by stepped into the street to avoid Gimpy, the dog instantly lunged toward a spot about three or four feet from his legs, to his left and just behind him. Gimpy seemed oddly to clamp his teeth around an empty space about a foot or so off the ground. "Ow!" The cry came from apparently nowhere, but near the dog. Omari was at this point only about forty or fifty feet away and could hear the shout of pain that no one in his visual field had emitted.

"Next to the man with the paper!" He shouted to his colleagues, and moving quickly by several people in the way, he yelled loudly, "Everyone down!" And the three Phi simultaneously aimed their guns at the space right in front of the dog, but hesitated for a moment, concerned they would accidentally hit Gimpy if he were to lunge forward. But just then, in that instant of pause, the dog yelped loudly and stumbled sideways. He instantly let go of whatever he had bitten and backed up quickly, barking hard again. Santiago, in his typically vindictive temperament, had sought to kill him on the spot in reaction to the painful bite. But the dog, apart from the one yelp, seemed now to be fine and unharmed. And at the same time that old Gimpy was scampering back, the Phi let loose with a loud barrage of gunshots.

Many people around them screamed and yelled out, and everyone scattered, diving for cover or protection, or just to flatten out on the ground where it might be safer. Eight shots rang out rapidly, with both succession and rough simultaneity. The men assumed they were firing at someone with extended proprioception and the ability to move and evade. So they directed their shots as well as they could to the center, left, and right all together, to remove any avenues of avoidance. There was nowhere at that moment for Santiago to go, as far as they could imagine, as they now emptied their guns, and reached for their backup weapons to continue.

The man with the folded paper in his hand, who had continued to walk rapidly forward, now dropped the news and turned and crouched with a revolver in his hands. He intended to return fire in that one vulnerable moment for two of the three Phi, as they were caught between emptying their chambers and getting to their secondary weapons. He aimed straight at Paki and pulled the trigger. But the trigger was stuck. It would not move back. He squeezed harder. Nothing. He smacked the gun in frantic frustration, and in that moment of distraction, Amon put him down with a single bullet to the chest.

The Maayufs had been doing their part in the situation. They had used their own power to thwart the would-be shooter. His weapon would not function because of them. But their main concern was the man's invisible master. They could feel the power near them, the presence of a formidable adversary, and they were well prepared for this, but they were at the same time quite surprised that they didn't sense the magnitude of force here that they had expected. The thought crossed their minds that this could be one of Santiago's top disciples invisibly present near them, and not the man himself. They had no idea what the Ring of Gyges was doing to his normal powers. He had also not yet drawn the true conclusion himself as to what was going on in his difficulties with power, even in the instant before the gunfire had begun.

Only Gimpy could at that moment see or sense Santiago, exactly where he was, and in his current condition. The Maayufs had long known that the lame little dog was different. But he was now exceeding even their greatest suspicions concerning the depth and power of his mind. On his own level, he was Phi. A low growl alone now announced his ongoing awareness and knowledge, but in the chaos and noise, no one heard him as he continued.

Miguel and Carlos had been trailing their colleague and the master from about half a block behind them, through visual contact with the man, their confederate, who was now down and dead on the ground. Neither of them could decide at first what to do. They had no idea whether Santiago had been shot or not. They could return fire and expose themselves to what was obviously superior firepower. Or they could simply seek to escape the situation. If Santiago was dead or severely injured, this might be a prudent plan. But if he was alive and saw them leaving him, a choice to play it safe in that way could, ironically, be their death warrant.

Their next move was going to be crucial. What then would it be? Should they attempt to take down at least two of the gunmen from behind, before they could even turn around? Or should they walk away? The stakes could not be higher, and with each passing second, a window of opportunity for either decision to be successful might be closing. Police would arrive, inevitably, and likely very soon. They had no idea that the captain and his two men were already running out the front door of the news building, having heard shots, and were now coming, fully armed and ready, directly toward them.

At the palace, the king was in a closed door meeting with Hamid, Layla, and now Hoda, who had recently arrived. A guard had been sent to find the boys and bring them to the session. Masoon was also on the way.

As they were talking, King Ali suddenly stopped in mid sentence and waited. He stared across the room, but his vision was focused elsewhere. Then he spoke. "They've found Santiago, thanks to Gimpy, our small dog friend from Dromeda, and our fellow Phi have engaged him and one of his associates with gunfire. The associate is dead."

"What of Santiago?" Hamid asked. "Is he dead, or still alive?"

The king took a deep breath and let it out, and then had an expression cross his face that no one could interpret.

33

AT THE PALACE

THE BOYS HAD EARLIER GONE DOWN TO VISIT WITH BHATI in her main sitting room. Before they arrived, Layla had taken Kissa and Hasina over to Hoda's office to get some things they might need for a later meeting with the king. And so Bhati had been alone for a short time when Walid and Mafulla arrived. Walid wanted to check in on her to see how she was doing, and the king encouraged him to go and do so. They had been together now, talking, for maybe half an hour.

Mafulla suddenly held up the index finger of his right hand, as Walid was about to continue in something he was saying, and by doing so, he stopped his friend in the middle of a word. "Sorry. But something just happened," he said enigmatically to Walid, and also to Bhati. "I didn't want to interrupt your thought, but something really big just happened." He had a look on his face of great concentration, as if his mind was far away. He dropped his head down a bit and rubbed his hands on his forehead.

"It's Ok. But what?" Walid asked at once. "What do you mean? What just happened?"

Mafulla looked up and said, "I'm not sure, but something important."

"Is it Santiago?"

"I think so, I mean, yeah, but ... I don't know for sure. Something's going on, or just took place."

"Where?"

"The newspaper offices, I think—somewhere around the newspaper. Outside, down the street, close to the building."

"Can you ... see anything?"

"I just saw a flash of a scene."

"What was it?"

"Omari and Paki and Amon basically unloaded their guns at something or somebody and it's likely our Mr. Invisible. And, I know this is going to sound really strange, but I think your old friend, Gimpy the dog, is playing some sort of role."

"Really?"

"Yeah."

"What do you mean?"

"He's there with somebody."

"Who?"

"I don't know. Maybe it's the Maayufs. But Gimpy's the only one ... who can see Santiago, or know where he is, I think. And it looked to me, in the quick vision I just had, as if right before the gunfire, our Gimpy bit him—and really, really hard."

Walid laughed loudly, despite his great concern, and said, "Gimpy bit Santiago?"

"Yeah, I think so."

"Awesome! Unbelievable! Good dog! Then what?"

"I ... can't tell."

"Is Gimpy Ok?"

"Yeah, yeah, Gimp's fine. I just didn't see any more."

"What should we do?"

"Tell the king?"

"Good idea." Walid turned and asked, "Mom, what do you think? Should we go to Uncle Ali?"

"Yes. It's a good idea. You boys should go right now and tell the king what you've just seen, Mafulla."

"Are you sure?" Walid said.

"Yes. Of course, Ali may have seen it too, or it might be new information for him. And it could be important for him to know. I'll be fine here on my own. I have a few things I need to do."

"Ok, Mom. But … you're sure?"

"Yes. And I think the sooner you get to Ali, the better."

"You're right. I'll see you in just a bit, Ok?"

"That's good. Now: Go."

"Back soon," Mafulla said, as he got up and made for the door. The boys then practically ran out of the suite and down the hall-way toward the king's rooms.

They at first almost bumped into a palace guard who had been walking toward Bhati's suite. He said, "Prince Walid! The king wants to see you as soon as possible."

Walid replied, "We're on the way there now."

"Very good! Thank you, Prince."

At the other end of the hall, they could see Masoon approaching. "Hey!" Walid yelled down to him and waved, as they walked forward.

"Hi, Prince," Masoon said.

"I heard you got Santiago's guys."

"Yes. They were determined adversaries and strong fighters. I was impressed by their skill and persistence. I'm sorry we had to take them down."

"But you're Ok?"

"We lost a man, regrettably, but I'm fine."

"I'm sorry for the loss."

"He was a good man."

"Many blessings on him for his sacrifice."

"Yes. He was brave."

"What's happening now?"

"I'm just checking in with the king to find out. My men are around the palace. His Majesty summoned me back here. He must expect our adversary to come this way soon."

"Yeah, I think so," Walid said.

"The dog Gimpy just bit him, good," Mafulla said.

"What? Who?" Masoon asked, with a surprised expression.

"Santiago. Minutes ago, I just saw a flash of something that was happening on the street near the newspaper offices. The little dog Gimpy from Dromeda bit Santiago on the leg."

Masoon, like Walid, couldn't help but laugh out loud at the revelation. "I knew he had it in him."

"He may have had even more in him for a second, but I'm sure he spit it out," Mafulla replied. And that made them both laugh again.

"Spit it out," Walid repeated, laughing some more.

"Sorry. I know this is serious stuff."

"No, it's perfectly fine, Mafulla," Masoon answered. "We depend on you to lighten the mood now and then."

"A little Mafoolery always helps," Walid said.

"Yes, well named, and aptly used," Masoon replied and looked back at Mafulla. "And is the dog Ok?"

"Yeah—other than what I'm sure is a very bad taste in his mouth. Santiago tried to kill him, but couldn't even really hurt him."

"Oh?"

"Yeah," Mafulla said, and then turned to Walid and added, "I forgot to mention that, because I didn't really see it, but I only sort of sensed it. And it sure surprised me."

"Wow, that's pretty amazing," Walid said.

"Yeah," Mafulla agreed. "Mr. Scary Power Man couldn't hurt an old lame dog."

"I wonder why."

"It could be that … The Gimpster is really Super-Dog in disguise, or … the invisibility stuff is somehow—I don't know—interfering with Santiago's powers. Or, maybe both!"

"Interesting," Masoon said. "And it's potentially a vital piece of information for us."

"Yeah, this could be really important," Walid insisted to his friend. "It might be crucial. Make sure to tell the king, first thing."

"Ok. You're right. I will."

"Should we go in?" Masoon motioned toward Kular's outer door.

"Yeah, thanks," Walid said.

Some distance away, Muriel al-Baki was in her kitchen having tea, and she thought she heard a knock at the door, and so went to check. Opening it, she was stunned at who was standing there. She said in a loud and rushed whisper, "What are you doing here?"

"He sent me to come tell you. It's happening now, or very soon, today. Go to the meeting place. He should be there within a couple of hours, at the latest. I'll join you there in a bit, to wait with you.

"Are you sure?"

"Yes."

"But this is all happening much faster than I thought it would."

"There are reasons. The schedule has been moved up. We have to adapt."

"Why?"

"I can't say. I have to go now. Just be there."

"Ok, I'll be there," Muriel said, and closed the door. She had to pack quickly and without her husband noticing what she was doing. He was in on all this to an extent, but had no real idea what the big picture was, or what Muriel was hoping to accomplish with Santiago. She decided to walk to the back of the house where he was reading and ask him to go to the market for a list of things. By the time he was back, she would be gone.

Two blocks away, Khata was sitting outside her house with her friends Ara and Cabar. Just a few minutes later, she happened to see the man walk by at a distance, the one who had just been Muriel's surprise visitor. She had never seen him before, but by intuition, or Phi insight, knew right away that this was not just some normal person walking down the street. She understood that something of importance was going on, and that he was involved. It was a deep and eerie feeling. Excusing herself for a minute from her two friends, she went into the house and found her mother. "Mom, I just saw a man walking down the street and had a really bad feeling about him."

"Who is he?"

"I don't know, but I think ... he just ... visited Muriel, and I have a strong sense that it's not good."

"Is he coming here, toward our home?"

"No, he's walking away."

"Ok, sweetie, thank you for telling me this," Rama said. "I should have trusted your feelings about Muriel from the start. So I completely trust what you're telling me now, even though I don't understand how you can have such feelings, or knowledge."

"Thanks, Mom."

"Why don't you girls come in for a few minutes? I'll walk over to the Adi house where Layla told me the king has some radio equipment set up, and I'll pass this information on to them for the palace. I can be back within fifteen or twenty minutes, tops."

"That sounds good," Khata said.

"Can you describe the man to me?"

"Yes, he had on a western business suit, dark grey, and with a blue tie, I think, and a white handkerchief in his chest pocket."

"Tall or short?"

"He was tall and thin."

As Rama quickly picked up her bag from a chair near the door, she stopped and said, "Now, first, before I go, I have to ask: Are you sure you're not in danger here at the house?"

"I don't think so," Khata said.

"You don't think so?"

"Actually, I'm pretty sure I'm not. As far as Muriel knows, we're totally in the dark about her."

"True. But you're sure you don't have any feelings of an immediate threat to you or any of us, from this man or Muriel?"

"None at all. Like I said, he was walking away. And he didn't notice me. I'm positive."

"Ok, then, but still I think you should get the girls inside. Maybe bake something together. Or, you can figure out what to do, and I'll be right back."

"Sure thing, Mom."

Santiago's anger toward the newspaper had accomplished exactly what Leem Hadad, Reela, and the king had hoped—apart from the deaths, of course, which were unanticipated and tragic. But it had caused him to do something that was not a part of his original plan, and contrary to his own best interest. By stopping at the newspaper and causing the damage there, he had alerted everyone to his location and timing. Otherwise, no one could have known exactly where he might be and when he was planning to strike at the palace. Shapur could certainly see things concerning Santiago with his new ability, but not often in a broad enough context to pinpoint the man's location. Now, they had a good sense of his relative position, the direction of his movement, and his unusual methods on this day. They also could predict roughly when he would get near the palace. By his need for revenge on the paper, he had given up most of the element of surprise that he would otherwise have had on his side.

He had evaded the many bullets of the three Phi by dropping to the ground as soon as he felt the impending shots on the way. The men had aimed at and around normal torso height, and were using all their ammunition to prevent the proprioceptive avoidance moves that they had most frequently seen and done. And those were all movements that involved a quick twisting of the upper body and possibly slight dips, but not very often a full drop, flat to the ground, which always put a man at a disadvantage, making it more difficult for him to get up and move quickly with a wide range of options. But in this case, they had been wrong and had missed him with all their shots. He had then scrambled away from the spot where he dropped, and from the little dog that had spotted him. And he was now jogging farther from the general danger, expecting his two men to follow in the direction they knew he'd be going. All he had said was that their next job would be at the palace, at the side gate. And they had seen maps. So they would know, or could quickly figure out, which way to go.

At that point, Santiago's hostile, frustrated, and repeatedly offended follower Miguel decided to make a move that no one would have expected. He pulled out the knife that he had been given earlier at the museum and stabbed Carlos in the back. The man, who had been walking slightly in front of him, then fell forward to his knees on the ground, and Miguel yelled out, "He has a gun!" He pointed frantically at Carlos as he moved away from him and into the surrounding crowd as quickly as he could. Omari first saw the pointing arm and, looking at Carlos, noticed the pistol that had just dropped out of his belt and onto the street.

"Stop where you are!" The guard yelled at the fallen adversary and moved toward him, at this point completely ignoring Miguel and his sudden disappearance down the street. Paki and Amon followed, and at about that time, the captain and his men converged on the wounded criminal as well. Gimpy started barking again and had turned around, facing a new direction as he saw Santiago slowly jogging away, down the street.

Paki looked over and said, "What is it, boy? What do you see?"

Miguel was now safely away and yet still walking in the direction he thought his leader would be going. He had already abandoned the cause for his own escape, but had an explanation ready that he believed Santiago would accept. He wanted the chance to betray the man one more time and in a much bigger way that could lead to his defeat. At present, he had no idea exactly what that would require, but he moved forward on mostly hope, along with his own form of both resentment and fury. He was every bit as determined as his so-called master. But his determination now was to bring the man down and see it happen. Yet he, like the king, would soon be up against a formidable opponent who had spent decades of hard work to make himself unbeatable by any other human being he ever might face. He was determined that no one would be able to bring him down.

Omari and Amon were tying up the injured man, who was now bleeding profusely on the street. As Amon explained to the shocked onlookers that they were palace guards responding to a crime, Sab Maayuf called out to Paki, "Do you have transportation, my friend?"

"Yes, a truck nearby."

"We need you to get us to the palace. I believe our foe is headed there. I have it on the best authority," he said as he pointed to Gimpy.

Down the street now a few blocks away, Miguel was walking briskly when he heard a voice near him whisper loudly, "Slow down."

He turned to his left where the sound had come from, and looked about. The voice was now closer as it said, "Slow down and explain yourself, if you want to live another minute."

He decreased his pace and said, "I had to do it. I had to give up Carlos so we could get out of there. It was the only way I could create a distraction big enough."

"Carlos was a good man for me. I might have needed him."

"I didn't trust him," Miguel said. "He'd been entertaining some serious doubts recently about what we're doing."

Santiago pondered this for a moment. He had experienced some troubling sensations that there might be discontent among his men, but he couldn't pinpoint who might be disaffected. "All right," he said. "But from now on, we don't sacrifice our own. We harm only others."

Miguel knew that this was a lie and that Santiago would be prepared to sacrifice him at any moment when it might seem the expedient thing to do. But he was relieved that his reasoning for now had been accepted, and his own treason had not been detected.

"Where are we going?"

"The side gate of The Golden Palace—I told you that already," the voice hissed. "I'll let you know more when you need to know."

At the palace, a call had come in with new information. A quick plan had been hatched and the king, after a period of meditation and surprising discovery, had sent two people he trusted out on what could be an important related mission.

The piano teacher's plan had worked. She convinced her husband to go to the market with a long list of things they needed. As soon as he left the house, she began to pack the one bag she'd been told she could bring along. It just took a while to find one thing she really wanted to take with her. Then, within thirty minutes, she left the front door to walk the twelve long blocks to her designated meeting place. She was inwardly shaking with excitement over the reality of what all this could mean for her. Santiago would make her a queen. She would have all the power and recognition she had ever wanted. It was just mere hours away now. Then, everything would be right, and wonderful. Everything would be justified. With Santiago, she could redefine the image of greatness in their time, and perhaps, for all time. Those were the thoughts that swam through her head as she made her way down the street, completely unaware that she was being watched.

After only about five minutes on the park bench, gazing at people walking by, and alternately pretending to read a book, Muriel noticed two boys she had seen at the palace on the occasion of the king's birthday party. They were crossing the park and talking to each other. She thought nothing more about it and returned to her book. When she heard a nearby noise and looked up again, they were walking over toward her with big smiles. "Hi," Malik said. "You're Muriel, right? Khata's piano teacher and the famous concert pianist—I recognize you from the recent birthday party."

"Oh, yes," Muriel said. "How nice to see you," she lied.

"It's nice to see you, too," Haji said. And then he added, "You were great at the party. I really enjoyed your playing. It was super amazing in every way."

"Thank you so much. It was a joy to be there."

"There's been a change in plans," Malik suddenly said.

"What do you mean?"

"There's been a change. He's not coming. We were sent instead."

"I'm sorry. I'm confused. I have no idea what you're talking about."

"Yes, you do. We're with you now. The master sent us."

Muriel just looked very confused and wary, and began to scan the park area as quickly as she could without being too obvious about it.

"He needs you at the palace right away."

"What?"

"Osvaldo. The master. He needs you at the palace. It's been arranged through our contacts. We'll get you in."

"What do you mean?"

"It's all about to happen, a bigger thing than he had anticipated. And I think it's possible he wants you there to witness it. He didn't tell me everything. You know how he is."

"Yes."

"You'll also want to be a part of what's about to happen. It will be a once-in-a-lifetime experience."

This connected with Muriel's fantasy perfectly. But still, she just said, "Oh, my. I'm not sure about any of this." She glanced around the park again, searching for what she could not have specified.

"We don't have much time," Haji kicked in with an urgent tone of voice.

"But there … was a plan."

"All good plans can change. Things will still play out as they should, but even better," Malik explained with a smile. "We've been instructed that if you were hesitant about this message, or the fact that we're the ones delivering it, I should tell you that he wants you to be there to share in the true greatness, as the royalty you're meant to be." Malik paused for a second and then added, "The Royal Family Clutter Room has yielded treasures beyond his expectation."

"Oh, my." Muriel stood up, still a bit off balance, but now immensely reassured because, she thought, how else could they know this tidbit of information, if not from Santiago himself.

"We don't have much time," Haji said.

"We do need to hurry," Malik said, adding, "Here, let me get your bag for you. You'll need it later. At the palace, everything will become clear."

34

THE INCURSION

THE KING AND HIS TOP ADVISORS HAD DEVELOPED A PLAN. They would make it relatively easy for Santiago to get onto the palace grounds and into the palace, but very difficult for him to get even near what he wanted. And they would make it totally impossible for him to get out, at least, in a normal physical, or bodily way. More than eleven Phi and many other resources of various kinds would be in position and awaiting his incursion, in whatever form it might take. It was time for the ancient legend to play out and finally come to an end. But they realized the monster might know a few things that no one else did, and so the outcome of what would happen on this day was not a foregone conclusion. It was still possible that another great loss could be experienced, and more than one royal funeral would have to be held during this same week.

The classrooms were empty. The administrative offices were, too. The entire staff, apart from palace guards, gardeners, drivers, and a few crucial assistants, had the day off. Khalid had been asked to spend the day at the Adi house with both his sons, who worked as chefs in the palace kitchen, where they would be protected by a security detail that had been increased for the occasion.

Walid and Mafulla were walking down the hall at a good pace. "So, we get to guard your mom," Mafulla said. He added, "And that feels deeply right to me."

"Yeah, it does to me, too," Walid replied.

Mafulla then remarked, "I'm glad we didn't get split up this time."

"I think the king understands how we work," Walid explained.

"Yeah, and yet—go figure—he still lets us do things together," Mafulla said and turned to his friend, doing his best to punctuate his words with the tried and true double eyebrow jump.

"Ah, to hear the sound of sweet Mafoolery in the air," Walid commented, and then smiled. "Are you worried?"

"Yeah, of course. I hope you are."

The prince let out a big breath and said, "Yes. Good. Me too. But the king would not approve."

"Well then, maybe we're just highly concerned, with a twinge of very serious heebie-jeebies. And that's Ok, right? The king's never spoken out explicitly against the heebie-jeebies. And, I mean, this guy's legendary," Mafulla explained.

"Yeah, well, but so are we."

"Ha! Good point. I just hope our legend is more justified than his. I mean, the nickname itself sort of gets to me: The Monster. That doesn't make it sound like a trivial challenge."

"Yeah, 'The Monster' is a pretty scary nickname."

"I'd feel a lot better if the ancient legend referred to him as "The Cream Puff," or "Snuggles," or "The Weakling.""

Walid had to laugh at that. But he also said, "Hey, it isn't just us defending the fort today, cowboy."

"True, and I have to keep reminding myself of that, but if the situation gets bad, we could end up all alone with you-know-who and be forced to rely on our wits."

"That could be bad," Walid said, playing along.

"Yeah. I think I'm at least one wit short of what's needed."

"At least," Walid agreed. "But another thing for us to remember is that, with the king around, we're never really alone."

"All right, I'll go with that insight."

"You should."

"Yeah. In fact, this little factoid will provide for today's perfect mantra: The king is really here. The king is really here. Whatever I might tend to fear, the king is really here."

"Not bad. Now, keep saying it until it governs your emotions."

"Good tip," Mafulla replied. And then a second later, he said, "Hey, do we know where the real Book of Phi and Ring of Phi and Stone are being kept today?"

"No, and I think the king wants it that way. You know, the most senior Phi can protect their thoughts and inner knowledge. They can totally shield what they know. We're not quite there yet."

"But it's possible that some of that stuff is in your mom's suite, right?"

"Yeah, the king asked dad to hide some of it in an old medical bag, back a while ago."

"So, and I'm just trying to get my bearings here," Mafulla said, "it's possible that the famous monster guy could end up coming through our door to get something he really wants."

"True. But, remember."

"Yeah, the king is really here, and there, and everywhere," Mafulla said. And he somehow both grimaced and grinned at the same time.

When they got to the outer door of Bhati's suite, the door was ajar. Walid's heart rate went up instantly. He looked at Mafulla and slowly opened the door a bit farther. The anteroom was empty. No one was at the desk. And the inner door was completely open. But then, they were the most surprised by what was now in the doorway.

"What in the world is this?"

"Come in," a voice called out.

"Kissa?"

"Yes. Come in. How do you like our new decorations?" She stepped into view.

Walid and Mafulla still stood in the anteroom, staring at what had caught them completely off guard. "What is this?" Walid said.

"Beads," Kissa answered. "Glass beads—a whole curtain of them in really nice colors, nearly ceiling to floor. Aren't they beautiful?"

Long strings of multi-colored beads reached from the top of the doorframe all the way to the floor, across the entire opening, and four or five layers thick. "Yeah. Very ... different," Walid said.

"Yes, indeed," Mafulla agreed. "Belly dancer beads."

"What?"

"It's a common term for those beaded curtains that they have in places where belly dancers perform."

"How would you know that?"

"I hear things. I'm well informed." Mafulla did a facial expression of superior knowledge. But Walid looked skeptical.

"Come on through," Hasina said from inside, as she now also appeared on the other side of the door.

Kissa added, "Just stick your arms out in front of you and part the new curtain of beads. "Oh, but first, close that outer door, Ok?"

"Sure," Walid said, and tentatively swam his arms through the loudly tinkling beads. Mafulla followed close behind.

"That's something I've only seen in movies," Mafulla said.

"And it's very clever, don't you think?" Kissa said. "Even genius."

Walid replied, "What do you mean?"

"Well, in case the lovely Hasina's planning to do a dance for us all, the mood is already set," Mafulla said.

"Ha!" Hasina said. "You've apparently seen far too many movies."

"So what's it for?" Walid asked again.

"It's a warning device," Kissa said. "Remember, invisible isn't the same as intangible. If Santiago tries to come in to this room, the beads will announce his presence. He can't get by them or through them without moving them. We'll either hear them or see them move apart, or most likely, both, and then we'll know exactly where he is."

"Oh. Wow, that is clever," Mafulla said. "An invisible man detector."

"Yep, and a simple one," Kissa said. "The king's had them temporarily installed at crucial points around the palace, along with flour on the floor and sand and other things, here and there."

"Flour and sand?"

"Yeah, to show his footprints."

"Jeepers," Mafulla said. "How come none of that ever crossed my mind?"

"Wait," Walid said to Kissa. "Out of kindness, maybe you shouldn't answer that."

"Hardee-Har," Mafulla responded.

"How's my mom?" Walid asked Kissa.

"I think she's fine, but a little worried about the man who killed your dad being allowed onto the palace grounds and even into the building itself today. I think she has total trust for whatever the king is doing, but it still uneasy about letting the monster into the house at all."

"I can certainly understand that."

"But the king has a plan," Hasina said.

"Yeah, fortunately."

"And the king is really here," Mafulla added.

"What?" Kissa and Hasina both looked puzzled.

"Oh, that's Maffie's little mantra today, reminding himself that wherever we are, the king is with us, in spirit and power."

"Oh, yes—very good. So's mom."

"That's also very reassuring," Walid said.

Mafulla looked puzzled and said, "Yeah, but my mantra could get way too complicated. 'The king and Hoda, Layla, Masoon, and Hamid are really here.' See what I mean? It's kind of a tongue twister."

Hasina smiled and just shook her head in the 'here-we-go-again' mode of nonverbal commentary. Walid paused for a second at this point and said, "So, what are we supposed to do?"

"You're the prince," Kissa answered. "You tell us."

"Oh, Ok. So, where's mom now?"

"In the back, resting."

"Good. So, why don't you girls go back there with her, as something like a second line of defense? Mafulla and I can stay up front here and be the first line."

"I'm not sure about that," Kissa replied, with great kindness in her voice.

"Why?"

"I think we should let her rest. If we go back there now, or soon, then first of all, we'll disturb her. And she probably won't get any more rest. You know how she is. She'll want us to feel welcome and she'll talk to us. And I think she needs whatever rest she can get right now. Plus, maybe we should be up here with you guys, to prop up and sort of strengthen the first line of defense."

"Ok, Ok, that's a plan. If by some remote chance, our problem man comes in here, he'll have all four of us to contend with at the same time. United we stand, and everything."

"That sounds good," Kissa responded.

"Yeah. It sort of sounds better than my first plan." In response, Kissa just smiled.

Down the street from the side gate into the palace grounds, the entrance normally used by service vehicles, a bread delivery truck was slowing down and pulling into a line of other cars and trucks waiting to be waved through the gate. Some were being sent away for now, it seemed, and yet others were being let in. As the bread truck slowed more and came to a stop, its left back door opened ever so slightly and quietly and Miguel Abad wiggled in, and then the door closed softly behind him. Santiago stood there near the rear of the truck, unseen. And as it now crept forward again toward the guard who was speaking to each driver, he walked along beside it, on the side opposite the gatehouse. Three other guards stood back a few feet, watching each of the arriving vehicles.

When the truck pulled up to the gatehouse, the main guard spoke for a few seconds to the usual driver, a man they knew well, and the truck crept forward, but only several feet, so that the back bumper was now even with the head guard. The man pulled open both rear doors and peered into the back area of the truck. Miguel thought he was hidden, but not well enough. "Hey! Who are you? What are you doing back here? Come out immediately," the guard shouted, while pulling a service revolver from his holster. Two of the other three guards reacted immediately and converged on the back of the truck. They jumped in and pulled out the now struggling Miguel, who fought with all his might.

"It's not me you want!" he shouted. "It's Juan Santiago, who's with me! You have to believe me! He's invisible and standing somewhere next to this truck! He's a murdering criminal on his way to harm the king! Use your arms and you can touch him! Then shoot him! Don't give him a chance to use his special powers!"

The guards looked very skeptical and then suspicious, but the two who had just climbed into the back of the truck now jumped back out, once Miguel was shackled, and began to move their arms around in front of them, as if feeling the air. And yet, just that second, the still struggling Miguel turned red and gagged, and before anyone could notice it happening, a hidden knife was pulled from his belt and used to slit his throat. He dropped as the knife did, and that unleashed a tumultuous cacophony of loud chaos around the gate. A fourth guard still manning the gatehouse began shouting for reinforcements and five or six uniformed guards came running from various directions. The gate partly opened, the men ran out to the truck, and Juan Osvaldo Santiago slipped onto the grounds unseen, barely dodging everyone by the power of the magic ring.

Within seconds, the guards were all fanning out now inside the gate, searching the air for resistance, waving their arms and swinging police batons in front of them. Santiago laughed to himself at what he saw as the clumsiness of their pathetic efforts, and he walked quickly toward the palace. He found himself gloating already. These pathetic primitives couldn't stop him. The highly advanced traitor couldn't, either. No one can now, he thought triumphantly.

He felt a slight but ever so faint wave of dizziness as he walked onward. His skin began to itch, first on his arms and neck. But again, it was so minor as to almost avoid his conscious notice. He did feel it, but then brushed it off. When grabbing Miguel's knife, he had reached around the man's clothing, and may have touched something that was producing a minor allergic reaction. He didn't normally come into physical contact with his men or even get very close to them, if he could help it—the dirty vermin that he really considered them all to be. And this was the reason, he thought to himself. An itch, a passing light-headedness, and a vague sense of nausea only came over him momentarily as he continued toward the back of The Golden Palace.

He had no idea what the king had brought onto the palace grounds and had been hiding in a large garden shed until the alert had been issued at the gate. But now, completely unnoticed by Santiago, more than a dozen men had begun to come out of that shed, some distance away, and they walked quickly in groups toward the three gates of the palace compound, pushing in wheelbarrows hundreds of large bags of sand. If Santiago had turned around, he would have seen the iron bars of the side gate now closed and four of the men pouring and spreading sand across the entrance road that he had just used. It was this that was already causing, even at a distance, the reaction he was feeling. He, of course, had no idea that if he got any closer to the source of his problem, the mildly uncomfortable sensations that he had felt just now would become exponentially more severe, and then completely debilitating.

The sand had been brought into Cairo by military trucks the previous day as an insurance measure. And now it was part of a strategic plan. What Santiago didn't know was that every possible exit from the palace grounds was being surrounded by a line of sand that had spent years, and in most cases, many centuries in contact with the base of the Great Sphinx on the Giza plateau, a short distance from the capital city. And, according to legend, this was the one place in Egypt, or for that matter the world, where the monster could never go. The king knew that there must be a reason, and it seemed logical that there would be consequences if the monster got near the place, or perhaps even close to anything from the place. So now, sand from that sacred spot had been brought to him, to surround him. And it would likely act as a barrier better than any other wall or fortification that could ever be put into place. Normal men could walk on it. Phi could hold it in their hands and even feel a sense of serenity and positive power. But the monster alone could never come near it.

A slight line of this sand was going to be spread along the entire perimeter of the walls, once the gates had first been fortified with it. The king certainly could have had it put around the walls earlier and prevented Santiago from entering the grounds. But it was better to dictate as many of the terms of confrontation as possible. And with him inside the gates, the king's plan could now begin to unfold.

From Bancom to Naqid to Masoon, the report had just come in to the Ali's rooms that Santiago was currently on the palace grounds. The gardeners were doing their jobs. Everyone was in place. The king was speaking with Hoda.

Masoon came in from the anteroom and interrupted to say, "I'm sorry, Majesty, but word just arrived that he's here by way of the side gate. He entered apparently alone and unseen, having killed one of his own confederates who betrayed him at the gate."

"Yes," the king replied. "I felt the act of violence nearby, and I sense his presence not far away, but … but far less presence and power than I would have expected."

"Do you think he's somehow masking his incursion?"

"No, actually, I don't, beyond the obvious invisibility. I suspect that his recent choice of jewelry, his new ring, is having a wholly unanticipated side-effect."

"Indeed?"

"When Mafulla told us of Santiago's failed effort to kill or even injure Gimpy, I didn't want to rush to judgment. We've long known that the little dog is, in his own way, one of us."

"Yes, Majesty. You're right."

"That alone could have explained Santiago's failure."

"That was my first thought as well."

"But on further reflection, I believe there's more at work here and it's of great interest to understand."

"You think it's the ring?"

"Yes, I do."

"Why?

"Well, in the *Republic*, Glaucon talks about the ring as if he's convinced that anyone who wears it and uses it will be taken down to a state of amoral selfishness, something that he believes secretly characterizes every man, at his core. The ring strips away what he thinks are the only motivations we have to follow socially accepted rules, and it thereby removes any veneer of morality."

"Yes. I recall that part of the story," Masoon said.

"It may be that he was very wrong about what exactly the ring does, in order to attain its famous result."

Masoon quickly replied, "I've always been sure that his conclusions were wrong about how people would act if wearing such a ring. I know that his smug confidence about the universality of ungoverned behavior that would result from such a scenario was misplaced. He was way off in that belief."

"Yes, I'm quite confident you're right about that," the king responded. "But I believe there's also something more. As the philosophers say, we each have an essence, and various essential properties that constitute our core identity. And then around this core, during our lives, we grow to have vastly many other properties that are not essential to the precise individuals we are. They could have been different. In those ways, we could have been different. Perhaps a ring that can make a man's fundamentally inessential outward shell, or his precise physical body, disappear can also rid him of anything else he's acquired that's not essential, or deeply necessary to his basic humanity as an individual personal soul."

"What do you mean, Majesty? I'm not sure I quite follow you."

"Glaucon was probably right to believe that many people who do the right things mostly do them for the wrong reasons. Once those inessential reasons, desires and fears that are not intrinsically related to the actions in question, but are connected only with matters of discovery and punishment, are stripped away, something important happens. The wearer of the ring is reduced, not necessarily to amorality or immorality, as Glaucon claimed, but perhaps rather to his essential basic nature and its direct relationship with the moral or ethical, whatever that might be. And in that state, he has to grapple with moral considerations in a new way, not doing a calculus of costs and benefits, but basing his choices on his own sense of how he wants to live and what he wants to become. And if he doesn't truly accept the path of goodness, in his fundamental human nature, his conduct will show that."

"I can see that interpretation as a potentially deep reading of the ring story," Masoon commented.

"Yes, and this is where we get to what's of most interest to us now," the king commented. "The stripping away of inessentials, of everything not germane to the core of being human, and of anything not strictly necessary for being the human individual or soul that you most essentially are, could then by the same logic of reduction, eliminate any unnatural, supra-human powers, any augmentations of the merely human that might also have been accumulated in any way at all."

"Oh, I see what you're saying," Masoon responded with a tone of fascination. "So, perhaps, when someone like Santiago puts on the Ring of Gyges and uses it, it makes anything vanish from sight that's not essential to the human soul he is—his clothing, his skin, his hair, his particular anatomical organs, even the brain cells in his head."

"Yes."

"And along with all this, which makes for his invisibility, it causes certain other things to vanish or disappear as well—emotions, attitudes, thoughts, and powers that aren't a natural part of who he as a man is, at his essential core."

"That's right."

"And so, all the extraordinary spiritual power he may have accumulated over these decades through unnatural means also begins to disappear, or becomes invisible, or somehow inaccessible, or—to put it another way—unavailable to him."

"Yes, that's exactly what I suspect. But it may not totally eliminate his power all at once, as it does his visibility. It may, in a sense, take longer to reduce or eliminate such arduously acquired extra baggage of the spirit. Perhaps it gradually diminishes at least the very upper reaches of what's been accumulated, and then goes deeper."

"So then, he may get spiritually weaker with time—weaker in his extra powers, the longer he uses the ring."

"Exactly."

"In this way, the ring that he thought would give him extra power will actually give him less, taking away much that he would otherwise have."

"That's correct. It's an unexpected turnaround. And, of course, that's the way it works with many artificial things that our fantasies tell us will bring us great good and pleasure, and power, and status. Those very things in reality can have the opposite effect, actually reducing and diminishing us in ways we never anticipated."

"And as a result," Masoon said, "We have an adversary now who, as long as he remains in the power of the ring and stays invisible, is also becoming only a shadow of his former, much enhanced self. So, the ring is reducing his power."

"That's correct. And at some point, he may realize that the source of his invisibility is diminishing him in these other ways. So I would expect him to reverse the ring when he plans to act decisively, and become fully visible once more."

"Will he then confront us with his full power? Will it come back as completely as his visibility?"

"We'll see. I have an inkling about that, as well, but I'm not yet sure of the answer."

Naqid came into the room. "Your Majesty, the enemy has entered the palace through the back doors and has apparently made his way toward the main staircase."

"The men saw the doors open?"

"Yes, and there are now footprints."

"So that part of the plan is working."

"Yes, Majesty, he's leaving footprints on the darkened flour the men had spread on the floor. But because of the low lighting you also suggested, he may not himself have noticed the tracks he made, or realized what's being done."

"Excellent. So, he's coming up the main stairs?"

"Yes, that's what we think. His tracks went toward the basement door initially, but then stopped and turned. He must somehow know that the basement room was a trick and a trap."

"That's fine," the king said. "We're prepared for that. Please release our special guest with instructions to walk toward that staircase."

"Certainly, Your Majesty."

35

SURPRISES

SANTIAGO HAD INDEED GOTTEN INSIDE THE PALACE, AND from Muriel's recent reports, he knew where the basement door was located. He headed straight there, but when he came close to his intended destination, he felt an odd sense that it was a trap. It was almost like he could discern at a distance the souls of many strong people waiting for him there. Even with his reduced powers, he was alert to trouble and leery of what he felt. This could not be right for him.

The surprising problem was that his inner mental vision of what was ahead was not clear, and that was both new and unexpected. But the vague warning he felt was enough to bring him up short. He then concentrated with all his power, seeking to determine where he should go instead. And in his efforts to probe into the minds of anyone in the palace who might know where the things were that he was determined to possess, he found a weakness. He discovered and accessed a shadow of information, unprotected. As a result, he changed direction that very instant, looking for the nearest staircase. Rather than going down for the treasure he sought, he would have to go up. This was also a surprise, but then he expected a few surprises along the way. These people were not stupid. They were fairly clever and had some measure of power.

But precisely how much, he had no idea. He didn't care, though, because he had supreme confidence in his own access to power, when it could be properly unleashed and directed toward those who might dare to stand in his way.

He was especially surprised at how empty and quiet the palace seemed. But he had heard it was a day of official mourning for the member of the royal family that he had so recently dispatched into the next world. So, it could be that everyone had been given the day off. And yet, where was the king? If he were here, then there would surely be more soldiers around, more guards, and even more attendants. Maybe he wasn't in the palace at all, but elsewhere. Perhaps it was the perfect day to come and steal great treasure from the place. Santiago smiled. He felt a little giddy. It could be that the entire universe was finally conspiring in favor of the ascendancy to ultimate power that this day might bring.

He saw a large staircase up ahead. Quickening his pace, he began to climb the stairs and felt himself closing in on his goal. Then, near the top, he experienced a surprise of such a magnitude that it disoriented him momentarily and caused him to lose his grip on the bannister rail he had been holding.

He said, "What?" He stopped at the top step, with his right hand now again on the railing to catch his balance. Forgetting his need for stealth, he spoke above a whisper to the figure walking toward him on the second floor. "You!" The woman stopped in her tracks and looked all around her. "You!" He nearly spit out the word with a tone of total disgust. Her face grew alarmed.

"Who is it?" She trembled.

"Your true master, you miserable traitor!"

"What? Where are you?"

"I'm invisible for now, but I can see you quite well here in the palace and home of my enemies! You deceiver! You've helped lay a trap for me! You've betrayed me!"

"No!" She looked about frantically and then tried to focus on the origin of the sound in the air, maybe ten feet in front of her and at the top of the stairs.

"Liar! Turncoat! I've caught you!"

"No! I've done everything as you said! You told me to come here to be with you!"

"Lies! Pathetic, stupid lies! You're really with the king! You have nothing better than that to say for yourself, you snake?"

"I've done as you said!"

"You've done no such thing!"

"You sent word of a new plan and I obeyed!"

"I did no such thing!"

"The boys told me!"

"What boys?"

"The boys you sent! I swear!"

"I won't listen to any more of this nonsense! No one betrays me!" And as he said that, he lunged toward her. She could hear the rustle of his clothing and smell the sharp report of weeks in the desert, and then feel the shock of his grip as he physically grabbed her. He pulled her and threw her toward the top of the long marble staircase. She screamed and flew over the first few steps and her left foot caught the red-carpeted tread on the third or fourth step down. And then her arm hit the bannister and she tumbled out-of-control, arms flailing, legs giving way. Finally, she hit hard and collapsed on the cold stone and went limp as her bruised and beaten body rolled to a stop, arms and legs akimbo, her head twisted grotesquely on her neck, unmoving.

When she and Shamilar were little girls, their parents doted on them, wanting only the best for them in their lives. Their father was a good man, a cloth merchant who made a decent living. Their mother kept the house running. The two of them had met years before in the marketplace. Then, for weeks afterwards, they seemed to run into each other again and again. Finally, a courtship started. And when they eventually announced an engagement, all their friends rejoiced.

The early days of their marriage brought hard work, but also a measure of bliss. The ordinary daily problems we all face became easier for them to bear and to solve. The small joys that were always available around them became more noticeable and entered their hearts more easily. When their first child came, not quite a year into their new life partnership, a happiness they never could have imagined accompanied the newborn. Muriel was named for her grandmother on her mother's side, and was a beautiful baby who soon became a sweet toddler and then a delightful and kind small child. Her love of music was clear from a very young age. When her mother sang, she smiled and gurgled, and soon sang along. A sister quickly joined their little family unit, and Shamilar was also everything they could have hoped for. Seeming more serious than her older sister, she was nonetheless a fun loving child, and she appeared to be endlessly entertained by her sibling, who was always performing for her and making her laugh. Their parents were determined to raise them in a happy and healthy environment, and prepare them for a wonderful adolescence and adulthood.

Muriel had begged for music lessons. In particular, she loved the piano and wanted to play. It was a sacrifice, but her parents were dedicated to developing the talents of their two girls. A few years later, the family was blessed with a son. At that point, Shamilar became a little mother to her small brother, rehearsing for the role she most hoped to play in the future. Muriel seemed, by contrast, to be jealous of the attention the new baby was receiving from everyone in the family and throughout the surrounding neighborhood.

It's often hard for a firstborn to accept what feels like a demotion to a less than favored status. But Muriel was not unkind to her brother. She just often did little things to keep her distance, to the extent that she could. And she tried even harder to please her mother and father with her accomplishments at school, in her music lessons, and at home. Every simple drawing became a masterpiece to show her parents. Their attention was more important than ever. She basked in their praise and coveted more. A need began to grow in her soul. And because this artificially felt need got out of control, she now lay broken on a cold marble step. There were so many steps along the way that she could have taken instead of the ones she chose. But little by little, her choices led to this.

The scream brought palace guards into the area, raking the air around them with long rifles. Two appeared from upstairs and six more from below. Santiago realized that they had clearly heard the rumor of invisibility because of the weak and traitorous Miguel. Or, so he thought. First Miguel, and now Muriel. The monster was merely confirmed in his long held belief that ordinary people were not to be trusted, ever, but merely used as long as necessary and then consigned to their proper fate. He quickly moved away from the stairs, evading the guards again, and he silently searched for the private quarters of the king.

Santiago smiled. "This is what I was born to do. This is where I was born to be," he said to himself. "This is the brink of my fine destiny and its greatness."

Bhati had fallen asleep on top of her bed, over the covers. Her body and soul were so tired, so worn out, so utterly drained of energy that she slid down into the deepest sleep of her life. And she dreamed. She was on a camel in the desert and there was an oasis just ahead of her. As she approached, a breeze began to blow out of the north, a cooling breeze in the heat of the late afternoon. She felt some sort of anticipation or sense of expectation, without knowing why, or of what.

There were beautiful trees at the edge of the oasis and they were now swaying in the light wind. Through the trees, she could see someone in the distance approaching. It was a tall man wearing white. She felt a sense of positive energy. As he got closer, she experienced a deep stirring in her heart. Then she saw! It was Rumi! He waved to her with a big smile on his face. She couldn't believe what she was seeing. She waved back and signaled the camel to kneel so that she could slide down and put her feet on the ground and run to her husband, as he also began to run to her.

"You're here!" she shouted with immeasurable gladness.

"Yes! I'm here and I'm so thrilled to see you like this!" he answered.

She began to cry, and at first couldn't speak more. Then she said, "I didn't think I would ever see you again, except in photographs, and in that hazy way our memories have of presenting us with those we love after they've … gone." The exuberance that she now felt in her heart could barely be contained in words and gestures as she got to him and touched him and felt his solid, true reality, and embraced him and squeezed him against her, while he was doing exactly the same.

"I'm so sorry," she said.

"No, I'm sorry," he replied. "I wish I could have saved you some other way."

"Walid tried," she said.

"Yes. I saw. I had to intervene for you both. I had to try, as well."

"You did. You saved us."

"I know. I know and I'm glad, but I'm so very sorry to be away."

She held him at arm's length now, squeezing his hands with hers, and she looked deep into his eyes and said, "In waking life, I can no longer touch you and hear you. But, sometimes, I think I feel you near me, very near."

"I'm closer than your skin," he replied. "I'm with you all the time."

"Can you see us?"

"Yes, and feel you, and sense what you think and feel and do."

"Is it?" She stopped in the midst of her question.

"Yes, it's everything good that you can imagine, and so much more."

"What's it like? What do you do?"

"Normal words can't say these things. Our words were made for the part of it all where you and Walid still live. But here, those words fall far short. They can't begin to describe this next adventure, like a baby can't understand the things of adulthood. You must have trust and faith that all will be well beyond your wildest hopes. We're kings and queens in a new way. We're all kings and queens, and there are no enemies, and no revolutions. No one is inferior. No one is evil. But there are things to do and ways to grow and so much more than you can imagine."

"You do well with these words that fall short."

He laughed. "Yes. I try, but I know that the words only spark and can't convey what my heart can share with yours."

"Please, show me something to soothe me and give me peace."

They looked into each other's eyes and Rumi took her hand. He led her into the trees and along a shining path in the sand. And up ahead she could see a sparkling pool of water and small houses all around. And there seemed to be music in the air. But if she had been asked, she would have said that it was a music she could feel, more than hear. They walked up to the edge of the pool, and it was still and clear. And Rumi said, "Look into it, my special Bhati."

And she did. And she saw herself and him reflected in it, and then she saw her parents and his parents and some other older relatives and a few friends and former neighbors from Dromeda who had gone on many years ago, most at advanced ages. And yet they were all now young and strong and they looked happy. And then, what she saw, she also felt in the depth of her spirit, and it washed over her with soothing waves of bliss that were somehow both in her and over her and moving through her at the same time. And she suddenly thought, "I want around me now a mountain and a river and snow on top of the mountain." And then in the next moment, there it all was, laid out before her and on all sides of her. She was not now looking into the pool at the oasis but standing beside a fast moving river and looking up to the white cap of a high rugged mountain that rose up in front of her, covered at its peak with snow.

She was stunned and in awe of what she saw. Then, she said, "I want the seashore now," and in the next blink of an eye, she was standing on soft sand next to the bubbling foam of newly arrived warm ocean water. And she could look out and see the next waves and whitecaps coming toward her in rows. Many shells were on the beach all around her feet and seagulls barked their happy cries into the air. And there were birds in the distance circling something farther down the beach. And she was stirred with a need to walk across the sand in that direction. Then, as she did, she had a sense of mission come over her and a feeling of purpose and meaning. Rumi was with her, but now he just watched her, as he slowly followed behind.

She walked and walked. She looked back at him and he smiled

and she continued on. And then, forty or fifty feet away, she could now see a body curled up on the sand at the edge of the water, without movement or signs of life. It was a woman, about her own age, or a bit older. She was partially covered by the sand.

Bhati walked up closer. She recognized this person in the next moment as a lady she had met recently and only once. It was Shamilar's older sister, Muriel. And she looked like she was asleep. But bruises were all over her body—terrible, dark bruises. Bhati bent down over her and said her name. But there was no response. She reached out and touched her shoulder and spoke her name again, and her eyes opened and she looked startled and then scared.

"Bhati? Bhati Shabeezar?"

"Muriel, what are you doing here?"

"I'm so sorry," she said.

"What?"

"I'm so sorry. I was so wrong. It was all so wrong."

"What was wrong, my dear?"

Muriel slowly sat up and looked around and then began to cry. She said, "I let my heart run wild and my fantasies enslave me. I wanted so much and I didn't know who to trust."

"We all make mistakes," Bhati told her in response. "But mistakes can be corrected."

"It's too late, now," Muriel said. And she sobbed.

"It's never too late," Bhati reassured her with a sense of certainty that seemed to come into her from beyond her. "The spirit is the means of transformation, flowing from the source of all. You have all the power it takes to own the life you've had, and now reject the bad choices and accept for good the transformation that you need. You can change."

"It can't be true," Muriel said, and her weeping grew softer.

"It is true. And it's beautiful. And it's good. It's the connection, the unity that you need to feel a part of, if you'll just release all the bad and embrace the good that's freely offered to you."

"I want what I've not allowed myself to have. I no longer want what I've so wrongly chased, but what you're describing to me."

And Bhati saw the bruises on Muriel's body become lighter and smaller and, within seconds, just vanish.

While Bhati was experiencing all this, Walid was in his mother's front room, looking out the window to the palace grounds below. Mafulla walked up to him and said, "Do you see anything?"

"Not much, just a few gardeners spreading sand around the inside of the wall."

"No invisible bad guys?"

"None that I can see."

"Good answer."

Kissa and Hasina were sitting on the large sofa in the room. Kissa said, both to Hasina and to the boys, "The only thing that bothers me a little bit is that we're separated from mom and the other Phi and don't even know where they are."

"Some are in the king's rooms," Wald answered.

"Yeah, and still, remember: The king is really here," Mafulla said, and Walid had to smile.

"What's that?" Kissa said and turned her head slightly to the side.

"What?" Walid responded, looking puzzled.

"Very faint ... at a distance—is it music?"

"I don't hear any ... wait ... yeah, maybe ... barely."

"Beautiful music," Hasina nearly whispered, "far away."

Mafulla listened and then whispered, in response, "This is a crazy surprise. I wonder what's going on."

"Shh." Walid held his right index finger to his lips and stood motionless and silent. They all listened, concentrating their whole attention. The music seemed to grow louder and closer.

Finally, Mafulla whispered, "Ok, this makes no sense at all."

"What do you mean?" Hasina asked, also in the most hushed of voices.

"We're on the verge of a potentially violent confrontation with a really bad character, and beautiful music begins to play in the palace?"

"I agree," Walid said. "This is too strange."

"But it's really nice," Kissa said. "It's strange and wonderful."

"Yeah, and why? What could possibly be going on?" Walid was clearly thinking through all the scenarios he could imagine for what this could be, and any reason that it might be happening. And he was doing all this as quickly as he could.

"It's getting louder. And it sounds like … an exceptionally good string quartet. Where would they be?" Kissa walked toward the door.

"Should we go look?" Hasina asked, and she also took a couple of steps in the direction of the glass bead curtain. And then she paused.

"Wait, let me," Mafulla said and walked by the girls, carefully and slowly parting the curtain of tinkling beads.

Walid took a couple of steps in the same direction and paused and said, "Remember the Triple Double."

"Oh, yeah."

Hasina then whispered, "Prepare, perceive; anticipate, avoid; concentrate, and control."

"I got it," Mafulla whispered back. "We're in the perceive part." He stepped into the anteroom and got right up against the outer door, and then opened it ever so slightly in order to peek out down the hall in the direction from which the music seemed to be coming. He scrutinized the hallway for no more than a second, and then quickly closed the door and now locked it. Parting the beads again, he came back into the room and said, "Well, I couldn't see anything at all."

"Nothing?"

"Just an empty hall."

Hasina said, "It sure sounds like there are musicians down the hallway, and not far away—somewhere near the king's rooms."

"Yeah, but the king wouldn't do something like this. He wouldn't surprise us like this, not now, without preparing us and letting us know what's going on."

Walid said, "Come back into the room, away from the door for a minute." And they all followed him back into the main sitting room. He added, "I need to think for a second about this music."

Mafulla said, "I have a strange feeling that it's all inside our heads, and the apparent direction and location are just part of the trick."

"That's spooky. Do you think it's from Santiago?" Hasina asked, with a look of apprehension on her face.

"Yeah, absolutely" Mafulla said, as there was a sudden, loud BOOM and the locked outer door they just left seemed as if it had been kicked in. The wooden door swung violently and fast on its hinges and then hit hard and bounced off the wall behind it as the music swelled to a much greater and almost overwhelming volume, as if an orchestra was with them in the room, playing at full force.

The adrenalin jolt that shot through each of the young Phi was instant and, for a moment, both unnerving and confusing. Their bodies were reacting before their minds could wrap around what had just happened. Walid grabbed Kissa, as Mafulla did the same for Hasina, and they all jumped back from anywhere near the beaded curtain.

In the next second, the four of them pulled out the service revolvers they had been given for any potential confrontation, as they continued to back farther away from the now open outer door and get ever closer to the wall behind them. All eyes were on the beads. Then the window behind them popped loudly with a cracking sound, as if a bullet had shot through it. They all turned around instantly to look. Walid lifted his left hand up in an instinctively protective movement, at first squinting beyond his hand and toward the window. But as he looked, he suddenly noticed out of the corner of his eye the shiny back of his Reverso watch, which had been flipped over in anticipation of any action. And in its nearly mirrored surface, around the engravings, he could see the beaded curtain now behind him silently part, as if on its own.

36

THE CONFRONTATION

"THE INNER DOOR!" WALID SAID AND TURNED, PULLING OUT his gun and aiming it back and around toward the now reclosing bead curtain.

"I see it," Mafulla said, as he also twisted around. Kissa and Hasina at the same moment caught a glimpse and began backing up more and to the side, getting as far from the door and the beads as they could.

"Show yourself!" Walid commanded.

"Certainly." The word came out of nowhere, as far as they could tell. Then, in the next instant, Juan Osvaldo Santiago stood in front of them, fully and clearly visible, with a sneering smile across his face.

The boys raised their guns at him, preparing to fire. "Who are you?" Walid asked, in a mental fog of sudden confusion. It was the ring. The man just laughed in a cold and evil way.

Walid hesitated for a second and then, as if through a mist of fog, began to remember everything that had just happened, and said, "Are you Juan Santiago?"

"Yes, indeed, I am."

"The real Santiago?"

"Yes. I'm happy to say that I'm as real as I can get, which is too bad for you."

"How ... did you get in here?" Mafulla asked, and as soon as the words were out of his mouth, he instantly recalled what they had just seen and heard.

"I walked. And I used a few simple tricks."

"What tricks?"

"Well, I hope you enjoyed the music. It certainly did the job. I found the occupied room. Oh and, by the way, your little toys won't work against me, I'm afraid—your little guns."

"You have no power over us," Mafulla answered, glancing down momentarily at the revolver in his hand.

"You're sadly, pitifully, dangerously, and soon, fatally wrong."

"You can't even hurt a lame old dog," Mafulla said, to taunt him.

"Oh, you know of that?" Santiago chuckled and said, "Well, I hope you won't allow yourself to get too excited about it. It was just because I was, at the time of the unpleasant little bite, completely invisible. I believe it's my new ring, unfortunately. It gives, and it takes away. What can you do? But when I have invisibility, I don't need all the other powers. And when I want them available, all I have to do is turn the ring in the right way back around and allow myself to be seen—which is good, anyway, don't you think? I'd much rather let people like you see me kill them. It makes it all so much more deeply satisfying."

"You're an idiot," Mafulla said, and added, "a sleazy, stupid, pathetic and psychotic fool."

"No, no, you'll soon realize that, quite to the contrary, I'm a genius," the man replied. "You'll come to this conclusion when, very shortly, I see you see me see you soil yourself in abject fear, and you'll be the pathetic and foolish one. It will all be wonderfully worthwhile."

Walid spoke up at that point and said, "The only thing you're going to see in the next few minutes is us taking you into custody for murder."

Santiago laughed again suddenly and loudly. "I'm amazed that anyone can be so wrong about something of such great importance. But, rather than to continue insulting you like you deserve, and listen to your puerile attempts to return the offense, I would suggest that you give me a bag or box of special things that are here somewhere in a closet, I believe. There's a ring, in particular, another ring that I want, and if you can manage to give it to me within the next sixty seconds, you may be granted the freedom to live, perhaps even to see a new day. I can't promise anything, and even if I did, keeping promises bores me, but I might spare you all for an act of simple acquiescence and quick obedience. It would charm me."

"I have another idea," Walid said. "Why don't you get down on your knees right now and put your hands on top of your head?"

"Oh? Are you still angry that I hired some dimwitted street thugs to shoot and kill your precious father? Don't worry. They didn't really cost me much—well, not in the grand scheme of things. It was a good value. I like to rid the world of useless vermin, even when I have to pay slightly worse vermin to do the job." Santiago laughed again, a sound without mirth or true pleasure behind it, but only a perverse counterfeit glee in the deeds he was planning.

"Don't you dare speak of my father like that."

"I'll speak in any way I please. I take orders from no man, or little boy." Santiago paused and then said, "I know who you are, and I know who you think you are, and it will not be healthy for you to speak to me in such a way again. Once is entertaining, but twice can be deadly—for either you, or someone else here that you may care about deeply and pathetically."

"This is your last chance." Walid spoke with great inner agitation, but also firm confidence.

"Oh, well. Let's see how tough you are when you're watching your pretty little girlfriend die an agonizing death in front of you. It might at least be amusing." Santiago held his left hand up a bit and spread his fingers apart, sort of pointing his outstretched fingertips toward Kissa. And she immediately gasped and then grimaced as if she was in sudden, great pain, and she groaned.

"Ooooh!" she muttered, and dropped her gun lower, as she raised her other hand to her head and staggered, bending over at the waist.

"Kissa!" Hasina called out.

Santiago laughed again and held his hand out farther toward her, saying, "Now, it will become much more fun to watch!"

"No." A voice rang out over his last word, coming from back behind the young people and to the side. It was Bhati, walking out of her bedroom, saying, "No. I must interrupt."

"What?" He turned his attention away from Kissa, and she gasped again and began breathing fast, bent over and still in great pain. Everyone froze in place, stunned at Bhati's sudden appearance. And she then addressed Santiago with no apparent fear at all.

"I just spoke to your former friend, Muriel, and she wants you to know that she's fine. But of course, I use the word 'friend' loosely."

The man completely stopped what he had been doing, lowered his hand, and said, "What did you say?"

"Muriel is fine now."

"Muriel's dead."

"You don't understand what I'm saying to you. I just now, in the past couple of minutes, spoke to her. She's fine."

"I threw her down the stairs. She's dead on the steps."

"Oh, I know what you did. I know everything you've done. And you'll be much better off now to stop and listen, and let us explain to you why and how you're wrong in what you're currently doing and thinking. That way, there's still time. You can save yourself."

Santiago smiled. "I'm afraid that, now, you'll have to be the next one dead. And no one can save you, not even your mouthy little child here." The monster now lifted his hand, fingers spread wide toward Walid's mother, and in the next moment, a barrage of gunshots exploded in the room. Walid shot, and Mafulla, and Hasina, and finally, Kissa, standing upright again and holding her revolver with both hands. As soon as her gun fired, Walid got off a second shot, as did Mafulla. Santiago, as they expected, used a form of extended proprioception and physical evasion, but it fell short, and he was slammed back against the wall. His right hand jerked up to his left shoulder and then away, and he looked in shock at blood all over his hand. His upper hip, or lower side on the right was also showing blood.

"What?"

All four Phi suddenly bore down on him with the full power of their minds. And now, aware of what was happening, the king and Hoda and Layla did the same thing from where they were in the king's sitting room, mere moments before they would rush down to Bhati's suite. Masoon and Hamid instantly ran down the hall to her door and came in, nearly flying through the glass bead curtain. Santiago lashed out at them with a blast of force they both felt as it hit them, but that they then instantly deflected with only moderate effort. Their fast and aggressive assault, by contrast, could not be avoided.

The monster didn't expect to be met with real power from these new foes that he knew nothing about. They walked up to him from both sides and stared into his eyes. Masoon pulled a large curved knife from his belt. But he didn't use it. He focused all the considerable power available to him on the mind and soul of his adversary, as did Hamid. Walid, Mafulla, Kissa, and Hasina also joined in. The room seemed to grow darker. But it was still daylight through the windows. Santiago resisted as fiercely as he could. It took all the power he had available to him, but he was somehow barely managing to hold back the mental assault that was now nearly crushing him.

He could hardly think. His mind was more darkened than the room. But one thought broke through: "The ring. It's the ring!" he said to himself, and twisted it off his finger with what seemed to be the last thin sliver of physical power left to him, shoving it into a pocket. And at that moment, his side and shoulder wounds from the bullets slowly began to close. The bleeding stopped. His mind began to clear. Masoon grabbed his arm and jerked it behind him. But then, the great warrior gave out a loud shout, as if of sharp pain. And yet, the surprise did not deter his forceful hold.

Walid looked around and saw to his immense surprise that the furniture in the room was beginning to move slightly to one side, and then, before he could say more than, "Look out!" it all began to rise above the floor and rotate around the room. The various items moved slowly at first, and then faster, and faster, with lamps and carpets and vases and chairs and every other item in the room now up around their heads and beginning to spin faster. It was all like a huge tornado had fit into the space and was turning everything into a potentially lethal weapon. Bhati screamed out behind them as something almost hit her in the head, and then she fell to the floor. Hamid yelled out as if injured, and grabbed Santiago's other arm. Masoon, with a look now of pain on his face, clamped his hand over Santiago's throat and shoved him back toward the wall with a stunning force of physical power that could not be resisted. And then he hit the man, hard.

Santiago yelled in pain and ducked down and lashed out at Hamid. With his other hand, Masoon pushed his knife into Santiago's mid section, and the steel hurt him badly, but it would not fully penetrate his flesh. It was almost like a force field kept its point from completely piercing him. And, before Masoon could realize what was happening, the knife had somehow slid off Santiago and was headed straight for Hamid's side. But the doctor dodged it, as Masoon spun and aimed a mighty kick into the adversary's gut that connected, full force, and bounced him once more off the wall behind him. Santiago roared like a wild animal and the room became even darker. Masoon then hit him twice more, each time hard enough to kill a strong man instantly. And the monster fell to the floor. But he seemed to have an almost supernatural ability to rebound, and did something from the floor that made everyone momentarily freeze.

His eyes flashed brightly with an eerie light from somewhere beyond, and he shouted in a nearly strangled voice, "You all now die!"

And another voice, one familiar to everyone else in the midst of all this chaos calmly said, "No, just you." It was the king.

Mafulla yelled out, "The king is here!" And it was almost as if everyone lost consciousness for a mere split second, and there was movement and a rushing wind. And when Walid and Mafulla opened their eyes, they were on a shore, a beach, beside the sea. And Walid was dizzy. Mafulla's brain felt like it was full of thick mush. And Kissa and Hasina were right behind them, stunned and silent, and Bhati was lying there on the sand.

"Mom!" Walid shouted and ran for her.

"Bhati!" Kissa yelled and did the same.

After a moment that seemed like a minute, she stirred and looked up and said, "Children. I'm fine."

"Where are we?" Walid said, as he looked into her eyes.

"Where healing happens, I think," she said.

"Bhati! Friends!" An unfamiliar voice called out and everyone turned. It was Muriel al-Baki, Shamilar's sister, but looking strangely different. There was a glow about her.

"You," Walid said.

"Aunt Muriel—why?" Mafulla asked.

"Mafulla, my dear, I was so wrong," she said. "And I know now."

"Where are we?" Walid asked again in a spirit of confusion and almost panic, but this time to Muriel.

She pointed out to the horizon over the water and spoke in a haunting, almost musical voice and said mysteriously, "The Ocean … is the greatest of all bodies of water, because it's lower than all the rest. They pour themselves into it."

"What?" Mafulla replied.

"This is what I've learned," she replied. "And this is where you are—in a place of learning."

"But you were helping him," Mafulla said.

"Yes, but no longer. Now, I'm helping you," she responded. And at that last word, there was a rush again, nearly a roaring, and a sense of rain on their faces, and a movement of some sort, and they all felt that momentary lapse of conscious awareness once more. And they seemed to be off balance, and then it was as if the sun was bright on their faces and the wind was at their backs, and there was a great sound and a flash brighter than can be imagined, and then silence.

A loud wind howled outside the house where the rest of the Adi family was being guarded and kept safe. It boomed against the door and the walls. "Oh!" Shamilar exclaimed, and she stood up from where she had been sitting. "What is it?"

Shapur arose as well, and he said, "It's over."

"What?"

"It's over."

"What's over? What do you mean?"

"Santiago's gone."

"Are you sure?"

"Yes."

Just then, Reela came into the room from the back, and the front door opened. Badar Sakat said, "That was strange. Is everyone Ok?"

"Come in," Shapur said. "You and Mumar. Quickly."

Badar held open the door and said something outside it and Mumar followed him into the front room with a puzzled look, reflecting the expression on his brother's face. "It's over," Shapur repeated, now for everyone. "Santiago's gone. He's been defeated."

"What do you mean, gone?" Badar asked.

"He's no longer in this world," Shapur said.

"Are you sure?" Mumar asked.

"Yes, absolutely certain. I know it to be so."

"How?"

"The king," Reela said.

"Yes, the king," Shapur said, nodding his head. "But," he added, "there's other news that's not so … satisfying."

"Is Mafulla all right?" Shamilar asked quickly, with great concern.

"Yes, he's safe."

"What is it, then, my husband?"

"I'm afraid it's your sister."

"Muriel? What happened?"

"She's also gone." He walked over to Shamilar to put his hand on her arm. She looked uncomprehending.

"What do you mean?"

"Our Muriel had become confused, and was helping that man, Santiago, and in the end he turned on her."

She put her hands to her mouth and said, "Oh, no. Oh, my."

"He turned on her and pushed her down a long staircase in the palace."

"What was she … doing? But, is she … Ok?"

Reela spoke up and said, "We found out about her unfortunate allegiance and hoped that in the end we could help her escape it."

"Did he harm her?"

Shapur let out a big breath and said, with great kindness, "I'm afraid that he took her from this world."

"No!"

"Yes, sadly," Shapur said.

"She's … dead?"

"Yes, in the past hour, but she's in the next life. And I think she's been transformed."

"What do you mean?"

"I don't know all of this, but I feel that, somehow, Bhati helped her, Walid's mother, through her spirit, and Muriel has seen that she was wrong in serving the man, and in lying to all of us about it and, I think, she's new in spirit now."

"How do you know all this?"

"I have no idea. I just see it and feel it."

"I don't understand."

"I think Bhati can explain more of it."

"She's still alive?"

"Yes."

"But my sister is dead?"

"She's been taken from this world and is now spiritually trans-figured, and, for the first time in many years, she's fine. And she will someday greet us when we make the transition that has come for her so early, so very early."

"Oh, my sister." Shamilar began to cry, and Shapur put his arms around her and held her.

Badar Sakat looked at Reela and said, "Are we sure that Santiago's gone and is no longer a threat?"

"Yes. And all his men are dead."

Mumar said, "We should radio in and check with Bancom."

"Tell him we're all fine," Reela said.

Walid could hear before he could see. But at first, there was nothing to hear. Silence was all around him, cocooning him like the black formlessness behind his closed eyes, which for the longest time, resisted his opening them. He seemed unable to move at all. He ached all over, almost like he did after the bomb went off in the palace basement stairs, months ago, and worse than after the automobile accident, and much worse than after the hardest physical fight. He wanted to groan but couldn't make a sound. He suddenly became aware that he was lying on his back, face-up.

He heard a slight noise. Someone groaned and said, "Ow." It was Kissa's voice. That gave him the power to open his eyes and look quickly around him. They were all on the floor of Bhati's sitting room, sprawled out in various positions, as if they had been knocked off their feet. Without thinking, he moved and crawled over to Kissa.

"Are you Ok?"

"Huh? Oh. Yes, I think so. Are you?"

"Yeah. Hasina!" He turned and shook Hasina's arm.

"What?"

"Are you Ok?"

"I … I think so."

Mafulla, hearing her voice, came to and rolled over toward them and groaned and said, "What happened?

Walid suddenly remembered the danger they had all just been facing a moment before and he jumped up off the floor, staring straight at where their adversary had most recently been. Masoon and Hamid were also coming back to consciousness, both in prone positions on the floor. And just that second, they both leaped up as well, looking around, back and forth. The furniture was all in place. The paintings were once again on the walls. Sculptures and vases were in their proper locations, and everything was as it had been before the weird storm that Santiago had caused or unleashed.

The light level in the room had returned to normal, and even a touch brighter than it ordinarily would be from the incursion of the daylight outside. It was so odd. Walid didn't fully notice it at first, but the only thing that was really different was that the many candles that were always on display around the room had been lit. They flickered brightly and happily, dancing their light off the many polished and mirrored surfaces around them and elsewhere in the room. Hoda stepped through the glass-beaded curtain.

"Mom!" Kissa said.

"Where's the king?" she asked.

"What?"

"Where's Ali?"

"I don't … we got knocked out or something," Kissa said.

"The king isn't here?" Walid said in a voice of great perplexity. "He was standing right there and speaking, just a second ago."

"Did you see him down the hall?" Masoon asked Hoda.

"No."

"Check the rooms," he said, and Hamid moved toward the back of the suite. Walid and Mafulla both followed him, looking into bedrooms, bathrooms, and closets—everywhere.

"Nothing!" Hamid shouted.

"Nothing," Walid and Mafulla both said, as they came back into the main room, looking totally puzzled.

Walid glanced over at where the monster had been standing and said, simply, "Santiago's gone."

"Yes," Hoda replied, now in the middle of the room with them. "I felt him go. I felt his power leave this world. He's dead because of the king's power."

"But … where's the king?"

37

A SOLEMN SERVICE

THERE WAS NO SIGN OF ALI, NO TRACE AT ALL, AND NO indication of what had happened to him, or where he might be. Everyone was stunned, and now almost frozen in their perplexity.

In front of all who were standing there in Bhati's suite, Masoon now looked at Hoda and asked, "What exactly did you feel?"

She said, "I felt the king use great power, more power than I could ever access. I felt the surge. Then, I felt Santiago leave the world. I sensed his power go. His evil is banished into ... whatever's next for him beyond this world. He'll no longer bother us, or anyone here."

"But what about the king?"

"I didn't feel the king leave us at all. I felt no other power go away."

"Santiago took off his invisibility ring," Hamid said, in a voice that showed inner thought. "Could he have dropped it?"

"The king wouldn't have used it to disappear," Mafulla said, alert to his reasoning. "Not like this."

"No," Walid agreed with his friend. "I mean, why would he? And why wouldn't he tell us now, or reappear to us?"

"Well, where's the ring?" Hasina asked.

Kissa replied, "I think Santiago slipped it into a pocket. But now, there's ... no way to know."

"Hoda, you're sure you didn't feel Uncle Ali ... die or anything?" Walid asked, almost choking on this last word.

"No. There was no sense of the disappearance of his power."

"But."

"When any other person with power has died, anywhere in the kingdom, throughout my life since I was your age, I've felt it," Hoda said. "And the more power there is, the more strongly I've always felt it leave." And then she repeated the word, "Always."

"And this time, you felt no such thing?" Walid asked, for extra reassurance.

"Nothing. I felt Santiago's power go, but no other person with power. And I've known Ali a long time. I know the signature feel of his special power. I would have sensed its departure. I'm sure of it."

Just then, Layla entered the room, followed by Omari, Paki, and Amon. "Is everyone Ok?" Layla asked.

Hoda turned and said, "Yes, but the king has vanished."

Layla looked confused. "What do you mean?"

Masoon said, "We were fighting Santiago, seeking to subdue him and not kill him, at least at first, and he seemed to realize that it wasn't just using the Ring of Gyges that sapped him of his extra power, but also merely wearing it. And so he took it off, and things got crazy very fast. Then, in the midst of a strange storm here in the room, just when Santiago announced to us that he was going to kill us all, the king entered the room and said, no, that only Santiago would die. And right then, something happened that made us all lose consciousness, everyone in the room, and when we regained our senses, shortly afterwards, Santiago was gone, his ring was gone, and the king was also nowhere to be seen."

"I felt Santiago die," Layla said. "But nothing else."

"I sensed the same thing," Hoda told her.

"So, where could the king be?" Omari asked.

"He wouldn't just leave," Paki said.

Walid's mouth went dry. And his stomach seemed to drop through the floor. "The Ring of Phi," he said.

"What about it?" Hoda replied.

"The king told us long ago that there was a legend that it can't be used without a price, a cost. And he said it was reputed to be very dangerous, and that he used it only when he was sure it was necessary, and only for the good of others, and never just himself."

"Yeah, he did say that," Mafulla recalled.

"And, as far as I know, he's used it twice," Walid said, "I mean twice before today—in the palace with Farouk al-Khoum, to save Kissa, and in the compound outside Dromeda, to save all of us. If he used it today, it was time number three. But I didn't see whether he had it on or not, and I sure didn't see him use it."

"But there were extra precautions in The Book of Phi that he could recently read for the first time, weren't there?" Mafulla remembered.

"Yeah, but still," Walid said.

Everyone was silent for a few seconds. Then Layla spoke. "It's true that earlier, he had on the ring. I noticed it."

"Yes," Hoda said. "So we should probably assume that he used it."

"Well then, what should we do now?" Walid asked.

Masoon looked at Hamid and over at Hoda and Layla. Hoda nodded to him in a way that only he noticed. He turned to Walid, and he said, "I think we'll find him, or that he'll rejoin us when he can."

"You do?" Walid was still in shock.

"Yes. But until that happens, we can't have a vacuum of royal leadership at the top."

"What do you mean?" Walid responded.

"We need you to take up the role and duties, until he returns."

"Really?" Walid was having trouble understanding what he was hearing.

"Yes, Your Majesty," Masoon said, and he and Hamid dropped down to one knee, as Hoda and Layla bowed deeply and Mafulla's mouth fell open—the exact same reaction that Kissa and Hasina were having at the moment.

"What?"

"Walid, until Ali returns, for the present and up to our reunion with him, you're now the king."

"Wait."

"I know it will feel strange at first, very strange, but it's your job and you must do it, Majesty."

"You don't have to call me that."

"Yes, Your Majesty, I do. And I do so with confidence and great gratitude."

"But."

Hamid kicked in and said, "Hey, you're our buddy Walid, still, Your Majesty, but while King Ali is off doing whatever he's doing now—and it must be truly necessary or he would be here with us at this great, victorious moment, and I know that with all my heart—it's your role to take up. It's your job to serve as our king, and we as your advisors."

"I'm supposed to ... pretend to be king?"

"No, no, no. You're supposed to serve as our king," Masoon clarified. "There is no pretense."

Walid looked back at his mother and said, "Mom? I don't know what to say or think. Do you agree?"

She looked up at him with great seriousness and said, "Yes. Masoon and Hamid are right. It's your task, for the time being."

"But, I'm fourteen."

"There have been younger kings," Hamid pointed out. "And most of them, vastly less well prepared."

"Most of them, pretty terrible," Mafulla said without thinking.

"Because they were grossly unready, and not of the right mind or character to begin with," Hamid said, giving him a look.

"True, that's very true," Mafulla quickly said, recovering the proper tone of encouragement for this unexpected turn of events. He added, "They were really, really different from you, totally and completely different in every way ... except for the age thing, which is really superficial, when you think about it. I mean, unless you're a baby, which you're not."

"Plus, you're surrounded with the best advisors that it's possible to have," Masoon said.

Walid just said, "You think that Uncle Ali is really Ok?"

"I think he's fine and that he's doing something necessary for him to do. And what's equally necessary for you in this moment, and in the meantime, is to serve in his role for the kingdom."

Walid looked over at Mafulla, and the younger boy said, "Hey, Your Temporary Majesty, what can I say? You've been getting prepared for this your whole life, even when you didn't know it."

"Mafulla's right," Bhati said.

"And Masoon is certainly right about the advisors," Mafulla said, adding, "that is, Masoon, assuming you meant in your remark to include, centrally of course, me."

"Yes, of course, centrally," Masoon said with a serious face.

"This just seems wrong," Walid said. "Wrong in about twelve ways."

"Well, I'm not surprised at all that you feel this way," Hoda spoke up and said. "After all, we're amid great uncertainty right now, not having a clue where the king is, or exactly what happened as he acted to save us all from the intensely immediate threat that Santiago posed. And don't think for a moment that Santiago was anything like a normal man or an ordinary threat. He was blocked from accessing some of the power available to him through the unexpected constraints imposed by the Ring of Gyges, and then even more, through his own inner confusion about what was going on. He had no clarity until he took off that ring. Within a minute, or even seconds more, he might have been able to flatten this entire building and kill everyone in it unless the king had intervened as he did. There has possibly never been anyone among us so powerful with malevolent force as that man."

"But now the king's gone, and so is The Ring of Phi," Mafulla said in a voice of almost no tone.

"I'm not so sure," Hoda said. "There may be a way in which the king is here, still, and perhaps even the ring."

"I don't understand," Mafulla said.

"I'm not sure I do, either," Hoda admitted.

And at that moment, Gimpy the dog came walking through the glass bead curtain. He went straight to the spot where Santiago had last stood, and he sniffed it. Then he sneezed three times. Everyone had stopped talking to watch him. His tail was down, as his nose was to the floor. He was walking left and right and left and right and turning back toward the door and to where the king had stood when he came in. At that moment, Gimpy's sniffing seemed to get twice as fast, and his tail rose up, and started wagging. At that point, Sab Maayuf came through the door, and right behind him, his wife Meskhenet.

"Ah, good dog," Sab said. "Good dog. You know, don't you?" Gimpy gave one loud bark. And Sab patted his head.

"I'll take that as a good sign," Walid said.

"Me, too," Mafulla said.

And then suddenly, Walid remembered Sab's exalted senior role in Phi and said, "Sab, where's the king?"

"I spoke with him. I communed with him, briefly, as it all happened in here," Sab replied. "Our spirits made contact. Ali wants you to do his job for him."

"What's happened to him? Where is he?"

"That, I'm afraid, I can't quite say," Sab replied.

"You don't know, or you can't say?"

"Both, I'm afraid. This is beyond my full grasp, for now."

"Is he coming back?"

"I wish I knew the answer. I hope so. I suspect so. I even believe so. But this is something new for me."

"It would just be too much if my dad had to make the ultimate sacrifice, and then Uncle Ali—both because of the same stupid man."

"He was an evil genius," Hoda said. "He was a misled man, and a foolish man, but never confuse that with stupidity."

"I understand. But, what can we do ... without Uncle Ali?"

Sab said, "You'll never be given more than you can bear. You'll never be called upon to accomplish more than you can do. It's been Ali's task to prepare you for a day like this. And you now stand before me, and all of us, prepared for everything that you need to be and do."

"I don't feel like I'm prepared nearly enough."

"Our feelings aren't always the best guides. They can fool us on many occasions. They are misleading you right now. But you can gently correct them."

"Yeah, he's often talked about that."

"He's known for his wisdom," Sab reminded Walid.

"Yes."

"And, my young king, you're already known for yours."

"I have to sit down."

"Yes, please do."

The conversations continued in Bhati's sitting room for nearly two more hours, and then everyone moved down to the king's rooms where they talked more. Masoon took Kular aside and explained the situation to him as well as possible. Like Darwishi, Kular knew about Phi, and the king's exalted status within it. Masoon did all that he could to reassure Kular, and he took the news as well as could be expected, and really even better than could have been expected, calmly and with courage and hope, and confidence, following his great surprise. And he expressed his eagerness to serve Walid for as long might be needed, just as he had been serving Ali.

When the time came, now the next day, for the memorial service to be held for Rumi, all the palace staff came into the big ballroom downstairs, most with their spouses, and some with children, and took their seats. Mafulla's parents were there, and Reela, of course. Shamilar was sitting next to Bhati and had her arm around her. Leem Hadad was on the first row with Ibrahim and Ben. Even Ahira had come to show his support. Zaman and Rama El-Noor were on the second row with Khata. Khalid and Hoda were also up front with their older sons and Kissa. Walid looked out and could see Ara and Cabar with their parents, and Bakat and her parents, and there were Jabari and his mother, and Set with his parents. Bafur was sitting with his dad, Bashir, and his mom. There was a sea of sad and sympathetic faces stretching across the expanse of chairs. Malik and Haji were there as well, but they were in the side room off the front of the ballroom with Walid and Mafulla and the others who would speak.

Hamid was the first to ascend the stage that had been quickly built at the front of the hall. He began with the words, "The king has asked me to begin this service of memory in honor of our dear friend, the great physician Rumi Shabeezar, brother of Ali, husband of Bhati and father of our Walid." Hamid then went on to give a wonderful talk, full of both serious and humorous reminiscences and, ultimately, words that were both moving and inspiring to all who were present. Masoon spoke next. And then Sab Maayuf slowly took the stage and gave the most incredibly loving account of Rumi's life and family and history. There was not a soul present who wasn't deeply affected by this lavish tribute to a man who had lived with humble greatness and love.

Then, Hamid returned to the podium and began to recount the recent troubles that had been caused by a man whose life had long been anticipated in kingdom legend. He spoke of the man's history and quest for power, along with his many criminal actions of theft and kidnapping and murder. He told about how several brave members of their community had stopped or prevented so many of his intended actions. He explained that this was the individual behind the murder of Dr. Rumi. And then he went on to explain how this man, Juan Osvaldo Santiago, had more recently intended to take things from the palace that would aid him in subjugating the entire population to his own perverse uses of power.

Hamid recounted how, on the day of mourning just past, the man had come to the palace to do great harm, and that he had been resisted and stopped first by four brave young people— Walid, Mafulla, Kissa, and Hasina—along with Walid's mother Bhati, and then by Masoon and Hamid, and finally by King Ali. "There are mysteries," he said, "mysteries about this man's powers and about how they were stopped, and how he had to be taken from the earth so that he could never again threaten us." He said, "It was, in the end, accomplished by our wonderful king, His Majesty, Ali Shabeezar, opening himself up to greater powers than any evil intent can ever access."

Hamid paused for maybe ten seconds and then went on. "I

can't tell you exactly what happened in the battle to save the palace and the monarchy, and all our lives, because I don't know. No one does, except King Ali. And the surprising news I have for you today is that, in delivering us from the monstrous threat we faced, our Ali has somehow, in the aftermath of his heroic actions, apparently vanished from our midst—we think, for an important reason, and temporarily."

There was a gasp from around the room, and then a growing murmur of words, as people spoke to each other their shock and puzzlement and questions. After a moment, Hamid continued. "But, I want to assure you all that we're confident he's where he needs to be, off doing what he needs to do, and that he'll return, when the time is right and he has fully finished the job he started upstairs in this building in his effective confrontation with the great threat to us all."

He looked across the large room. "There are mysteries around us. There are mysteries within us. The adversary, the monstrous man who came here to harm us and actually to kill us all, brought with him many enigmas. But King Ali was able to cut through those puzzles and prevent his intended actions—apparently, at a price. We don't know all that took place. Even those who were physically present could not see what happened. But we do know that our king used greater power to stop this man, about whom there was an ancient legend. And to do so, he used a power, about which there are other legends. In the aftermath, both of them were gone. We have good reason to believe that the enemy died in the events that transpired, whatever they were. And we have just as good a reason to think our king did not. I can't explain this to you at the present time. But I can assure you of our confidence about it. Yet, King Ali's absence from among us now is undeniable. And we must live with it until he is able to rejoin us and take up again the causes of our governance and our lives together that are so dear to his heart."

There were again whispered comments heard throughout the room. Hamid went on. "It was King Ali's wish, expressed many times since he took the throne, that the next in line for the duties of kingship should be our beloved Prince Walid. And until our elder leader is able to return to us, Walid has agreed to serve us in this capacity." The whispers and many quietly spoken words again spread throughout the room in a buzz of comment. Hamid waited a moment and then spoke up, a little more loudly. "As most of you know, despite his age, our Walid Shabeezar is a young man of great wisdom, strength, and judgment. Many experienced and capable advisors surround him. And he has the distinct advantage of your presence as good friends and associates here in the capital and, for many of you, in the palace itself."

Hamid paused again. "All will be well as we await the return of King Ali, from whatever far place and task has claimed his presence at the moment. In the meantime, please rise to join me in welcoming to his new role, our currently serving monarch, His Royal Majesty, Walid Shabeezar."

At that, everyone stood up, and remained standing in silence, as Walid walked from the side alcove onto the stage. The closest friends of his in the front two rows then began to clap, and slowly the applause spread throughout the room. Then, it became louder and more spirited. Masoon stood next to the stage and lifted his right hand, palm up, in gesture toward Walid, now on stage, and said, "Long live the king!"

Many voices then repeated, "Long live the king!"

Masoon then said it again, louder: "Long live the king!"

And now everyone shouted thunderously, and with heart, "Long live the king!"

"Thank you. Thank you all. Please be seated," Walid said over the noise, with both hands in the air, and everyone did as he asked.

He waited as they were all seated and became still. He then said, "Thank you for coming to remember and honor my dear father. He will always be missed. And just as we were beginning to cope with his absence, another one suddenly has surprised us all— but one that we do believe to be of a temporary duration. We don't understand what has happened with King Ali, or why he's absent now, but in our hearts, those of us who have been closest to him are assured that all is well, and that he will return."

There was not a sound in the room as Walid spoke. He took a breath and said, "It was hard for me to lose my father, as you know. It's now terribly difficult to deal with the sudden disappearance of my uncle and wonderful mentor. But, along with my mother who sits here among us, thanks to my father's tragic sacrifice, they've prepared me for the next stretch of the road ahead of us. With your help, with your prayers and support and ongoing encouragement, I'll seek to uphold this role of leadership for as long as it takes to get us to the day when, hopefully soon, we can welcome back our benefactor and guide. Meanwhile: Long live the kingdom!"

At those words, everyone responded with an echo of the words: "Long live the kingdom!"

"May we all do well and prosper," King Walid said, more quietly, and then added, "For your vital part in our joint enterprise—past, present, and future—I thank you. I will depend on your help, and for it, I'll always be grateful." With those words, he stood looking at them for a few seconds, and nodded his head, and then turned and walked off the stage.

Everyone again instantly stood. Then, someone in the room yelled out, "Long live King Walid!" And then nearly everyone shouted these words back. The instigator loudly said it again, and once more, the gathered crowd repeated the words. This led to a loud outbreak of applause and foot stomping, started by Phi and close friends of the new king, and taken up by nearly everyone who was in attendance.

Jabari turned to Set and said, "Nice job, man."

"Thanks," he replied.

"You can yell pretty loud."

"Yeah, when I need to."

"It's terrible that King Ali's vanished, but it's awesome that Walid's taking over, in the meantime, as king."

"Yeah, my feelings exactly."

"I wonder, for how long?"

APPENDIX

The Diary of Walid Shabeezar
Unexpected Events

The ancient Greek philosophers kept saying: "Know Yourself." I always thought that would be the easiest thing in the world. After all, what's closer to me than me? I pay attention to what I think, how I feel, and how I react to the people and things around me, and in these ways I find out, to some extent, who and what I am. But I've learned that I need to listen to other people, too. Others sometimes see sides of us that we hide from ourselves, or just don't notice.

In this diary, I try to come to greater levels of self-knowledge, as well as knowledge of the world. I write down insights I have and things I learn from other people. Then I re-read what I've written, now and then, and I'm sometimes amazed to rediscover a bit of wisdom that had come into my life just to be forgotten quickly under the daily assault of new things to do and think about. I'm glad I keep this diary. And I've gotten a little more regular about it. It serves me well. And it then helps me to serve others better.

△ △ △

It's Ok to talk about important things. It's more than Ok. It's necessary. What amazes me is how hard it is in many situations.

Socrates pointed out something interesting and odd about the normal course of our lives. The least important things, we think about and talk about the most. The most important things, we think about and talk about the least. This is backwards and upside down!

I've come to believe that the most important thing of all in this world and beyond its borders is love. And we don't understand it very well. How often do we actually think and talk about it—I mean, in the normal course of our daily lives? Sadly, the answer is: seldom at all. And this is strange. No wonder we make so many mistakes about it.

Plato's Symposium is a dialogue about love. The characters in the dialogue say some pretty interesting things. Khalid had us read it and then I went by his house to talk to him about it.

I told Khalid about a new idea I had. Love isn't a feeling, but a rich state of being that gives rise to commitments, actions, attitudes, feelings, and thoughts. It's deep and powerful and lasting.

He agreed. And then he surprised me by saying that he thinks of love as first a force for good that comes from beyond us, dwells in us, and passes through us when we're properly functioning as created and creative spirits. We're the containers and conveyances of love. That was a new idea for me!

If you properly give, you always get, and most of all, you gain.

We begin life as the beneficiaries of others. We first receive and ideally then give. That's how we receive even more. And then we can give much more. And we grow, in a positive spiral of possibility.

If we allow it to, love creates in us a form of creativity that we can bring to the world. That's the creative force of love in action. It comes from the source of the universe, and animates us if we let it.

I asked Khalid how he knew he wanted to marry Hoda. He said, "The first time I looked into her eyes, I saw God." That sort of left me without words. And it's the way I felt when I first saw Kissa. I felt like I was going to fall into her eyes, into a depth of spirit I had never seen, an eternal, endless spirit of love. I saw just a flash. I mean, when it happened, I was in the marketplace and she was with her parents. But that was all it took. I sort of knew right then.

Khalid said this about Hoda and that first look he had into her eyes: "I sensed in that instant the loving embrace of the source for all things." That's what I felt, too, with Kissa.

It's a wild and transformative idea: The Ultimate Source of All loves us directly, intimately, and completely—and through each other. But it takes a special soul to reflect that love with blazing clarity.

When something is deeply and perfectly right, you'll know it. The most important things in life aren't a matter of just confused and uncertain guessing. Conviction will come.

△ △ △

We all have different gifts and responsibilities. But whatever our gifts might be, the corresponding responsibility we have is to use them well.

Every life gift or talent is important. Each is of great value. Develop what yours are without worrying about the gifts and talents of others. The world needs us all.

Not everyone who enters deeply into the fellowship of the mind is Phi. Phi talents and skills are distinctive and not as widely experienced. But the nobility of the mind and its royalty is, in principle, available to us all.

We Phi are guardians and pioneers. The fellowship of the mind that we represent and protect is an outpost of intellect, love, and creativity in this world that reflects the deepest realities existing beyond the world.

Membership in The fellowship of the mind is open to all who seek it.

Burdens can be blessings to those who receive them well. Blessings can be burdens to those who don't handle them properly.

Our profiles and clusters of talent are as unique as our fingerprints.

The key to a happy and fruitful life is to make the most of the talents you've been given and not go moping around about one you don't have. That's a paraphrase of Khalid.

Life isn't a grim competition of abilities and accomplishments, but a celebration of the wonders in us and around us, with each of us taking joy in our own form of being, and even more, in each other, doing whatever we can to make our time here worth celebrating.

Healthy competition is motivational. We compete to get better.

△ △ △

Even smart people can do stupid things.

Friends save friends from mistakes. But all too often, we allow ourselves to be saved only from some of the consequences of those mistakes.

Never be too quick to say, "This is terrible" or, "This is great." Things can turn out very differently from how they look at the start.

Many things and events in the world seem layered, with several diverse consequences and levels of significance.

Simplicity and complexity often happily co-exist.

Be alert. You never know what the next moment might bring.

The world is a tumbling kaleidoscope of patterns and events. When you're attentive and perceptive, you can benefit from the churn.

Things tend to happen exactly as they need to. The power that works behind all things can alone help us to accept that and be at peace.

△ △ △

It's always good advice to expect the unexpected.

To a surprising degree, how we handle surprise charts our path.

There are many ways to waste a life, and many ways to turn one around before the waste is complete. We had to confront some bad guys today who gave their lives for the wrong cause.

Where there's life, there's hope. Redemption is always possible. Transformation can happen. I really believe that.

There's an old saying. "Fall down seven times; get up eight." I've always thought of that in terms of failure, resilience, persistence, and the ultimate success that's right for us. But it can also be understood in terms of mistakes and redemption. Everyone falls now and then, and occasionally, a lot. It's vitally important to rise once more.

The harder you fall, the higher you can rise. It's like a ball bouncing. But not all of us rebound. Some stay where they fall. But that's never necessary. It's always better to bounce back.

Our friends sometimes have talents we would never suspect. But, as the philosopher Emerson once wrote, and as I've been discovering over and over, "Life is full of surprises."

Malik and Haji are Phi. I couldn't believe it. But then, again, I could. And yet it was still a surprise. I think it's an important thing for me to know, now that we're all apparently ready for such knowledge to be shared. Things happen when the time is right.

There are likely some important truths about the people around us that we don't know and would amaze us. We should ask more about people. And then listen—really, deeply listen.

There are some things that can be known properly only at the right time or in the right conditions. We often act as if we think that all truth is accessible to all people at all times, without any conditions for knowing having to be satisfied. But maybe some things can be known only if you're suitably developed and prepared, and in the proper position, and also it's the right time. This is something I should think about more.

△ △ △

I've often heard people say, "Timing is everything." That may be an exaggeration wrapped around a truth, like we often get in popular aphorisms. But, I do think that the element of timing is much more important in life than we tend to imagine. This insight counsels us to neither rush nor delay but follow the deeper rhythms as they lead.

Dance to the music you hear, whether anyone else hears it or not.

There's a phrase I've always loved: "When the time had fully come ..." and I think about it often. I believe it's in the Bible. The world is pregnant with possibility, but pregnancies have to grow and develop until the time is right for the new birth. That's maybe the way it is with many things. When the time is right, the right thing happens. If we try to force matters ahead of their time, we make a mistake. And if we lag behind, not acting at the proper moment, we make an equal mistake. When the fruit is ripe, that's when you get your best bite.

When the heat of the pan is just right, that's when you should cook your food. Not hot enough—you get problems. Too hot—you get problems. Just right is the key to almost everything. I learned this from Kissa's brother, Shumar. Wisdom can be found in the kitchen.

Wisdom can likely be found in every room of a house, because each room represents some facet or activity of life.

△ △ △

Trust the trustworthy. Have true faith in faithful people.

Honor the honorable with your thoughts, and they will honor you in return.

The right cosmic vision brings confidence and compassion. But the wrong worldview makes those things rare.

Without a helpful system of beliefs, we stumble in the dark. The best philosophy shines a light.

Truth illumines the path forward. Hope moves us along it. Love spurs us to take others with us as we go.

The best way to live is simple: Always learning, always loving.

Coincidence is often the disguise of destiny as it tugs and nudges us along on our path.

Be open to unusual, unexpected, and amazing help that will often come just when you need it.

There's much more going on in this world than meets the eye.

Wisdom is the ability to see more deeply and feel more properly.

We think we wait eagerly for good things to happen. And, certainly, we do. It's a completely new thought that, just maybe, special moments are waiting every bit as eagerly for us. That's the magic.

When it's time for a date with destiny, don't ever delay.

△ △ △

We had a hard workout with Masoon today. Advanced Phi training sometimes leaves me sore and drained for a while. But that's what it takes to get better.

Few people stretch themselves and try to break through their limits. Most of the limits we experience in this life are moveable. We can push them and expand ourselves, but only with great effort.

Sadly, we live in a world where too many people expect extraordinary results without extraordinary effort. When you invest in the right process, tremendous things can happen.

In exercise, I'm often asked by Masoon to try things that I then fail to accomplish the first time, and even the second time. But, with properly performed exercise, there really isn't any such thing as failure. Everything you do has results, whether it looks successful at the time or not. It's a process. And I've come to trust the process.

The only real failure is not to try. That's true in exercise and life.

△ △ △

Consistency is flexible harmony. It isn't about repetitive behavior at all. It's about coherence and deep congruence among thoughts, values, beliefs, emotions, attitudes, and actions.

The only way to be consistent with your highest goals and deepest values in times of change is to adapt and adjust and flow with the change, making sure to bridge what matters and what's new.

Consistency is power. I often like to think of it as flexible firmness.

Some people self-destruct through persistently inconsistent behavior. And there are only three possible causes of this: (1) Ignorance—They don't realize they're being inconsistent with their own goals and values, or (2) Indifference—They don't care, or (3) Inertia—bad habits have taken them over. We can defeat these things that otherwise would defeat us. We can defeat ignorance with information. And we can conquer indifference and inertia with a lively use of our imaginations. The imagination engages the emotions, and in this world, it's mainly the emotions that move the will. Remember this!

Mafulla recited the Seven Conditions of Success today, when we were talking about consistency. I had never understood it before, but you can't monitor and maintain consistency in your life if you don't' have a clear conception of what you're trying to accomplish and an emotional commitment to the importance of what you're doing. And, actually, all the other conditions for success the king told us about support the consistency condition. I wonder if that's true for each of the conditions—that all the others support each one? That's wild! I'll have to think more about that!

Mafulla's Summary: The Seven Conditions of Success: To position ourselves as well as possible for success in any challenge, we need a clear CONCEPTION of what we want, a strong CONFIDENCE we can attain that goal, a focused CONCENTRATION on what it will take to get there, a stubborn CONSISTENCY in pursuing our vision, an emotional COMMITMENT to the importance of what we're doing, a good CHARACTER to guide us and keep us on a proper course, and a CAPACITY TO ENJOY the process along the way. These seven concepts provide a great checklist, diagnostic tool, and guide for achievement.

Insight for the day: Fast thinking sometimes requires slow walking.

△ △ △

Fear is a visceral emotion that's not easily tamed. At its best, it arouses and moves us to action. At its worst, it impedes us or even shuts us down. It's not, in itself, a bad thing, but should be harnessed and controlled as quickly as possible.

The greatest souls don't need fear to move them to action. They do what they know is right, when they know it's best, and with the degree of energy or power they understand to be required.

Knowledge alone will not banish fear. Only perfect love can do that.

Imperfect love multiplies our fears. Perfect love transcends them.

There are wonders and mysteries in our world, layered and deep.

It could be that in life, meaning and mystery are related. Everything that's truly meaningful brings us up against a great mystery as well. The power of good exceeds the power of evil, but battles between the two are often not easy.

Evil sometimes seems to win, but the wise see more deeply the infinite resilience and power of good.

Our mental categories are filters for experience, but on occasion, I see things that far exceed those categories. I'm amazed I can take them in at all. But then again, the spirit is bigger than any artificial boundary.

Keep the borders of your thought elastic and flexible, able to receive the unexpected and the new. Stiff mindsets can't flex when that's required. Properly accommodating souls grow.

△ △ △

With most big problems, things seem to get worse before they get better. Knowing this helps us not panic or feel discouraged.

There's a reason for almost anything, and there may be some sort of reason for everything. Don't count on always figuring it out.

The wisest people avoid worry, but still have existential concern.

I saw Layla and, in conversation, she passed on to me an insight that the king had mentioned to her. I was saying something about how unenlightened so many people are and what widespread change the world needs. She repeated the king's words. Enlightenment takes place one mind at a time, one soul at a time, one heart at a time. And that one change alters everything. I like that idea a lot.

△ △ △

Don't be a box bound dweller. Think far outside the box!

The box of experience is good. It's necessary. We can't function without it. But it's just not all there is. And what lies beyond it can put into perspective what happens within it.

Our four dimensional universe is merely a single sliver or thread of reality. In fact, our life here is just a footprint of our overall existence, almost like a grain of sand in the desert—or a shadow that's simply flitting across the ground beneath an intricately engineered airplane as it wings across the vast and endless sky above.

I need to think and act out of the infinite resources that naturally belong to me as a spirit temporarily visiting here.

Everything reflects something deep and high and vast.

It could be that the entirety of reality is modeled by the famous novelty of Chinese Boxes—a box within a box within a box, and so on.

It's part of my job as a living, growing human being to keep my mind open to possibilities that lie far beyond the horizon of my current experience.

It could be that one of the greatest human qualities is openness. Too many people are closed off, in their minds and hearts.

△ △ △

We're all here to learn and teach from what we learn. Then, when we teach, we learn even more.

As we do, so we'll be. As we are, so we'll act.

We all have habits of thought, as well as of action. I should never let old habits hold me back when great new realities call out to me.

Pay attention to the breadcrumbs you occasionally see that mark the path to truth. Someone's left them for you to use. Follow them to find out where they lead. I got that from something Mafulla said.

Worry comes from perceptions, assumptions, and projections. It has no deep roots in the most fundamental realities. Remember that.

△ △ △

Mafulla said something funny about the mistakes we make and the stupid things we sometimes do. He said, "Maybe idiocy is the teeming swamp from which the flower of brilliance can blossom." I love it.

Mistakes can lead to mastery; confusion can lead to clarity; chaos to order; failure to success; humility to the heights; nobility to simple service—all nice turnarounds that life presents us. Almost anything can be a doorway into what on the surface seems its opposite.

We had a great workout with Masoon today. After all the physical exertion and some really spooky stuff he taught us, we enjoyed a great talk about imagination and its role in our lives.

The imagination can be our greatest ally or worst foe. It's up to us.

In the grip of imagination out of control, we have difficulty coming to realize that this is what's happening, because the imagination touches all our thinking. When we're imprisoned by its projection, we view everything through those bars. That's one reason why it's so hard to talk anyone out of a delusion. Their fantasy dream or nightmare filters everything they hear and see and think.

The imagination can be a great source of energy, for positive or negative results. It's a tool to be cultivated carefully and controlled.

Imagination out of control can derail any adventure. Properly used, it propels us to new heights. It's a prime example of the Double Power Principle—power for good or ill, able to help or harm.

△ △ △

The Epic of Gilgamesh is a great cautionary tale. This amazing man, Gilgamesh, is tall, strong, handsome, rich, and is a king. But he's totally self-absorbed and goes around using people for his own purposes and passing desires, with no concern for them at all. But then, he's confronted with a great loss and by the unavoidable fact of mortality in our world, and it eventually humbles and redirects him. The story illustrates the view that nobility and humility need to be balanced in a life, in order for truly great things to happen.

Without proper values, strong and talented people can goad each other into doing terribly wrong things.

Talent, power, energy, and vision need to be well harnessed and guided. Otherwise, awful harm can result from any of them. This is explained by the insight of the two powers.

To those of us who are overly ambitious for the things of this world, our mortality can be an important reminder and corrective, if we'll just remember and heed it.

△ △ △

When somebody's name pops into your head, you should contact that person and see how they're doing. They might have a need you can meet. Or you might have one for their help.

Thoughts that spontaneously appear are sometimes signs. Follow them to find what they signify. We sometimes glimpse only small shards of the mosaic that's there to be seen.

There are signals of need and opportunity all around us, if we can just calm the chatter of the mind and listen. Then, act.

A plan is good to have, even if it just gets you started. All plans should have flexibility built in.

The divide between life and death can sometimes seem as thick and sturdy as a massive rock wall, and other times as thin as newsprint. And yet, there are doors in the wall, and small rips in the paper. You can be on this side, overflowing with confidence and full of plans and, without warning, suddenly find yourself on the other side.

△ △ △

When we look at the surface of life, much of what we see is misleading. We need deeper perspectives to get to the truth. Light dances on the water, but it's not coming from the pond at all.

We can enjoy the surface of life without being misled by it. In fact, that's the only good way to enjoy it.

We live in a reality of infinite complexity and surprise.

The world isn't boring. We should never be, either.

While we're souls in physical bodies, our experience of the world is both enabled and limited by those bodies.

In the realm of appearances, it can seem that evil people have more power than the good—that evil can do damage and end lives in a way that no good person can reverse. But the king taught us that, while evil men can entice others to spiritual corruption and hold back the growth of many, the truly good can lead others in the ways of right and enhance the world much more. The power of good is greater.

We think the evil man can do the ultimate harm by killing someone. But in doing that, what does he accomplish? He sends someone earlier than otherwise expected into the next world and the next adventure, without the constraints and limitations of these earthly bodies. He forces a transition to a new life, which we have reason to believe will be better. His evil intent is transmuted and redirected to good. But he's still wrong to have done what he did. He's to be judged by his intention, and by his duties, not just by the most important consequences his act might have for others.

Why then do we judge and condemn murder? The transition from this world to the next was not rightly the killer's to cause. He violated a great duty in taking to himself such a choice. We're to remain here in this phase as long as nature allows and our possibilities for love, growth, and enjoyment still exist. No one else should ever make the decision for us—as long as we're conscious, or even capable of becoming conscious—of whether or not we're to stay on this life's path, at this point along the way of love and growth and earthly enjoyment.

Murder, like suicide under conditions of emotional pain, is deeply wrong because it's against the intent and purpose of our creation.

I asked the king then how killing someone in self-defense could ever be morally acceptable. He said that under the most extreme conditions, this equally extreme act can become what he called "a tragic imperative," but that it should be avoided whenever it's at all reasonably possible.

The test for moral action is whether something is consistent with the purpose of creation, the meaning of life—loving creation, or creative love. Anything that lovingly, creatively enhances life is right, and anything that at its core contravenes the wonderful requirements of loving creativity, or creative love, is wrong.

It's good to have a clear guide for action, but in the details, wisdom is always needed. There can't be a rule for everything. Discernment is important. Virtue, like wisdom, is a skill, and an art of life.

Mafulla asked the king why it's so difficult to do great good in this world. The king said that it isn't hard at all to do small things that are good. And, whenever done for infinitely valuable souls, even small goods are unlimitedly great in their effects. But for the truly difficult things, there is the compensating fact that struggle can itself be good for us. A noble deed that was hard to do can then multiply the forms of goodness that result.

This world seems made to challenge us and grow us. But the whole process depends on our reactions.

△ △ △

Before you pursue a goal, think through the consequences as well as you can, projecting what it would be like if you get what you want. For any potential path forward, consider all the angles and implications for others as well as yourself.

We're not always good at imagining consequences, but we should try our best. Some things seem fine in the abstract, but if they actually happened, we'd have real problems as a result. That's why we should also rely on the experiences others have had and have passed on to us in the form of recognized wisdom. Real wisdom can guide and correct our otherwise wayward imaginations.

The imagination is powerful. A wise imagination is powerfully good. You never know when an amazing opportunity will present itself. And when it does, you're often not sure what to do about it. But that's Ok. And that's where the power of thought and imagination can help. Sometimes we need to live with a new option for a while, in order to let it grow on us and in us.

Badminton isn't as easy as it looks. Most things aren't. Skill is the hidden factor in life that we don't often appreciate.

A simple game can be played with exquisite skill. Such is true in much of life. Skill matters. And skill can be developed.

Skill comes from experience. It's an essentially cultivated quality. Nothing will substitute for experience. From difficulty and hard work and talent, even the ideal of mastery can eventually arise.

△ △ △

Mafulla's dad died and then came back to life. I can't believe that I can write such a sentence. I didn't know that it could even happen. But I'm so glad he's back. He went somewhere when he was out of his body. And he told us an amazing story about it.

I wanted to write here what Mr. Adi told us today about his experiences beyond this world. But I can't yet. I need to just think more about it all, and process it.

There's something up ahead for all of us, and we can catch only the smallest, quickest glimpses of it in this world when we come across stunning beauty, or great kindness, or the gift of magnificent love. They're all pointers to something else that involves their perfection and completion and goes beyond it. I do know that.

I think Plato saw hints of what awaits us. He had intuition and insight to match his reason. He thought of this world as merely a shadow of what's to come. Some people now dismiss him as foolish in that idea and hope. I believe it's much more likely that he was wise. We easily think of the next life as involving a less substantial form of existence, modeling it on ghosts and vapors, as if spirits are less real than material things. But Plato and other wise people have thought in an opposite way: The next life will be much more substantial and full and robust in all its aspects than this one could ever be, even at its best.

We often view things as the opposite of what they are. But we can learn.

△ △ △

Many hands can ease a task, and many minds can solve a problem. When we tackle a tough issue with others we admire and trust, we spark each other to new thoughts and perspectives. And that can lead to new actions.

Diverse experiences and capacities come from richly diverse lives.

When you're trying to understand a complicated situation, and especially one in which deception may be going on, your first thoughts aren't always your best ones.

Complexity can show some patterns and hide others. We may have to dig deep to get to the truth.

Just because something is unexpected and surprising doesn't mean it isn't true. In fact, this can be the sign of a deep revelation.

Truth is often odd, and it sometimes comes at us from weird angles.

Unexpected things happen a great many times around the world every day. The miraculous may be more common than we think.

△ △ △

I haven't been able to write anything for two days, but I'll try.

When someone you deeply love dies, when someone you've known your whole life and depended on suddenly isn't there anymore, and especially when you lose a parent, it's first of all a shock. You feel like the floor is disappearing underneath you. Your ordinary reality dissipates like a mist. You're sort of hollow inside. And you feel really exposed in some way. But the biggest surprise is that it's not the total complete horror that you would have thought. To a properly oriented mind, it's not that sort of thing at all. It's almost like you can feel that this is a transition, and that it's one you'll also make some day, and that this person—in the current case, my dad—is just going first, and will be there for you when you go, or in my case, for me when I go, too. He'll prepare a way for me, like I'm sure someone has prepared a way for him. And then one day, I'll do the same for someone else. It's a cycle of love and responsibility in the great transition.

I'm the man now who has to stand up and take a lead to make the difference that my family is in the world to make. I'm the tip of the spear. I have plenty of support and love, but a new kind of responsibility as well.

We inherit from those who go before us much more than we think.

My mom has her own great journey in the world and I know she'll always help me, as I'll always help her. But dad's death feels like it's left a distinctive inheritance of responsibility to me.

I need to hold on to everything I've learned from my dad. I need to keep it close to my consciousness, so I can use his wisdom whenever I need it. And I know he'll still be there to ask, in my heart.

Death is universal, but it's always so particular—this person at this time for this cause in this situation, leaving these loved ones and these possibilities behind. There is nothing more general or specific than death.

Each death, like each birth, is a doorway into something new. Every ending is also a beginning. I believe this in my soul.

△ △ △

So, Plato wrote about a ring that makes a person invisible. What would you do if you could vanish from sight any time you wanted? Would you do anything different? That's an interesting question.

How does a person act when he thinks that no one's watching? This question gets to the issue of basic character. And it says something about the individual and society.

One of Plato's literary characters seems to think that the only guides in life are pleasure and pain. These things are certainly important motivators, but I'm sure there's something else as well. You can be attracted to what's true, good, beautiful, or harmonious even in cases where pleasure and pain don't come into play—or if one of them does, it's only as a side issue, and not as the prime mover.

Do I do the right thing, not for its own sake, but only because it makes me feel good? Or does doing the right thing make me feel good because I do it for its own sake? I'm convinced the latter is true.

I enjoy doing what's good precisely because it's good. I don't do what's good just because I enjoy it. That gets things backwards. And it grossly misrepresents the mindset of good people.

I think you can love pleasure and enjoyment, and still have motivations that go beyond their narrow boundaries.

You can live a life of principle without diminishing your experience of pleasure. You just have to pick the right pleasures in the right circumstances, the ones that won't do you harm, but only good. And who would want the opposite?

The properly formed mind takes a certain pleasure in intellectual

Truth, aesthetic Beauty, moral Goodness, and spiritual Unity, in all their manifestations.

△ △ △

One of the worst things in life is fear. Uncontrolled, it undercuts you. Fear, if left to do its work, makes a life narrow and small.

We never know what new adventure will await us on any given day. The best we can do is to be prepared to give everything that's in us, and with the right attitudes and values, move confidently forward, believing that we can prevail over any odds that may face us. That's why we're here.

We're here for adventure. We're here for a journey. And I think, we're here for many adventures and journeys. The path we're on now is preparing us for the next one, and often in ways that we can't even imagine.

Welcome any great new adventure with confidence.

We're alive here and now to flourish through challenge and opportunity. That's our calling and should be our joy.

Happiness is a moving target. And a time of sadness, now and then along the way, is natural.

I can't even begin to process yet what happened with Santiago and the king.

It's impossible to prepare yourself in advance for the magnitude of surprise that life can bring.

I can't get my head around what it will take to serve as the king in

Uncle Ali's absence. But we never feel truly prepared for the biggest surprises and changes that overtake us. And yet, indeed, life never throws at us more than we can handle. I believe that's a much deeper truth than most people realize. There's always a way. But to manage big challenges, we have to dig deep and allow the positive energy and power available from the source of all to flow through us for the good of others as well as ourselves. We may not have all the resources we might want, but we have access to everything we truly need.

I hope Uncle Ali is Ok and that he'll come back, somehow.

I believe that, ultimately, good will prevail.

I will maintain my confidence that love conquers all.

I will do what I feel called to do. And I'll seek always to be courageous and bold, and help others to be those things, too.

I'll seek to embody love in all that I do.

ACKNOWLEDGMENTS

I'm thankful, as always, for the distinctive process that has led to this book, as well as the others that have come before it. I suspect that many people think of creativity as an onerous challenge, and perhaps difficult out of all proportion to the ordinary course of work. But it can actually be the easiest thing in the world, once you've mastered a lot of stuff that already exists out there to be known. At its best, I suspect that creativity involves a flow of something from outside your ordinary conscious mind and into the stream of awareness that we tend to characterize of as normal thought. It happens like a genuine blessing. And for it, I'm grateful.

I want to thank everyone who has helped keep me happy and balanced and sociable during the most often solitary process of transcribing the movie in my head that has played for over a year and a half now. Thanks especially to the guys in the gym: Thanks to Don, Ed, Tom, Michael, Paul, John, Vinod and Pam, and my many other co-sufferers in the local cathedral of bodily exertion who supported me during the writing of this book. The exercise of the mind must be balanced by the exertion of the body. You guys sure help.

Ed and Bruce, thanks again for all the great editorial advice and ongoing encouragement.

You readers who write me about these books bless my soul. I always appreciate your kind words.

I want to thank five cats, one of them now departed and awaiting me, and three dogs, one also now gone off to the next adventure, and the human part of my great family as well, and as usual.

And I wonder: What, if anything, is next?

And then I remember. Much is yet to be revealed.

Tom Morris
Wilmington, NC

AFTERWORD

Beyond *The Magic Ring*

Beyond First, there was *The Oasis Within*, a short tale about a series of deep conversations and surprising events that took place as a group of men and camels crossed the desert in Egypt in 1934. Then there was The Golden Palace, the official Book One to a series of subsequent stories about these remarkable individuals, collectively entitled:

WALID AND THE MYSTERIES OF PHI

Then came *The Stone of Giza*. Next was *The Viper and The Storm*. Then, there was *The King and Prince*, and *The Mysterious Village*. This is Book Six in the official series. If you've read these books, I hope you'll love what's still to come. All the volumes together present a sprawling account of action, adventure, and ideas set in and around a richly reimagined Cairo, Egypt in 1934 and 1935, with a few sojourns farther abroad. They contain tales about life, death, meaning, love, friendship, the deepest secrets behind every-day events, and the extraordinary power of a well-focused mind. The events they relate will continue to interact with many classics of philosophy and literature. And you'll gradually discover in these books the outlines of a powerful worldview and a profound philosophy of life.

To find out more, visit **www.TomVMorris.com/novels** or go to **www.TheOasisWithin.com.**

The prologue and companion book to the series, *The Oasis Within*, as well as any book in the series, is available for large group purchases at special discounts. To find out more, contact the author through his oldest and most reliable email, **TomVMorris@aol.com** or through the contact page on his personal website. Tom is also available to speak with book groups via email, Skype, or any other means that would help in the discussion of these stories. Make a request, and speak to the author.

About the Author

Tom Morris is one of the most active public philosophers and business speakers in the world. A native of North Carolina, he's a graduate of The University of North Carolina (Chapel Hill), where he was a Morehead-Cain Scholar, and he holds a Ph.D. in both Philosophy and Religious Studies from Yale University. For fifteen years, he served as a Professor of Philosophy at the University of Notre Dame, where he was one of their most popular teachers. You can find him online anytime at **www.TomVMorris.com.**

Tom has been honored with the University of North Carolina's Distinguished Young Alumnus Award, as well as with honorary doctorates in recognition of his work. He has been a George A. and Eliza Gardner Howard Foundation Fellow, through Brown University, and a Fellow with the National Endowment for the Humanities.

Tom is also the author of over twenty-five pioneering books. His twelfth book, *True Success*, launched him into an adventure as a philosopher working and speaking throughout the world. His audiences have included many major companies and dozens of the largest trade associations. His work has been mentioned, commented on, or covered by NBC, ABC, CNN, CNBC, NPR, and in most major newspapers and news magazines. He's also responsible for the books *If Aristotle Ran General Motors, Philosophy for Dummies, The Art of Achievement, The Stoic Art of Living, Twisdom, Superheroes and Philosophy,* and *If Harry Potter Ran General Electric,* as well as many others. His most recent books include the philosophical prologue to the current series, *The Oasis Within,* and the subsequent books, *The Golden Palace, The Stone of Giza, The Viper and The Storm, The King and Prince,* and *The Mysterious Village,* as well as the current volume. He just may be the world's happiest philosopher.

Φ

www.ingramcontent.com/pod-product-compliance
Lightning Source LLC
Chambersburg PA
CBHW022203030726
47494CB00019B/39